CW00432299

STRATHALMOND

Best wishes

[signature]

STRATHALMOND

A Novel
by Alex Aitken

HIGHLANDER
PUBLISHING

Highlander Publishing
Canada
A Highlander Publishing Paperback

Strathalmond

This edition published 1999
by Highlander Publishing
Box 20030 Taylor Kidd P.O.
Kingston, ON, Canada K7P 2T6

All rights reserved.
Copyright © 1999 by Alex Aitken

Cover and interior design by Susan Hannah
Author photo courtesy of The Whig Standard, by Michael Lea

No part of this book may be reproduced or utilised in any form
or by any means, electronic or mechanical, including photo-
copying, recording, or by any information storage
and retrieval system, without permission in writing
from the publisher.

This work is a novel and any similarity to
actual persons or events is purely coincidental.

Permissions & acknowledgements appear on p. 432 of this book.

Canadian Cataloguing in Publication Data

Aitken, Alex, 1939-
Strathalmond

ISBN 0-9684094-0-7

Title.

PS8551.1775S77 1998   C813' .54   C98-931799-4
PR9199.3.A47S77 1998

PRINTED IN CANADA

*To my wife, Marjorie
who was around this story from the beginning,
and who made the telling of it happen.*

ﮏﮏﮏ

In the valley of the Beugh Burn at the edge of a town called Myrestane that lies just a few miles from Scotland's capital city, the House of Strathalmond still stands.

Houses, unlike people, don't fade away.

Contents

BOOK 1

∽ 1430–1460 ∾

Chapter One

ⵥⵥⵥ

It was eleven o'clock in the morning when Thomas Ingram
rode finally into view of the foreboding dark tower that was
Houstoun Castle.

He had been riding since dawn, coming from Leith and
skirting around the south side of the crag of Arthur's Seat to
follow the Pentland Hills westward towards the lands of the
Black Douglas. He had made good time and had time to spare
before his appointed meeting with the Earl. This was as he had
planned it. He wanted the time to view the land that would
soon be his.

Near to the castle, he turned his mount northward for
several hundred paces to a spot where the Houstoun Wood,
that surrounded the buildings, ended. There the land fell away
in a long gentle sweep into the valley of the Beuch Burn, a little
meandering rivulet that joined the River Almond some few
miles to the east. Ingram dismounted and, stretching to relieve
the stiffness of his long journey, he leaned against the wide
trunk of an ancient elm on the edge of the tree line and looked
northward across the valley.

It was a warm June morning in the year fourteen hundred
and thirty, and the sun had begun to disperse the early mist
that still clung stubbornly to the green grasses of the slope.

Across the valley the land rose steeply to the thrusting rock called the Crag-o-Binny that had lifted itself three hundred feet above the skyline. Away to the north and east the silver blue river Forth snaked in and out of view on its way to the Firth.

Thomas Ingram, reclining against the tree, relished the moment. He took in everything in his view, from Arthur's Seat, squatting in the morning mist over the city of Edinburgh, balefully and distantly eyeing its rival the Crag-o-Binny, to the black hills of Drumcross in the west that hid at their feet the little burgh of Bathgate.

In the foreground, where his eyes finally came to rest, he could see the ferm-toun of Myrestane, a mere cluster of farm dwellings, crowned on its northern side by the ancient church of St. Nicholas. Nearer still, and a mile to the west of the ferm-toun, at a spot where the Beuch Burn ran straight and true across a level and verdant clearing, he saw the great mansion of Strathalmond with its high narrow gables and the wide entrance at its gate.

In his mind's eye he saw it for Strathalmond was not yet built.

But soon it would be built, and he, Ingram, would build it. And there, where he gazed, there would it be.

Two red deer sprang with a quiet rustle from the trees and Thomas awoke with a start. Straightening up and stretching once more, he took his mare by the bridle and walked her back through the wood towards the castle.

In appearance, Thomas was an Ingram. From the lanky figure, and long face, with its big light hazel eyes and lantern jaw, to the over-large bony hands and long pointed fingers, he was unmistakably an Ingram. He was prematurely bald, but some long reddish wisps of hair still bounced up and down as he approached the entrance with his long, springing stride.

A castle guard who stood outside the entrance felt a sudden fear of this strange-looking, threatening man, covered from chin to ankle in a heavy cloak of an unfamiliar hide, bearing down on him with great bounding strides and leading behind him a sweating, weary grey mare. The guard's hand tightened on the sword at his belt as he took a few paces forward to meet the stranger. Then he was immediately relieved when Ingram smiled at him. It was a warm, disarming smile that dissolved all the menace of its owner. It was another Ingram feature.

Thomas looked up the face of the great tower and was overawed by its size and strength. He had never been so close to a castle of any kind but the ones he had seen from a distance or in paintings had never seemed so ominous as this. Even the great castle of Edinburgh, though larger and more elevated on its rock high above the city, didn't have the menace of this Douglas fortress.

Although only thirty-five years old, "old for a soldier but young for a merchant," he often said, Thomas Ingram had six ships at the Pier o' Leith that plied a trade with the Low Countries and the Baltic. Yet he had never, until now, had any cause to visit a castle.

Thomas' father had been a comrade-at–arms of Archibald, the fifth earl of Douglas and lord of Houstoun. Though Thomas had never met the man whose castle he now entered, Archibald had promised a grant of land to him, the more to be discussed when they first met.

Houstoun Castle was a tower-house. It had no outer fortifications, no moat and no curtain walls, but relied for its defences only on its elevated site and massive stone walls that were sheer and solid, unadorned by turrets and buttresses. The lower storeys displayed only a few arrow slits and no other openings. The narrow entrance, wide enough for just a single horseman to pass, had been purposely made unobtrusive and unwelcoming. On the outside of the wall a gate of heavy iron latticework hung in the centre of a frame of the same material that was anchored into the walls on each side and into the arched roof. Another gate of similar construction and proportions was placed on the inside face of the wall. There was no other way in or out of Houstoun Castle but through these two gates. Between the gates it was dark and damp and the sun never shone. Green moss had formed here and there on the great granite stones that supported the round arch above, and Thomas could feel the chill as he walked through.

The inner gate, like its outer counterpart, lay open and Thomas came into a dark inner courtyard, lit here and there by torches fixed high around the walls. The smell of dampness and stabled animals caught in his throat. A young boy emerged from the shadows and walked quickly up to him. Without ever looking up at the tall merchant, he took the bridle firmly from Thomas' hand and proceeded to lead the horse away, pointing as he did so with outstretched arm towards an iron door that also lay open to reveal a turnpike stair.

As Thomas approached the door, still marvelling at the sheer size and strength of the place, his host came down the steps to meet him. The two men could not have been more different in appearance.

Archibald Douglas was a diminutive man. He wore a short padded doublet, light blue in colour, long hose and pointed shoes. On his head was a wide-brimmed, low-crowned hat and Thomas immediately pictured him as a figure in one of the paintings he had seen of courtiers in the Court of France. He looked totally out of place in these dark, dingy surroundings.

The little man extended his hand and his small light blue eyes twinkled above the distinctive hooked nose.

"Thomas Ingram. You are welcome, Sir, to my house."

Thomas took the hand and found the grip surprisingly strong. But he still couldn't believe that this little man in front of him was Archibald, master of Douglas, lord of Galloway and of Annandale, Eskdale, Teviotdale and Lauderdale, and duke of the vast holdings of Touraine. In fact, he was the greatest magnate of the Scottish realm.

Still bemused, Thomas followed his host who moved nimbly up the dark spiral stairway of the tower, talking as he went.

"I dare say that this is your first venture into a house such as this. What think you of it? Would it not serve to repel even the most aggressive of assaults?" Ingram mumbled his agreement as he strove to keep up with the quick ascent of his leader.

"The Douglas seat is Threave Castle in Galloway, you know,

13

but it is remote from the capital and I choose, when possible, to live here."

They passed open doorways at three levels, Archibald all the while conducting a tour and explaining their access. On the first level were kitchens and servants' quarters. On the second was the great hall, and above it various private apartments. He pointed out the thickness of the walls, the strength of beams and buttresses, the dormers and the arrow loops for defenders.

Thomas, totally unfamiliar with the terminology of construction, merely nodded in approval, suitably impressed by the stronghold of the Douglas.

"And you see the stairs we mount, and the direction of their turn? This would defy the attempts of an enemy to handle a sword here. That is, in the most unlikely event that an enemy could ever reach here in the first place."

They emerged at last from the narrow stairway into a small chamber. Archibald called this his "thinking room", and it was comfortably furnished with cushioned chairs and tapestries, to the point of being cluttered. It was brightly lit by torches that aided the daylight coming in from wide slits in the walls on three sides, and Thomas was relieved to escape into fresh air and away from the stench of the ground level.

The Douglas relieved his guest of the long cloak.

"Camel hide, is it not? I see how the merchants can obtain the superior goods of the East."

When they had sat down and Archibald had poured generous cups of wine, he leaned forward fixing the little eyes on Thomas.

"Aye, I can see the resemblance to your father, though where you came by the long shanks I canna but wonder." He smiled and sized Thomas up and down for what seemed a long time.

Thomas' puzzlement gave way to intrigue touched with a certain awe.

"I told you I owed a debt to your father. That debt was no less than my life."

Thomas was astounded by this revelation. He knew that his father had died at the battle of Beauge, fighting in the service of the earl for the French King, Charles VI, against the English. He remembered the day the news had arrived, nine short years ago, and how he resolved then to make his fortune in trade, and avoid, as well as was possible, the hazards and griefs of soldiering. From a very early age his father had flickered in and out of his life, a phantom figure moving to and from one campaign or another, a man Thomas never really knew, but only the repeated family stories of his courage.

As if reading his thoughts the earl continued."You never knew your father, did you?" Again he smiled that little thoughtful smile. "Well, I did," he went on. "He served me and mine for many a year and through many a fray until he took that English pike at Beauge that was meant for me."

Thomas could think of nothing to reply. He just sat there thinking of his father and the little man before him, battling in a remote province with the forces of the English warrior king. A picture that was hard to believe.

Archibald arose and refilled their cups, as Thomas dragged his thoughts away from war and killing back to the comfort of the room and the warm generosity of the host.

Archibald briefly looked from the window slot before turning again to Thomas. "Aye, a brave man your father. And for you he wanted a peaceful and prosperous life away from the battlefields. Everything he had, and he had gleaned a fair fortune from the spoils of his campaigns, he spent educating you and setting you up with your first ship. You know that do you not?"

"I do", said Thomas, thinking that he did not, for he had always thought that his mother's family had been the instrument of his early success. Again he had the feeling that Archibald could read this thought, but the little man merely smiled and said no more on the subject.

"And now we will get down to the business at hand, Thomas Ingram of Leith. As I indicated in my letter summoning you here, I plan to make you a grant of land in the valley of the Beuch burn for the purpose of building a house, a house that your father wished for you."

He walked to the window. "See there! There is the Beuch and there is where the house will be, so that whenever I look from here I will remember your father and the return for his great service to me, poor return though it may be."

Ingram arose and joined him at the window. He began to express his thanks when the Douglas raised his hand to stop him. "Not yet. No words yet Thomas until you have heard the full terms of the grant, for it comes with a service to me to which you will be bound. Come with me now."

He led the way out of the chamber, back down the narrow stairway and into the great hall of the castle. Thomas took little notice of the size and grandeur of the hall as he wondered about the service. There was no mention of this in the letter.

A servant was summoned who, after some whispered words from his master, scurried away.

Archibald motioned Ingram to a chair at the end of the huge banquet table, while he remained standing.

A few moments later the servant returned, ushered a boy into the hall, and left. Archibald, with a deft little hand movement, and inclining his head towards the boy, invited Thomas' attention to the newcomer.

He was a rosy-cheeked handsome boy with dark blue intelligent eyes and a shock of curly black hair. Thomas judged him to be around eight or nine years old, and while he began to wonder why he was here, the boy walked right over to him with no visible shyness.

"Who are you, sir? I'm Ranald. I'm pleased to make your acquaintance. Why have you no hair? Where did you come from? Are you a Douglas man? I have a goshawk, and it can catch rabbits for the cook. Do you have a hawk?"

Both men began to laugh, as Thomas tried to decide which question he would answer first. Archibald interrupted.

"This, my friend, is Ranald 'the Questioner'. Ranald, this is Thomas Ingram of Leith. He is a merchant and a trader and has his own ships. He is going to take you back to Leith with him and show you his ships."

Thomas, perplexed, started to get up as Archibald continued.

"And you will go and live with him and he will be your father."

Then, to Thomas, "The other side of the bargain. Now, I think, we will eat."

The Douglas had a way of terminating a conversation, and Thomas, still trying to take in what had been sprung on him, was quite happy not to pursue the matter further at that time.

Servants came in and proceeded to move benches up from the walls of the great hall to one end of a long table. Archibald's wife entered the hall, a big severe-looking woman whom her husband introduced as the Lady Euphemia. Behind her came two boys, one about the same age as Ranald and very like him in looks, and the other a bit younger and bearing a striking resemblance to Euphemia. The boys, William and David Douglas, were introduced to Thomas as their sons, and they immediately earmarked a seat on the bench alongside Ranald "the Questioner", scrambling up on it noisily as servants began to bring in the food. Archibald Douglas sat, elevated by several cushions, in a large high-backed oak chair that had been placed for him at the head of the table. Thomas sat on a cushioned bench next to Euphemia and facing the unruly boys.

The volume and variety of the food placed before him gave Thomas further indication of the wealth and resources of the Douglas: a joint of beef, various cuts of pork, mutton, and venison, two pheasants, several wood pigeons and a platter containing fish baked in meal. The boys focussed on the sweets consisting of nuts, preserved fruits, honey and herbs set on a large platter. Their eagerness to grab for it was quickly abated by a stern look from Archibald. Two large flagons of wine were placed next to the host who leaned over and tore a leg from the plump pheasant, hungrily devouring it as the fat ran down his chin and dripped onto his doublet. At this signal the others began to seize and consume items from the plates, occasionally using the short daggers, provided with small pewter plates at each place, to cut anything that was too large to be pressed into the mouth. Choice pieces were offered, one to another, and Thomas ate heartily with an appetite built up from his long journey, and enhanced by the sheer quantity and quality of the food in front of him. Only Euphemia ate with any dainty reserve, having set a lace bib of foreign origin under her chin to catch any drops as she popped small pieces of meat and fish into her mouth with long delicate fingers.

Conversation went on all the while. Archibald talked of nothing but trade and where Thomas' ventures took him and had he ever been at the fairs at Brugge or Antwerp? He poured generous measures of wine into Thomas's goblet, saying that it was the best Gascon wine brought from Calais. Thomas was impressed by the knowledge his host displayed about the Merchants of the Staple, who traded in English wool, and the counting houses and exchange rates. Archibald Douglas, nobleman and landowner, was even acquainted with the depreciation of the currencies, and the problems faced by traders in trying to decipher the relative values of the coinage produced in the marketplaces of France and Flanders, and the Baltic trading cities of Lubeck, Stralsund and Danzig. To Thomas's astonishment, Lady Euphemia joined in the discussions, asking how Thomas fared with the Andrew guilder of Scotland, the much debased Arnoldus gulden of Gueldres, the Carolus groat of Charles of Burgundy, the David and the Falewe of the Bishopric of Utrecht, the groats of Limburg and Milan, the English Ryall, the Florin Rhenau of the Bishopric of Cologne, and the French Louis d'or.

They talked for over an hour after the boys had left in the care of a well-rounded, elderly man whom Archibald described as their tutor.

As the table was being cleared by diligent and silent servants, Euphemia also took her leave and Archibald and Thomas adjourned to the "thinking room", where more wine was poured and the subject of Ranald "the Questioner" was again brought up.

It was clear that Archibald knew a great deal about Thomas. Not only about his commercial ventures, but also that he was married to Margaret, a daughter of John of Akyne, a trader and ship owner from the Burgh of Linlithgow, and that they had a three-year-old daughter called Marjorie.

"So now Thomas I will tell you about the other part of our bargain," the Earl went on, and Thomas was mildly bemused by the assumption that a bargain had already been made.

"You will spend tonight here as my guest, and in the morning you will take Ranald back with you to Leith. I want you to raise him as your ward and tutor him to your trade, so that he will grow to be a man of commerce, safe from the distress and danger of these times. You will give him your name, for his own will not serve him well I am thinking, and when he is of age or when he marries, only then will you tell him who he really is."

He looked Thomas in the eye, reading the question forming in his mind, and added, "Ranald Douglas, my own son."

Thomas' confusion left him speechless. Why did Archibald want him to take this boy, his own son? Why train and tutor him for a merchant life? What distress and danger? And the biggest question of all was how could any trade or tutoring benefit a Douglas, especially one who was already heir to the greatest estates in Scotland?

Archibald continued. "What I will tell you now is for you alone to know, and I tell you because you are your father's son and I have trust in you as I had in him."

He then went on to explain that the boy Ranald was his illegitimate son, conceived prior to his marriage to Euphemia, who was the daughter of Sir Patrick Graham of Kincardine. He and Euphemia had three children, William and David, the boys Thomas had met earlier, and Margaret who was three. Little Margaret, he said, was the successor to Galloway and all the lands that had been acquired by his grandfather, Archibald "the Grim". He smiled and flicked his black hair with the back of his fingers.

"This is what we Douglases inherited from Archibald "the Grim," the colouring of the Ancient Picts rather than the Celts. We are what you might call, the Black Douglases."

Thomas was enjoying this Douglas story, and was forming

a growing attachment to this amiable and humorous earl of Douglas. He was still overawed, however, by the sheer wealth of the Douglases, and not least by the fact that a three-year-old girl held title to all the lands of Galloway. He was anxious to hear more about how he, successful perhaps, but still a humble merchant when measured against the House of Douglas, could possibly figure in the story.

Archibald grew wistful and somewhat serious.

"For a long time now I have had a premonition concerning the future of the Black Douglas line," he said. "Our power and influence is great and will grow even stronger, and there will come a day when it will threaten the Stewarts and the very throne on which they sit." He watched Thomas' reaction to this almost treasonable comment before continuing.

"I have no fear for myself but for my children and my children's children. I fear that day which will surely come. There is nothing that I can do to prevent it or to save the Douglases from it when it does. The boys you saw this day are Douglases. They are seen to be Douglases, my heirs, and what is more, the heirs of a lineage that goes back to the Bruce. Some say, even now, that the Douglas claim to the throne is better than that of its present tenant. One day that claim will be tested, or the Stewarts will take steps to see that it never is. But there is one Douglas that I can save from this portent I have of strife and warfare, and that is Ranald, since none save Euphemia and myself, and now you, knows his identity. His poor mother died bringing him into the world."

At this point Archibald arose and refilled the wine while Thomas experienced a strange mixture of unease and gratification. Archibald came straight to the point.

"For Ranald I want freedom from the ties that Douglas parentage would thrust upon him. I want him to grow up in your world and not mine. I want him to learn the skills of commerce and finance and not the arts of war. When his time comes, I would like to see him die in bed, surrounded by the trappings and mementoes of a successful merchant rather than in the wet dawn of some cold and bloody field of battle. I have determined that you, Thomas Ingram of Leith, and perhaps you alone, can give him that. For that, you will have my eternal gratitude and my present favour."

He went to the window that looked out onto the valley.

"Your house, down there, will be built without delay. I will supply the land, the materials and the masons that will build it to your specification and desire. You will take Ranald on the terms I have stated."

The little man approached Thomas and extended his hand to seal the bargain. Thomas took it.

Early the next morning, when the sun had risen over Scotland's capital and scattered the mist that clung to the valley of the Beugh, Thomas took a parting look at his estate of Strathalmond as he turned the horse's head eastward for Leith. The boy, snuggled in the saddle against him, black curls brushing Thomas's cloak from the continuously turning head, laughed and chattered his way into Thomas Ingram's heart.

"Is it far to go to your house? Are your ships there? Can I go on a ship? Do you have hounds? Could I have a hound?"

Chapter
Two

᪽ ᪽ ᪽

The great house of Strathalmond towered four storeys above the green open fields and the newly planted trees that Thomas Ingram had set out to line the long approach to its door. Tall chimneys rose above the slated, pitched roof with its crow-stepped gables. To the south, a dark line of young yew trees marked the limits of its expansive kitchen gardens, and to the east, some hundred paces off from the house, a lofty dovecote embraced the incessant cooing and the sporadic panicking of dozens of fat wood pigeons. Three deep and languid fish stanks on its western flank served to secure for its cooks a constant supply of fresh fish for the table.

Thomas stood at a window on the third floor viewing the results of the finished work with a feeling of entire satisfaction. Nowhere in these lowlands: not in the capital, not in the new and thriving burghs, not even on the hill, where the Douglas castle looked down from its fortified domain, was there such a house as Strathalmond. Close by, on the northern side of its towering walls, the whoops and shouts of children carried on the summer breeze.

They had made a dam across the Beugh burn and the young David Douglas, skinny and bare-arsed, ran across the bank and leapt, whooping, into the centre of the muddy pool to the obvious delight of his little sister Margaret and her friend Marjorie Ingram. The girls paddled, skirts raised up, around the side. On the far bank, Ranald Ingram, who had been entrusted by his father with the supervision of his sister and their guests, hunched over his model sailing boat, brows knitted in concentration. David, eager to impress the girls and delighted with their response, returned time and again to the bank to repeat his performance.

Eventually the interest in David's performance waned and Marjorie, leading her friend by the hand, crossed the burn with unsteady steps over the stones below the dam to reach her brother.

"Is it ready, Ranald? Is the boat ready?"

Ranald looked up at the golden hair and light blue eyes set in the round picture-perfect face. The more he looked at Marjorie Ingram these days, the more he felt an awakening urge to get closer to her somehow. He wasn't sure how. Was this what he should feel for his beautiful little sister?

Well, she wasn't really his sister. Ranald knew that just as he knew that Thomas Ingram wasn't really his father. But from the day that he had been taken from Houstoun Castle to the house in the Port of Leith, he had been called Ranald Ingram, and Thomas had told him that he was to call him father, and Thomas's wife, Isabella Ingram, mother, and that Marjorie was to be his little sister. From that day to this nothing more had been said. In the years that followed, Ranald had been brought up as the son of a wealthy merchant, tutored by Master Matthew, a strict and scholarly friar that his father's friend Bishop Kennedy of St. Andrews had introduced to his family. Whenever he had managed to escape the attentions of this disciplinarian, he had spent his time on the docks, talking to his father's sailors and looking over their ships and questioning them on the ports to which they sailed. Lately, now that he had turned sixteen, he had pestered his father to be allowed to sail with them, and Thomas Ingram had said that soon he would be.

"Is the boat ready?" Marjorie shook his shoulder with a dainty little hand.

"Not boat . . . ship," Ranald said rising to his feet and pushing the mop of black hair up off his forehead.

"This is a model of father's first ship, the "Isabella of Akyne", a sailing model. You see her sails!" He held out the intricately designed little merchant ship, pulling a string to raise the sails, then crouched down on the bank to set it in the water of the dam. David, having swum across to see the launching, looked on with admiration. The little ship twisted and turned for a few seconds before, gathering the breeze on her sails, she set off straight and true across the dam, to cheers and clapping from the exuberant onlookers.

A mile or so up stream, two boys, side by side on identical grey ponies, moved quietly and carefully from a dark clump of trees into the sunlight. They looked skyward along the rim of the wood. A heavy wood pigeon, glistening blue with an urgent whirring and flapping of its powerful wings, broke from the trees to their right and bore towards them. One of the boys, with a quick and silent movement of a mailed arm, raised and loosed a peregrine falcon. William Douglas, called William of Houstoun, the son and heir of Archibald, and his younger cousin, Will Douglas of Abercorn, watched as the flashing blue peregrine rose into the sky and wheeled around to take its bearings, large luminous eyes blinking in its squat, square head.

The attention of the boys was transfixed on the falcon as it spotted the pigeon and drew itself up to swoop. The pigeon, sensing the danger, beat its strong wings faster, and angled away from the trees. The peregrine dropped like a stone, turning and swirling in the air to meet its prey straight on in a final mortal collision of blood and feathers. The Douglas cousins cried out with glee, urging their mounts forward across the grass to the little killing ground.

The boys looked alike, both dark-haired with dark blue eyes, and both below average height. None of the Douglases were big men with the single exception of James "the Gross", the younger boy's father. Though of fairly tender years, both had the commanding and somewhat arrogant bearing of the Douglas line, and both displayed that carefree and keen relish for the hunt that had been bred through generations of men who possessed their land and meant to hold it against all challengers. They were, of course, both treated as men by their elders, since the Douglases knew, more than anyone, how circumstances might force manhood and leadership upon them with no warning given.

At fourteen, Archibald Douglas' older son, William of Houstoun, was already dreaming of the day when he would ride into Edinburgh at the head of a thousand men, and let the guardians of the new king, a poor disfigured little six year-old that had been crowned the year before, see what impressive power the Douglases could muster. Why his father had not seen fit to do this before now, William couldn't imagine. He knew that his great uncle James would have done it, had he been earl of Douglas. More and more, as he grew older, William of Houstoun had come to adulate James "the Gross", and had found frequent reasons to visit the stronghold of James at Abercorn, and hear his tales of the raiding and pillaging of his youth. His own father's early days were bland by comparison.

William of Houstoun sometimes wished that he could have been James' son, and he would have been envious of his present companion were it not that he reminded himself that he, William of Houstoun, was the one of royal descent on both his father's and his mother's side. He thought what a king he would have made, as the two dismounted to find the falcon astride its ripped and bloody prey.

Will Douglas of Abercorn had no such daydreams. The world for him was a delightful round of riding, hunting and hawking, and learning the skills of sword and lance. He enjoyed the company of his older cousin and had looked forward to this visit with his father to the new house of Strathalmond, built, they said, by some merchant friend of the Houstoun Douglases.

Earlier in the day he had met the merchant's son, Ranald and he had taken to Ranald right away. Will Douglas of Abercorn was like that. His first meeting with a stranger raised in him an immediate like or dislike, that had always proved, on further acquaintance, to remain unchanged. He had taken even more to Ranald's pretty sister, prettier than that other cousin of his, the scrawny little Margaret, to whom he was already betrothed. His father had told him that Margaret was heir to the lands of Galloway, and that she would blossom in due course, but he knew she would never grow into so desirable a flower as Marjorie Ingram. He thought it unfortunate that all that beauty was wasted on a merchant's daughter.

The two boys, retrieved the falcon and set off along the burn toward Strathalmond.

The ship's determined voyages across the rippling water of the dam, after Ranald had explained how the set of sails and rudder could make it sail against the breeze, continued to fascinate the onlookers, as the two Douglas boys road up along the bank.

Without a word, William of Houstoun drew his spear from the sheath on his saddle and threw it down at the ship. The long steel point pierced sail and hull, driving the small vessel below the water to pin it to the bed of the burn. Margaret began to cry as the others looked up in surprise at the newcomers, their eyes squinting against the sun.

Moments later, Ranald, taking the bank in several long bounds, leapt on William of Houstoun carrying him out of the saddle. The two rolled kicking and struggling on the grass, the falcon screeching and pecking as it freed itself from the thrashing pair. They rolled over and over and Ranald's superior size and weight gradually gave him the upper hand. Soon he pinned the younger boy beneath him, and as his temper cooled he slowly got to his feet glaring angrily at William of Houstoun. William pushed himself backward along the ground with his feet and then quickly got up, reaching as he did for the dirk in his belt. At that moment, Will Douglas of Abercorn, who had dismounted and moved toward them, seized his cousin from behind grasping his wrist to immobilise the weapon.

"Cannie man. Cannie!" he said. He held the smaller boy firmly for a few seconds as Ranald backed slowly away, all the time eyeing the dagger.

"He'll die for that," William of Houstoun retorted, struggling to release himself, but to no avail. "No man assaults a Douglas and lives to tell it." Will Douglas of Abercorn spoke softly in his cousin's ear.

"Another time, man, another time. Right now we are guests at Strathalmond and, anyway, the lad is unarmed. What would our fathers think if you killed the son of our host? Put up your dirk and calm yourself. Would the heir to Douglas want to kill a child minder? Would it not be like skewering a lassie?"

This prompted both boys to laugh and, unseen by his cousin, Will Douglas of Abercorn motioned with his head to Ranald, indicating that he should take off. Ranald, thankful for the signal, turned and went back down the slope to the dam where Margaret cried more sorely than ever and the others looked on fearfully.

At the insistence of Will Douglas of Abercorn, both Douglases mounted up and galloped off towards the house without looking back.

∾∾∾

The great hall, located on the second floor of Strathalmond above the kitchens, had been prepared for its first banquet. The two oak tables, long and wide, were set out in the form of a "T", the cross piece forming the head table. These were laid with every kind of meat, game, and fish available from the Lowlands of Scotland, and a selection of wines and other delicacies, accessible only to a wealthy merchant, from the trading nations of Europe and the East. The sumptuous décor, ornate fireplaces, and exquisitely carved chairs, completed the picture of the most elegant dining room in the country.

Thomas Ingram's family and upwards of forty guests had been directed to their seats at the table by a retinue of servants under the direction of Isabella of Akyne, and now the servants moved around silently dispensing the wines under her ever watchful eye.

At the centre of the head table Thomas sat between the highest ranking guests: the tiny Archibald, earl of Douglas and lieutenant-general of Scotland and Ingram's secret benefactor; and the huge figure of the little man's uncle, James Douglas of Abercorn, earl of Avondale, whose girth had already attracted the description of James "the Gross". He was the father of Will Douglas of Abercorn. Also at the head table were Isabella, the hostess of the evening, her father John of Akyne, Euphemia Douglas, the wife of Archibald Douglas, Sir John Forrester of Corstorphine and various other landed noblemen, friends of the Douglases.

Lined on each side of the other long table were landowners, merchants, sheriffs and representatives of local burghs, friends of the Ingrams and the Douglases, the two Douglas boys and Ranald Ingram.

Opposite the boys, almost as if the seating arrangement had been carefully planned, sat two men of the clergy. One of these was Thomas of Stowe, the familiar local primate of St. Nicholas Church, a cheerful, red-faced cleric who had already quaffed three full goblets of the rich Gascoigne wine, and was trying to attract the servant's further attention. His companion, thin and sallow-skinned, with a hawkish face and surprisingly kind, grey eyes, had been introduced as Master Anthony, the visiting Papal Legate from Rome, and he was studying Ranald, an engaging little smile on his thin lips.

The sounds of eating, knives on pewter plates and the manual tearing of meat from bones, the clinking of goblets, loud belching and riotous laughter mingled with shouted conversations back and forward in every direction across the tables, grew to a crescendo. It echoed from the great stone walls around the room.

James "the Gross", a mountain of flesh with a high-domed bald head crowning little pig eyes, a bulbous red nose and big widely spaced teeth in his cavern of a mouth, held the floor, as was his custom. William of Houstoun leaned forward to hang on his every word.

"Archibald!" James spluttered, pulling around in his

chair, a capon leg gripped firmly in his fist. "When will we see the Douglases free Scotland fae that mealy-mouthed bastard Crichton? Eh? Man if ye're auld grandfaither was alive, auld Black Archibald "the Grim", man it wid be a grim day for Crichton. He widna be able tae hide behind that wee laddie o' a king if Black Archibald was alive."

The din in the room subsided as faces turned on the earl of Douglas. Murmurs of anticipation awaited his reply to this clear insult.

William of Houstoun's eyes shone with excitement. His feelings of shame for his father and exultation for James "the Gross", his Douglas hero, suddenly bubbled up in him, raising him to his feet. "Aye, death tae Crichton!" he screamed out, looking wildly around the tables for support.

Earl Archibald rose slowly to his feet and surveyed the room, his eyes finally falling on his host. When he spoke it was with a slow quiet deliberation that barely concealed his anger. "Allow me, Thomas Ingram, to beg your pardon for the unguarded remarks that the wine brings to the lips of my kinsmen. One of them might plead youth and inexperience as his excuse. The other, it grieves me to say, has no excuse." He glared at James "the Gross" for several long seconds in the total silence that ensued.

The huge earl of Avondale, gripping the meat in one hand as he wiped the dripping fat from his chin with the other, smiled at Archibald through his big teeth and laughed derisively. Without replying, he seized a flagon of wine, filled his cup to overflowing, and turned his attention to John of Akyne on his other side, filling his cup also. "Fine wine John. Drink up man!" he laughed, as if signalling the end of the matter.

The tension around the room instantly eased, and the guests returned, relieved, to their conversations and their eating and drinking. Few noticed the young William of Houstoun turn and stomp angrily out of the hall, followed by his cousin, Will Douglas of Abercorn.

Archibald sat down and looked at Thomas Ingram. "Dangerous times, Thomas. You remember what I said?"

Thomas Ingram did remember that earlier conversation years ago. "Distress and the danger" had been Archibald's words then. He was talking about the dangers inherent in the ongoing feuds among power-seeking factions of the Scottish nobility. Each sought its place in a shaky hierarchy under an even shakier crown on the head of a child. The little king was the pawn of two less than noble guardians, Sir William Crichton and Sir Alexander Livingston. Each of these two saw the power that could be had by possessing the person of the king, and all of Scotland, noble or not, saw the ever more vocal and challenging power of the Douglases. All of this, thought Thomas Ingram, was brewing danger. Finally understanding Archibald's fears, his eyes were drawn down the table to Ranald.

∾ ∾ ∾

Ranald Ingram had been little affected by the events of the last few minutes, save only that they had been an annoying interruption to his conversation with the foreign priest, Master Anthony. Ranald had never met anyone like Master Anthony. The recent busy preparations for this dinner, the earlier fight with William of Houstoun, and even the persistent longings concerning Marjorie Ingram, had all been banished from his mind by this encounter with the priest. He had taken little food and no wine, nor had Master Anthony, and he was desperate to get down from the table and away from the din and clatter, as he had so much to ask his new companion. So when Master Anthony suggested that Ranald might show him the garden, it was an answer to a secret prayer.

It was one of those rare summer evenings in the Lowlands, warm and windless, with only the deep-throated cooing of pigeons carrying on the air. The two young men walked around the kitchen garden and made their way along the line of yews, moving away from the house. They walked south along the side of a ripening field of oats and up the hill to the edge of the woods that fronted Houstoun Castle.

They were strikingly different in appearance; Ranald of

medium height and broad-shouldered, with a ruddy complexion and a mop of raven hair; Master Anthony slimmer and taller, head erect and lips that smiled. The legate questioned Ranald on the attributes of Strathalmond, its location and its views, what was being cultivated in its garden and how the dovecote was maintained. He asked about the castle of Houstoun that overlooked them, and whether Ranald spent time there in the company of the young Douglases. Ranald was well aware of the elevated status of a Papal Legate. He dutifully answered the enquiries that he saw were made with a genuine interest, but he felt that there were more important things to discuss, and he was anxious for his turn to ask the questions.

The priest, almost imperceptibly, turned his enquiries to more personal things. He asked about Ranald's training in his father's business and about his life here and how he filled his days. He commented on Ranald's little sister and how pretty she was, and he noted the sudden blush that came to Ranald's cheeks, and his little smile flickered larger for a moment. Ranald seized on the subject of ships and trading and told how his grandfather, John of Akyne, was presently petitioning Henry VI of England for the return of two of his ships that had been taken by English pirates in the North Sea off Yarmouth.

They came to a young walnut tree, and looked across the open landscape towards Edinburgh. Master Anthony hefted up his long robe and sat down on the grass. "Now Ranald Ingram, you have been dying to question me all evening. Fire away with your questions and I will do my best to answer them, poor though my knowledge may be."

Ranald needed no further prompting, and his questions came fast and furious, his face alive with anticipation, his blue eyes shining. "What is it like to live in Rome? Is it true that the Arab trading ships have no nails? Have you ever been to the marts of Genoa or Venice? Yes, Venice. What is Venice like?"

"Hey man! Hey!" the priest held up a hand, laughing all the time. "One at a time."

Ranald stopped short, regarding the other closely, his face full of expectation.

Master Anthony leaned back, his hands on the grass, and gazed across at Houstoun Castle, considering his reply.

"Before that castle was built, two hundred years ago, when there was nothing here in these chilling, bleak Lowlands of Scotland but woods and wild grasses and maybe the odd clay hut, Venice was the proudest city on this side of the world. I say this side of the world, because even Venice could not match the cities of Cathay in size or splendour." He looked round at Ranald. "But you asked about Venice. Imagine its merchants in their great stone counting-houses rising between the canals, checking their sacks of cloves, mace and nutmegs, cinnamon and ginger from the Indies, ebony chessmen from Cathay and musk from Tibet. Picture, if you can, the dealers in jewels, pricing diamonds from Golconda, rubies from Badakhshan, and pearls from the fisheries of Ceylon. See in your mind the silk merchants, stacking bales of silk, muslin and brocade from Bagdad and Malabar. Mariners from every nation and port in our world converged upon Venice. Red-haired ladies, perfumed and bedecked with all the brocades of Persia on their backs, trailed up and down the marble steps of their palaces. And parades; can you imagine their parades?" The priest bent forward closer to Ranald, motioning with his delicate hands as he described, in almost confidential tones, the parades of Venice. "First come the navy, sailing past in the harbour, fifty galleys and other smaller craft, with their crews cheering and shouting from the decks. Then come the guilds on foot: first the master smiths, with garlands on their heads and banners and trumpets; then the furriers apparelled in samite and scarlet silk, with mantles of ermine and vair; then the weavers and the master tailors in white with crimson stars. Then the master cloth workers pass, carrying boughs of olive and wearing crowns of olive on their heads; then the fustian makers in furred robes, and the quilt makers with garlands of gilt beads, their white cloaks sewn with fleur-de-lis, marching two by two. Then come the makers of cloth of gold, all in cloth of gold and their servants in cloth of gold or of purple, followed by the mercers in silk and butchers in scarlet, the fish sellers robed and furred and garlanded, the master barbers and the glass workers, garlanded with pearls and carrying flasks and goblets of the famous Venetian glass. That, Master Ingram, is Venice."

Ranald was spellbound. He was transported from the now darkening gloaming of Strathalmond, a slight chill growing on the breeze, to the sun-filled casements opening onto the canals and the blue harbour of Venice.

"You must be...sad to be here Master Anthony," he uttered quietly.

"No, Ranald, not sad. Perhaps a shade despondent. For you see, this Scotland is a land of strife and all its heroes are warriors. The good Abbott Bower tells us that every day its citizens are robbed and pillaged. You saw and heard young William of Houstoun tonight talk of war and violence. He listens too much to his uncle. That is what is sad."

The priest got to his feet and brushed the grass from his robes. "You are the fortunate one. You are protected from all that, and someday you will see Venice for yourself. But it gets chilly. Come, let us return to the house. I have a gift for you that I think will interest you."

They walked slowly back towards Strathalmond, Ranald beginning again to pour out his questions. "What of the cities of Cathay? What were they like? What were they called? Have you ever been there?"

"Tomorrow is time enough for that," smiled the legate as they passed through the great oak door into the house.

The next morning Master Anthony gave Ranald Ingram the best present of his young life. It was a book about the life and travels of a young merchant called Marco Polo, and it answered all his questions about the great cities of Kinsai and Sugui and the wondrous palaces of the great Tartar emperor, Kublai Khan. It captivated Ranald's interest for a long time, long after Master Anthony had collected the Papal dues from the parish of St. Nicholas and all the parishes of the Lowlands, and returned to Rome.

In the months that followed, much of Ranald's time was

taken up under the tutelage of the friar that his father had hired to teach him Latin, French and counting, and that friar took his duties most seriously. Thomas Ingram took Ranald frequently to the Port of Leith, personally supervising his apprenticeship as a merchant, showing him how wool and hides were packed for shipping, how prices were set and paid, and introducing him to his colleagues and the masters of his ships. Ranald loved to walk along the dock behind the tall bounding figure of his father in the hide cloak. It made him feel so important.

At the same time, the lives of the young Douglas cousins were a constant round of hunting, hawking and horsemanship, and practising the skills of sword and spear. Ranald took every chance he could to join them for, in a way, he envied their freedom, and he found that, notwithstanding their opportunity for constant practice, he could hold his own with them in all their pursuits.

Ranald's skirmish with William of Houstoun was forgotten — not so much forgotten, perhaps, as relegated in his mind to a matter of little consequence. Will Douglas of Abercorn was his favourite, and the bond between these two, that had been formed on their first setting eyes on each other, grew into a strong and enduring friendship.

William of Houstoun talked all the time of his rank and his entitlement, and of how he would someday make up for the lack of courage of his father, the earl, and be a man like the Black Douglas, or his great uncle, James "the Gross". Ranald would look at Will Douglas of Abercorn and smile and say nothing, but he felt bad when he heard the boasting, for he liked Archibald Douglas, who was his father's friend and was no coward.

When they were alone, Ranald would tell Will Douglas of Abercorn about the merchants of Leith and his father's ships, and how, in the coming year, when he would be seventeen, he would get to sail to France. Then he would tell him about his book on the travels of Marco Polo. He could tell that his friend was interested and excited, and he wished that Will Douglas of

Abercorn was heir to the earldom of Douglas, and not his bragging young cousin, William of Houstoun.

One night, after dinner, as his parents and sister and he lingered at the table, tasting a new delicacy called dates that his father had brought back from the Port of Leith, his father addressed him with a serious look. "You're spending a lot of time with the Douglas boys these days, Ranald?"

"Aye father," replied Ranald.

"Aye, maybe the learned friar isn't keeping you busy enough, I'm thinking."

Ranald sensed a certain displeasure in his father's voice, but he said nothing and the subject was pursued no further.

Chapter
Three

❧ ❧ ❧

In June 1439, six months after the dinner at Strathalmond, Thomas Ingram received a summons to Houstoun Castle from Euphemia Douglas. It was an urgent call to say that her husband was very ill with fever and would he come without delay and bring Ranald.

It was mid afternoon and Ranald was with his tutor, Master Matthew, in the large well appointed room at the top of the house that looked south up the hill to Houstoun Castle. The room served the cleric both as a living chamber and study, and it was also the schoolroom for his single pupil.

Master Matthew was first and foremost a scholar, well versed, not only in the laws and dogmas of the Church, but also in Latin and French, history, geography, counting, and the writings of literary men and philosophers. He was one of the most educated men in Scotland and had accepted the position of tutor to the young merchant's son partly out of a duty to his principal, Bishop Kennedy, and partly for the remuneration and accommodation that afforded him the opportunity to pursue his own studies in relative comfort. He was a heavy, ungainly figure in his mid forties with a head that was too big for his body and an expansive wrinkled face.

In the beginning he had set the design of the relationship,

authoritative disciplinarian and silent attentive pupil. Within a very short time Ranald's infectious good nature, his intelligence, his voracious appetite for learning and his constant questioning, had dismantled that relationship and replaced it with mutually exciting and rewarding dialogues, in which each had become, at the same time, an educator of the other.

Among many other things over the last few months, they had discussed the Great Pestilence in Europe that had decimated families and populations, disrupted trade and destroyed whole institutions, a plague that had no known cause and no effective cure and had been called the Black Death. It had arrived in Europe from the East around a hundred years ago, and its rampant devastation through cities and countryside, sparing no one it touched, made many believe that the world was at an end. And it still returned, to this place or that, every few years, and the fear of it, and its reported horrible effects, were never far from the minds of men. Now, on this bright summer afternoon at Strathalmond, Ranald was to see it for himself. The urgency of the request and the mention of the word fever could mean only one thing in these times, and Thomas immediately called Ranald from his studies, the two setting off up the hill to Houstoun Castle.

When they arrived at the Douglas stronghold, they were shown into the great hall. The banquet tables had been removed and dozens of people stood around in groups, engaged in the solemn and subdued conversations of a funeral party. All the Douglases were there, the local priest, some burgh officials and many others that Ranald did not know. William of Houstoun, with his usual angry expression, stood near a window looking out. Next to him, Ranald's friend, Will Douglas of Abercorn, was engaged in conversation with his father, the monstrous figure James "the Gross", the only man in the room who was seated. Lady Euphemia Douglas, tall and dignified as ever but with swollen red eyes, came over and took Thomas' arm, leading him away from Ranald and talking all the time in hushed tones. Ranald was left alone in the middle of the room, puzzled by the occasion and ignored by the crowd. Once he caught the eye of Will Douglas of Abercorn who gave a slight nod of acknowledgement then returned his attention to the conversation with his father.

After what seemed like a long time in this solitude, Thomas Ingram returned and placed an arm around Ranald's shoulders. He led him back to the entrance where Euphemia stood erect, her hands clasped in front of her and a pained expression on her face.

Thomas Ingram's voice was quiet and serious. "Ranald, the earl of Douglas is gravely ill and he has expressed the wish to see you. He is in his chamber on the floor above."

Ranald looked from his father to Euphemia, and before a question formed on his lips, she spoke. "Ranald, my dear husband is not long for this world. Because of his illness he has denied all access to the chambers above this hall, and no one may go to him now." Her voice quivered and she blinked her eyes to loose the tears that had swelled up in them. "He said to me that he wished he could have seen Ranald "the Questioner" just one more time."

Ranald stood in silence, suddenly overcome with sympathy for this great lady, and perplexed by what she said. His thoughts raced and he looked again at his father, his eyes questioning.

"It's plague, Ranald," Thomas Ingram whispered. "There is danger now for everyone in this castle. The earl has directed that all the rooms above this hall will be fired, and everything in them burned when he is gone. Then all we can do is pray to God for our own deliverance."

He gripped Ranald by the shoulders, turning the boy to face him. Ranald was speechless and, for the first time in his young life, stricken with panic. All the stories he had heard and read about the pestilence ran through his head: the horrible deaths of its victims; the mass burials in unhallowed graves; bodies of men, women, and children left to rot in their houses and in the streets of their cities; the marching, murderous swath of death.

"Ranald!" His father's voice pierced through his nightmare.

"Ranald, Lady Euphemia has asked if you would go to her husband to grant his last wish. I can't tell you the reason for that wish, but say only that there is a reason, and I can't tell you to go. But I have to tell you that it is a last wish of a fine man and my friend. You alone must decide."

There was a finality in the words. Ranald looked around, trying to take it in. It seemed like the crowd in the great hall, nodding and talking in whispers, in pairs and in groups, slowly receded into a mist, leaving only himself, his father and Euphemia standing at the stone stairway, his father's intent stare and anxious frown and Euphemia's clasped hands. His thoughts fixed on the description he had read with Master Matthew from the pen of Agnolo di Tura of the plague in Siena. "It is impossible for the human tongue to recount the awful truth. Father abandoned child, wife husband, one brother another. And so they died and none could be found to bury the dead for money or friendship".

And this was his father's friend, and he would die alone and be burned with all his possessions in the top of his castle.

"I'll go father," he said. "I'll go now," and before the others could speak, he turned into the stairwell and quickly mounted the stairs, two at a time lest delay should weaken his resolve.

Ranald passed through the open doorway of Archibald Douglas' "thinking room", where Thomas Ingram had passed years before. At once a foul smell caught in his nose and throat causing him to retch. The incense that burned in the darkened room — juniper, rosemary and pine — made it hard to see, but did nothing to breech the awful smell of putrid flesh. Ranald moved forward slowly, peering to accustom his eyes to the shadows. Then he saw him, a small boyish figure, stretched on his back on a large bed, white and naked in the poor light. Ranald halted abruptly, trembling with the shock of what he saw. Archibald, fifth earl of Douglas groaned with pain as his open eyes regarded the boy.

Ranald's eyes moved from the beads of perspiration that stood out on the man's brow and glistened on his chest, to the large black and suppurating gland boils that ringed his neck and heaved out from his armpits and from his groin. Even in the poor light Ranald could decipher the slate blue colour of asphyxiation on the earl's grotesque face. All the stories of the pestilence had never prepared Ranald for this, and though he tried to look away, he found that he couldn't, and he just stood there staring at what was once a man. The victim's eyes shone and the eyelids blinked twice, very slowly, to Ranald. It was the only way that the earl could show his thanks. Then, with a supreme effort, Archibald lifted a hand a few inches from the bed and waved it — at once a farewell and a motion to leave. A tear ran down into the pillow.

Ranald backed slowly out of the room, still staring at the earl, then he finally turned and shuffled down the stone stairway, past the great hall and out into the sunlight.

༄ ༄ ༄

After the death of the earl of Douglas, Ranald steeped himself in his studies to such an extent that even Master Matthew was impressed by his efforts. He rarely went out, except on business with his father to the Port of Leith, or to visit other merchants or suppliers of wool and hides that would be shipped by the Ingram fleet. His only outside interests were Will Douglas of Abercorn, whom he would strive to meet whenever Will was at Houstoun Castle, an interest known all too well to Thomas Ingram, and the clandestine regard that he paid to Marjorie. He would watch her from his window when she was alone in the garden. Sometimes she would look up suddenly and he would pull back from the window.

By the Spring of the following year he had recovered from the ordeal of his meeting with death. He no longer imagined that he could smell its smell, or see the black smoke from the pitch and brushwood fires that clung to the high walls of Houstoun Castle, and seared the innards of its high chambers. The snow went, and the cold mist that had clothed Strathalmond, and the valley of the Beuch renewed itself in a parade of green grasses and lilac, wild flowers and cooing doves. Now, whenever he saw

40

Marjorie, he downed tools and contrived by every means to meet her, as if by accident, as she crossed the lawns or knelt to pick flowers by the edge of the trees.

Marjorie Ingram had blossomed from the pretty little girl playing at the dam into a bewitching beauty. She was a different person. Although he had grown up with her, Ranald couldn't remember the girl he had played with before. He felt that he was meeting her for the first time; the first time she wore that white dress, the first time he could smell her hair and feel weak when she smiled at him, the first time he had felt like this. In the house he avoided her. He hid from her in his study and arranged, when he could, to eat on his own, declaring that his work demanded it. He longed to sit near her, but imagined that his parents would see him and know. Did Master Matthew know?

Thomas Ingram leaned back in his chair, stretching his long legs and running a hand over the bald dome of his head. He and Ranald sat in the well-furnished library of the house that Thomas used as his study. This was the place where he entertained his business colleagues, and instructed Ranald on the merchant's trade, the acquisition and transporting of goods and the counting of profits and losses. The women of the house, Isabella and Marjorie, never entered this room, as they were never, at any time, included in any matters pertaining to the business. Whether things were going well or otherwise, whether cargoes yielded a handsome profit or were lost or pirated in the North Sea, no elation or concern was demonstrated or discussed at the family table as such matters were the sole province of Thomas and his son. The same rules applied to the politics of the time, and how the family was, or could be, affected by the constantly changing alliances and factions in this much-troubled country. This latter item was to be the theme of Thomas' lecture to his son on this particular night.

"Now then Ranald, Master Matthew considers his work here is done and he will be returning to St. Andrews at the end of the week. What do you think of that?"

41

"I think, father, that Master Matthew is the best judge of that."

"Aye, no doubt," Thomas grunted, as he reached for his brandy glass. "Anyway, he did a fine job while he was here, and I will be recommending him to his master, Bishop Kennedy."

Thomas smiled. He was pleased that Master Anthony would be recommended, and he knew that this was as close to a compliment to his own achievements as he was ever likely to get from Thomas Ingram.

"But you know, Ranald, there's a thing or two that I want to say to you." He paused briefly. "Bearing further on your education, one could say."

Ranald was attentive. He had not seen his father so serious since that day at Houstoun Castle.

"You're seeing too much of the Douglas boys."

The question jumped to Ranald's lips. "Why?" His father quickly put the glass back on the desk and lifted a hand to interrupt.

"Ranald, listen to me now! They are fine boys and I have no complaint against them, but they make dangerous friends for you, and I want you to steer clear of them . . . at least, for a while."

Ranald was taken aback. He had always felt that Thomas had something against his spending time with the Douglases, but had never dreamed that it would come to a directive like this. While he struggled with it, Thomas continued.

"These are uncertain times. Young William of Houstoun is no longer William of Houstoun. Now he is William sixth earl of Douglas, and because of who he is and the power he has inherited, he has made powerful enemies."

Seeing Ranald's confusion, Thomas decided that he must be specific to make his point. "You know of the tug-o'-war between Sir Alexander Livingston and Chancellor Crichton over the possession of the person of the young King James. Livingston had him in Stirling Castle and Crichton had him kidnapped and returned to Edinburgh. Now, Crichton, having the king once more in his control, has made a pact with Livingston;

Livingston, his former enemy! Now why do you think he would do that?"

Ranald didn't have the faintest idea, and he didn't know what all this had to do with him being forbidden to see his friends. Thomas went on. "There is only one reason for that pact; the young earl of Douglas . . . your friend. He is a kinsman of the king and his father was lieutenant-general, a post that young William sees as his. Believe me Ranald, it is a position that Sir William Crichton will try to see that William never gets."

Thomas could see that he had not yet dispelled the confusion in the boy's eyes.

"Crichton doesn't have the power to take on the Douglases face to face, so I have great fears that he will come at the earl some other way, some back-stabbing way. Now do you see what I mean? I want you away from these boys, and out of the way of Crichton when he makes his move."

Ranald was speechless. He couldn't believe what his father had just said, but he knew that Thomas Ingram was astute in these matters, and was suddenly fearful for his friends. Thomas spoke again, his voice low and serious. "Ranald, you will keep to yourself what I have said to you tonight, and you will do my bidding in this and stay away from Houstoun Castle."

∿ ∿ ∿

Ranald saw no more of the Douglas boys that summer, nor did he venture up the hill to Houstoun Castle. With his tutor gone, he had time on his hands, time that he spent, whenever possible, with Marjorie. When he wasn't with Thomas, learning the merchant's trade, or putting in the study time that his father directed, he and Marjorie would play games on the lawns or take long walks in the warm summer afternoons along the Beugh Burn to its source in the hills at Drumcross, or climb on the Crag of Binny. Marjorie loved to go to Binny and stand on the top, pointing out the distant hills to the north, across the Forth River, and the great castles of Edinburgh and Stirling.

Ranald liked to go there too, for on the climb up, he could take her hand or put an arm around her slim waist to support her. The merest touch of her: her smile, her fragrance, her melodious laughter, pervaded his senses. Soon, he thought of little else but when next he would be with her. The Douglases, the trading ships that he so loved to visit, even the tales of Marco Polo that had been constantly read and re-read, were all blotted out by one single thought of Marjorie. Perhaps — dare he wish it — one kiss, one touch of these sweet, laughing lips. And it came at last.

Ranald's dirk had carved into the smooth bark of the walnut tree the tryst that he longed to make, "R. L M". He was replacing the dirk in the sheath at his waist, his other hand brushing off the loose bark shavings that clung to the thin stem, when a delicate white arm encircled his waist from behind. He turned and looked into the lovely shining eyes. Suddenly all the pent up passion of the summer exploded. He took her in his arms and kissed her mouth. It was warm and soft and he kissed it again and again. And Marjorie kissed Ranald, and they held each other, standing there by the little walnut tree at the edge of Houstoun Wood, until the sun fell below the high gables of Strathalmond.

∾∾∾

As the warm summer days gave way to autumn, and tenant farmers, and lesser folk that gained their living from the land, harvested the oats and barley on the strip fields of landed estates and cottar farms, the inhabitants of Strathalmond became conscious of the increasing activity around Houstoun. Large groups of men, many of them mounted on sturdy, short-legged garrons, travelled noisily along the southern boundary of Strathalmond lands to and from the castle.

Ranald had no direct contact with the Douglases, but there was much talk among the servants of how William of Houstoun was entertaining the riders at Houstoun Castle, and venturing out himself, at the head of ever increasing bands, around the sheriffdom, from the Burgh of Linlithgow along the estuary of the Forth, by Abercorn and Cramond, to the West Port of the capital itself. The traffic along their boundaries became the subject of conversation between Ranald and his father. "'Tis no concern of yours, Ranald, but now you can see the young earl flexing his muscles, and I have a strong fear that he might enrage the wrong people," Thomas said.

At the celebration of Martinmas, following the Mass at St. Nicholas Church, Ranald and Marjorie took a long walk in the brisk November air to the Moor of Drumshorling, that long sweeping expanse of scrub and fern on the estate of Houstoun, lying to the south of Houstoun Castle. As they emerged from the woods that bounded the moor on the north, the sight that greeted them caused Ranald to tighten his grip on Marjorie's hand and draw her protectively to him.

Upwards of five hundred horsemen wheeled back and forth in the swirling ground mist, whooping and calling out commands and waving long lances hung with fluttering pennants, the steel tips shining here and there in the watery sunlight. Further off, foot soldiers, in loosely assembled columns, moved at a steady march across the moor.

As the couple stood there, transfixed at the sight, one of the riders broke off and galloped straight towards them.

Ranald saw that it was William of Houstoun, earl of Douglas. He sat high on a heavy horse and he wore a leather doublet fronted by a triangular gusset of chain mail. A linen overshirt displayed the red Heart of Bruce above the Lion Rampant, the arms of the sixth earl of Douglas. He turned his mount with a deft pull on the reins, so close to Ranald and Marjorie that several divots of soft earth sprayed up causing the pair to cover their faces. The earl gave a loud guffaw as he turned the horse again to face them. "Think ye that ye could unseat me now, Ranald Ingram?" he sniffed and raised his head, the young boyish face turning to a sneer.

Ranald recognised the copied mannerism of James "the Gross", and was suddenly afraid. He didn't reply.

"Nay! Not ye, nor a thousand like ye. Not James Stewart,

nor Crichton nor all the jackals that slink at their backs. Look ye!" Half turning in the saddle, he pushed a gloved fist straight into the air above his head. At the signal, the ranks of warriors assembled behind him let forth their fearsome battle cry that carried away across the moor.

"A Douglas! A Douglas! A Douglas!"

Ranald put his arm around Marjorie's shoulders and she leaned, trembling, against him.

"Nae a question. Eh? Ranald 'the Questioner' is fair oot o' questions. Eh?" William said, as he swung around to face his men. Then, as a parting shot, he looked back at Ranald. "Ah'm bound for Edinburgh Castle in two weeks at the invitation of the king, and Ah'll warrant young Jamie Stewart will have nae questions either." Laughing madly, he rode off across the moor to the Douglas army.

Ranald guided Marjorie back through the trees toward Strathalmond, embracing her and consoling her in silence. The shouts behind them rang out in the clear morning air; "A Douglas! A Douglas!"

ᘏ ᘏ ᘏ

At the dinner table, Thomas Ingram sat with a silent frown as Ranald recounted the run in with the earl of Douglas. Now and again he cursed under his breath. "The young fool. Bloody young fool."

Later, when they were alone, Isabella looked up from her sewing at her husband who sat by the window, looking out, still wearing the frown that had clothed his face throughout the evening. "Thomas, I think you must do something to curtail these strolls of Ranald and Marjorie."

Thomas Ingram looked up, awakened from his reverie. "Oh that, m'dear. They have no fault in that. They weren't to know that William Douglas would be practising for battle on Drumshorling Moor."

Isabella returned to her work, setting another careful stitch and drawing the needle up towards her. "I'm not talking about Douglas, my love," she replied, looking up. "At least, not William Douglas."

"What then?" Thomas' interest grew. Isabella gathered up her cloth and threads and placed them in the basket beside her chair.

"Our daughter and Ranald Douglas." It was the first time either of them had ever referred to their adopted son by that name.

Thomas sat in silence for a long time, eyeing his wife, his mind working. "Oh! You're not saying .... you don't mean ...."

"Aye, that's exactly what I mean. What world do you men live in?"

Thomas became agitated. "But ... but that .... cannot be ... I mean ... it just cannot be!"

Isabella spoke in a quiet, level voice, almost a whisper. "I'm afraid that it can be," she said. "And it is. You just have to look at them. They are stricken with love for one another." Thomas Ingram was perplexed. He looked around the floor in front of him, his head moving from side to side.

"What will we do?" he demanded. "What will we do?"

"There is very little we *can* do," Isabella replied.

∾ ∾ ∾

Two weeks later, as the family were at dinner in the sumptuous dining room of Strathalmond, Thomas watching his children at every turn with a new kind of interest, the double doors burst open and a servant retreated into the room, propelled by the forceful entry of Will Douglas of Abercorn. Thomas got to his feet, signalling to the servant to release the intruder, whereupon William advanced from the entrance and stood facing the family, agitated and tearful.

"The earl is dead! William and David are dead, murdered by that bastard Crichton!" he cried out.

A few moments elapsed while the import of what he said sank in, then Thomas and Isabella rushed to the young man, consoling him and leading him to sit down at the table. Ranald was staggered. He just stared at William while Marjorie pressed a fist to her mouth, her eyes wide and frightened.

When, by the tender ministrations of the Ingrams, Will Douglas had partly recovered his composure, he proceeded to tell what had happened.

"I tried to warn them, William and David. When William got that invitation from Crichton — sent under the king's seal — to dine at Edinburgh. 'Beware!' I told him. 'Crichton cannot be trusted'. But you know William of Houstoun. He was always a hot-head, and since he became earl, he's been worse than ever. He wouldn't listen to me, and, to make matters worse, he took a thousand men with him to the capital and flaunted his power in the face of Crichton. God! I should have stopped him." Will Douglas wrung his hands in agitation, his eyes wildly searching the stone flags of the floor.

"You shouldn't blame yourself," Thomas said gently. "And I doubt if you could have stopped the earl of Douglas."

" Michael, William's manservant, told me what happened," Will went on. "The men-at arms were billeted around the city and the boys entered the castle alone apart from Michael and another servant. Crichton and Livingston were both there and the laddie King. Right after the dinner, Chancellor Crichton put a bull's head on the table, then six of his men seized William and young Davey. They dragged them out of the hall into the courtyard, shouting treason, and hacked them to death." Will shook his head and began to cry. "They cut their heads from their bodies," he sobbed, looking up at Thomas Ingram.

"And the king," Ranald began.

"The king!" Will's voice rose. "Michael said that he just stood there greetin'. He's just a wee laddie — a frightened wee laddie."

Will leaned forward, his head in his hands, silently crying. Ranald went to him and embraced his shoulders. The women sobbed into napkins. Only Thomas Ingram spoke.

"A sad day for the Douglases", he said quietly. "And a sad day for Scotland".

Chapter Four

༄ ༄ ༄

After a hard gallop along the shore from the small burgh of Queensferry, the two young men slid from their saddles, laughing and panting, and collapsed side by side against the north wall of Abercorn Castle.

"Another win for the merchant," Will Douglas said with a grudging frown, his eyes full of merriment. "You are in the wrong trade, you know. Anyone who can ride like that should be a soldier." He reached inside his leather doublet and extracted a silver coin which he flicked to Ranald Ingram. Ranald laughed.

"Now that you are earl of Douglas, maybe I should let you win the odd race I am thinking."

The two relaxed on the short grass, their backs against the castle wall, looking out over the estuary of the Forth that sparkled in the August morning.

"You know, from the top of this tower, on a clear day, you can see the Palace of Falkland, right . . . there," Will said, pointing across the water. "They say it's the king's favourite place."

The two friends gazed where he had pointed, the mention of James Stewart evoking memories of William of Houstoun and young David and their cruel murders at the Black Dinner, and of James "the Gross", who everyone now knew had conspired with the murderous Crichton in that affair to become earl of Douglas himself. His gluttonous appetite had rendered him bed-ridden in the year before his death, and he had taken no pleasure from the title that he had so wickedly acquired. Now Ranald looked at his son, Will Douglas of Abercorn, now the eighth earl of Douglas and his friend. Ranald wondered how so likeable a man could have issued from such a villainous father.

On first sight Will and Ranald looked like brothers due to the black curly hair and the same dark blue of the eyes. But Will was broad and powerfully built with square jaw and eyes that fixed and penetrated an onlooker, while Ranald Ingram, a shade taller, was slim of build with eyes that laughed and he had the small delicate hands and facial features of his real father, Archibald Douglas.

"So, tell me Ranald! How is the romance with that gorgeous creature that you hide away at Strathalmond?" Will said.

Ranald blushed. He wished that he had never confided in Will Douglas his love for Marjorie Ingram. He had told his friend that he was adopted by the Ingrams as a boy and that Marjorie and he were not brother and sister.

"What does Thomas Ingram say to it?" Will went on, amused at his friend's discomfort. "Though if it were me that was so fortunate as to capture that particular flower, I wouldn't care a damn what her father thought."

"Shame on you, earl Douglas, married at Lent to the Fair Maid of Galloway," Ranald laughed.

Will's hearty guffaw pierced the morning stillness. "Married, Aye! A maid, Aye! For God sake man, she's but a wee lassie. She's only eleven years old. Aye, Lent was the perfect timing for that marriage. A betrothal arranged by my scheming old father to secure the Lordships of Bothwell and Galloway, the reunification of the Douglas lands. Not that I am complaining, mind you, but it will be a long time before I can crawl into her wee bed. You, on the other hand, have no territory except what you might carve out among the sheets with that fair-haired angel you are courting. I would be happy to give you Bothwell and Galloway for her right now, and I would go down and sweep her into my saddle and away to Threave and live happily ever after." He smiled fondly at Ranald. "But alas, her heart is pledged to another. You're a lucky bastard, Ingram. A lucky man, and I have to live like a monk, earldom and all."

"You're no monk, Will. Not from the stories I've heard. I think there isn't a plump thigh between here and Houstoun that doesn't have your finger marks on it." At that the earl clapped Ranald on the shoulder and they both dissolved in laughter.

After some further philosophising on the subject of girls, Will became serious. "So when are you going to tell your father about you and Marjorie Ingram? You're not getting any younger, you know. What age are you now? Twenty is it?"

Ranald looked down, frowning and playing a blade of grass in his fingers. "It's difficult," he mumbled.

"Would it help if I were to go with you to see him," Will said.

Ranald looked up quickly. "No! Not you! I mean, no . . . . . it wouldn't help."

Will didn't miss the anxiety in the denial. "Not me. Why not me Ranald?" His eyes fixed on Ranald's and he read the concern in his friend's face. Ranald looked away as Will pressed on. "Why not me?"

Ranald looked back slowly at the questioning eyes. He knew that he could not go back now. He had said too much and he must tell the truth of the matter.

"Will," he said, "Thomas Ingram doesn't know that I keep company with you." He watched the Earl's puzzlement slowly turn to hurt as he continued. "I was forbidden years ago to keep company with any Douglas. My father, for some reason, thinks there is danger in it. I haven't obeyed him Will. He doesn't know I'm here."

"Danger?" Will said. "What danger? Where is the danger?"

"I don't know, exactly. But I think it has to do with the feuding and hatred in the country among Douglases and Crichtons and Livingstons. I think that, but I don't know". Ranald saw the hurt look on the other's face. "But that makes no difference to me Will," he hastily added , grabbing Will's arm. "You and I are friends and I will always see you. Father is getting old, you know. He is seeing ghosts where there aren't any. I wouldn't have mentioned this except to explain why you can't help me with Marjorie. That, I must do myself, and I will do it when I'm ready."

Will was silent for a few moments. Then he spoke quietly. "Whatever the danger Thomas Ingram imagines, there is none to you, but it is not right for you to disobey your father, Ranald. You must away now, back to Strathalmond, and steer yourself clear o' me in the future."

"No!" Ranald almost shouted the word. Then in a serious voice, "No. I pick my friend and I see my friend and that friend is you, Will Douglas. That is an end to it."

"I think not," said the Earl, getting to his feet, "for I have planned a raid on Crichton's castle at Barnton for this day week. If there is danger to come from that, you can have no part with me. Obey your father!"

Ranald rose up steadily, his face red, and his look demanding and serious. "I will go now, but I will ride with you on Barnton in a week." Before the Earl could reply, Ranald leapt into the saddle and rode off southwards to Strathalmond without looking back.

 барана

The tower-house of Barnton overlooked the river Forth a few miles to the west of Edinburgh. It was the home of Sir George Crichton, Admiral of Scotland and Sheriff of Linlithgow, a cousin of Chancellor Crichton, the murderer of the young Douglases. Chancellor Crichton, for whom Will Douglas nursed a rankling hatred, had his home in Edinburgh Castle, a stronghold which, even with the Douglas strength, was unassailable, and could never have been attacked anyway as long as King James II was in residence. To strike at the Crichtons, the earl of Douglas chose Barnton. By a series of machinations emanating from a need for Chancellor Crichton to answer to the king for an alleged default, Will Douglas, acting as the king's lieutenant- general, had the opportunity to advance his considerable force against a Crichton. He cared less for the Chancellor's default, contrived or otherwise, than for the chance to act out his own very personal agenda in avenging the murders of his cousins.

It was revenge that filled the mind of the Earl of Douglas early on the morning of the twentieth of August in the year 1444, revenge against Chancellor Crichton to be taken against his cousin, an innocent in the deed perhaps, but a Crichton nevertheless, and one that he could get to.

A cold wind blew in from the Forth, carrying a heavy rain that soaked the three hundred or so mounted troops as they circled and formed ranks on the flat land to the south of Abercorn Castle. Will Douglas, on a heavy, dappled-grey horse, his bright coat of arms on his breastplate, rode in and out through the ranks shouting orders to the men. He could have raised thirty times the force, but he knew that what he had mustered, mainly from his Lothian lands, with a few captains from his headquarters at Threave in Galloway, would be sufficient to assault Barnton and he would use no more than was needed.

There was no element of surprise planned and Will well knew that news of his coming would have already been delivered to Barnton, just a few miles distant, by any number of local tenants seeking some small reward. There would be no time, however, for any force to be assembled by the Crichtons in defence of their castle. This was why Will Douglas had raised his men in Lothian rather than announce his coming in a long march from Galloway.

As the troop was assembled for departure, Ranald Ingram rode out of the trees to the south. He pulled up short when he saw the assembled men. He peered through the rain at the serried ranks of horses, the long bristling spears, banners and pennants here and there and the helmets and armoured vests. Urging his mount forward he could make out two small cannon mounted on carts and some apparatus of slings and large stone balls. His excitement of accompanying his friend turned to apprehension. He suddenly realised that he had given no thought to the venture he was embarking upon. He had looked forward for a whole week to an adventure with the Douglas, something different from his trade missions around the wool merchants and the farmers who grew oats for export. It was going to be exciting and he had told Thomas Ingram that he was going to a friary north of Perth to negotiate a wool shipment. Now, seeing the horsemen move slowly off, Douglas colours fluttering in the wind, Ranald was suddenly afraid.

As Ranald's hands trembled on the reins, Will Douglas rode up, commanding and resplendent in his armour with its blue and white coat of arms. He wore no helm and wet black curls were plastered against his forehead. Above the breastplate, a mentonniere plate was fastened, rising to cover the lower part of his face.

Ranald stared at him. This wasn't the friend with whom he hunted birds around Abercorn and talked about girls on warm afternoons. This was a warrior, riding before an army on a dark plain. The cold wind sent a shiver through his body.

"Hail to you, Ingram!" Will called through the rain. "What brings you here?"

Ranald's sense of excitement and adventure had now all but evaporated and he could think of nothing to say.

"Be off home, man! This day's work is not for a merchant. Get back to your accounts and your customers."

Ranald's face flushed with anger. He was being dismissed like a child.

"I said I would ride with you to Barnton, and ride I will," Ranald retorted, his voice trembling.

Will moved right up beside him, at once dropping his arrogant, commanding posture and regretting the insult to his friend. "You should obey your father, man. There could be danger for you in this, and I would want no part of that."

The unspoken apology gave Ranald courage. "I am going," he said, and he reined his horse around to set off after the column. Will leaned over and grasped Ranald's arm.

"Then you will go," he said, "but you will ride in the rear and when we get to Barnton you will stay back and watch. This is my command. Do you take my meaning?"

Ranald nodded without looking at the Douglas, tears mixing with the rain on his face.

The ensuing raid on the tower-house at Barnton was sudden and deadly. Ranald Ingram, an unarmed civilian observing from the rear, was introduced to a new experience, one that caused him to bring up the contents of his stomach and to swear to himself that never again would he disobey his father. He watched the events unfold as pictures in a book, as the pages are turned by some unseen hand: the Douglas horsemen galloping to the gate; the few defenders going down beneath the hooves of the horses or impaled on the long spears of the attackers; heads severed by swords and arms and legs twitching on the headless trunks. He saw the battering ram cave in the studded oaken door, while servants, who had earlier poured hot steaming liquid from the walls, were cut to pieces in the courtyard within. Here and there he heard the screams of women as they were brought down and raped by groups of Douglas men, and he shut his eyes when he saw a child of no more than three years being waved in the air on the end of a lance.

Soon the tower-house was ablaze, the flames licking at the rain from the narrow windows. The small cannon were brought up to blast the stone work from the inside at close range, and a huge swinging stone ball was erected to finish the demolition. All the while cries of "A Douglas" "A Douglas" rent the air.

Before it was dark, Barnton Castle had ceased to exist. The Douglas force had turned again for Abercorn, leaving behind them only a smouldering ruin and the plaintiff sobs and cries of what remained of the Crichton household. Long before that, Ranald Ingram had ridden off to the south-east and crossed the river on his way to Strathalmond, his stomach sick and his head pounding.

That night and for many days thereafter Ranald couldn't rid from his mind the images of Barnton. He launched himself into his work and his studies and said nothing to his parents or to Marjorie about his experience. He heard that Will Douglas had returned to Galloway and was relieved not to have to see him, or try to reconcile the friend he had made with the fearsome commander of that bloodthirsty host.

A few weeks later Strathalmond was awakened in the middle of the night by the thundering of horses and the yelling and shouting of riders. Ranald arose at once and went to the window of his chamber. The pictures of the Barnton raid rushed back into his mind as he stared out at a score or more of mounted men urging their horses along the edge of the grounds and past the gates of Strathalmond towards Houstoun Castle. Some held aloft flaming torches, and their lit-up faces flashed past in the night like an army of caterwauling spectres.

He rushed down the winding staircase to the main hall where he met Thomas Ingram in his long shift, peering through the side of the large window as he tied the silken cord around his waist. Servants were assembling, dishevelled and confused, and Isabella appeared, one hand clutching her breast in abject alarm. Marjorie followed, half hiding behind her mother as she grasped the back of Isabella's night gown.

"They're passing!" Thomas whispered, looking around to Ranald. "I think it's a raid on Houstoun."

He turned back to look out the window as Ranald joined him.

The horsemen had passed, and now Ranald could see the brushwood flares they carried closing on the granaries and outhouses around Houstoun Castle. Thomas opened the door, and he and the others watched and listened to the now distant shouting. Suddenly a ball of fire lit up the night sky; then another.

"They're burning the granaries," Thomas shouted.

Isabella moved behind her husband and pulled him by the shoulder. "Come back into the house!" she shrieked. "Come in and shut the door. It's none of our affair, husband." Ranald strode forward and clanged the heavy door shut. He turned back into the room, white faced and trembling. "It's Crichton," he said. He fixed his gaze on the stone tiles at his feet. "It's revenge for Barnton." Then he looked at Thomas. "Can I talk to you and mother?" he said.

∾ ∾ ∾

The next day, after a night of guilt-ridden, fitful rest during which Ranald pondered on what he intended to say to his parents, they assembled in Thomas' study that overlooked the stone dovecote on the east side of the house. Ranald stood by the window while Thomas and Isabella eyed him in an expectant silence.

"Last night I might have brought much grief to this house," Ranald began. "I was at the destruction of the Barnton towerhouse with Will Douglas."

He looked away as Thomas leapt up from his chair, and Ranald was to witness the Ingram rage at first hand and for the first time in his young life.

After what seemed like an endless barrage of loud and unrestrained remonstrations, interspersed with accusations of disobedience, stupidity, carelessness, and callousness, during which Ranald stood immobile, staring at the floor, Isabella came forward and gently spoke to Thomas as she led him back, somewhat exhausted, to his seat. After a long silence, wherein Thomas avoided Ranald's eyes while Isabella moved to comfort her son, Ranald continued.

"I humbly beg your forgiveness, sir, for disobeying you. I was scared at Barnton; scared out of my wits. Will Douglas is my friend but I could never again ride with him. I know that now. You need have no fear of my disobeying you in this ever again."

Isabella looked at her husband with a little smile on her lips and squeezed his arm. Thomas didn't react, nor did he look at either her or Ranald.

"I want you to send me to Brugge on our next sailing, to work there for a while and learn about the markets." Ranald said. Now Thomas Ingram did look at him, the anger vanishing from his face. "And I ask for the hand of your daughter,

Marjorie, so that we may be married on my return."

Thomas and Isabella just sat there, speechless, staring at Ranald, their faces lacking all expression. Ranald, whose courage finally failed him, mumbled something to the effect that he must attend to his work, and took a quick leave of them as they were still trying to take in his announcement.

∾ ∾ ∾

"Marriage!" Thomas Ingram kept repeating the word. "Marriage!"

Isabella poured out two goblets of wine and returned to her chair. She laughed at her husband's inability to advance the conversation beyond that single word.

"Come, Thomas. That adopted son of yours and our lovely daughter are in love. Anyone can see it. The servants, even the doves in the dovecote can see it. It was only a matter of time until he plucked up the courage to ask for her hand."

Thomas seized the goblet and took a large swallow. "But marriage?" he repeated.

"And why not marriage?" Isabella replied. "Marjorie isn't getting any younger. What did you have in mind for her? And who better for a husband than Ranald? He is your protégé, the son you never had, and you have said many times that he is becoming a fine, skilful merchant."

"You know why not, woman. He is a Douglas." Thomas grunted.

"Is that the reason that you would deny him, Thomas? Is that the only reason?"

Thomas had to think for a moment. He looked at Isabella who raised her eyebrows. "Well?" she said.

"Yes . . . yes I suppose it is," he said, suddenly realising that there was no other reason except perhaps the reluctance of a father to part with a daughter, something that was too silly for him to admit.

"So, he is a Douglas, though he does not know it," Isabella persisted. "But he is an Ingram in all his endeavours. He was raised as an Ingram, as your son. He had one involvement with the Douglases that he has regretted. He admitted it, and he got such a fright that he won't repeat it. You heard him."

All the time she was speaking Thomas was thinking. She was right. Ranald had confessed to disobeying him and keeping company with Earl Douglas. He got a fright and maybe it had cured him. Maybe, even when his true identity was made public — and it had to be — if there was to be a betrothal to Marjorie, whom everyone thought was his sister, maybe there would be no tie to the Douglases and the danger that surrounded them. He would be seen to be a merchant in the Ingram enterprise, the son of Thomas Ingram, an important burgess in Edinburgh and a shipowner. Ranald Douglas would be seen as an Ingram. One day he would inherit the Ingram business. What more could Thomas want for his daughter?

Isabella broke into his thoughts. "I am right, am I not?" she said. "There's no reason to refuse Ranald's betrothal to our daughter. In any event, you can then send him to Brugge, at his own request; send him for six months if you want to test his love and his promises."

Isabella's logic was undeniable and Thomas finally agreed to grant Ranald's wishes. He knew that his resolve was malleable in the hands of this lady he had married, but she was rarely wrong in these things. Yet the concern still lived at the back of his mind. Ranald Ingram was a Douglas.

Ranald tried hard to put recent events from his mind and concentrate on his studies. He confined himself to his chamber and avoided contact with Marjorie in spite of his longing to be with her, to encircle her slim waist and nuzzle his face into her slender neck and the delicate fragrance of her hair. Pictures jumbled in his mind of Will Douglas wheeling through the smoke among his vicious plunderers. He saw again the blazing granges of Houstoun against the black sky, the anger in Thomas' face, the supplications of his mother, and he himself, standing there and boldly asking for the hand of Marjorie Ingram. Had he gone too far? Had he hoped for too much?

When his father finally summoned him to his study, he felt a great sense of relief. Now there would be a resolution of all that happened in the last few weeks and he would know how things stood.

Thomas Ingram was composed when Ranald entered the room. Ranald suddenly thought how old he looked, sitting back in his high-backed couch, smaller looking than the giant, striding figure on the dock at Leith. Thomas' long face was marked with some small wrinkles around the eyes, and his long hands seeming skeletal as they lay on his lap, joined at the finger tips. He smiled the Ingram smile and Ranald relaxed.

"You had much to say of late, Ranald", he began. Ranald was silent. "Much that needed saying, I think. You are a man now, and it is right that you should speak your mind. Indeed you would be no Ingram if you did not. You have courage, Ranald Ingram, and you have a good discipline of mind, and I have some things now, of my own, to say to you." Ranald waited, expectant and apprehensive.

"You will go to Brugge as you have requested, and we will talk further on this later as I have some ideas concerning some new trading ventures that we should explore. Further to this, I want to offer you a partnership in our business. You are ready for it, and I need you now to take over from me as my duties as burgess take time away from our other ventures."

Ranald was overjoyed. A partnership! New trading adventures! Thomas went on. "I give my consent to your betrothal to my daughter."

Ranald couldn't believe what he was hearing. As he tried to speak, Thomas raised his hand. "And, hear me well! I don't say that I have no concerns in this matter, but I have agreed to it on the understanding that your association with the Douglases is no longer an issue, and that you have learned your lesson."

This was the best day of Ranald Ingram's life. Betrothed to Marjorie, his own beautiful Marjorie, and a partner with Thomas Ingram of Strathalmond.

"One final thing, Ranald, before you explode with your own good fortune as you stand there." Ranald was barely listening now. What final thing? Did he not have everything he ever wanted?

"As you know, you came to Strathalmond as a boy, the son of a friend of mine whom I chose to raise as my own son." Ranald nodded, his interest growing.

"Do you remember where we first met?" Thomas continued. Ranald had thought about that meeting often when he was younger and the present conversation brought the memories back to him. He recalled a large house with big kitchens, where he spent time with a fat red-faced lady who was always tasting soup or stew from a large pot and letting Ranald taste it. Often it was hot and burned his tongue. Then a little man would come and shout at the lady and take Ranald into a big garden.

"I remember some things," he said.

"A man, perhaps?" Thomas said. "A little man?"

Ranald nodded. Thomas looked seriously into Ranald's eyes. "That man was your father."

Ranald tried to picture clearly the little man in the garden, but he couldn't see the face. "Who? . . ." he began.

"You met him a few years ago at Houstoun Castle," Thomas said, searching Ranald's face. "The plague?"

After a few moments Ranald was suddenly back in that awful room, with the posies and the overpowering smell and the little naked man on the bed. "My father?" he croaked, feeling his legs go weak beneath him and catching hold of a chair. "My father?" He sat down heavily.

Thomas' voice was quiet and steady. "Your father. Archibald the fifth earl of Douglas."

Ranald sat in a half stupor as Thomas went on to recount the whole story of his original meeting with the earl and the arrangement that had brought Ranald to Strathalmond. "And now you can see why you were called to his bedside that terrible day," Thomas said. "So that he could take a last farewell of his son."

A strange mixture of feelings flooded through Ranald. He sat in the chair looking at Thomas then turning his head to the window that opened towards Houstoun. He was neither happy nor sad. After the initial shock of the news he didn't feel anything. Eventually he spoke.

"A lot is clear to me now, father. Why you are so concerned by the Douglas name. Why you have feared for me." Gathering his thoughts he continued. "You need have no fear. I am Ranald Ingram and that will always be my name, and you will always be my father." He stood up and moved to Thomas, reaching out his hand. Thomas took it in his own and embraced his son, sheer pride and joy beaming from his eyes.

Chapter
Five

꙰ ꙰ ꙰

Shortly after the revelation of Ranald's true identity, a feast was held at Strathalmond to mark the betrothal of Ranald Douglas Ingram of Strathalmond and Marjorie Ingram. It was attended by all the local dignitaries, various burgesses from the city, business acquaintances of the Ingrams, family members from Leith and Lanark and the ever present cleric, Thomas of Stowe, the professional reveller.

News of the betrothal had been announced far and wide, that had declared Ranald as the son of Archibald the fifth earl of Douglas, and it was no surprise therefore when a servant admitted the latecomers, a dark powerful quartet in leather jerkins and high riding boots spattered with the mud of their journey from Threave — William the eighth earl of Douglas and three of his brothers.

Will Douglas strode right up to Ranald at the high table. He bowed slightly to Thomas and Isabella, before thrusting out his hand to grip Ranald's in a strong handshake.

"Congratulations, cousin Ranald Douglas!" Turning to Marjorie, he delivered a low and graceful bow. "Your bride to be is even fairer than I remembered. May you both have a long and happy life together." Then, looking at one of the table servants, he called out, "Is there a seat at this feast for the men of Galloway?"

Places were soon laid, and the Douglases joined in the occasion while the other guests could not hide their awe. They had found themselves in the company of the most powerful family in Scotland. Ranald received smiles and nods of pleasure and esteem, and even Thomas Ingram found himself sharing in the reflected glory of the occasion. After years of misgiving about this family, Thomas was suddenly lording it before his important associates — sheriffs and burgesses of the Lowlands — for the Douglases were little less important than the king of the realm, if that, and here they were in Strathalmond, guests at Thomas Ingram's table. Isabella, so wise and unperturbed on most occasions, now fluttered like a butterfly to the attentions of Will Douglas and his brothers.

After the meal, Ranald and Marjorie found themselves alone with Earl Douglas in an ante-room off the great hall. Will again pounded Ranald's hand. "So, cousin! I might have guessed it. See! Marjorie," he laughed, tilting Ranald face up with a hand under his chin. "Most clearly a Douglas, and I'll warrant you are glad of it."

Marjorie bristled. "Were he a Douglas, Sire, I might have little cause to be glad. As it is, he is an Ingram, which is all that I desire." The barb in her tone was ignored by the Douglas, who merely smiled and screwed up his face in an affected wince.

"A flower most certainly, Ranald, but no wall-flower I see." Will Douglas quipped.

At that point Marjorie excused herself saying that she had to attend her mother, and the two new-found cousins were left alone.

"I've missed you Ranald since our little escapade at Barnton. I had hoped that you might have ridden over to Abercorn when I was there."

Ranald's silence didn't go unnoticed, and Will went on. "Ah, I see. The old problem. The dangerous Douglases. Am I correct?"

Noticing Ranald's uneasiness, Will caught him by the shoulders. "Look, my friend! I understand it and I understand Thomas Ingram's concern. Believe me now! We live in different worlds. I know that. Your immediate business takes you to the markets of Brugge and Antwerp to make deals for the flow of goods. Mine takes me to the general council at Stirling to outlaw the Crichtons. But we are friends, are we not? And as your friend I can help you. Tell me what I can do to assuage the fears of your new partner, Thomas Ingram? Did I hear it right? You are now a partner with Thomas Ingram?" Will smiled.

All the happy warmth of his comradeship with Will Douglas filled Ranald once more, ousting the doubts that he had felt at Barnton, and he gushed forth his latest trading plan that would justify Thomas Ingram's trust in making him a partner.

"I can see the signs, Will. I can read things in the times that will profit us in the future. Wine! Will. The clarets of France. The doors to French wine will be closed to England but not to the Scots. You know what that means, Will? The wine that England needs, and will sooner or later sorely want, can be had from us, Will."

Will laughed heartily. "Enough!" he cried. "Enough, I say. What do I know of wine except how to drink it? But if you need my help, you need but ask."

The two hugged each other, happy in their friendship.

"Come, Ranald Douglas Ingram! Is there no wine at this feast? And remember this. To the next raid of the Douglas on Northumberland, you, my friend, are not invited."

∾∾∾

In the autumn of that year Ranald set off for Europe, embarking on the busiest period of his career so far. He planned to study the markets, gain a full understanding of the workings and financial dealings of the Company of the Staple in Calais that monopolised the English wool trade, make business contacts for the Ingram enterprises and develop his own plans for the importing of French wines through Scotland into the much larger English market. These plans hinged upon Ranald's belief that, in a very few years, the predominance of the Port of Bristol as the centre of the wine trade would decline, due to the loss of English landholdings in France and the denial of French wines to England. When this occurred, Ranald would be ready.

Back in Strathalmond, life was equally as busy for Marjorie Ingram. The wedding date was set for early in June of the following year. Marjorie's education, which had included reading, French, song and scripture, and had always been addressed to the finer points of manners and deportment for a young woman of her class in society, now found a new emphasis in light of her impending marriage.

Thomas Ingram had, for some years, owned a town house in Edinburgh which was found to be necessary for his increasing duties as a burgess of that city, and he had decided that he and Isabella would move there after the wedding, leaving Strathalmond as the home of Ranald and Marjorie.

In the upcoming months, Marjorie, under the guidance of her mother and Dame Elizabeth, a tall spindly woman who always wore black and rarely smiled, learned the skills of running a household and pleasing a husband. Dame Elizabeth, a mixture of housekeeper and chaperon, was at Marjorie's side every hour of every day, correcting, cajoling and reprimanding.

"When we go to Mass each morning, at the Church of St. Nicholas, you will bear your head upright and your eyelids low and without fluttering. You will look straight in front without looking up nor glancing from place to place, nor stopping to speak to anyone on the road," Dame Elizabeth instructed. "And have a care that your hair, wimple, kerchief and hood and all the rest of your attire be decently ordered, so that none who see you can mock you, but may find in you an example of fair, simple and decent array. And on our return from Mass, you must see that the maids are employed upon their work and you must interview Master James, the steward, arranging with him the menus for dinner and supper."

Marjorie was soon to discover how full were the days of the wife of a merchant, whose household employed upwards of twenty-five servants. After Mass each day and the checking of household chores and menus, she and her maids would take out her dresses and furs from their chests, spread them in the garden or shake them in the breeze, remove any spots or grease stains and be ever watchful for moths and fleas. Fleas were the constant bugbear, and a good wife required to know how to catch them and dispose of them and keep her husband's bedchamber free of flies and his bed free of fleas. The menu for dinner, which was served at ten o'clock in the morning, would depend on the time of year, and whether it be a meat or a fast day, and the good wife needed to be familiar with the menus and the supervision of cooks and kitchen staff, and of the acquisitions of supplies from the provisioners and markets.

In the afternoons of spring and summer she would spend time in the garden, giving advice to the gardeners, picking and arranging flowers, weaving garlands of thyme and rosemary or gathering berries for the table. She might also ride out hawking with other ladies of the district.

In winter, after supper, a good wife might sit under the carved beams of the hall, mending her master's doublet, embroidering a vestment for the priest, or making a hanging tapestry for the bedchamber. In the evenings, on the return of her husband, she would be expected to bring bowls of warm water to wash his feet, and comfortable shoes to ease him. She would listen to his words and admire his labours, and perhaps she would tell him how she passed her day and ask his advice on any small problem that she might have with the servants or the provisioners. At the end of the day she would accompany her husband around the house, ensuring that the servants were in bed, locking the doors and putting out the candles, for a good wife must be thrifty and not wasteful in the burning of candles.

All this was impressed on Marjorie, and it was made clear to her that her constant attention to her husband, both in and out of the marriage bed, the keeping of his secrets, the careful and charitable management of his household, and the pleasing of his guests, would keep him contented and keep his attentions from roaming to other women.

Like his father Thomas, Ranald Ingram, an important and wealthy merchant, had to be seen to be charitable: in the giving of alms to the poor, in patronage to the church and in the making of gifts of jewels, wine, and game to his peers, and to his leading retainers. Thereby he maintained a high social profile, and this expansive generosity was nothing more than was expected from him. On a special occasion, such as his upcoming wedding to Marjorie, a more than usual display of dignity and wealth would be called for from Ranald and his father which would show itself in the size and quality of the wedding banquet.

In the Spring of the year, as the wedding day approached, Marjorie's instruction turned towards the planning of the banquet. The feast would be a day long affair, incorporating dinner in the morning, after the nuptials at St. Nicholas Church, and continuing until the evening supper. Isabella and Marjorie, with the invaluable help of Master James the Steward, set out to plan the affair, the staff that would be required for the occasion, and the menus for the feasts.

Four big men from Myrestane would be hired as ushers to keep the door, and control any guests who might have too much wine and ale. Squires would be recruited to serve at the dresser in the kitchen for the handing out of dishes, and at the hall dresser for the distribution of spoons, and cups, and the pouring of wine for the guests. Two senior table servants would set out the silver salt cellars at the high table, the gilded goblets, spoons, ewers, alms mugs, and sweetmeat dishes, and show the guests to their places. Each table would have a waiter and two servitors. A flower girl would make chaplets of flowers for the guests, and there would be women to see to the linen and deck the bridal bed, which would be blessed in a special ceremony. The floors of the great hall would be strewn with violets and green herbs, and flowering branches would be gathered in the morning to deck the walls. A good stock of candles would be laid in for the tables, and great torches to be set in the sconces on the walls, or carried in procession by the guests, for the supper would end with dancing, singing, wine and spices and lighted torches. Minstrels would be hired and acrobats and mimes to entertain the company, and Master James said that they should not forget to engage a clerk to keep track of costs and make the accounting for the wedding.

Marjorie enjoyed her part in the menu preparation. The maitre d'hotel and his cooks would visit butcher and baker, poulterer and saucemaker, vintner and spicer, and the wafer maker who would prepare the small wafers and pastries that so delighted Marjorie and her friends. Many courses and dishes would be served with rich, highly-spiced viands. There would be beef, mutton and poultry, venison and game of all kinds, black puddings and sausages, eels and herrings, round and flat sea fish and fresh water pike, pottages — spiced and unspiced, meat and meatless — roasts and pastries and diverse sauces. Nor would they forget to serve slops for those without teeth or with weak stomachs.

Meat dishes would be flavoured with vinegar, verijuice and wine, cloves, cinnamon, galingale, pepper and ginger, and the always favourite almonds.

Sweetmeats made with honey, or jams derived from carrot or pumpkin, would be sifted with sugar, and wafers would be filled with candied oranges.

The instruction on the wedding feast menus made Marjorie's mouth water.

When the last of the wet snow had long since gone from Strathalmond, and the land bloomed green with the scent of hawthorn and the eternal promise of May, Marjorie Ingram was no longer a girl of leisure, but had herself blossomed, like the spring, into a capable and confident virgin bride. What she would learn of pleasing her husband in the bed chamber, she would learn on the night, for Dame Elizabeth, who had spent most of her life in a convent, was not qualified to speak on that matter, and Isabella did not see it as a fitting subject to be discussed with a daughter.

Ranald Ingram, on the other hand, had received the appropriate fatherly talk from Thomas, and was encouraged, over a flagon of ale, to seek out, during his stay in France, some courtesan who would teach him the skills of pleasing a wife.

"And an older one," Thomas had said. "The more breeks she has unfastened, the better!"

Ranald travelled extensively between Calais and the different markets in Flanders. He watched the activities of the English Merchants of the Staple at the mart in Calais, where they brought in the famous Cotswold wool, collected and paid the duty to the English Crown, and sold it to the dealers for the Flemish cloth makers. He noted, with considerable interest and admiration, the activities of the Merchant Adventurers, who cared little for the monopoly of the Staple, and made their profits by direct dealing in wool and hides, discounting prices and denying the English King his duties. He talked with the masters and crews of the English wool ships, learning how often they had to evade Scottish pirates or lose their fine wool shipments, although he reminded himself of the many cargoes that had been lost to the Ingram fleet along the English coast. Like Thomas, Ranald cursed the wars and political intrigues that caused trading to suffer, but, if wars were inevitable, the trader must learn to see its advantages and be quick to act.

At three of the great market fairs in Flanders, the Bammys Mart in October, the Cold Mart in winter and the Pasque Mart at Easter, Ranald made his contracts with the dealers from Leyden and from Florence, Genoa and Venice, to load his ships for the Port of Leith with rolls of satin and silk, mink furs, Gascon wine, ginger, saffron, and Holland cloth.

In one short season, he learned about the flow of goods and the intricacies of the money exchanges, and had become a familiar face in the markets. He enjoyed the colour and excitement of Calais and Flanders, and when it came time to leave that bright and vivacious arena and return to his relatively bleak homeland and its clanging of arms on sullen rainy mornings, Ranald was sad. Yet he was all the time thinking and planning, and he knew he would be returning soon to France, for the key to his success would lie in Burgundy when the time was right.

In that same season in which Marjorie Ingram acquired her wifely skills and Ranald made his trading plans, the earl of

Douglas resolved that his attack on Barnton had been ill-advised, and that in future he would think before acting. Though not yet twenty, he had learned much of the art of the politician and of making pacts that would suit his own ends, and unmaking them for the same reason.

The influential Bishop Kennedy, formerly an ally of the Black Douglases and the Livingstons of Linlithgow, now became an enemy, joining with the earl of Angus on the side of Crichton. The Black Douglases and the Livingstons, having now aligned themselves on the side of the king against Crichton, Bishop Kennedy and Angus, moved in November, with the young king in tow, to besiege and take the Castle of Methven in Fife, a stronghold of their new enemies. Then Will Douglas, riding into battle as he loved to do, at the head of Livingstons, Crawfords, Ogilvies, Robertsons and Hamiltons, ravaged and pillaged the land from Fife to Angus and chased Bishop Kennedy into the safe haven of St. Andrews Castle.

The Douglas power continued to grow, and even the curses of Bishop Kennedy, invoked in the name of the Church and the Holy Father, had small effect on Will Douglas. He certainly made no reference to either enemies or curses in his intermittent letters to his friend, Ranald Ingram, in which he restricted his discourse to the hunting of stags and wild boars rather than the hunting of men along the English border. He looked forward to Ranald's replies, with their talk of trading in the foreign markets, and he sometimes pondered upon how preferable might be the life of a peaceful merchant to the responsibilities and constant risks of a Douglas chieftain.

Ranald and Marjorie were married by Thomas of Stowe in the Church of St. Nicholas at Myrestane at the beginning of June, and there followed the most magnificent feast day ever to take place in the shire of Linlithgow. Will Douglas and his brothers, Hugh, Earl of Ormond, and Archibald, Earl of Moray, had a favoured place at the high table. The great hall of Strathalmond was filled to bursting with every kind of dignitary, and the stables with the best mounts in the country. Between the feasts, which were served in relays, the gardens were arranged with tables of wines and sweetmeats, and the colourful robes of ladies vied with the hanging summer blossoms. Various acrobats entertained the guests, and a storyteller, a lank, grey-haired giant, who lived on the Drumshorling Moor, held them spellbound. The music and dancing continued well into the night.

When Ranald finally closed the door to the bedchamber, high in the west range of the house, he turned to find himself captivated anew by the shining eyes of his lovely bride. He suddenly knew how useless and inappropriate had been his sojourn to the house of the woman in Calais, and he struck the memory of it from his mind as he took Marjorie in his arms.

Chapter
Six

ʚʚʚ

A few years later, on the third day of July in the year 1449, the Ingrams and the Douglases attended another wedding. This one took place at Holyrood Abbey in the City of Edinburgh between James II, the nineteen-year-old king of Scots, and Mary of Gueldres, a princess of the House of Burgundy and the niece of Philip the Good, Duke of Burgundy, the most powerful nobleman in Europe.

As usual the match was formed on sound economic principles, in that it would solidify the Franco-Scottish alliance, and grant Scottish merchants favourable status in all the Burgundian dominions, not least of which were the rich trading cities of the Netherlands.

James had come out of his minority — a time when he was pushed and pulled from one castle to another by the contending factions around him — as a clever and determined monarch with a resolve to establish his supremacy once and for all. He came out of his nuptials with a dowry of sixty thousand crowns, to be paid from the coffers of Philip of Burgundy over a two year period, an infusion of funds that the crown sorely needed.

James' own promise, to bestow on his new wife an annual income of five thousand pounds Scots together with the earldoms of Atholl and Strathearn, was not foremost in his already scheming mind.

Will Douglas caught up with Ranald below the elms that fringed the abbey grounds. Ranald and Marjorie were laughing, along with Thomas and Isabella, at the frolicking little black-haired twin boys that Marjorie had given her husband three years earlier.

"Ranald Ingram!" Will Douglas called out, as he pushed his way through the melee, goblet in hand. "If you can pull yourself away from your beautiful family for a while, I have someone you would just love to meet."

Casting a big smile in the direction of Marjorie and her parents, Will led Ranald firmly by the arm along the edge of the crowd and through a narrow gap in the high hedge that was guarded by two burly ushers. It opened into a small private garden. There, by a fish pool, stood the unmistakable little dandy figure of the king, flanked by Mary of Gueldres and a tall and handsome man who was talking earnestly to the bride and groom. King James turned towards them.

"Ah, Earl Douglas, you have found your friend, I see."

Ranald and Will bowed. "Yes, Your Grace," Will said. "Allow me to present Ranald Ingram, merchant of the Port of Leith and your most faithful subject."

"Indeed," said James, his little eyes moving from one to the other. "My bride and her uncle, Philip Duke of Burgundy." he said, with a flourish of his arm.

Ranald bowed low, straightening up to regard Mary and her uncle. He found it difficult to determine which impressed him the most, for they were each striking in their bearing and their presence. Mary of Gueldres was a tall, big-boned woman with thick straw blond hair that bubbled out from beneath her peaked bonnet, and smiling grey eyes. She was a prize indeed for this little weasel-faced monarch, Ranald thought. But if she commanded Ranald's attention, her uncle commanded it more. Philip of Burgundy's appearance was arresting. He was tall and straight, with broad shoulders and a large head that he carried high like a red stag. His long straight hair, that had the grey sheen of armour, was gathered in a broad azure ribbon behind his head. He had a long straight nose and a wide, thin-lipped mouth that made little smiling movements in conjunction with his clear blue eyes. He delivered a small, almost imperceptible bow to Ranald, the eyes widening slightly.

"I am most pleased to make the acquaintance of the Scottish merchant of whom I have heard so much from my friends in Flanders. I trust that your venture there was profitable." He spoke with only the merest trace of an accent.

Ranald could still hardly believe his good fortune in meeting the man that could be so influential in his plan. He glanced briefly at Will before replying. He knew that this was a critical opportunity for him. Ranald's quick mind determined that his response must be calculated neither to fawn nor to seek to impress, but merely to give him the chance of a further meeting, in private, with the duke. He had to improve his knowledge of Philip's background, what kind of man he was, what things were important to him and what exactly was his status in France.

"Profitable, Sire and most enjoyable, for Flanders is a delightful place and I have longed, since my return, to have the chance to talk further of my stay there. I look forward to returning to it."

Philip smiled graciously. "Perhaps you will have that chance. Now especially, wouldn't you say, Your Grace?" he said, looking at the king.

At that point, the queen spoke. "Indeed. I am so pleased that you found my country to your liking."

With a quick look towards James, who was already showing the signs of being excluded too long from the conversation, Will Douglas bowed low. "If you will permit, Your Grace, we will take our leave, for you have many guests to meet. We wish you and your lovely bride much health and happiness." With that he retired backwards from the royal presence, Ranald quickly joining him, and the two left through the gap in the hedge at which they had entered.

Walking back towards the abbey, Ranald couldn't contain

his excitement, nor Will his amusement.

"What think you now of Will Douglas?" Will laughed. "Did I not say I would help you in your wine plan? It's still a plan, I hope?"

Ranald nodded his head slowly, smiling happily. "Never more so," he said. "And you have helped me more than you know. But come!" He caught Will by the shoulders. "I have to talk to you."

"Your wife and children . . . " Will began.

"They are all right. They will be all right for a while," said Ranald.

Ranald urged Will through the crowd of revellers and over to a quiet spot by a high wall some distance from the main building. Will, as he went, signalled to a servant who rushed forward with flasks of wine. Once seated on the grass by the wall, flagons in hand, Ranald "the Questioner's" questions came, fast and furious.

"What did Philip mean by 'especially now'? Can you tell me about the duke of Burgundy? Do you think I will have another opportunity to talk to him?"

Will laughed, amused as always by his friend's gushing questions. "Ranald, you have an excellent mind for trade and dealing, but your naivete in other matters sometimes amazes me."

As Will went on, Ranald hung on his every word, eyes shining with excitement.

"The marriages of kings and those of noble birth are contracts of convenience. This marriage, apart from replenishing James' coffers, is meant to restore the Auld Alliance with France from a commercial aspect. You should see that. You are faring well at the markets of Calais and Flanders, man. Who do you think controls these territories?" Will looked at Ranald under raised eyebrows, a little grin forming on his lips.

"The duke of Burgundy?" questioned Ranald. "Surely Flanders is a long way from the Duchy of Burgundy."

"That fine-looking nobleman that you just met controls Flanders, Brabant, Limburg, Luxemburg, Hainault and Holland as well as the Duchy of Burgundy. There is little trade that moves in Arras, Calais, Lille, Bruges or Ghent that he has no hand in. Philip of Burgundy, my friend is a veritable guardian of chivalry, a patron of the arts and immensely rich. If you want to trade in wine, or any other commodity for that matter, he is your man. It is clear that he has heard of you and now you have met him. I wish you every good fortune in advancing yourself with him, but you should not seek to do that here for your ideas, I think, should not be made too apparent to our beloved monarch."

Ranald could see that Will Douglas was anxious to end the discussion there. He had made an invaluable contact for Ranald, and it was now up to Ranald to make what he could of it, although he feared that, without a further meeting with Philip, that might not be much.

Later, after the wedding supper, Will Douglas bade adieu to Ranald and Marjorie, and he and his brothers set off back to Galloway. Ranald returned with his family to Strathalmond but not before he had arranged to meet there with Thomas Ingram in the near future, since he was keen to discuss his plans with his senior partner.

∾∾∾

It was over six months before Ranald's talk with his father could take place, owing to Thomas' busy schedule as a burgess and Ranald's need to return to Calais on another trading venture.

The two partners relaxed in the study after Thomas' arduous ride from Edinburgh through a January blizzard. A log fire blazed in the hearth throwing its cosy warmth through the room as the wind whistled and moaned around the shuttered windows of Strathalmond. Marjorie came in with a tray containing a flask of brandy that Ranald had brought back from his last trip, and two fine crystal glasses. Thomas was pleased to see how contented she looked and how her obvious happiness enhanced her striking beauty. She gave her father a brief peck on the cheek and then left them to rejoin Isabella and the children.

The decisions affecting the Ingram enterprises were all made by the two owners, and usually over a glass or two of brandy. The advantages of having only two principals in the business were that these decisions could be made quickly and effectively, no other consultation being required, and that full disclosure of each one's concerns could be made and dealt with, leaving no harboured grievances. Both men had their own perception of their own and the other's strengths and weaknesses, and as these perceptions had always been freely declared at their meetings, they felt that their decisions were all the more valid. They each valued the other's strengths and accommodated the weaknesses, since they knew that the combined effect of their abilities and their natures served the business well.

Sometimes they had disputes, and the brandy exacerbated them, but in the end an agreement would be made and the dispute never again mentioned.

Thomas much admired his son's entrepreneurial spirit which, in Ranald, was combined with exceptional ability and natural intelligence. What Ranald lacked in his judgement of people, Thomas put down to his youth and lack of experience. The heroic and faultless picture of Thomas Ingram that Ranald had grown up with had sustained a few blemishes in recent years, but what Ranald viewed as a lack of willingness to seize opportunity, an over-cautious attitude to new business arrangements and even a slightly too moral approach to profit taking, were made up for by the same predisposition that gave rise to them; Thomas Ingram's honesty, good judgement, and reputation for fair dealing.

"So, Ranald, you'll have seen that two of the Livingstons were hanged lately and their heads cut off at the Castle hill".

"I heard about it," Ranald said carefully, already guessing why this subject was being raised. Thomas was now going to make the point that the Livingstons had been great allies of Douglas, the conclusion being that this is what happens to Will

Douglas' friends. This 'I told you so' attitude was very typical of his father, and it annoyed Ranald even when he could see it coming. He reacted.

"I suppose that you are going to say something, Father, about the friends of Will Douglas."

"I am saying no more," Thomas said, slightly put out by his conclusion being seized from him. "All I am saying is that King James is wasting no time in getting rid of his enemies, now that he has come of age."

Ranald knew that there was truth in that, and he was glad to let the subject end there. He didn't bother to raise the fact that Thomas had entertained several Livingstons at Strathalmond, when it had suited him, and no one was more flattered than Thomas Ingram to see the Douglas brothers at Ranald's wedding banquet.

"In any event, the earl of Douglas is now one of James' loyal supporters." Ranald said.

"Aye. For now he is," Thomas replied. Then Thomas, getting up to refill the brandy glasses, moved on to business.

"Your introduction to the duke of Burgundy could be a very fortuitous thing for us. Did you meet him again after the wedding?"

"No," Ranald said, noting that Will Douglas' part in the introduction was conveniently ignored. "He returned to France right away. I fear that I may have little chance of renewing our acquaintanceship."

"I'm sorry to hear that. I've been thinking of late that this idea of yours to increase our wine imports has a lot of merit, and Burgundy is certainly the man to know for that."

Ranald's excitement grew. Now he had Thomas on the right subject, and he had questions for his father touching on the political matters that Thomas knew so well. "Tell me, Father, what you think about the possibilities of increasing our trade in wines; bringing wines to Leith and exporting them to England? What I want to do is devote some of our ships exclusively to the wine trade. I want to build a wine fleet."

Thomas thought that it was a marvellous idea and could

be very profitable. He was very proud of Ranald for his astuteness in coming up with it, but he didn't want to appear too keen at this stage. He would examine the matter carefully to determine its viability. That was Thomas Ingram's way.

"There are two things to consider," Thomas began, taking another sip from his glass. "Firstly, will the French refuse to ship wine to England once England loses its territories in France, if they ever do lose them? At this time they still hold Gascony and Normandy and the Port of Calais." After a short pause he went on. "But I think that they will lose them, and soon, and the loss of the clarets from the vineyards of the English kings around Bordeaux will be a great blow to their trade."

Ranald concentrated on every word as Thomas continued.

"The second thing — how to get the French trade when that happens? And this you have answered yourself, Ranald, in four words — the duke of Burgundy!"

Ranald poured more brandy as if to lubricate the flow of encouraging comment from his father.

"Yes," Thomas continued."I think he is the man that can make your plan happen, on the French side where you would have to begin. Later you will have to make an English contact. Apart from the duke's huge influence in France and his obvious interest in Franco-Scottish commerce — witness the wedding dowry — he is no friend nowadays to the English. In fact he abandoned his alliance with England fifteen years ago."

Ranald was constantly impressed by Thomas' knowledge of these alliances and who was treating or not treating with whom.

"Yes, you must find a way to meet with Burgundy again, so that we can advance this plan of yours." Thomas concluded.

Thomas smiled the Ingram smile, and both men stood up and clinked their glasses in a silent toast to each other.

ભ ભ ભ

After the execution of the Livingstons and the forfeiture of their lands and goods, a new triumvirate had formed to run the affairs of the State, under King James to whom they had pledged their allegiance. This comprised the old enemies, Chancellor Crichton, Bishop Kennedy and Will Douglas. Such were the fickle allegiances of the times upon which Will Douglas was becoming a practised master.

This was the year that Pope Nicholas V had declared as a jubilee to celebrate the end of schism in the Holy Church, and the roads of all pilgrims led to Rome. One such pilgrim was Bishop Kennedy. Another was the earl of Douglas. Will Douglas, however, had more reason to make his pilgrimage than ever entered the mind of Pope Nicholas. The road to Rome passed through the lands of Burgundy, and the road back, for Will, would pass through the court of the English King, Henry VI.

In the summer of 1450, Will Douglas and his small retinue arrived at Strathalmond. In his letter to Ranald Ingram to announce the visit, he had said that he wanted to discuss a small proposition that may be of interest. Ranald, delighted as always to entertain his friend, laid out the best table for him and tried to guess at the nature of the proposition.

"Burgundy!" Ranald cried out, as he and Will Douglas walked in the garden.

"How? When?" Ranald sputtered.

"Burgundy, the palace of Philip the Good, then Rome, to see the Holy Father, then London and Henry VI on the way home. Can I take it that you are interested, then?" Will smiled.

"Interested!" Ranald exclaimed. This was too good to be true and his thoughts were racing as plans took shape in his head. Will, enjoying every minute of this, continued, his blue eyes sparkling and the dark curls flicking up in the breeze.

"Now, can we talk business, my friend. I need ships for a thousand men and horses, Leith to Calais, and provisions on board. The trip to Rome and back will take six months, and I need ships for the return, Calais to the Port of London. Are you with me? Can Ingram provide them?" Ranald's head was nodding vigorously.

"Yes, yes, yes, anything. When do we go?"

"October," Will said. "I have already announced my coming and Rome waits to see the Douglas." He laughed.

"And Burgundy?" Ranald quizzed.

"Yes, Burgundy also." Will replied, drawing a folded letter from his doublet. "I wrote to Philip to announce the coming and this is his reply. I took the liberty of mentioning that Ranald Ingram, the Scottish merchant, would be among my retinue. You see the reply." He held out the letter which Ranald almost tore from his hand, his eyes greedily devouring the narrow script.

"...and I shall be pleased to renew my acquaintance with the merchant, Ranald Ingram, of whom you speak so highly." Ranald read out the words, his joy bubbling over. He embraced Will Douglas in a tight hug, the letter grasped in his hand.

∾ ∾ ∾

There was no such joviality when Ranald later announced his impending trip to Marjorie and his parents as they sat at the supper table.

"No! Fifty times no!" Thomas Ingram blustered, his big face reddening.

Isabella, looking sheepish, lowered her eyes and looked at the table, while Marjorie's alarmed stare moved from her father to her husband.

"But the duke of Burgundy, father! The opportunity!" Ranald implored, feeling a sudden rush of anger himself.

"No! Not with Douglas! How many times do I have to say it?"

They sat there for what seemed like an age, two angry men glaring at each other.

Marjorie, recovering from the shock of her husband's announcement, spoke, almost in a whisper. "It is such a long time," she said. "Six months."

Ranald thought hard of a way to persuade his father. "Father, listen to me," he said at last. "I know your concerns about Will Douglas. Now he is the king's man but tomorrow he may not be. He's proud and independent and showy, and he will cut a swath across Europe as if he were himself a king. I know that. But look at it this way, father. What harm can come to Douglas or his followers in France or in Italy? Tell me that! There is no danger for him there. He is a guest, a pilgrim no less, and he travels in the king's name. What harm? What danger there? If there is danger for Douglas, it is here in Scotland, not in France. How then should my joining him concern you? It's safe, father. As safe as Strathalmond."

Thomas grunted and looked at the floor. He was bound to admit that Ranald's argument was sound. Will Douglas and Ranald would be out of Scotland. It was hard to see how Ranald could come to any harm, and Ranald finally had the chance to meet with Phillip of Burgundy. Still, Thomas remembered the little Archibald Douglas and that day that he parted with his son, his own flesh and blood, and the reason for it.

Thomas looked up. "We'll see," he mumbled, "We'll see."

ໜ ໜ ໜ

All through the summer the excitement grew as plans proceeded for the embarkation of a thousand men and horses on the Ingram ships. Provisioners were consulted, accountings were taken, decks and holds were cleared, and accommodations were planned in and around the port for the assembly of the small army. No such fleet had graced a Scottish port since the arrival of the fourteen vessels that had escorted Mary of Gueldres from the Netherlands on her way to marry James Stewart, the Scottish king.

Across the Forth, in the Palace of Falkland, that king was laying his own plans, plans that necessitated the absence of the power hungry earl of Douglas from the realm, if they were to have any chance of succeeding.

Chapter Seven

~~~

Ranald stood on the deck of the "Lady Euphemia", a two hundred ton vessel, captained by John Fraser, the firm's oldest and most experienced master. Her crew of fourteen, including cook and boatswain, moved busily around the deck, attending to their duties and mouthing silent curses at the press of men and horses that continually impeded them. This was an entirely new cargo for Ingram's sailors, a cumbersome, noisy, jittery mass of men and beasts, staggering on the moving deck as they tried to take shelter from the cold North Sea wind laced with its biting salt spray.

Ranald looked back along the tilting rail at the flotilla of ships off their stern, bobbing and rolling on the heavy sea, loaded to the line with men and horses.

"Would you look at them!" Will Douglas shouted into the wind, as he approached Ranald with a hale and hearty laugh. "Who would believe that these were the men that rode with me, barely a year since, across the English Border, and burned the towers of Alnwick and Warkworth? Man, they couldn't burn incense right now. What say you, Ingram?"

Ranald had a fleeting image of the Douglas horde raping and pillaging their way into England. He forced a little smile. "They're not sailors," he said.

The two stood at the rail looking into the wind.

"What will Henry Plantaganet say to your raid on his province?" Ranald said, fixing Will with a serious look.

"Never a word, man. Never a word. The English burned Dumfries and Dunbar, and I burned Alnwick and Warkworth. It's a game man. Never you fear, my friend. Henry has more to concern him than a few pitiful holdings on the windswept moors of Northumberland."

Ranald smiled. Nothing was a problem for Will Douglas. The devil-may-care ebullience of the Earl was almost contagious.

"He has just lost Normandy to the French," Will went on. "Just as Thomas Ingram predicted. A wise man your adoptive father, Ranald. He should have been a politician, or a military commander perhaps."

Ranald tried to picture Thomas Ingram as a military commander, but with no success.

"Your ship's master says we will dock in Calais before dark. I must away and organise this white-faced retinue of mine back to dry land before they are sick all over your fine oak decks." Will left with the jaunty swagger of a master mariner.

Some time later, on the flat fertile plains of France, the same men that had huddled in misery on the rolling decks of the Ingram ships, now rode high on their battle horses, a long column of conquerors, their banners and pennants flapping in the breeze. The eighth earl of Douglas, flanked on either side by his brothers, the earls of Ormond and Moray, and in the rear by several Scottish lords, knights and lesser noblemen, riding under the Royal Standard of Scotland, passed into the Duchy of Burgundy to the cheers of onlookers who had gathered in the little fields to await the spectacle. Ranald, riding by choice in the rear of this magnificent column, followed only by the pack horses and supplies, was puffed up with pride.

This pilgrimage to Rome of Scotland's finest had been known about in advance, and every town and village all along the route had turned out to bid them welcome and cheer them on. Lodgings had been provided for the leaders, and encampment areas for the rest. Provisions had been stored for them, and the entertainment of musicians, players, and acrobats, was abundant at every stop over on the way, for these were no English banners that graced the train, but those of England's old enemy and therefore France's friend.

Since the channel crossing, Ranald had seen little of Will Douglas. The earl had been occupied, along with a select few others of his own rank, with copious introductions to local dignitaries, and banquets given in his honour. Ranald was not perturbed by this, for he didn't give it a thought. He had come to meet only one dignitary, and he took pleasure in watching the accolades being bestowed on his friend.

Besides, he had no time to spend with lords and their ladies. At each stopping place Ranald had sought out the local traders and merchants, learning what goods they handled, from which source they were provided and at what prices. He had many invitations to look around their storehouses, and he relished the free and open discussions on trading matters, and the willingness of his hosts to answer his endless questions.

As the procession passed through the countryside, the word of their coming went on ahead, and Ranald began to find his own little welcoming committee at each stop. He was "Ingram the Merchant" whose grandfather had died at Beauge fighting for France against the English. By the time they reached Dijon and the palace of Philip, Duke of Burgundy, Ingram the Merchant had already become something of a celebrity, and, before their camp was made, he was spirited away to a banquet of local merchants.

While Ranald was receiving such approbation from his counterparts in France, things had not gone so well for the Douglas. His brief visit to the Court of the French King, Charles IV, en route to Burgundy, had been planned by him as more than a social call. He knew that Charles had been instrumental in arranging the match between King James II and Mary of Gueldres, and he knew why. Charles' aim was to strengthen the alliance between Scotland and France, and hopefully Burgundy; all to be allied against England. Will thought the time favourable for him to seek to recover the lands of Touraine for the Douglases, lands that were lost to them on the death of Archibald, the former Earl of Douglas and Duke of Touraine.

Charles was a gracious host and pledged his friendship to Will, but he turned a deaf ear on Will's attempts to recover Touraine. It had reverted to France and there it would remain. Will discovered that Charles had grown as a warrior himself of late in his sojourns against the English and, in the politest fashion, he made it clear to Will that he was dedicated to recovering French territory and not giving it away.

Will Douglas, on reflection, had not really expected any other answer, but he thought that his petition was worth a try. And all was not lost. There was still Philip of Burgundy, who might be persuaded to plead in Will's cause, so when he and Ranald came to the banquet prepared in their honour by Philip the Good, both men were in the best of spirits, and each had his own agenda.

Every wealthy man of the time, be he nobleman or merchant, landowner or burgess, was ostentatious in his hospitality, and both Will Douglas and Ranald Ingram knew this, expected it, and had witnessed and enjoyed its results on many occasions. Ranald and Thomas Ingram had been entertained at dinners where Edinburgh's leading merchants and administrators had sought to outdo each other with every kind of exotic delicacy, while there was not a castle or a palace in Scotland in which the earl of Douglas had not been an honoured guest at one time or another. But this day, for both of them, was to be different.

From the morning they arrived until late into the evening, Will and Ranald were mesmerised by the sheer splendour of the occasion. Neither had ever experienced anything approaching the lavish surroundings, the sumptuous table that overflowed with every kind of food and drink, the displays, indoors and outside in the gardens. They saw every variety of players, musicians, mimes and ballad singers, wild and exotic animals with their trainers, and tournaments of jousters set high on battle horses, the afternoon sun sparkling on their full plate armour. Ranald and Will were spellbound.

Philip of Burgundy sat in a high, exquisitely carved chair, taking in the proceedings. His tall frame shone in a long cloth of gold robe, hair swept up beneath the huge circle of a black hat from which a black silk scarf dropped from crown to shoulders. Now and then he would look up to a gallery, built to be filled with his subjects who had attended in droves to witness the wealth and power of their duke. Philip of Burgundy acted like the king that he believed he was born to be.

The festivities went on all day, every performance out-shining the last, until the guests wondered what possible display could follow to impress them more. With concentrated interest, Will watched the procession of knights in armour and their detailed, meticulous rituals. Oaths were sworn to God and to the One True Faith. Then a squire would approach holding a live pheasant, and after much incantation and doxology, oaths would again be sworn by the knights, this time to the pheasant and also to the duke of Burgundy, their secular leader. This procedure was repeated before each contest, and on each occasion Philip would stand erect and bow to the knights.

Will Douglas was impressed by the skill and courage of the champions in the lists, and was often on his feet cheering the collisions of men and horses. Ranald preferred to walk around the courtyard, enthralled by the performances of jesters and magicians. It was a day such as neither of them had ever witnessed or would witness again, save at the palace of this remarkable duke.

Late in the evening, as the festivities continued under the flickering lights of a thousand candles, Ranald and Will sat in Philip's private chambers, sipping the best Gascon wine that either had ever tasted.

"Chivalry!" Philip declared, raising his glass. "That is the thing that is needed these days."

He had discarded the golden robe and the headgear and was dressed in a simple white robe that fell to his feet. Ranald remembered the grey hair, pulled back from the temple, and these blue, dancing eyes.

"You know what I am saying, My Lord Douglas," he continued.

Douglas, dressed as always in leather doublet and high boots, for he disliked hose, regarded his host with a serious and unswerving gaze.

"Chivalry is a thing much changed, Your Grace. But today we witnessed what it used to be. Your tournament was stupendous."

The large head flicked up as the duke sniffed in annoyance. "What it will be again, sir. The next crusade will be no mere tournament."

Will threw a puzzled look at Ranald who was toying silently with his glass.

"Crusade, Your Grace?" Will replied.

"Crusade. Of course, crusade. It is my determined intent to bring the forces of Our Lord to the relief of Constantinople, and banish the Turk from Christendom once and for all. I have pledged my life to it," the duke exclaimed.

"Indeed, Your Grace. A laudable pledge indeed. And you may count on Douglas for such humble assistance that he can give," Will said.

Ranald was struggling to understand this conversation about chivalry and crusades. When he caught the brief wink from Will Douglas, he began to wonder if their host was slightly mad, and this was the man whom he had come so far to see.

Will spoke again. "But the hour is late, Your Grace. With your leave, we would take our rest and look forward to your company on the morn when we might pursue these matters."

Philip, who seemed prepossessed, waved an acknowledgement, and a servant, appearing from nowhere, guided Will and Ranald to their chambers.

"He's mad!" Ranald said, once they were alone. "A crusade to Constantinaople? Mad!"

"Don't excite yourself, man," Will replied, smiling. "Mad he may be, but also the duke of Burgundy. And now we know his weak spot, do we not?"

In spite of the wine and brandy he had imbibed, Ranald

could not sleep. He kept thinking about Philip the Good and his wealth and his influence and his irrational obsession with chivalry and crusades. This was the man with whom he wanted to talk about serious things, real things, like wine trading and profits. Then he thought about Will, and how he winked at him and how quick Will Douglas was to see things. And he thought about how different they were, his friend and he. It was a long night.

He was still thinking in the morning when he joined Will in the palace grounds.

"How can a man, an intelligent man, a wealthy and powerful man, pay such homage to ritual?" Ranald said.

"Come, come Ingram. It happens all the time. Even in your world, I'm sure."

Will watched Ranald's puzzled look and went on. "What about your societies of merchants, or the many guilds of tradesmen like the silversmiths or goldsmiths? Do they not have their little rituals? They have ceremonies that dictate entry into their bands, where they swear allegiance to the group and to each other. Why they even swear oaths to certain tools that they use. What's different about an oath sworn on a bird?"

"But the duke of Burgundy," Ranald began.

"Why should he be different from anyone else?" Will countered. "Look, Ranald, most men are joiners, perhaps all of us. We need a kinship with others of a certain group. Rituals are merely the outward aspects of this need. It has nothing to do with wealth or power or intellect. Philip of Burgundy is no less influential in your cause just because he likes to wallow in self-conceit and the admiration of others. This chivalry thing and the notion that he will lead a new crusade is part of his need to be like a king. Only kings begin crusades and inaugurate Orders of Knighthood. It is as simple as that. It makes no difference whatever to your plan."

Ranald thought about this and realised that Will was right. He also realised that he had received a lesson from Will Douglas in the sizing up of men and their motives. It all seemed so clear to him, that he wondered why he had been concerned in the first place.

"Ranald, I think that since you are apparently so well received here in Burgundy, you should remain here while I proceed to Rome. You need more time with the duke, and I'll return this way when you can join us again. After all, Rome is not your target. It's filled with clergymen, politicians and intrigue. More my style, wouldn't you say?"

Ranald was delighted at the suggestion for he had thought about this course himself. "And Philip?" he asked.

"Oh, have no fear, man. Philip will have someone to entertain. But a word of advice. Humour him, but don't underestimate his wit or his ability to make you a very rich merchant." Will laughed and they shook hands cordially.

℘℘℘

"So who looks after the Douglas estates while the earl makes his pilgrimage?" the king asked, looking across the long bench at the Crichtons.

"His brother, John Douglas of Balveny, Your Grace," Chancellor Crichton replied.

"Ah, so," James intoned, looking up at the high ceiling of his Palace of Falkland as if searching for inspiration in its cornices.

The two Crichton cousins looked at each other in anticipation. They were similar in appearance, both short and stout with thinning hair and heavy jowls. Chancellor Sir William Crichton and Admiral Sir George Crichton were members of the most formidable baronial family in Scotland, and natural survivors of the period of strife that surrounded the young king's minority. They had finally arrived where they wanted to be. Now the king was of age and ready to take Scotland in hand, breaking the hold of the Douglas usurper. The Crichtons would be at his side.

"An opportunity, perhaps, Your Grace," Chancellor Crichton ventured carefully, phrasing the words as neither question nor statement.

Before any reply, George Crichton spoke. "I have heard

91

reports that the Balveny tenants are unruly, Your Grace," he said, watching the reaction. "It is said that they are mocking your efforts to establish the rule of law."

At that, James' eyes flashed with sudden anger. "Mocking, you say. Mocking me! I'll give them mocking." James pounded a fist on the table and the birthmark that covered the left side of his face went from red to dark purple.

He glared at his two advisors. "Douglas again! By God I'll give them mocking!"

The Crichtons sat back, contented with their morning's work.

All through his adolescence James had watched the positioning of the magnates of his realm with growing fear. His studies of the not too distant history of his English counterpart, Richard II, a pretty, fun-loving boy, whose weakness as a monarch had ended him up in the Tower of London, were strong in James' mind. Richard was a king who had lost his kingdom and his life at the hands of greedy and powerful noblemen who attacked in packs as wolves attack a stag. James had poured over Richard's last words from his prison cell, so often that they haunted him.

A wondrous and fickle land is this, for it hath exiled, slain, destroyed, or ruined so many kings, rulers and great men, and is ever tainted and toileth with strife, variance, and envy.

And there was no lack of that strife and envy here in Scotland: Gordon, Sinclair, Livingston, Forrester, Crawford and Ross, all feigning allegiance when it suited them and not one of them to be trusted; and the most troublesome, the most powerful...the Douglases.

The king's face still shone with anger as he sat down to supper with his wife.

In the short time since their marriage Mary of Gueldres had come to know her lord and master very well. So well, in fact, that she had already begun to regret having set sail to this violent country. James had seemed in the beginning so endearing, so much like a child whose unhappy youth had made him vulnerable and in need of a good woman. Now he had the haunted look of a man forever looking for the devil at his back, and prone, at any moment, to fly into fits of anger at these invisible demons.

Mary thought of her father, and her uncle, the kindly and confident Duke of Burgundy, as she looked at this angry little man across the table.

"Earl Douglas has ever protested his loyalty to you my dear. Perhaps Admiral Crichton has received erroneous reports, or the tenants merely lack the strong hand of their master. Perhaps Lord Balveny does not have his brother's authority with . . . ." Her words were cut off by James lifting a wine flask and shattering it against the wall.

"Earl Douglas! Loyalty! That for his loyalty!" he shouted as he threw another flask, his face burning.

The Queen sat quiet, looking down at the meal in front of her as her fiery little husband strode out of the room.

∾∾∾

When the subject was trade, Ranald Ingram found Philip of Burgundy to be a fascinating companion.

"A wine fleet, you say. What a marvellous idea." Philip leant forward in his chair. "The wines of Burgundy and Gascony shipped through Calais to the Port of Leith, and then transported overland to England. My dear Ingram, now I know why my merchants in Dijon are so excited about you."

Then a shrewd look appeared on the Duke's face. "But of course you would need the wines, in great quantity, and their safe passage to Calais, would you not?"

Ranald's preoccupation with the subject that was dearest to his heart, talked freely without any regard or thought to the social gulf between himself and the duke.

"I would, Your Grace. In short, I need you."

Philip smiled. "Then, if this thing is to be done, we would

require to come to some … accommodation, yes?"

"Indeed so, Your Grace," Ranald said, now in full flood. "But there is one other matter to consider. For the volume of wines that are contemplated, I would have to know the position of England as to its import."

"Not Scotland?" Philip said.

"There will be no problem as to Scotland, Your Grace, since King James will have the duties arising from the imports, and thereafter from the exports to points south of the border."

"And he needs the cash, I'll wager," Philip said, half to himself. "And England? Would there not be a further duty to Henry Plantaganet?"

"Yes, Your Grace," Ranald went on, planning as he spoke, "but Henry might not think it fitting to import French wine from me, especially if such imports direct from France were closed to him."

Philip laughed in a strange high-pitched giggle.

"Give no thought to England, Ingram the Merchant. Let your partner attend to Henry."

"My partner?" Ranald questioned.

"Philip of Burgundy", the Duke said, putting out his hand.

Ranald took the proffered hand uncertainly as he began to think that this was all a dream and he would wake up soon.

∾ ∾ ∾

Later, as Ranald and Will made their way back across France to Calais, Will's congratulations were loud and earnest.

"One of us, at least, was successful. The wary old fox would not shake my hand in partnership. The lands of Touraine will never be mine, I fear. France is France I think, for Charles and for Philip. On that point they agree, even if they agree on little else. But what did I tell you? Is this not the most lucrative partnership the Ingrams have ever made? I am happy for you, man. Now we visit Henry Plantaganet, although I think that your work has been done already. If your Philip says that he will attend to Henry, you can rely on it that your plan will be fulfilled. For me, there are other matters to discuss in England."

Ranald had no idea what his friend was talking about. "What matters?" he said.

Will gave that flick of the dark curls. "Nothing for a merchant to know, my friend. Nothing for a merchant to know."

Chapter
Eight

∾ ∾ ∾

It was still dark on the bare, flat land around Abercorn.
Blustering wind and rain rattled the door and the little windows of the cottage as Lang Tam o' Nyddry pushed his way into another day. He pulled his cloth coat closer around his neck and made his way around the corner of the little stone-built house. He was building a lean-to barn against the gable of the cottage with heavy grey stones from the shore of the Forth. The wind whipped at his tall, emaciated frame as he grasped the stones and placed them with big gnarled hands. Now and then he would stop and wipe the rain from his face and his one good eye. Half of Tam's face had been caved in by a kick from a horse that had broken his cheek and blinded one eye forever.

Inside the cottage, his wife, Mary, kindled the open fire, stopping now and then to throw a handful of oats onto the earthen floor that were quickly seized by a dozen or so crowding chickens. She was a small wrinkled woman, old for her years, but with a cheerful face. She sang in a low continuous humming fashion as she worked.

Lang Tam and Mary had been together for twenty years, during which time they had raised three sons, and Tam had come from being a landless hired man to being a tenant of the Douglas estate at Abercorn. Mary was proud of her husband's achievement. It meant that his service had been good, and valued by his masters.

Now they were secure in their cottage, and Tam's advancing years excused him from giving any further military service to the earl. Their youngest son had died of plague. The other two were hired out, as their father had been before them, living sometimes at home and more often away, since they frequently had to travel outside the shire in search of work.

Lang Tam, by dint of hard work, had advanced himself well in the forty years that had elapsed since he was hired out as a boy in the district of Nyddry. He had a one quarter share of a plough team, a heavy wooden plough and the six oxen that were needed to pull it. Soon the ploughing season would begin and the thirty foot strips of land that lay in the rich earth of the Forth Estuary would take all his time. Mary would look after their two cows, the hens and the sheep, tend to the churning of butter and cheese, the carding and spinning of wool, and the cutting and hauling of peat from the bog to fuel the fire in their little cottage. They were able, with the contributions from their sons, to pay their rent and supply the produce demanded of them by the Castle of Abercorn.

Lang Tam o' Nyddry was respected among his peers. He had given faithful service to his Douglas masters, Will Douglas and his father, James "the Gross", before him.

When Tam was younger, he had marched behind the Douglas horses, his long pike on his shoulder, sometimes as far as Stirling or Perth, and once into the border country. He had returned with a sack or two of barley or perhaps a lamb or a firkin of ale, taken in the rout of Douglas enemies, and he and his neighbours had sat around the fire, drinking and telling stories of the fight while the women roasted the meat. These were good days when he was younger.

But the best day for Lang Tam o' Nyddry was the day that Will Douglas had called upon him at his little cottage and asked him how was the harvest, and was his family well. James "the Gross" had never done that. The eighth earl of Douglas had called upon Lang Tam o' Nyddry.

A watery sun came peeping up through the dark clouds and the rain came down harder, soaking through Tam's under-shirt and into his bones. He worked on, laying flat stones and then heavy round ones in layers as the wall took shape. Towards midday he stopped and was making his way around the house to the door when he saw a familiar figure approaching, waving to him as he came.

It was Donald o' Inshmachen, a neighbouring tenant on the estate and a co-owner of his plough team. Tam held the door open to admit his short, fat friend, who entered the cottage, all out of breath and wiping the rain from his red face with a pudgy hand.

"It's the King's soldiers," Donald gasped. "They've laid siege to the castle."

He sat down heavily, pulling off his hood, his great stomach heaving as he tried to regain his composure.

"Siege?" Tam said. "The King's men?" Tam was having difficulty understanding.

"Aye, Tam. Two hundred, maybe three hundred of them. They're all around Abercorn." Donald was still breathing heavily.

Mary had poured two tin mugs of ale which she set down on the little table in front of the men. Donald grabbed a mug and took two large swallows, wiping his mouth on his sleeve, before continuing.

"There is a man there with the soldiers. He was reading an order saying that all the tenants, cottars, and hired men of the earl of Douglas must come to the Castle of Abercorn with no delay, by order of King James."

"What could this be about, Donald?" Tam said, as he took off his wet shirt. Mary handed him a cloth with which he wiped his thin body, then she gave him a dry shirt from a wooden stand near the open fire.

"There is no telling," Donald said. "But it's a serious thing, for the soldiers are all round the castle and they are letting no one leave. I was to go post-haste and bring in all the others from the estate. That's what they said. And it's the King's order."

"Then we must away," Tam said, pulling on a heavy hide cloak that fastened under his chin and fell to his knees. Mary put a restraining hand on Tam's arm, a sudden concern in her face. The old worry flooded back that she had had years ago, whenever Tam had shouldered his pike to join a Douglas. Tam covered Mary's hand with his own.

"Have no fear, Mary. Lang Tam o' Nyddry will come to no harm, for he is a good tenant o' Earl Douglas. That is the earl's own words to Tam."

The men went out into the rain, leaving Mary at the door, wringing her hands, the fear still in her eyes.

Tam was amazed at the size of the force of soldiers assembled before the gate. He could also see riders in a single long column circling the walls on all sides. The gate and heavy entrance door were closed, and Tam saw a few men atop the tower shouting something into the wind. Men from the estate were gathered in a group, pressed in by the horses of the riders. Two soldiers broke off from the group and rode towards Tam and Donald with spears at the ready. They signalled, with threatening movements of the spears, for them to join the others. When all the stragglers had been so assembled, they stood in the rain, waiting and watching.

After a short time, a group of men-at-arms approached on foot dragging a cannon that was mounted on a short gun carriage. Donald looked wildly at Tam.

"Holy Mother!" he exclaimed. "They're going to blow in the walls!"

Tam didn't look at Donald but kept his eyes fixed on the soldiers. "Not the walls, Donald, for that cannon is too light. The gate. They are lining it up on the gate."

Tam looked up and saw some more figures appearing on the tower. They were clearly agitated. Then a voice called out in the rain.

"Surrender in the name of the King! Surrender, or we blow down the gate!"

The small cannon had now been drawn up to the gate, and its handlers were busy preparing it to be fired, bringing heavy stone balls from somewhere in the rear.

Tam felt a twinge of the old excitement of battle. Would that the Douglas were here, he thought, instead of on a pilgrimage in a foreign land. Then would Lang Tam o' Nyddry get his pike. But Tam realised that Douglas was not here, only the castle staff, and there was nothing for it but to open the gate.

A sigh of relief arose from the assembled estate workers when they heard the clang of iron and the loud groan of the oak door as it swung back on its heavy hinges. The gate was lifted and the mounted men quickly moved in to take the castle.

Later, the castle staff, caretakers, servants, cooks and housekeepers, stablemen and gardeners had been assembled and stood with Tam and Donald and the other estate workers, all looking, one to the other, with puzzled and fearful expressions.

The ranks of soldiers opened and a little rider advanced to face the assembled crowd. He wore a colourful doublet and a large round hat, and carried at his belt a jewelled dagger. He had a small pointed face, and Tam could see that it was blemished by a red mark that ran down one side from brow to chin. That he was not a Douglas, Tam could tell, but, judging by the effect on the soldiers, he was some kind of important figure.

A tall officer, in full armour and mounted on a battle horse, rode up to take a position to the right of the little man. He took a vellum document from his belt and, eyeing the assembled workers, began to speak.

"Know Ye that the Castle of Abercorn and all the Estates of William, Eighth Earl of Douglas, are now forfeited to the king." He paused and looked around the audience."By order of the Crown and of the Parliament of Scotland, all subjects, formerly employed in the service of the earl of Douglas, and of his kin, the earls of Ormond and Moray, John Douglas of Balvenie and all others who hold lands of, or otherwise conduct themselves in the service of, the Black Douglases, shall hereupon swear an oath of allegiance to His Majesty King James II of Scotland, thereby denouncing all loyalties and allegiances to the aforesaid Black Douglases and all their heirs and successors."

The tall officer glared around the crowd, and Tam could see a smirk on the face of the little man with the jewelled dagger. The assembled servants and farmers jostled uncomfortably, unsure what the fine words meant and anxious to get out of the rain. There was a long silence.

"What does it mean?" Donald said to Tam. "Swear allegiance to the King. How do we do that? Tell me and I'll swear it, for one master is the same as the other, Tam." Those standing nearby heard Donald's words and nodded vigorously. But they weren't like Lang Tam o' Nyddry. Earl Douglas had never greeted them and wished them well. Tam pulled himself erect and spoke out in a clear loud voice.

"Lang Tam o' Nyddry swears allegiance to none save Will Douglas." This colloquial use of the earl's name made Tam feel close to his lord and master, as if the Douglas and Tam were standing there side by side; as if Tam were young again and standing behind the Douglas standard on some wind-swept moor.

The little man's smirk vanished and anger flared in his eyes. He turned slightly in his saddle and nodded to the officer who had replaced the paper in his belt.

Without a further word being spoken, the tall officer, urging his mount forward through the crowd of soldiers and servants, rode up to Tam. In one quick flowing movement, he drew his sword and plunged it into Tam's chest, with such force that the point of the blade emerged through the back of the old hide cloak. He withdrew the sword. Tam's mouth opened, as if to speak, then it spouted a frothing stream of blood as Lang Tam o' Nyddry sank onto the wet earth and rolled onto his side, one wide sightless eye staring up at Donald.

Back at the little cottage, Mary had a sudden feeling of panic. She ran to the door and looked out into the rain. She moved to the corner of the house, looking out in every direction. Through the rain she saw the rotund form of Donald o' Inshmachen, running and stumbling towards her. He was alone. She turned to the half-built stone wall of the barn, then she grasped the wet stones with her hands and leaned her face against them, a long moan coming from her throat.

∾ ∾ ∾

At the same time as the king's men were making a round of all the Douglas castles in the Lothians and the border country that lay south of the capital, laying siege and swearing all free tenants to the Crown, Ranald Ingram was on the docks at Calais, supervising the preparation of his ships for the return from France. Ranald and Will Douglas were both in good spirits.

"So, Ranald, you will not be joining me at the Court of Henry Plantaganet?" Will said, as they sat in a hostelry near the docks.

"No, Will. I fear I've been absent from Strathalmond long enough. I will sail to Leith. My plans are well advanced."

"And you have no cause now to talk to an English king, especially when your new-found partner in Burgundy will have more sway." Will grinned. Ranald had come to recognise how quickly his friend could assess a situation.

"You are wise, my friend," Will continued. In any case Henry VI is a weakling, they say, and not the power behind that throne. I doubt if it would serve anyone's purpose to talk to him."

Ranald looked up with surprise. "But do you not sail to England to see the man?"

"To see two men, Ingram. Two men. One for show, and the other for, shall we say, profit?"

The Douglas had lost Ranald. What other? What profit?

Will, seeing the perplexed look on Ranald's face, laughed heartily and drank the remainder of his ale. Then, looking around the room, Will leaned over like a conspirator and whispered in Ranald's ear. "Richard, Duke of York." He sat back with a satisfied smile. After a few seconds, and seeing that Ranald was still perplexed, Will's laugh erupted again, so loud that it caused all others in the hostelry to look round with interest.

ϿϿϿ

Two weeks later Ranald was back at Strathalmond, back in his comfortable study with Thomas Ingram. He had returned, filled with high spirits and desperate to tell his father of his success with Philip of Burgundy, but his homecoming had been marred by the news of an attack on Houstoun Castle and the trepidation it had caused to his wife and his household. Marjorie and Isabella had joined them in the study and the events were recounted at length.

"It was terrible, Ranald," Marjorie said. "Soldiers everywhere and horses galloping past our gates on their way to Houstoun."

"But they didn't threaten you?" Ranald said anxiously.

"An officer rode up to the house. Master James went to meet him and the officer asked if Strathalmond was part of the Houstoun Estate of Earl William Douglas. Master James told him that it was not, and that it was a freehold estate belonging to Thomas Ingram, a merchant of Leith and a burgess of the City of Edinburgh. The officer then asked if there were any kin, servants or employees of the Douglases within the house, to which Master James answered that there were not. Then the officer left. It was a terrifying time for us Ranald. The shouting and galloping of horses went on for two days and nights and the fires from the outbuildings at Houstoun burned through the night. The gate of the castle was smashed by a cannon and Master James said that all in the household were forced outside of the walls and made to give an oath of allegiance to the King."

Ranald's face grew dark with anger as he listened to Marjorie's account of the occurrences, and when she finished he embraced her.

"It was most fortunate that the officer did not know that you are a Douglas, Ranald. A lot has happened here since you left." Thomas Ingram said. "King James has ridden on all the Douglas houses and some have not been let off so lightly as Houstoun."

Ranald's anger was mixed with a lack of comprehension.

"Why would the King do these things?" he uttered, looking at Thomas.

"Because of fear," Thomas replied. "He's afraid of your friend, Will Douglas. And that fear is being kindled by his advisors. Aye, I can well see the hand of Crichton in this."

Thomas said no more as he did not want to further upset Marjorie and Isabella, but he was deeply concerned. It had always been just a matter of time until James would be forced to take on the Douglases. Now it had begun, when Will Douglas was absent, and the cunning Crichtons could play the King like a fiddle. Thomas feared for his son and for Strathalmond.

Later, when the women were gone, he expressed his fears to Ranald. It was no longer merely a matter of avoiding Will Douglas. Now they had to be careful in all their dealings and take no part in the quarrels of the state. The reports that thirty free tenants had been murdered in the last two weeks caused a shiver to run up Ranald's spine.

Thomas was, of course, delighted to hear how Ranald had been received in Burgundy, and the partnership with Philip was more than he could ever have hoped for. He agreed that Ranald's decision to leave the dealings in England to Philip was entirely correct, and he was relieved to hear that Ranald had not accompanied Will Douglas there. He told Ranald this, and the reason for his relief, for if his son was to avoid the coming struggle between the Douglases and the Crown, he would have to have all the information that Thomas Ingram could give him.

"England is a divided country," Thomas began. "It has lost France; it has a weakling for a king; the Crown is drowning in debt, and only last year a leader of its rebellious peasants, a man by the name of Jack Cade, occupied London and murdered the Treasurer." Thomas smiled an aside, "The perfect time for you to wrest the wine trade out of Bristol and into Leith, I think." He settled back in his chair and went on as Ranald listened with interest.

"To tell it briefly, there are two contenders for the throne, Edmund Beaufort, Duke of Somerset, and Richard, Duke of

York. As I speak, they are evenly matched in men and arms. Make no mistake, there will be war before there is peace, and to gain an upper hand, either of these two men will seek to add a further name under his banner. That is the way I see it. And what name will serve better than that of Douglas."

Gradually things were becoming clearer to Ranald. "Richard of York," he interrupted, and Thomas slowly nodded his head.

"But what gain would there be to Will Douglas to ally himself with York?"

"Ranald, Ranald," Thomas said, "Think on it, man! There is an old saying that one favour is deserving of another. If your friend were to assist York in gaining one kingdom, it might be seen that York could make the way for Douglas to gain another." Ranald was horrified.

"You mean here, in Scotland. But surely, father, you are wrong. Will Douglas has no mind to usurp the throne of Scotland. You don't know him. He is loyal to James Stewart. How can you think that rebellion would ever be his intent?"

Thomas smiled. "It's not what I think that's important. It's what James Stewart thinks, or rather what he is encouraged to think by his trusted advisors."

"Crichton!" Ranald said with a sudden anger in his voice.

But no, he thought, composing himself. Whatever lies Crichton might be spinning, the King must know that he has the loyalty of the earl of Douglas. He must ... then why are his forces laying siege to Douglas castles? No, this is the work of Crichton. When Will Douglas returns, this perfidy will be laid bare and James reassured of the Douglas allegiance. Then Ranald's mind went back to the conversation in the hostelry at Calais. Two men! Richard, Duke of York!

Thomas Ingram could see his son's dilemma and he felt a sudden regret at having tarnished Ranald's heroic perception of his friend. "But come," he said. "I may be wrong. Who can decipher the intrigues of noblemen and kings? We have plans to make. Let's discuss the building of the wine fleet for it seems to me, from what you are telling me of Philip of Burgundy, that the time is right to make the contracts."

The mention of the wine fleet brought Ranald back to the real world of trade, back from the useless speculation on politics, pacts and mere possibilities.The two Ingrams talked on into the night about the sealing of bargains with the Gascon wine growers, the writing up of an agreement with Philip of Burgundy and the details of freighting the wines across France and shipping them from Calais to the Port of Leith. Soon, Ranald gave no more thought to the earl of Douglas.

Chapter
Nine

∾∾∾

May came to Strathalmond once again, and the dark days of winter, their chill and their bleak loneliness, when Marjorie Ingram had longed for Ranald, vanished like the snow off the dovecote gables. Ranald was at home now, and apart from the occasional trip to Leith to oversee the fitting of the new fleet, he worked in his study or walked with her and their children in the garden. All through the Spring they had entertained visitors, emissaries from Burgundy — delightful, sophisticated gentlemen who had praised Marjorie's cuisine and enjoyed her singing and her riddles. Her life had never been so full or so good, and watching the enthusiasm of her husband at his work filled her with happiness.

The raucous call of rooks filled the air as they built their high colonies of nests in the tall trees of the driveway. No more news of raids or sieges came to trouble their house, and Marjorie wished that there could be a great wall around Strathalmond, and she and Ranald could live within it forever, in peace and tranquility, praising the Lord and the Holy Virgin for the bounty that had been bestowed on them.

At the Church of St. Nicholas, where she walked every day, Marjorie offered her prayers to the Blessed Virgin and to her Divine Son and Lord in the Holy Sacrifice of the Mass. At

Candlemas she had strewn on the altar the delicate snowdrops — emblems of purity — that had pushed up through the snow around Strathalmond, for they had bloomed to remind her of the presentation of Jesus to the temple. Now she nurtured her own little garden that was sheltered against the north wall. It was her garden of the Holy Mother, and the warm sun was spreading all of nature's beauty at the feet of the Mother of God.

Marjorie had turned over, with her own hands for it was a token of her love, the little square plots of earth between the paving stones that fanned out from the small statue of the Virgin Mary. Often she knelt in the sun, adoring and caressing the colourful blooms, the emblems of her devotion: violets for humility and daisies for innocence. Fragile blue harebells, Our Lady's thimble, adorned the borders. On two sides of the garden, purple flowering clematis reached up rough wooden trellises to make the Virgin's bower that peeped over tall hollyhocks — the staffs of St. Joseph. In a half circle around the feet of the statue, innocence and purity were marked by beds of marigolds interspersed with the white purity of lilies, while, in the centre, roses of white and red filled the air with their fragrance, and irises, the symbol of the birth of Christ, stood tall and straight.

Ranald came round the side of the house and stood by the wall, watching her as she knelt among her flowers. He looked up at the azure sky and down the long line of yew trees, and at the rich green grass that curled against the walls.He thought how much love there was in Strathalmond, and how much he loved Marjorie Ingram.

They walked hand in hand across the grass and through the trees until they came to the mill that sat down in a hollow by the Beugh Burn. They watched, dreamily, as the huge miller helped a local tenant to empty a load of grain into a hopper, then they turned and made their way back along the burn to the place where they had played with the little ship so many years ago.

"Do you remember the 'Isabella of Akyne'?" Ranald said.

"Well now she has become a fleet, the first wine fleet, ready to sail for France."

She squeezed his hand, and he bent down and kissed her full, soft lips, pulling her against him. They sat down on the bank and Ranald's thoughts went to that day and his first meeting with Will Douglas.

"I heard lately that Will Douglas has had trouble." Ranald squinted up at Marjorie in the bright sunlight. A brief shadow crossed her face.

"The King's army has destroyed his castle at Craig Douglas on the Yarrow, and he is now called to Parliament to attest his allegiance to James Stewart. Parliament meets at the Tolbooth next month."

"I am sure it will go well for him, Ranald," Marjorie said, anxious to change the subject. "Come, let's get back to the house." Ranald got up and followed his wife up the small hill to Strathalmond, thinking as he went that Will Douglas had only one friend here.

※ ※ ※

In the present turn of fortunes, it seemed to King James that the earl of Douglas had few friends anywhere these days. The King felt secure for the first time in a long while. His confrontation with the Douglases had paid off, and while he felt that he owed a debt to the Crichtons, he was not prepared to follow their advice to its conclusion that aimed at the death of Will Douglas. James may have been rash on occasion, but he wasn't stupid, and while he had manoeuvred the powerful earl into a position of atonement before the Parliament, he knew that the Douglas was still a force to be reckoned with, and could still bring many squabbling noblemen behind the royal banner. Besides, he admitted to himself, he liked Will Douglas as a man, if not as an adversary. These were James' thoughts as he strode up and down the great hall of Edinburgh Castle, watched by his wife and the two Crichton cousins.

"So, Lord Douglas will come before my Parliament on the

twenty-eighth of June to answer the charges brought against him, and he should have an advocate to plead for him. That I have resolved, for I am not a man to put down another without fair hearing." James finished his little speech, feeling a certain pride in himself and glaring at the Crichtons. After a few moments, Sir William Crichton replied.

"Your Majesty is a generous and merciful ruler, even to his declared enemies," he said in his silky voice, "but where, I wonder, would one find an advocate in this cause?" He smiled to his cousin. The King pondered on Crichton's words, thinking that perhaps he was right. Who, in the face of recent events, would wish to be identified with a usurper of the Crown?

"Here!" Mary of Gueldres spoke the word clearly and with commitment, and before the others could recover from their shock, Mary continued.

"I will be advocate for Earl Douglas before your Parliament, for I know him to be no usurper, and a loyal and faithful servant of James Stewart of Scotland." She looked steadily at the Crichtons who visibly wilted under the stare of her grey eyes. Then she raised her chin and smiled benignly at her husband. For a few seconds James was non-plussed, then he resumed his pose of the placid leader and smiled briefly at Mary.

"Then it shall be," he said. "The Earl of Douglas shall have the representation of my Queen."

Will Douglas rode to Fife for an arranged meeting with the Queen at Falkland Palace. On the way he pondered on the turn of events that had occurred since he had set off on the pilgrimage to Rome, and on how his status and his loyalty to James had been undermined in the interval. He knew that the Crichtons had never been his friends, that they had the ear of the King and that they would take every chance they could to discredit Douglas, or worse. What caused him to wonder, however, was the motivation of James in attacking Douglas lands when he was away on what was, after all, a royal errand — harrying and murdering his tenants — and forcing him now to come before the Parliament like some guilty boy. His wondering turned to anger and he dug his heels into his horse's side.

What did the King want of him? When had he ever given James cause to think that the Douglas was anything other than a loyal subject? He had made no pact with the Duke of York, even though the latter had tried hard to persuade him to do so, nor had he taken steps to avenge the recent raids on his castles, for the King was led into that course by Crichton. That was how things appeared to Will on his way to Falkland. Perhaps it would become clear to him when he met Mary of Gueldres.

He reached the palace in the early evening. It lay nestled in the Lomond Hills, ringed by the Forest of Falkland, a quiet and serene retreat that had been acquired by James for his wife. It was a country home for them, where they came to hawk and hunt stags and wild boar in the woods, and to relax in the evenings, playing chess and listening to the music of fiddle and lute. It was an escape from the noise and smells of Edinburgh and it was a favourite place of Mary's. She stayed here often, while her husband was busy in the city, and she had selected this place to meet Earl Douglas, the King having agreed to their private meeting.

On entering the room, Will bowed low, and the Queen rose to offer her hand which he kissed gracefully. She smiled and directed him to a couch that faced her own high chair. They both sat, eyeing the other.

She struck Will Douglas as a rare beauty. She was not exactly attractive, not even of feature or delicate of frame, but a beauty none the less. It was a handsome, feminine kind of beauty, Will thought, that came from the large face and wide mouth, the yellow hair, thick and unruly, and the grey, smiling eyes. Will saw a strength in her that made him glad to have her for his advocate.

Looking at the Scottish earl, Mary's thoughts were more of an intimate nature. Even though a Queen of Scots, this handsome creature, with the wide shoulders, the dark curls and the deep blue, arrogant eyes, was one Scot that she might willingly exchange a crown for. Breaking the reverie, Mary began.

"The issue, My Lord Douglas, is your allegiance to your King. It seems that there is doubt about that in some quarters."

Will was immediately impressed by the direct approach of this lady.

"There are some quarters in which it will always be in doubt, My Lady. The quarters of Chancellor Crichton." Mary smiled at the pun. "Outside of that there should be no doubt about my loyalty."

"I need no convincing of it, Lord Douglas, but I fear that my husband, and Parliament for that matter, will require more than an honest aspect and an earnest protest of your allegiance to be convinced." Mary said.

"More, My Lady?" Will replied, furrowing his dark brows. "What more?"

"I take you to be a man of your word, Sir," Mary continued in a level voice, "and men of their word have often difficulty in understanding how anyone can doubt them. Dishonest men have no such difficulty, since they expect no more of others than that same deceit that they themselves employ."

In spite of his growing displeasure at the thought of his own pledge not being good enough, Will was warming to the intelligence of the Queen. If he needed an advocate, no one was better suited to the task than she.

"So men that cannot accept you, at face value, as an honest man, must need some assurance of your position beyond your own attestations." Mary went on.

"What more then?" Will repeated. "My Lady, you know that at the time that I left for Rome, I was in the king's service along with Chancellor Crichton and Bishop Kennedy. I went on a pilgrimage, still in that service, and the Holy Father himself commended me above all pilgrims. When I returned, my lands had been invaded and my people harassed. I could have expected that from Chancellor Crichton but never from James Stewart. Now I am to go before Parliament and give some proof of my loyalty to the king, and you are telling me that my own words attesting it are not enough. What else can I do? I am the one who was most grievously wronged, and I am the one who has to make some amends. My Lady, I am frankly at a loss to know what is expected of me."

Mary watched the earl's anger and confusion grow by the second. She had an answer for him, the only answer, for she knew her husband, and she knew his weakness. James Stewart was no Will Douglas. But she weighed her answer carefully, for the man before her was a proud man, and pride was also a weakness.

"I will tell you, My Lord Douglas, what you must do," she began, "and while you will not like it, I must ask you to bear with me and hear me out before you speak." Will Douglas relaxed on the couch, commanded by the serious aspect of his advocate.

"Much of what I am about to say is of a very private nature, but, since I say it as your advocate, it carries with it the privilege accorded to that relationship. That privilege bars me from reporting it, and it also bars you, and I rely on your word that it will go no further." Will nodded, and Mary continued.

"When we go before the Parliament, you must offer to resign all your lands and holdings to the king." Will started upright in his seat, and Mary raised a jewelled glove to restrain him. He sat back reluctantly.

"My husband, Lord Douglas, is not like you. He is not a confident ruler, assured of the loyalty of his subjects, strong and sure in his position. James Stewart is a weak man, haunted by the spectres of nameless faces of nobles that would take his crown, crying out silently for one true friend. Men like Chancellor Crichton need only whisper in his ear, for him to give faces to these ghosts." Mary paused and regarded Will with imploring eyes.

"The stronger you are, my lord, the stronger you appear, makes my poor husband cringe with fear. He fears you and he distrusts you as he distrusts everyone. He grew up, listening to the viper tongues of men like Crichton. Now he is a man, and he tries to escape his fear by deliberate acts of what he thinks of as courage, raiding and pillaging a strong man's holdings. But all he lacks is a true friend, Lord Douglas. You must be that friend for I see no other around me. You must show him that all that you have you will assign to him, and if you do that, you will do a greater service to him than you can imagine, and to me."

What an exceptional woman, Will thought, forgetting for the moment his own predicament. Would that he could have had Mary of Gueldres for a wife instead of the Fair Maid of Galloway.

"Resign my lands to the King?" he said. "This is the only way to convince him of my loyalty?" Mary nodded. She knew that the Douglas pride would find this solution of turning over half of Scotland to James very hard to accept.

"A temporary measure, my lord." Mary continued. "I am convinced that such a voluntary assignation of lands, made at the outset of this meeting with Parliament, would clearly show the trust that the Douglas has in his ruler. It would stop the mouths of the Crichtons for good. And then, when your allegiance is no longer in doubt, James will be persuaded to return your lands and your position in the realm."

"Persuaded?" Will said, raising his eyebrows.

"That will be no great feat. My husband's trust in the Black Douglas will be restored, and, remember, he wants you as his subject, for you are the most influential magnate in Scotland. You can restore the security that my husband lacks, and it is the lacking of it that makes him act like a petulant child. You must trust your advocate in this, Will Douglas. It may come as a blow to your pride, but you are a bigger man than to let pride rule you. In any event, if your allegiance is true, then so must be your trust."

Will had no answer to this final point, and Mary knew it. That he was able to subjugate his pride was more flattery than fact. Mary had no doubt that she could recover his lands if he followed her advice, but she could offer no guarantee of a King's actions. Will thought for a long time on Mary's proposal before he answered.

"Then it shall be done," he said, as he rose and bowed again. He had decided to go with her, and he was anxious to take his leave before the Douglas pride changed his mind.

∿ ∿ ∿

And the earl of Douglas did go with his advocate. He did resign his lands to the king as a pledge of his allegiance and the king did restore them. Mary of Gueldres had made a good assessment of her husband's actions; good, but not perfect.

A different man from James Stewart, a stronger and wiser man, would have accepted his victory graciously, thereby healing the hurt pride and the loss of face of Will Douglas. However, instead of cementing a friendship, James Stewart created an enemy when, in restoring the lands to the earl, he declared that he did this "notwithstanding any crimes committed by the said William, Earl of Douglas or by occasion of forfeiture or of treason, treachery or otherwise". Will Douglas was enraged by these words, and no less by his loss of the Earldom of Wigtown and the Lordships of Stewarton and Dunlop that were not returned to him.

In the months that followed, the dark anger of the Black Douglases still clouded Will's face as he set about to recover the titles that had not been returned. When he did recover them he made a point of announcing himself, wherever he went, as William, Earl of Douglas and Avondale, Lord of Galloway and Earl of Wigtown. Will Douglas would not be made a fool of by a fool.

Now he was in Scotland and he would make no more pilgrimages to a Pope, but rather to the duke of York, and the earls of Crawford and Ross. There were pacts to be made and there would be no more resigning of his holdings, only to be insulted. Let James Stewart try to command him now.

Inevitably, James Stewart did try.

∿ ∿ ∿

Mary of Gueldres sadly reflected on the faults of high born men, as she sat in her private chamber in Edinburgh Castle listening to yet another tirade from her husband. This one concerned a certain gentleman called MacLellan, who, for some reason, had been imprisoned in Douglas Castle. It appeared that the king had commanded his release, and Patrick Gray, MacLellan's uncle, had travelled to the castle bearing the king's order to effect the release.

James paced up and down, eyes blazing, gripping a rolled up missive in his hand, which he repeatedly peered at as if it contained some secret that he couldn't decipher. Then he approached Mary, waving the document in her face.

"Listen to this!" he shouted. "Listen to this!" Mary waited in silence.

"When the supper was over, Gray handed my order to Douglas. My order! Sealed with my seal! He delivered it into Douglas' own hand and asked that he might take the person MacLellan into his charge." Mary, long since tired of the ranting, affected an interest.

"And what did Douglas say?" James cried, his face purple. "What did he say?" He waved the paper again at his wife.

" 'You are come a little too late.' That's what Douglas said. 'You are come a little too late. Your sister's son is lying over there, but he is missing his head.' And then he said that Gray could take the body and do what he liked with it." James walked across the room and then returned, glancing all the time at the paper as he went.

"Missing his head!" he shouted, throwing the paper down at Mary's feet. "That's your earl of Douglas for you! A wicked man! But he will make no fool of James of Scotland. That, you will see!" He glared one more time at his wife before turning briskly and leaving the chamber.

Oh, the frailties of men, Mary thought, wishing she could be anywhere but here.

Chapter Ten

༄ ༄ ༄

For the great mass of the population, the merchant and the farm worker, the craftsman, tradesman and labourer, the power struggles and the skirmishes that permeated the Scottish scene were looked on as not much more than games played by kings and nobles. They were akin to tournaments, played on a grand scale. They were the meat of tales told around the fire at night, or songs sung by travelling balladeers on feast days, when the rest of the population got a break from their daily grind.

The lives of ordinary people were affected by these power struggles. The lives of Lang Tam o' Nyddry, and many others like him, were extinguished, and their families' lives changed forever. But the ordinary commoner had no recourse against a king, nor had he any influence in the decisions or actions of those who wielded power and used it, often to the extreme detriment of others.

It was for this reason that Lang Tam's widow bore her grief in silence. Her older son, Huw o' Nyddry, came home to take over his father's cottage and tenancy, and neither of them dwelt on Tam's untimely death or the cause of it, for they were too busy surviving. It was for the same reason that Ranald Ingram devoted his full time and attention to his work and the Ingram wine fleet, giving little thought to the activities of the king or the Douglas.

Everyone, of course, merchants and farmers alike, knew well the lengths to which these two powerful factions had gone. It was now an open conflict, but a conflict that the common man, rich or poor, tried to ignore in the hope that it would not affect him. Only Thomas Ingram, among these low born citizens, continued to be concerned, for his son was a Douglas.

It was in February that Ranald met his friend Will Douglas again. The earl had come to Houstoun Castle with upwards of two hundred mounted soldiers, and he had been in residence there for a week before Ranald received an invitation to join him in a hunt. It was to take place at the castle a few days later.

"This will test your skill, my friend, with the horse and the spear," the invitation said, and Ranald could readily picture Will's mischievous grin.

Whatever the problems Will Douglas may have had with the king, they were never brought up by the earl in these occasional meetings with Ingram. The Douglas had always insulated their friendship from his other life, and only commented on that when Ranald questioned him.

The hunt began in the early dawn of a dark chilly morning at the edge of Drumshorling Moor, close to where Ranald and Marjorie had been accosted by William of Houstoun years earlier. Ranald rode up to join the Douglas who was standing in his saddle calling out directions to several teams, each consisting of a man and three dogs of the heavy mastiff breed. The teams were deploying themselves in different directions as they were instructed.

These hounds were not for the stag, Ranald realised. They were too heavy and too slow. There was only one quarry for which they were suited.

"Good morning, Ranald Ingram," Will said cheerily. "You are ready to prove yourself I see."

Will looked with some admiration at Ranald's horse, a strong lean animal, as fine as his own. Summoning a retainer, Will reached down and took from him a long spear which he tossed to Ranald.

"You will need this, I think," tossing back the curls at his temple, "for Mr. Boar."

Ranald was taken aback. "We are hunting a wild boar?" he said.

"Not any boar," Will laughed. "This fellow has eluded me for close to a year, but I have finally sought him out. He's a big one, fifty inches at the shoulder, and about five hundred pounds of him. So I called for my friend Ingram to see to his dispatch." Will was enjoying the look on Ranald's face.

"We are not using the bow?" Ranald said, seeing that Will carried only a long spear, apart from the sword that was sheathed near his saddle.

"This is not a lady's hunt, my friend. Besides the bow is a useless weapon unless you want to kill our fine mastiffs that would be sure to get in the way. No sir, the spear is the weapon of choice for this quarry."

Ranald had never hunted wild boar. He was a skilled rider and experienced in the deer hunt, but he knew the boar was by far the most dangerous of animals, and for that reason he had avoided it. Most hunters of boar would use the crossbow, even at the risk of injuring their hounds, to avoid coming into close quarters with the beast. But Ranald knew that Will Douglas was not most hunters. In this, as in everything he did, Will had to be the best. Ranald, in spite of his growing fear of the hunt, was glad to be included by his friend because it meant that Will had a high regard for his ability even though it was unproven.

As the hunting party set off, out of the Houstoun woods and onto the moor, Ranald felt a brief stab of conscience at the thought of what Marjorie and Thomas would think of this escapade.

Trotting side by side across the soft bog land along the edge of the forest, Will explained the hunt. The boar was a night forager, so if they did not find him in the early hours he would be back in his den, and the hunt would be abandoned. They had to approach him from downwind, for a boar could smell a man or a dog at a hundred paces. In front of him, spaced at intervals along the margin of the trees and then running off at a right angle across the moor, Ranald could see the teams of men and dogs that waited in position.

"These are the relays," Will said, pointing out the teams. "When the boar is roused we will chase him up and the first relay man will loose his mastiffs into the hunt. The boar will be driven ahead of us, and at each relay point, as we pass, another set of dogs will join the chase so that fresh dogs will always strengthen the pack. Clever, wouldn't you say?" Will smiled. "But we must ride hard to get to the boar and protect the dogs for he is a murderer of dogs."

As they passed two relays without incident, and Ranald was gathering courage as he thought about the brilliance of this strategy, a shout went up from Will Douglas.

The boar had surfaced. In the same instant, Ranald saw him rise from the long grass, a huge black ball that took off along the trees with alternate grunts and snorts. Three enormous mastiffs followed, leaping and barking in excitement.

The Douglas took off at a gallop, dropping his long spear into the horizontal position and Ranald followed suit.

Two more relays of dogs were released as the boar passed them, bearing down on the fleeing animal with savage energy. Before reaching the next relay, the boar turned to the right into the moor. Hardly had Will and Ranald changed direction, than he turned left again towards the trees.

By now all the dogs had been released, and they barked and squealed in headlong flight through the tufted grass, on every side of the galloping horses.

"He's drawing them into the wood!" Will shouted through the clamour of dogs and horses. "He's going to make a stand!"

Ranald's fear returned. Tales he had heard of the wild boar at bay flooded his mind. He gripped his spear more tightly and forced his horse slowly through the trees.

As he emerged into a small clearing, he saw a dozen or so mastiffs, big and muscular with frightening jaws, circling the boar that had turned to face them. It was heavy and squat, its red eyes flaming in the black hair of its great head, and wide, curling tusks circling up and down in a slow, threatening challenge.

"Now you have him, Ranald!" Will's voice came from behind.

As he spoke, one of the mastiffs, a large brindled male, yellow eyes blazing and a fearsome growl coming from the wide muzzle, leapt forward onto the boar, seeking its throat. The boar dropped its head low and the mastiff tried to sink its teeth into the hard cartilage between the shoulders. Ranald watched as the boar shook the dog loose, and, with a single sideways sweep of its long curved tusks, ripped the belly of the mastiff open, so that its intestines spilled out in a purple, green pool into the forest floor.

"Go now, Ingram! Spear him now!" Will's voice broke through the morning air like a battle cry, and Ranald levelled his spear and urged his mount forward with a vicious kick. At the same time the boar charged forward towards him.

The long metal point of the spear penetrated the boar half way down its curved hairy back, and drove in and through the soft tissue below. The boar raised its head in mid charge, its tremendous weight pushing the spear up and back at the rider. Ranald, still grasping the long hilt, was heaved over the high back of his saddle. The spear shaft broke and he crashed to the ground, winded by the impact. He looked up helplessly as the great boar trotted forward to within four feet of him, the broken spear protruding from its back.

Ranald was transfixed with terror. He felt the blood drain from his face as he lay, unable to move, hypnotised by the tiny red eyes. The razor sharp tusks slowly began their curious circular motion, then the boar charged. Ranald shut his eyes and put his hands over his face. He smelled the sickening musky odour.

Suddenly there was a loud cry, the pounding of hooves and a long swishing sound that ended in an ear-piercing squeal.

Will Douglas, standing high in the stirrups, brought down the great two-handed sword with such a force that the wide blade severed the boar's head from its body. Ranald grunted as the headless torso rammed against his chest, hot sticky blood gushing over his face and neck. He opened his eyes to see the boar's head on the ground beside his cheek, the small eyes twitching.

Later in the great hall of Houstoun Castle, Ranald still shivered spasmodically as he gulped the brandy.

"Have another drink," Will said, refilling the goblet. "You will be fine in a minute. Man, what a story to tell your grandchildren!" Will rose and went to the hearth where he lifted the boar's head by one tusk, holding it up.

"Take this back to Strathalmond, lest they don't believe you."

Warmed by the brandy, Ranald slowly recovered his composure. "You saved my life," he said, in a matter-of-fact tone, looking balefully at the great head. Will threw the boar's head back into the central hearth and bowed gracefully.

"I thank you, sir, but you did all the work. All I did was cut off the devil's head. In any event, I think that you can fairly say that you were bloodied in your first boar hunt." He laughed and gave Ranald a friendly punch on the shoulder. Ranald smiled sheepishly.

"Have supper here," Will said, "and then you can go home and forget all about it. Anyway, I want to hear what progress in the wine import business."

∾ ∾ ∾

At supper Ranald and Will were joined by James Douglas, a younger brother of the earl and the twin of Archibald, Earl of Moray. He was dressed in the black frock coat of a cleric. Winking at Ranald, Will introduced him as the next Bishop of Aberdeen.

"You didn't know that we had one of these in the family — a cleric — did you Ranald? James here is matriculated at the University of Cologne in the Faculty of Arts."

"I see," said Ranald. "He is the one with all the brains in the family."

Will let out a loud guffaw. "You see what I told you, James. Ranald Ingram is as great a wit as he is a boar hunter."

They all three now laughed, and Ranald felt a happy glow from being in the company of Douglases, particularly since Will had introduced him to James as Ranald Douglas. It was a feeling of comfort in being family. Ranald looked at his new found cousin with interest.

James Douglas was a shade taller than Will, and slimmer. He was finer of feature, with short black hair cropped close to his skull and narrow blue eyes that shone with mirth.

"But look you, Ranald," Will said, waggling his index finger. "Though he may be a priest, he is also a warrior. Ask your partner, Philip of Burgundy, the next time you see him, which Scottish knight put his Burgundian champion in the dust in the lists at Stirling not long since." He nodded slowly, glancing at James.

Ranald, well fortified with brandy, looked at James with appropriate awe.

The night drove on with merriment. Will had earlier sent a servant to Strathalmond to announce Ranald's intention to take supper at the castle, and Ranald launched into a discourse on the wine fleet that was now a reality.

Three ships plied already between Leith and Calais, unloading thousands of casks of Gascon wine and paying duties to the King on each one. Philip of Burgundy had made his connections with the English importers, and the wine left Scotland for the English market, loaded in shipments to York, Bristol and London, paying even more duties to the king. Plans were laid to increase the fleet to sixteen ships within the month.

"You see," Will exclaimed, looking to his brother, "the beneficiary of all this commerce is my friend James Stewart of Scotland."

Ranald suddenly thought how ironic it was that James Stewart was benefiting greatly from the wine trade that Will Douglas had been so instrumental in developing, especially now that that Douglas and the king were such declared enemies.

"Someone should tell the king how the earl of Douglas contributed to his fortune," Ranald said.

"Indeed," replied Will, "and that someone will be myself when I visit him at Stirling Castle a week from now."

"You are going to see the king?" Ranald said with surprise.

Will grinned. "I have been summoned into the royal presence, my friend. But never fear, I have insisted on a guarantee of safe-conduct and it has been assured."

Ranald felt alarm as his mind darted back to another occasion when Douglases were summoned into the royal presence; the night of the Black Dinner. Will, guessing what Ranald was thinking, quickly interrupted.

"Don't concern yourself, man. The murdering Crichton will not be present, and, in any event, *this* Douglas is no careless boy with nothing at his back but his own arrogance."

At that the cleric spoke up. "There is nothing for Earl Douglas to fear, Ranald. Now that the Black Douglases have united with the earls of Crawford and of Ross and could sign a pact tomorrow with Richard of York, I think that James Stewart will have a care how he entertains Will Douglas."

Will threw a scolding look at his brother. "Don't listen to our cleric, Ranald. I have no pact with the Yorkists. Not yet, at least. Richard of York is, at this moment, camped with his army at Dartford and facing the Duke of Somerset and his Lancastrians who have, I am told, an even larger force at Blackheath." He laughed.

"Now I think that, were my grandfather, Archibald "the Grim", here, he might advise that the Black Douglases wait to see the outcome of that stand-off before rushing into any pacts in England."

Ranald was beginning to feel uncomfortable with all this talk of pacts and armies. This was the other earl of Douglas and not the one he knew. He was aware that the earl's brother had launched them into the present subject, and he was slightly surprised that a cleric, a student of the arts, could be so ready to talk of power struggles. But then he was another Douglas.

Will, seeing his friend's obvious discomfort, changed the

subject back to the hunt, and Ranald was relieved as the day's events were recounted again for the tenth time.

∾∾∾

Stirling Castle was not a favourite place of Mary of Gueldres. It had none of the calm domesticity of the Palace of Falkland. It was a symbol of the bitter strife that had dominated the country's history for three centuries, and it was filled with ghosts. Mary would not normally have chosen to accompany the king to such a place, but he was meeting the Earl of Douglas, and she felt it a duty upon her to be there. She had great hopes that this meeting would enable a reconciliation between these two rivals for the power over Scotland, that it would serve to forge a bond between them. She believed that, deep down, they had a mutual regard for each other and it was only pride, and the whisperings of jackals, that had made them enemies.

She knew that the choice of location was made by Chancellor Crichton. He was the Guardian of the Castle of Stirling and he would go to any length to keep her husband within his influence. For this reason, more than any, she had to be there.

As they rode up the steep incline from the little town of Stirling, Mary looked around at the splendid view. Stirling Castle was built on a great outcrop of volcanic rock high above the Forth Valley. To the north Mary could see the rounded hills of Perthshire, and to the east the river meandered across the valley floor to the sea, passing the spires and towers of Edinburgh.

Mary could see the bridge, far below, where Wallace and Murray had cut Surrey's English army in two more than a century earlier, and the Bannock Burn where another Douglas, Sir James "the Good", had ridden side by side with the Bruce on another sad day for England. Nothing but war and rumours of war cried out from the ancient walls of this elevated fortress, Mary thought, but perhaps the day that was coming would bring peace and a new comradeship.

At every opportunity, Mary had tried in her subtle way to assure her husband of the good intentions of Will Douglas. She had set about to remove the spectres that haunted him and to relieve his fears. In recent days she had the feeling that she was succeeding, for James was in good spirits and gave every outward sign that he would welcome Lord Douglas as a loyal and faithful subject. Mary knew that he liked Douglas, that he admired his manliness and his wild, proud passion for life, and this, in spite of all the cajoling of Chancellor Crichton and his scheming cousin, would win James Stewart over. And Mary would be there to deflect the destructive, poisonous, canker of the Crichtons.

These were her thoughts as she rode through the gates of Stirling Castle, and she smiled to the king. James Stewart returned the smile. When he met the earl of Douglas, he would assure him that the king of Scots was his friend as well as his prince, and that the time had come for them both to begin from the beginning. The Douglas would sever the bonds that he was reported to be making, and give his whole allegiance to his king, and he, James, would be gracious and accept this oath of loyalty, and the two together would be a new and all powerful force in this land of Scotland.

But once inside the great walls, Mary had a sudden feeling of foreboding. The castle itself seemed to sneer down at her from every side. Looking up, she thought she saw a figure at a high window. It looked like a woman in a green dress, who stepped forward and bowed, holding out something in her hands as if showing it to her. Mary looked away and blinked her eyes. When she looked back, the window was empty. Mary shivered, and urged her mount closer to her husband.

Chapter Eleven

❧ ❧ ❧

Marjorie Ingram found out about the boar hunt just as wives find out most things. Servants are not close-mouthed, and the news soon travelled from Houstoun Castle down the hill to Strathalmond.

"You could have been killed!" Marjorie shouted angrily.

"I would have been, had not Will Douglas saved my life," Ranald replied.

"Will Douglas put your life in danger in the first place," Marjorie countered. "I don't know what you were thinking of. You have never been on a boar hunt before. Why do you endanger your life with the likes of Will Douglas? He is looking for ways to get himself killed. Why do you want to join him? What does he care for his family? He has no children to be left fatherless." Marjorie was becoming more enraged by the minute, and Ranald decided to keep quiet and weather the storm until it blew over.

"I wonder what Thomas Ingram will say when he hears about this boar hunt with Will Douglas," Marjorie continued.

Ranald could just imagine what Thomas would say, and he wondered briefly if he would rather not face another boar than his father.

Eventually Marjorie's anger died down, and after a few hours of sulking when she said not a word to him, life at Strathalmond gradually returned to normal.

Ranald showed appropriate remorse and apologised profusely. Marjorie got him to swear that he would go on no more dangerous ventures with Will Douglas, and she said that it would serve no purpose to report the matter to Thomas Ingram, much to Ranald's relief. In a day or two all was forgiven and forgotten, but Marjorie inwardly rejoiced that her husband was safe, and Ranald took a secret delight in having shared the excitement of a hunt with Will Douglas that would be talked about for years to come.

∾ ∾ ∾

Supper with the king, in the splendour of the great hall of Stirling Castle, was a lavish affair. It was attended by fifty guests, their seating arranged, in order of rank, around the table that faced the elevated chairs of James II and Mary of Gueldres. The highest-ranking guest was the earl of Douglas and the lowest, the sheriff of Linlithgow with Chancellor Crichton fitting somewhere in the middle for he was not of noble birth. Mary was pleased that The earl of Douglas sat closest to her husband and herself, while Crichton was far enough down the table to be out of range of their conversation and away from the ear of the king.

Stationed at intervals around the walls, Will could see men of the king's guard, and he recognised their captain. It was Patrick Gray, the uncle of MacLellan, who had come to Douglas Castle to take his nephew, and had left with a headless corpse. Will smiled at Gray who sharply turned his face away.

The supper went well. The king was in good fettle and engaged with gusto in the small talk conversations with his guests. Will, a master of small talk and a gifted storyteller, gave his thrilling version of the boar hunt which exaggerated the courage of Ranald Ingram and downplayed his own involvement.

"Ah, that was the young merchant whom I met at my wedding," James intercepted. "Now a wine trader of some significance I hear."

"Of great significance, Your Grace," Will said, reaching for his wine glass.

"This fine Gascon wine was most likely brought from France in an Ingram ship."

"Then we are most glad that the boar did not dispatch Master Ingram," James said, to the laughter of all the company.

Mary recalled Ranald Ingram as an engaging young man who was obviously desperate to meet her uncle, Philip of Burgundy. An enterprising merchant, she thought.

All through the supper the conversation was light with much joking and laughing. No mention was made of the very recent skirmish in Edinburgh between a group of Crichton's friends and a small force of Douglases, and Mary was thankful for that because it had so enraged James at the time. The talk got onto England, and the growing threat of war there between York and Lancaster. The King was a supporter of Lancaster, which was the side of Henry VI. Everyone present at the supper knew that Henry VI was childless and that Richard, Duke of York was, without question, his heir, but they also knew that the Duke of Somerset had his own ideas about that.

For the Scots at the supper, it was a far off struggle that made a good conversation piece, much like the betting on a tournament. Richard of York had committed treason but was too strong to be punished. On the other hand he was, at the present time, too weak to tackle the much larger force of the king. He had gone to London to accuse Somerset, and the outcome was a conference with Henry. The parallel with the Scottish situation was altogether too obvious for James to ignore when the subject came around.

"Richard of York has finally seen the wisdom of disbanding his army," James said, smiling at Will Douglas.

"Yes indeed, Your Grace," Will replied." It is a wise commander who avoids a fight when the odds are overwhelming."

By suggesting that Richard of York had disbanded his forces because of the likely defeat by a much larger force, rather than because he had been called upon to disband by Henry, Will had turned James' point right around. James, however, ploughed on.

"He disbanded, Lord Douglas, at the request of his king, and in exchange for a free pardon for the Yorkists and the bringing to trial of Somerset."

James looked pleased with himself. Mary was worried about the trend of the conversation for she knew that both men did not care to lose an argument.

"Aye, Your Grace," Will said, "a free pardon. And that is why Richard of York was made to ride into London before his king's column, much like a common criminal. He was merely exercising his free pardon, no doubt."

This was followed by a great roar of laughter from the guests who were enjoying what had suddenly become a contest of words between the earl and the king.

"In London, at St. Paul's, your Richard of York made an oath that he would form no assemblies in future without his king's command. So the matter is at an end." James said this with a smug look that signified finality.

Will had not missed the reference to the Yorkist as "your Richard". Looking around the company, he raised his glass, in the motion of a toast.

"Aye, time will tell, Your Grace. Time will tell." A few sniggers and muffled approvals ran round the table.

At that point heads began to turn to a troupe of acrobats, whose performance had just started in a cleared area at the end of the long table. Wine glasses were being replenished by servants, and Mary breathed a sigh of relief that the dangerous discussion was finished. Will laughed and joked with the guests near him. The king feigned an amused interest in the leaps and somersaults of the troupe, while he seethed inside.

As the evening grew merrier and the guests grew drunker, Mary of Gueldres excused herself to her husband and retired to her chamber. Tired from her long day, she was relieved that the supper had gone so well, in spite of the risky subject of York and Lancaster, and she wanted to be fresh in the morning when the conference between her husband and Will Douglas would begin.

Some time later, during an interval in the entertainment, James adjourned to a little anteroom off the great hall that served him as a study. From there he sent a note by one of the guards requesting the earl to join him. Then he sat at the small table, trying to compose himself. He had ordered a flask of brandy and two glasses, and a chair had been set for the earl opposite his own. Not wishing to say his piece in public, where Will Douglas might turn serious comment into jokes for the amusement of others, he would have his say in private, and he would have it tonight. He would know where the earl stood now, this very night.

When Will Douglas entered the room, James asked him to close the door and take a seat, then he poured two brandies and sat back in his chair with a little smile.

"So you think Richard of York a fool to disband and swear an oath to his king, Lord Douglas?"

"Not a fool at the time, Your Grace, but only on hind-sight, for I think were he asked to do it now, his answer might be different."

"And at supper you said that time would tell. Do you think that York will not abide by his oath?"

Will could readily see where this conversation was going. The king had a notion that Will knew something of the plans of Richard of York.

"Your Grace, I have no knowledge of Richard's plans. My expression was derived from mere common sense. In a land where powerful factions contend, anything may be the outcome. Oaths, I fear, are not what they used to be."

At that last remark James bristled, and Will wondered just how naïve this monarch was. He had made it clear to the king that royal commands alone had little value. Lands where there was contention among magnates included Scotland as well as England.

Will suddenly felt sorry for James Stewart. Here was a weak man, unsure of his status and uncertain of his support, looking south and seeing his counterpart, Henry Plantagenet, standing like a stag at bay amid savage hounds. Will's own animosity left him and he resolved to help the king, to explain the state of Scotland to him, and, if James would but understand it, to offer him the full support of the Douglas.

"Sire," Will continued, "There is no truer, more loyal subject of Your Majesty than the man you see before you. Forget Richard of York. Forget the English and Henry Plantaganet. But look you to Scotland and the condition of its governing."

James listened with a new interest as Will continued.

"You have, in this land of Scotland, noblemen, strong men, violent men, men who have little concept of commonwealth but only of their own ultimate power over the little monarchies that they have built up. They are also frightened men, for they see you, James Stewart of Scotland, King of Scots, as an enemy. They think that you might usurp that power in their little kingdoms and thereby cheat them of their birthright."

At that point Will stopped, watching James with a searching look. Had he said too much? Was this King of Scots capable of understanding him?

"Pray continue, Lord Douglas," James said without expression.

"And so they make pacts with each other, these noblemen, in the hope to grow their strength to such an extent as to ensure their safety." Will said.

"From the king?" James said. "Safety from the king?"

"Yes," Douglas said, thinking that now he must press the point to its conclusion.

"From the king."

"And your own pacts with Crawford and Ross? Do you say that these are made to protect the earl of Douglas from James Stewart? And your meetings with Richard of York? Do you tell me that these also are merely a defensive strategy, and not an attack on your king?" James was growing angry.

"Yes! Yes! Yes!" Will shouted. "That is indeed what I say." Will had resolved to serve this little man, and to educate him. How could it be so difficult for the king to understand what he was saying?

"The bonds I have made with Crawford and Ross are not made to threaten you. Douglas must be free to make his own decisions for his own security." Will continued.

"Then, if they are not made to threaten your king, you must break them. These pacts have no place in a Scotland that should be one country under one prince." James retorted, his anger growing.

" Should be, perhaps, but is not!" Will exclaimed, losing control of his own temper, because this little king was too stupid to understand the realities of the situation. All he could see was some idyllic land, where he manipulated all the power and the nobles had no right to make bonds.

James' birthmark went purple and his eyes flamed with rage as he got to his feet.

"Will you break your pacts with Crawford and Ross?" he shouted at Douglas.

Will sneered at the king. "I will not," he said quietly.

James stood there for a second, his lip quivering and his whole frame rigid.

"Then if you will not, I will!" As he spoke, he drew the little jewel-handled dagger from his belt and, reaching wildly across the table, he plunged it into Will's throat.

Eyes wide with surprise, The Earl of Douglas tried to raise his hands to the dagger that still protruded from his neck as a fountain of blood spouted out over the table and onto the king's sleeve. James screamed and staggered back, knocking over the chair that fell back onto the floor with a loud crash.

At that point the door burst open, and Patrick Gray rushed in, his long-shafted poleaxe at the ready. Gray was quick to survey the scene, Will Douglas dying where he sat, his jerkin soaked with his blood, and James, standing back whimpering, his whole body shaking.

Gray swung the great axe high over his head and brought it down on the Douglas, shattering his skull, the grey red tissue of brain and bone spattering across the table.

Gray looked with a vengeful smirk at the body of Will Douglas with its shattered head. It was revenge for his nephew, MacLellan; one head for another. He then turned to the other guards that had rushed into the room. He closed the door and had two men lead the king, who stood gabbling in shock, to his bedchamber. Then Gray himself, assisted by two other guards, lifted the body of the Douglas and heaved it unceremoniously from the narrow window of the study into the garden below.

∾ ∾ ∾

The death of the earl of Douglas shocked the nation. Rumours of how it happened abounded, but while the reason for it was lost in the many versions of the event, it was the idea of a man being murdered while under a guarantee of safe conduct, and while accepting the hospitality of another, that offended the conscience of the people. Petitions arrived in the Parliament calling for an inquest into the affair. One petition, that of Ranald Ingram of Strathalmond, called for the deposal of this "tyrant". James Stewart hid himself away in his apartments, while the Queen cried softly over the death of Will Douglas.

James Douglas abandoned his studies and his clerical garb and put on his armour. Riding with six hundred men to Stirling, he burned the town and dragged the safe conduct pass, that had been issued to his brother, through the streets, tied to his horse's tail. Then he made his own declaration that neither he nor his would ever give obedience to this king, and that he would have his revenge for the murder of Will Douglas.

The king, hearing this, put aside what feelings of guilt he had for the death of Will Douglas. He emerged from his castle hideaway, as angry and vicious as ever, persuading the Parliament that the murder of the Douglas was justified by his treason, and setting his sights on his enemies. James, the ninth Earl of Douglas, was one. Ranald Ingram, the merchant who wanted to depose the king, was another.

And this time there would be no mistakes, he thought, no taking of castles and then returning them. This time he would destroy them. And it had occurred to him exactly how he would do it.

∾ ∾ ∾

Huw o' Nyddry was soon to discover that his move back to his father's cottage meant that he had no earnings from being hired out, and that became, in a very short time, a serious problem. His younger brother was hired out and could barely support himself. Huw had to find a way soon to put food on the table for himself and his mother while still maintaining the tenancy. It was coming time for the ploughing, and Huw needed something soon to supplement the family income. So when he heard that men were being hired for money in Edinburgh, something to do with quarry work, Huw packed a little cloth bag with food for a few days and set out on the long walk to the city.

He entered by the West Port early the next day, among jostling crowds of tinkers carrying their tins and pots for sale on the streets, oxen pulling carts of hay and farm labourers guiding litters of squealing pigs to the market. The foul stench of the place made Huw wretch, and beggars in rags with blinded eyes or missing limbs grasped at his shirt. Now and then a shower of piss would splash into the narrow cobbled street from some high window.

As he pressed through the crowd, a young woman in a torn and faded red robe pushed him into the mouth of an alleyway. Opening the robe she pulled Huw's hand against a naked breast as she sought his mouth with her own. She reeked of ale, and a mass of purple scabs clung to one corner of her mouth. Huw, in a sudden frenzy to escape, pushed her violently away as he turned and ran into the narrow alley. Her curses followed him. The alley opened into another street where Huw could see a tavern, its doors already open for trade. He went in and flopped down on a stool, the smell of the woman still in his nostrils.

Huw sat in the tavern for most of the morning, watching customers come and go. Around noon, three young men entered, one of them nodding to Huw as they took stools around a broken-down bench. Huw could see from the dried mud on their hands and the cut of their clothes that they were workmen, and he soon engaged them in conversation.

"I heard that there is quarry work to be had in Edinburgh?" Huw said.

The youngest of the three, a youth of no more than fifteen years with a shock of red hair and small, pearly white teeth replied. "That there is," he beamed. The other two grimaced at him as if they did not want him to speak, but the red head carried on.

"It's not in the city. It's out by the Silver Burn, a full day's walk from here. That's where we are heading." He looked around proudly at his companions.

Huw's heart leapt.

"Would it be all right for me to join you fellows?" he asked tentatively. Red head looked at the others who merely shrugged, now that the job site had been revealed.

The quarry at the Silver Burn was a large bite out of the green slopes of the Pentland Hills. Huw could see dozens of men working at the rough face, wielding picks that broke off great ragged lumps of rock. These were being filled into heavy carts that then joined a slow procession down the slope to a flat promontory where other men hammered and shaped them. The hiring was a formality. Work was clearly abundant here, and it was for cash money, payable at the end of each day. It wasn't for farm wages that came in quarterly and were whittled down by debts owed to the master of the estate.

Huw was elated. At dawn the following morning he set himself to work at the face. It was heavy work, but it was for cash. Talking with the other men, he discovered that this work was being paid for by the king himself.

Huw made no tie between the king and the man who had been responsible for his father's death, and even if he had, this work was for cash money.

"They take these stones down yonder," an old man told Huw, "and them that you can see with the pointed hats, them are stone masons, and they shape these stones into great big balls. Them are cannon balls, m'lad, for the king's bombards."

Huw wondered what a bombard was, but he didn't wonder for long as he had to get back to work.

Chapter
Twelve

ல் ல் ல

"You sent this! " Thomas Ingram shouted, waving the document in the air. "You were so stupid as to send this petition to Parliament. And you signed it "Ranald Douglas Ingram!" Ranald was seeing the Ingram rage once again. Thomas stomped around the room, crushing the document in his hand. "Do you have any idea what this could mean for the Ingrams? Do you?" Thomas shouted.

Ranald felt his own irritation rising. "The king murdered my friend. What am I expected to do? Forget it?" he roared back at his father. "He should be deposed for his cruel villainy."

"Deposed?" Thomas went on. "And how do you propose that would happen? It would take a different Parliament from this one to legitimise that. You should have left the petitioning to the Douglases."

"James Douglas is a fool," Ranald said. "All he has done is burn the town of Stirling for revenge. What use is that? How does that revenge Will Douglas? James Stewart must be brought down. That is why I made the petition, and I made it in the name of a Douglas. This Douglas! And I would do it again!"

Thomas Ingram shook his head and sat in his chair. He knew that this fight was going nowhere. Ranald saw it that he had a duty to his friend, and in other circumstances what he did would have been laudable.

"You are right, Ranald," he continued quietly. "Sacking a town makes fools of the Douglases and their allies. It shows mere pride instead of wisdom. The wise thing would have been to do what you did, petition to get rid of the king."

Ranald looked up with surprise as Thomas went on."But it was for the Douglases to do it, and not a mere merchant. Perhaps, and I say only perhaps, James Douglas, at the right time, when the horrid deed was fresh in Scotland's mind, could have changed the Parliament and had the petition succeed. That, I suspect is what your friend Will Douglas would have done. Now it's too late. By his acts James Douglas has grown weaker and James Stewart has grown stronger. There is only one course for the King now, and that is to finish the Black Douglases, once and for all." He looked down at the paper in his hand."I only pray that he does not count Ranald Douglas Ingram as one of them."

Ranald listened to Thomas Ingram and felt ashamed. Not because he had petitioned, but because he hadn't thought it out first. Perhaps he could have prevailed on James Douglas to do the petitioning. How he wished now that he had consulted his father in the beginning.

"Do you . . . .do you think that the King might seek his revenge against Strathalmond?" Ranald stammered nervously. Thomas said nothing, but merely looked at Ranald and shook his head in anguish.

∾ ∾ ∾

Huw o' Nyddry was a good worker, and the quarrymaster was quick to notice it. So when another big job came up, Huw was the first to be recommended, and he soon found himself at Edinburgh Castle where he was selected to be a foreman of a squad of men.

The capital buzzed with excitement. Something was about to happen that all could watch. It would entertain the population and give some light relief to their daily drudgery.

Bellmen, at every gate leading into the city, rang their bells and called for workmen to take wages, while others sized up the long line of applicants, feeling their arms and shoulders and checking on their sobriety. Huw and the other foremen were led through the castle gate into the wide courtyard where Huw first laid eyes on the two bombards.

They were cannon, the biggest cannon that Huw had ever seen. He had seen cannon, the kind that were brought up in a siege to smash the gates of castles, large and heavy enough to be handled by a dozen soldiers, but never anything like these. Now Huw understood what a bombard was, and the purpose of the huge stones that he had dug from the quarry and the masons had shaped into great round balls.

The master of works, a short rounded figure of a man standing on an elevated platform, addressed the foremen. He began to explain the work and the wages. He said that every man there was in the pay of King James of Scotland, and the two bombards that they saw before them were to be taken to certain places near the Burgh of Linlithgow. This was all they were required to be told, and even this may have been unnecessary, for most of the Edinburgh men being hired had no idea where Linlithgow was. Huw knew, and he was glad that the work would take him close to home.

The bombards would be mounted on what the master of works called cradles, which were huge carriages of iron and wood, each set on four thick, iron-rimmed wheels, and these cradles would be drawn by teams of oxen, six oxen to a cradle.

The work to be allocated to the squads in the foremen's charge varied. Some would go ahead of the bombards to clear the way and smooth out the road, filling any holes and marking any soft earth to be avoided. When the cradles were in motion, they would not be stopped for impediments and these squads would ensure clear passage. Others would accompany the bombards, making any last minute repairs to the road, assisting the wheelwrights should there be a breakage of wheels, and ensuring the safety of the mountings on the cradles.

The master of works then indicated to the foremen whose squads would go on ahead and whose would remain to accompany the bombards. Finally, of the foremen of squads to remain, he selected six, whose squads would load the bombards on the cradles. Huw was among the six. The work was to start the next morning.

That night in the tavern, spending some of the silver that he had earned in the quarry, Huw met an old soldier who had seen service in France, fighting the English. That, at least, was what he said, as he sported the red stump of what had once been his right hand, and blinked one watery eye constantly when he spoke. Although he wore the ragged remnants of a quilted gambeson, Huw didn't believe him. The taverns were full, tonight, of workmen with money, and this "old soldier" was trading tales for drink as fast as he was able. Huw, after buying the old man a mug of ale, was intent on ignoring him, until he heard the word "bombard" mentioned in one the soldier's stories. Huw caught him by the sleeve.

"Bombard, you say?" Huw's interest grew.

"Aye," said the old man. "At the siege of C———. I was there, I was. And that bombard, that very one that is lying up there at the castle, "Mons Meg" they call it, I saw them fire it! The "Muckle Murderer" is what the soldiers called it."

Seeing the expectant young faces around him, the soldier pushed his empty mug across the table, blinking his eye. It was quickly filled.

"It can throw a three hundred pound gunstone two thousand paces!" he announced, and he reached for the mug and took a long swallow. He wiped his mouth with his sleeve and looked around him, chin up and lips pursed into the pose of a knowledgeable expert. This was his night.

"And the castle wall," Huw said urgently, " did it breech the wall?"

The old man smiled. "It went through that castle wall like a poleaxe through a cheese." The old man cackled, his watery eye blinking wildly and his sinewy hand, with its long black fingernails, pushing the mug back out across the table.

Early the next morning, Huw and his squad assembled to load the bombards onto their cradles. The huge barrels were lifted using pulleys that were mounted on a robust scaffold, then lowered slowly onto the cradles, the men steadying them to prevent them from swinging.

Huw noticed the group of six men who directed the operation and whom the master of works had introduced as gunsmiths from Flanders. These men would accompany the bombards on their journey, and it was their function to direct the loading and the firing. They fussed around the weapons like mother hens with chicks, gabbling furiously in Flemish as they eyed the men of the squad with disdain.

Once in the cradles, the bombards were secured by large wedges of wood that were hammered in along the sides between barrel and cradle. The pulleys were removed, and the first team of oxen brought up and hitched to Mons Meg. She would go first, the master of works said, and the other would follow a mile or so behind so that any unforeseen stoppage of the first team could be relayed to the second in time for it to be stopped.

He explained that the only major slope between the castle and the ultimate destination of each bombard was the descent from the castle to the West Port of the city. The route would be out of the castle gates and along the short street called Castlehill into the Lawnmarket, then right and right again down the narrow steep slope of the Westbow into the Grassmarket. Continuing west through the Grassmarket, the bombards would leave the city by the West Port.

In the afternoon, the first team of oxen pulling its mammoth load left the castle. It was led by the master of works and accompanied by three of the Flemish gunsmiths, two wheelwrights and several squads of men including Huw and his squad. It trundled through the gates and into Castlehill. The squads who had gone ahead had cleared the narrow streets, and dozens of Edinburgh's citizens gawked and cheered from high windows.

Once it had made the turns into the Westbow, the oxen were unyoked for the sharp descent. Long ropes had been fixed to the front of the cradle above the great wheels, with huge wedges attached at their extremities. These were checked so that the wedges could be pushed under the leading wheels in the event of a runaway. At the back of the cradle a further six ropes were attached, each one long enough to allow for five men to grasp it so that the bombard was lowered down the slope, proceeding under its own weight with thirty men from the squads holding it back. Any sudden acceleration was quickly arrested by those in front dropping the great wooden wedges below the wheels. The men behind would then take the strain while the wedges were removed, and the load would advance once more.

In that way the bombard, Mons Meg, descended into the Grassmarket. The oxen were yoked up and the team proceeded westward under the towering rock of the castle, to the cheers of the crowds that had now come from all parts of the city and the surrounding villages. As the rumble of the great iron-rimmed wheels of the cradle on the cobblestones filled the narrow street, most of the men in the squads returned to the castle to enable the descent of the second great gun.

From the royal apartments of the castle, the king of Scotland and his Flemish queen looked down at the procession of the bombards far below. For James this was the realisation of a dream that had begun when, as a boy of seven, his father had shown him bombards, imported from Flanders, and piqued his interest in artillery. Now they would see some action.

The guns moved at a slow grinding pace past the castle stables and out through the West Port into the countryside. Here, the great wheels sank into the soft earth of the track that led west towards Linlithgow, and the oxen strained in the harnesses.

James grinned. In two days he would follow with his soldiers and the wagon loads of stone cannonballs, and Mons Meg would sit before the Castle of Abercorn, the large fortress of the Black Douglases that was second only, in size and importance, to their stronghold at Threave. The other bombard would turn off south to the lands of Houstoun.

Once out of the city streets and into the rutted tracks, progress was slow and ponderous. The squads, with pick and shovel, had to loosen stones from the fields ahead of the guns to fill in holes and depressions every few feet along the way. The work was continuous and exhausting. Huw and the other foremen arranged breaks for their men in relays, so that the progress of the cradle was unhindered. The little master of works flitted back and forth from the leading bombard to the other in the rear, issuing directions and stopping all the time to stamp a foot on the track repairs with a constantly worried look. The Flemish gunsmiths in their long cloaks and wide floppy hats rode aloof on their ponies.

Just before dark, the motley column made its first overnight stop at the tiny village of Dean, where the track crossed the river that flowed north to the Port of Leith. By now they had attracted followers, provisioners with their carts of food and ale to supply the workers, entertainers with their flutes and magic tricks, and women of the city who had an ever ready eye for men with cash.

At every night stop, new teams of oxen would be supplied at the cost of the local sheriffdoms as commanded by the king, and every shack and outhouse became a doss-house for the labourers.

The master of works gathered the foremen together to lay the plans for the morrow, pointing out defects and how they would be cured. The next day, he said, should take them to the lands of Gogar. Thereafter the track divided. Mons Meg would proceed towards the Burgh of Linlithgow, passing through the little settlements of Kirkliston and Winchburgh. The second gun would move south and west towards Drumshorling Moor. The forward squads, that were clearing the way of main obstacles, would be divided equally at the separation of the ways.

For the first time Huw wondered about the actual destination of Mons Meg. Its purpose was clear enough, but where exactly would it be used? He made a mental note to request this information from the master of works the very next night.

Another day of backbreaking work led the guns and their long procession of followers to a place called Gogarstane, where a prehistoric stone marked the junction of the roads. Here the crews made camp, to sleep where they could find a dry spot.

"Pray, sir," Huw said, " Where are the bombards to be fired?" Huw asked the master of works in private, after the latter had concluded his nightly meeting.

The little man looked wary. It was not in his mandate to give out this information.

"You will know, soon enough, Huw o' Nyddry," he said. Then, seeing Huw's downcast look, and thinking, because this was the best of his foremen and they were out of the earshot of the others, he continued. " This is between you and me, you understand," he said in a quiet voice, looking around furtively. "Mons Meg will lay siege to the Castle of Abercorn. The other is bound for Houstoun."

The news shocked Huw. "Abercorn?" he muttered. "But that is where I live. I am a tenant of the estate of Abercorn." The other shrugged his shoulders.

"The king's orders," he said. "All Douglas houses are to be razed to the ground."

Huw was speechless. He stared at the huge cannon, and his mind went to how Lang Tam o' Nyddry had died on the orders of the king. And now he, Huw o' Nyddry, was taking this cannon back to Abercorn for the king, this time to destroy the castle.

"I cannot go further," he said, looking at the master of works. "Not to Abercorn".

"But you must," the little man said, in an anxious voice.

"No!" Huw said with finality. "Not for you and not for the king. I must take my wages and leave you here."

The master of works was thinking fast. He saw that Huw was determined. He didn't want to lose his best foreman when they had so far to go and come back. Besides, if Huw were to leave there would be questions, and it would come out that he had told the destinations of the guns, contrary to the king's orders. Suddenly his face lit up.

"You and your squad can switch to the other bombard," he said. "Then you will not go to Abercorn." He looked expectantly at Huw.

Huw was relieved by this solution. What the king did elsewhere than at Abercorn was of little concern to him. It didn't affect him. This way he would not be giving up pay. This promised to be a long job, and the money would keep his family for a whole year. Huw nodded eagerly to the master of works.

In the morning the squads were switched and the whole caravan divided itself into two. The master of works was happy with the solution, for he could not accompany both bombards. He put Huw in charge of the whole column that would take off south-west, while he himself would go with Mons Meg.

"Tomorrow you will pass through Nether Gogar and proceed as far as Westfield before dark," he told Huw. "Thereafter you will cross the River Almond and take the track that runs north and west. That way will bring you to the ferm-toun of Myrestane and the Castle of Houstoun. Once there you will deliver the bombard to the soldiers of King James."

Huw, in his new-found role as acting master of works, and at a new rate of pay that had already been established, moved off with the gun, the clearing and road-fixing squads in front and the long line of wagons and camp followers trailing out behind. The bombard had no name, but it was identical in every way to the one they called Mons Meg. Huw decided to call it 'Myrestane Mary', after his mother and his destination.

Although the distance to Houstoun was shorter than that to Abercorn, the track that Huw found himself on now was in very poor repair. Many holes had to be filled in, and in some places the way narrowed to a mere path, barely enough to let a single rider pass. At these places the road had to be built up from nothing to the width of the cradle and more, and the sides shored up with timber to prevent them from crumbling under the great weight. As a result, Mons Meg sat on a slope facing the Castle of Abercorn while Huw was still two full days from Houstoun.

The passage of the bombards across these Lowland tracks had been reported back to Edinburgh Castle on a daily basis by the king's messengers, and a substantial force of royal troops, accompanied by wagons containing barrels of gunpowder and the heavy gunstones had already arrived at Abercorn.

Patrick Gray, the king's captain, delivered the call to those within the walls to surrender the castle. As before, none of the Douglases were present, and at the sight of the great bombard and the large contingent of soldiers, the gates were opened and the castle emptied of its residents.

The king rode up, dressed in his dandy clothes, his little dagger at his side, and dismounted to stand beside the gun as the Flemish experts began to direct the loading ceremony.

At the same time, at a point where the track ran past a church at Nether Newliston, the bombard, Myrestane Mary, lay at an angle as the edge of the track had collapsed under the weight of the wheels on one side. Huw had directed that the oxen be unhitched from the front and hitched to the side of the cradle, and he was directing the men to pull from the front and push from the rear while the oxen pulled the cradle up from the side. The strategy succeeded and the gun was once more centred on the track, but more time had been lost.

Houstoun Castle was still two days away.

Chapter
Thirteen

∾ ∾ ∾

When the first gunstone from the bombard shook the thick wall of Abercorn Castle, causing a long crack to appear across the top of the entrance gate, a rider was sent post-haste to Houstoun. From there the news was soon relayed to Strathalmond.

By the time Thomas Ingram and Isabella had arrived from Leith, summoned by Ranald Ingram, many more great gunstones from the thundering gun had shaken Abercorn Castle. One of the towers had crumbled and fallen, and the king had returned to Edinburgh, for Abercorn would soon be destroyed. More riders rushed to Houstoun to update the terrible news.

On his way from the city, at a point not far to the east of Myrestane, Thomas passed the column led by the largest cannon that he had ever seen. He recognised it as a bombard, the gun that he had only heard about in his father's tales of soldiering in France. When he and Isabella rode up the drive to Strathalmond, they passed servants, loaded down with their belongings, heads down and doggedly trudging away from the house.

The family was in the great hall. Ranald was talking earnestly with Master James, the steward, while Marjorie stood at the window clutching the children.

Isabella rushed to her daughter while Thomas, ignoring Ranald, caught the steward by the arm. "What news of Abercorn?" he said.

"It is being cast down, Sire," Master James said. "I fear that nothing will soon be left of the Douglas Castle of Abercorn."

"God save us!" Thomas whispered, raising his eyes to the ceiling. He looked at Ranald. "And another devilish gun is at Myrestane."

"It is making for Houstoun Castle," Ranald said calmly. "The king means to end the House of Douglas."

"Aye, Houstoun Castle, and what of Strathalmond?" Thomas looked at Master James. "In the news, was there mention of Strathalmond?" The steward shook his head.

"Only that the second bombard will attack Houstoun."

"Why do you say Strathalmond, father," Ranald began, with sudden alarm.

"The House of Douglas, man! Your words! Do you think the king forgets that you are a Douglas? God, Ranald! Why are the servants leaving this house? Tell me that!" He looked at the steward. "Why, Master James?"

Master James dropped his eyes and said nothing, while Ranald had a look of shock on his face. "What's to do, Thomas?" Ranald said.

Thomas Ingram grew irate. "What's to do?" he shouted. "What's to do?"

Marjorie approached them as he went on, his voice growing louder.

"You ask me what's to do? I took you, a Douglas, into my house, and made you an Ingram. At your father's wish I did that. I told you time and time again to steer your ship clear of the Douglases. But did you listen to me? No! I permitted you to marry my daughter and let you stay in this house, but did you keep away from Will Douglas? No!"

Everyone stood in silence, the steward looking uncomfortable as Thomas ranted on.

"No! Your friend was murdered by the king, and what did you do? You petitioned Parliament to depose James Stewart and signed yourself Ranald Douglas! And now the king triumphs and his cannon is at your door, and you ask me what's to do!"

Thomas looked around with wild eyes and everyone was silent. Then he motioned to the steward.

"Get a flask of brandy. That's what we'll do, for there is damn little else we can do. Maybe tomorrow there will be no brandy . . . and no Strathalmond."

In the midst of the tirade, Isabella had ushered the children out of the room. Now Master James rushed off for the brandy, glad to escape the family quarrel.

Marjorie stood, staring boldly at her father, her wifely duty struggling with her fear of the truth in his words.

Ranald turned on his heel and strode from the hall.

∾ ∾ ∾

The last mile of Huw o' Nyddry's journey, from Myrestane to Houstoun Castle, was mainly uphill and was the most gruelling part of the whole trek. The oxen sweated and staggered under the load, and the initial excitement of the men had long since evaporated. Now all Huw wanted was to deliver the bombard and have a break from the work until it was time to return it to Edinburgh.

Huw received his instructions from the master of works from messengers who rode from Abercorn, and the latest messenger brought the news that the Castle of Abercorn would soon be destroyed and that the king, himself, and the master of works would then return to the capital. Huw was to deliver the gun to Houstoun Castle and await the soldiers who would arrive soon to take over.

Reaching the top of the hill, Huw could see the tower of Houstoun Castle rising above the trees. Since hearing the messenger's news, he had a sense of sadness, thinking about Abercorn and his father, and how Lang Tam had been so proud of his visit from Earl Douglas. Now the Douglas was gone and his great castle was gone. They were gone just as Lang Tam o' Nyddry was gone. Now this fine castle of Houstoun would follow the fate of the other, Huw thought, and he had delivered the bombard.

But this kind of thinking was not normal for Huw, and soon his mind went back to the wages. Anyway he didn't know the Douglases nor the King of Scots. What did he care about the destruction of the castles of great men?

As the bombard advanced through the wood to the castle, Huw heard the hoof-beats of horses and he turned to see the approach of dozens of soldiers. They skirted round the column and passed by Huw, a tall rider in front, in helmet and full armour, giving him a brief wave with a gloved hand.

At Houstoun, as at Abercorn, there was no Douglas army to defend Douglas lands. The Black Douglases, though not yet defeated, were seeing the royalist power grow and their own alliances crumble. James Douglas was fully employed at his Border stronghold, and the force that he had sent to defend Abercorn and Houstoun had had to withdraw before a superior royal army.

In the morning, the tall mounted figure of Patrick Gray delivered his message to those within Houstoun Castle. It was to the effect that any who surrendered and came out through the gate now would be granted the king's mercy. Those who chose to remain would be hanged. To emphasise the point, he said that Abercorn Castle was destroyed and its defenders already hanged.

Those within the walls were not ready to question the truth of this, even though it conflicted with what messengers had reported. There was no Douglas force to defend them. All they saw was the bombard at the ready, and within a very short time, a long line of men, women, and children poured out of Houstoun Castle, straining under their belongings and anxious to receive the king's mercy.

From the edge of the wood where the land sloped down to Strathalmond, Ranald and Marjorie Ingram stood watching.

What Thomas Ingram had said in anger the day before was still going round and round in Ranald's mind. It was all his fault. Thomas was right. These enormous guns would be the finish of Houstoun and maybe Strathalmond with it. If only he had listened to Thomas. If only he hadn't sent the petition to Parliament. If only...

Marjorie squeezed his hand. Her eyes moved from the line of people leaving the castle, to the soldiers, mounted and ready, and finally to the bombard. She looked at Ranald, terror in her face.

"It's all right, my love," Ranald said gently. "The cannon is a threat. You heard the officer threaten, but there were no hangings at Abercorn. Abercorn is not destroyed."

He put his arm round her and pulled her against him. He could feel her slim body tremble. "See them now! They are evacuating the castle and walking through the line of soldiers. No harm has come to them. Now there is no need to use the gun."

As they continued to watch, they could see some activity around the bombard. Three men, in what Ranald recognised as Flemish hats, appeared to be examining it and making hand signals to some of the soldiers. Then a big wagon was brought forward through the crowd of soldiers and evacuees from the castle, and halted next to the bombard. Ranald could see great round stones being unloaded onto the ground. There were four soldiers in the wagon who stood, two on each side of a sling-like apparatus that had long wooden bars at each end. The stones were rolled onto the sling which was then heaved up by the soldiers lifting the bars. The sling was rested on the side of the wagon and the stones rolled over to drop to the ground. Four more soldiers on the ground used a similar sling to carry the stones over to the gun.

"God!" he whispered to himself. "They mean to fire it!"

Ranald gently turned Marjorie around and started to lead her away. "We must get back to Strathalmond. There is nothing more to see here. Everything will be all right, I'm sure." Marjorie, letting herself be led away but continuing to look back, was more afraid than ever.

"Are you sure, husband? What are these stones?"

They were almost back at Strathalmond, Ranald still trying to reassure Marjorie, when the first deafening explosion shook the ground beneath their feet.

ოოო

Huw o' Nyddry watched the operation of the bombard with fascination. There was a lot that he already knew about the gun from having been responsible for transporting it. He knew that it weighed more than the six oxen that pulled it, and that it made just three miles a day subject to breakdowns. Now he learned more as he watched the Flemish gunsmiths.

The gun had been removed from the cradle and set in its firing position with a large mound of heavy timber shored behind it. The great weight of the gun and the support of the timber would absorb the recoil, Huw learned.

The powder was poured into the powder chamber from casks that had a specially shaped spout. The chamber could take over one hundred pounds of powder but it was never filled to more than three fifths of its capacity, one fifth being left empty and the other packed with a wooden plug. Huw watched the soldiers load a gunstone into the muzzle of the bombard. A sling made of iron mesh, similar, Huw thought, to chain mail, was laid down on the ground and the stone rolled on to it. The ends of the mesh were then caught together and fixed to a strong rope that was taken over a timber tripod and hitched to a horse. The horse walked forward and the gunstone, in its iron hammock, was raised level with the muzzle of the bombard. From there it was pushed into the opening by two soldiers.

Huw then saw a metal bucket that the men called the fire bucket, and from which the long-handled torch was lit that was used to fire the powder. All of these operations were closely supervised by the Flemish gunsmiths who attended to the sighting and firing.

When the first gunstone was fired, Huw staggered back in amazement. The blast was deafening, and the huge gun lurched back to crunch against the timbers. Huw saw the wall of Houstoun Castle shake and seconds later he heard the deep, solid thump of the gunstone against the castle wall. The ground shook.

Then the gunsmiths washed out the powder chamber with

water from a barrel, to prevent any sparks remaining from igniting the new powder to be loaded, and the whole procedure began again.

After a while the loading and firing seemed to run to a smooth schedule, and the walls of Houstoun Castle crumbled under the onslought. Huw o' Nyddry had seen enough.

๛ ๛ ๛

All that day and all the next day the thunder of the great bombard rent the air and shook the earth. The family of Thomas Ingram had moved into a small chamber on the north side of Strathalmond, furthest from the noise, but they could still hear the periodic blasts of powder and the heavy thumps of the gunstones against the castle walls.

Most of the serving staff had now left, and Isabella, accompanied by Master James, had taken the children to the inn at Myrestane.

In the evening of the second day, Master James returned, his face white and his hands trembling as he entered the chamber loosening his cloak.

"We must leave Strathalmond, Sire," he said. "We must leave now."

Ranald gave the steward a searching look. Master James was agitated, and it was not like him. Something must have happened.

"The officer, Sire," Master James continued. "He stopped me at the gate."

Ranald and Thomas exchanged fearful looks while Marjorie gripped her husbands arm.

"He asked if this was the house of Ranald Douglas, and I said Ranald Ingram. Then he said Ranald Douglas Ingram, the traitor to King James."

Master James grew agitated. "Sire, they plan to cast down Strathalmond! That officer said that you are a Douglas, Sire, and it is the order of King James that your house be destroyed by the great cannon, and that any person refusing to leave will be hanged, or they can perish in the rubble. Sire, we must leave Strathalmond now!" Master James flopped down into a chair, staring wide-eyed from Ranald to Thomas.

"When?" Ranald said quietly.

"Sire?" the steward questioned, looking up.

"When must we leave? Did the officer say when?"

Master James shuddered as another loud crack resounded. "In two days from now. We have two days to be out of Strathalmond, for then it will be destroyed by the bombard."

Thomas Ingram sat back in his chair. "I will not leave Strathalmond," he said. Marjorie raised her head and looked straight at Ranald. "Nor I," she said.

Ranald looked around the room: at the steward who sat with head bowed, at Thomas gazing vacantly at the wall, and at Marjorie who smiled a little smile at him, her head erect and her eyes shining with an inner courage. For a few moments he stood there in silence, his mind racing. Then he moved quickly to Marjorie and kissed her hard on the mouth.

"Two days," he said. "We have two days." Then, looking at the window, he said, "There are still two hours of daylight. Look after father. I must go to Edinburgh. If I am not back in two days, leave Strathalmond and take Thomas Ingram with you."

Ranald rode away from Strathalmond as the great gun still roared. He rode as he had never ridden before, driving the courser hard out of the gates and down through the sleepy cottages of Myrestane to the open road that led to the capital. Pictures flashed through his mind as he felt the strength of the horse between his thighs, gobbling up the miles before dark: Marjorie's face, erect and proud, strong and beautiful; Thomas Ingram, large and strong, with the domed head and big gap-toothed mouth, smiling and wise; Will Douglas, broad and dark and laughing.

As the last light faded from a clouded sky, Ranald Douglas walked his horse to the stables of the inn near the Mercat Cross in Edinburgh. He had two days.

∿∿∿

On the morning after her husband had departed for Edinburgh, Marjorie Ingram stood in her little garden, the garden of the Blessed Virgin Mary. The small white Candelmass bells had passed, and daisies and Easter lilies heralded the coming of summer. Marjorie knelt down on the dew-covered grass and asked the Holy Mother to protect her family and save her house from the evil of men. A little robin, with its red breast and bold demeanour, hopped in front of her, stopping to give her an inquisitive look as if she were invading his territory. Marjorie looked up along the trellis, where the new buds of the purple clematis prepared for their summer shower, and over to the green row of yews. Was it all to be lost forever? Was there to be no more Strathalmond?

A tremendous crash shook the earth and the robin flew up and over the wall. Marjorie looked up the hill towards Houstoun Castle and heard the distant shouts and cheers of men. Another day of bombardment had begun.

∾ ∾ ∾

Ranald Ingram rose early after a restless night. Dreams, one flowing into another, had wakened him continuously from shallow sleep; mixtures of nonsense, vivid terrifying pictures. In them, he saw the bombard being wheeled into his warehouse at the dock in Leith and pointed at the boxes of wine that were stacked to the roof. Then Thomas Ingram came forward with a lighted torch and tried to light the powder. Will Douglas arrived and was showing Thomas how to hold the torch. William of Houstoun, fully armed, was riding across the Drumshorling Moor and King James took his dagger from his belt and touched it to the bombard. The gunstone flew out and obliterated the distant horse and rider. Marjorie and the children were in a room with Mary of Gueldres and a soldier came in pulling the bombard. Ranald arose to escape more dreams.

He made his way up the slope of the narrow Lawnmarket, wending in and out between carts loaded with hay and the rickety stalls of peddlers who were setting out their wares, then passed through Castlehill to the gates of the castle. There he was stopped by a guard who asked his business. He waited while the officer of the castle guard was called, and after much discussion he was admitted into the guard room within the castle and asked to wait. He waited there for a long time.

Finally, in mid-afternoon, a servant appeared who led him through the inner courtyard and into a long narrow hall where the servant asked him to wait and pointed to a bench against the wall. He waited.

Ranald sat in the hall for what seemed like an eternity. Nobody came in. Now and then he would get up and walk to and fro, looking at portraits of ugly men on dark canvases. Then he would sit again. The day passed into evening, the first day of grace, Ranald thought.

He began to worry about the message that Master James brought from the officer. Had he got it right? Was it two days to leave Strathalmond? Would Thomas Ingram leave? Could Marjorie get him to leave? Two days. Now the first of these days had almost passed and Ranald had done nothing. He could do nothing.

As Ranald began to think he must return to Strathalmond, to save his family at least, the servant returned.

"The Queen cannot see you today, Sire," he said in a flat voice. "You must return tomorrow."

"But tomorrow will be too late!" Ranald started.

"Tomorrow, Sire," the servant repeated. "You must leave now."

Ranald was thinking about the time, trying to calculate. Tomorrow would be the last day. Should he leave now for Strathalmond before it was too dark to travel? Was this attempt to see the Queen a useless venture? If he went home now, he could ensure that Thomas and Marjorie got out of the house?

"Will Her Majesty see me in the morning?" he asked in desperation. The servant looked bored.

"Tomorrow, Sire," was all he said.

Chapter Fourteen

≈ ≈ ≈

The next morning the sky was overcast and it was raining steadily. Huw o' Nyddry and his squad came to the site of Houstoun Castle early, for he had received instructions that the bombard would be moved that day.

What had once been the high and imposing tower-house of Houstoun Castle was now no more than a shell. The facing wall and the high section of the tower had collapsed into a huge rounded pile of stones and rubble from which long timbers stuck up at odd angles. Only the sides remained, scarred and shaken, the ancient stones grimly holding up.

The crowd of locals, who had assembled the day before to stand glassy-eyed watching the destruction wrought by the great gun, had not returned, for it was all over now. Most of the soldiers had returned to Edinburgh leaving only a small force with the tall officer.

Huw noticed a group of women huddled together in the rain. They were crying. He had seen them the night before and they looked as if they had been standing there all night. He walked over to them and asked who they were. They told him that they had been servants in the castle and now they had nowhere to go, no work and no place to sleep. They were a mother and two daughters. The mother was small and thin, her face lined with wrinkles and her hands clasped to her thin chest. She reminded Huw of his own mother. The two girls clung to her, weeping and wailing. They were not much more than twelve or thirteen, Huw thought.

As the bombard was being primed once more, this time for its final assault on the skeletal remains of the castle, Huw stood back from the wretched women. He saw them shiver in the rain, and their miserable belongings, wrapped in a sheet, lying on the ground in front of them. They huddled closer and cried out as the first crack of the bombard split the morning air. These were no great people from great houses, Huw thought, and for the first time he felt ashamed of what he had done for wages.

Down the hill, in Strathalmond, Marjorie Ingram served a glass of brandy to her father on a silver tray.

"We must pack our things now, father," she said quietly. Thomas Ingram stared at his daughter, his eyes red and heavy. "Ranald?" he said.

Marjorie shook her head. "He has not returned, father. We must do as he says, now, and be ready to leave Strathalmond."

Thomas struggled to his feet. "I will walk in the garden," he said. "Will you show me your garden, daughter?"

Marjorie brushed a tear from her eye, and, taking her father's arm, she led him out of the little room, through the great hall to the garden. At the door, Thomas Ingram put his hand on the high vertical beam of the entrance, looking up its length, like a builder complimenting himself on his work.

❧ ❧ ❧

When Ranald Ingram passed through the gates of Edinburgh castle for the second time, there was no delay at the guardroom. The same dull servant appeared and led him inside to the same long room. Ranald sat in the same place as before and the servant left. Ranald removed his hat, shaking off the rain. As he did so, the servant returned and led him up a flight of stone steps to the royal apartments, saying he would take his cloak.

Mary of Gueldres sat in a high, ornate chair and she smiled

as Ranald bowed before her. "I am happy to see you again, Ranald Ingram," she said. "Sit, please. Your visit has an urgent purpose, I think."

Ranald felt relieved, not only to receive an audience early in the day, but also that the queen came straight to the matter in hand. He lost no time in recounting the events of Houstoun and the danger to Strathalmond. He told her what the officer had said, that they had only until this evening to be out, and Strathalmond would be demolished by the bombard.

"The king is not here," she said. "He has gone to the Parliament." She paused, fixing her eyes on Ranald's, then went on. "He was here yesterday, but as you requested a meeting with me, I felt it better to see you in his absence."

"I appreciate your forethought, Ma'm," Ranald replied. "I fear, however, that time is now short."

Ignoring this, Mary continued. "You are the Ranald Douglas that petitioned Parliament, are you not?"

Ranald's heart sank. "Yes," he said.

"And the good friend, I think, of Will Douglas, were you not?" Mary continued. Ranald nodded.

"Then you must know the reason for the king's command, sir."

Ranald remained silent in the face of this sudden formality. There was nothing to say to this. He was thinking frantically what plea he might make when Mary spoke again.

"I have sympathy for you and your family, but there is nothing that I can do to change the king's order." Mary looked, with a sad expression, at the rain pattering on the window. "I was an advocate once for Will Douglas, and it did not serve him well at the end. All that I can do for you," she said, looking back to Ranald, "is urge you to go now and take your family out of Strathalmond. You can save their lives even if you cannot save their home."

Ranald was shattered by the finality of her last remark. He racked his brain for something to say. There must be something more.

"But what can your husband gain by destroying

Strathalmond, Ma'm? It is only a merchant's house. It carries no threat to the King of Scots."

Mary grew agitated. She knew that. Good God it wasn't a matter of gain for her husband, but a matter of retribution. Did this merchant not understand that? Was he not the intelligent trader that she had heard about from her uncle and from others? She got control of her feelings in a moment.

"It is not a question of gain," she said. She could not go further. She could make no criticism of her husband, even when her heart went out to this Ranald Ingram, this stalwart friend of Will Douglas.

Ranald's mind searched for an answer. He could see the queen's predicament. She supported him but she could not comment on the decisions of her husband. It wasn't done. She couldn't intercede for the Ingrams of Strathalmond. She couldn't make a case to take to the king. It was not a question of gain. That is what she had said. What then? Think! Ranald Ingram. Think!

"If not gain," the words came out, Ranald's mind working as he spoke, "perhaps it is a question of loss, Ma'm," he said. Mary was puzzled.

"Go on," she said.

"My father, Thomas Ingram, has vowed that he will not leave Strathalmond," Ranald began, knowing that everything depended on how he would put his argument. "Even now, I may be too late to remove him by force from the house, and force may be the only way." Mary was listening with growing interest.

"If Strathalmond is destroyed, and Thomas Ingram with it, then I fear that the Ingrams will be destroyed, and all their enterprises."

Mary of Gueldres could see immediately where this was going for her mind was as quick as Ranald's.

"Pray continue, sir," she said, hoping that she was right in her surmise.

"You may know, Ma'm, that the Ingram wine fleet is now forty ships. We have a contract with Philip of Burgundy. By his valued endeavours with the wine dealers of London and Bristol, we ship to the Port of Leith fifty thousand casks of Gascon wine every month. Thirty of these we export to England, for you are aware, Ma'm, that there is now no wine traffic to England from France."

Mary was elated. She strove hard to keep the feeling from showing on her face. It was true, all that they had said about this young Ranald Ingram. Why else would he be a partner of her Uncle Philip? Now he would refer to the duties paid to her husband on this fantastic wine venture. Now she had something to take to James.

"And the duties to the king are substantial Ma'm, substantial, and continuing."

What a marvellous man, Mary thought. The duties are continuing so long as the Ingrams continue to trade. What a clever man!

Ranald leaned back. His plea was made. He looked at the queen, hoping that it had been enough for her to intercede with her husband. He hoped that there would be time.

The queen called for a servant. Her face impassive, she took a quill and wrote something on a vellum sheet. When the servant arrived, she gave him instructions to take it to her husband at the Parliament without delay, adding that there would be a reply, which he should bring to her at once. The servant left and Ranald relaxed in his chair. He looked at the window and saw that the midday light was fading.

"A glass of wine, perhaps?" Mary of Gueldres said, as they waited. "It is ironic that the bombard that threatens your house was a gift to the king by Philip of Burgundy, my uncle, and your present partner in trade." She smiled.

∾ ∾ ∾

By mid afternoon the rain had stopped, and the last walls of Houstoun Castle had been levelled. The few onlookers of the morning had gone home, and only the old mother and her weeping daughters still stood there, staring at the ruin.

"Get your squads organised, and move the bombard down the hill to yonder house through the trees!" the tall officer shouted to Huw. "We will demolish it before dark."

Huw walked over to the old woman and her daughters. He took the mother's bony hand and pressed a silver coin into it, then, turning away, he shouted to the men.

"Get to it boys! Bring up the oxen!"

လလလ

Thomas Ingram sat a long time in the little garden. He never knew it was so beautiful or so peaceful. After a while he no longer heard the blast of the bombard or felt the tremor at his feet. Since the moment that the tower of Houstoun Castle collapsed, Thomas never looked up the hill again.

He had been too hard on Ranald, little Ranald "the Questioner". He felt bad that he had lost his temper and blamed Ranald for the plight they were in. He, Thomas, was the one that brought Ranald into his house. He had always known the risks of fraternising with the Black Douglases. He should have done more. Now he was doing nothing but sitting in the garden while Ranald was away trying to do something. Thomas did not know what, but it would be something. Ranald was the achiever while Thomas was only a critic.

Thomas listened. There was no longer any sound of the bombard, and there was no longer any castle. Then it dawned on him what that meant. Houstoun was destroyed and they were bringing the bombard to Strathalmond. He must do something. He rose and made for the house. He must collect Marjorie and any valuables they could carry and leave Strathalmond. At the door he collided with Master James who was leaving, carrying his goods.

"All the servants have left, Sire," James shouted. " The gun is coming. Save yourself!"

"Where is my daughter?" Thomas called back at him, catching the steward by the sleeve. "Where is she?"

Master James shook his head, pulling himself out of

Thomas' grasp. "I don't know, Sire," he spluttered. "She left. I think I saw her leave, down the driveway."

Thomas pushed passed the steward and into the house.

He crossed the great hall with long strides, calling out Marjorie's name as he went. Signs of the hasty exodus of the servants and staff were visible everywhere: overturned benches, mugs and plates lying here and there on the floor, odd pieces of clothing, wrapped in blankets, dropped and discarded in the scramble to leave. Thomas bounded up the stone stairs to the upper apartments.

"Marjorie! Marjorie!" he shouted continuously, throwing open the doors on the upper levels. He rushed back down the stairs and out into the courtyard at the rear, still shouting her name.

Then he stopped and listened. Strathalmond was as quiet as a tomb.

ოოო

Not far from Edinburgh Castle, King James was attending a session of Parliament when the messenger delivered the letter into his hands, as he had been directed to do. James glanced at the seal and opened it at once. He immediately recognised the Queen's flowery hand and laconic style. The missive was brief and to the point.

Mary said that the commercial interests of Scotland were, as the king had ever pointed out, of crucial importance. She reminded him that these interests, in particular the trade with France, solidified as it was by their own marriage and the agreements with her uncle, yielded the coffers of the Crown abundant revenues. In no venture, she went on to say, was this more proven than in the growing wine fleets of the Ingrams of Leith, and the import of Gascon wines into Scotland and on to England. The revenues from the Ingram trade were, at this very moment, at severe risk, arising from the threatened destruction of the house of Strathalmond by the bombard. For this reason Mary implored the king to cancel the destruction order and thereby save the Ingram trade. She wrote that, while she knew that her husband had good personal cause to destroy the house, she also knew that he would put his country's interests before his own as he always did. She then invited him, should he agree upon the wisdom of this course, to send to her his confirmation of the withdrawal of the destruction order by the messenger who awaited his reply.

James did not have to think for long. Ranald Douglas Ingram's petition still goaded him, but his wife was right. He could not risk losing the lucrative duties. If he did, Parliament and its auditors would hear of it. Was not the father, Thomas Ingram, a burgess in the city?

James quickly scribbled a new order to his officer, appended his seal and handed the paper to the waiting messenger.

∾ ∾ ∾

Huw o' Nyddry was, by now, something of an expert in moving the bombard. While the soldiers that remained set about retrieving gunstones from the ruin and loading them into the wagon, Huw supervised the hitching up of the oxen and turned the cradle carrying its murderous machine down the hill towards Strathalmond. The slope was gentle and the ground soft which meant that there was little risk of a runaway. The descent would be effected in the same way as that from the castle in Edinburgh, except that the it would be safe, Huw thought, to have the oxen in front as the wheels would sink into the earth and they would be needed to pull. Huw was right in his assumptions, and the team moved down the slope at a slow, steady pace.

Huw was out in front of the lumbering gun, some distance away and close to the gates that led into the driveway leading up to Strathalmond. He was examining the ground and marking, with wooden stakes, a route to avoid soft or marshy areas, when a woman emerged from the line of trees and hurried up to him.

She wore a long white cloak, and Huw could see wisps of

fair hair peeping out from under the pointed cowl that covered her head. As she came close, Huw saw a beautiful face, marked with worry, smooth white cheeks wet with tears and eyes that were sad and searching.

"Please, sir," she said, her voice cracking with emotion, "Please don't destroy my home."

Huw o' Nyddry was nonplussed. The woman wrung her hands, her eyes pleading, crazed with grief.

"Please!" she repeated.

Huw moved back, away from her. This was a lady, the lady of this fine mansion. What did she want talking to Huw o' Nyddry? No fine lady had ever talked to Huw. He looked around for somebody, anybody. The bombard was still on the slope, oxen straining, and men on the ropes were shouting and cursing. The soldiers were nowhere to be seen. He looked back at the face of the woman.

"Please, sir!" she cried.

"I must go," was all he could think to say. He moved back, shaking his head, as if she were some witch, sent to put a spell on him. "I have to go." Then he turned away and walked off quickly towards the bombard.

After a dozen or so steps, Huw stopped and looked back. The woman was still standing there looking after him, hands clasped together. In the cowl and long cloak, she looked like a monk, framed in white before the great dark shadow of the house behind her.

The sky had cleared, and the sun was low in the west when the bombard was hauled up to a point about thirty paces short of the gates at the end of the drive leading up to the house. The men sat down on the grass, relaxing after their efforts, and the oxen were unhitched and herded off to the side. Huw leaned against the gatepost and watched the sun's rays highlight the roof and peek through the steps of the gables. The woman was gone.

This was a beautiful house, Huw thought. Why should it be necessary to destroy it? He thought of the servants and the family that lived here, and his mind went back to the misery of the old woman and her daughters standing homeless in the rain. Then he thought about the lady in the cowl and he knew she was the lady of this house. She had pleaded with Huw o' Nyddry for her home, but what could he do? He was just the acting master of works. It is the soldiers she should beg. The officer is the one to plead with.

The officer rode up behind Huw, leading the wagon that contained the gunstones and powder. He stopped between the gates and leaned forward as he peered at the house.

"It looks quiet enough," he said. "Maybe they have all left."

He cast a look at Huw, then, as if not wishing to appear over anxious to commence the bombardment, he urged his horse forward. "I suppose that I should read the king's order again," he said, looking back at Huw as if seeking support.

With that, he rode forward up the drive.

Inside the house, Thomas was frantic. He had looked everywhere but couldn't find Marjorie. Where had she gone? Why had she left without telling him? Perhaps she had gone to Myrestane, but why had she not said? Thomas was back at the main door, trying to decide what to do, when he heard the voice outside. He could make out some of the words.

"...by order...King James...house...Ranald Douglas......be destroyed....leave...refuse to............hanged..."

Thomas opened the door and stepped out. He strode forward until he stood right in front of the horse. The officer, now putting away the order, made to rein the horse around, turning away his face. He was not comfortable reading orders when so closely confronted. He was used to making these pronouncements to a building, the more distant the actual recipients of the order, the better.

Thomas Ingram's big hand grabbed the horse's bridle. "What is this you say, sir?" his voice boomed. "This is the house of Thomas Ingram. You are on my land, sir. Be gone from here! Be gone, I say!"

The officer was suddenly panicking. He tried to turn the horse that writhed and swayed as Thomas held fast to the bridle. The officer reached a hand to the hilt of his sword and Thomas's free hand grabbed his wrist. In a mad frenzy, the officer freed his foot from the stirrup and aimed a rash kick at the big merchant. His boot caught Thomas on the side of the face and Thomas fell to the ground, losing his grip on the horse and rider.

Huw, watching from the gate, took a few steps forward. He saw the officer whirl the horse round and come towards him at a gallop. As the tall man lay on the ground, Huw saw the white figure of the lady rush out from the trees beside the drive to kneel beside the fallen man. She cradled his head in her arms and he heard her long cry of anguish.

"Get that bombard in position to fire, now!" the officer shouted to Huw, his face contorted with rage. "Now!"

Chapter
Fifteen

࿏ ࿏ ࿏

Ranald Ingram couldn't stop fidgeting in his seat and looking at the window. The light was beginning to fade. He got up, bowing to the queen, and walked across the room, then he returned to his seat. Mary of Gueldres' placid, almost serene, smile was the only calming influence on Ranald as he waited for the messenger from the king. Time passed slowly, as on a ship becalmed at sea. Once or twice he decided to take his leave and hasten back to Strathalmond. Maybe the message was not coming. Maybe there was no message.

As Ranald stood up for perhaps the tenth time, there was a knock on the door of the chamber and the messenger appeared, walking in quick mincing steps to the queen. He handed her the sealed paper. Ranald's heart stood still, his hands clenched into fists.

Mary opened the seal, and her face beamed as she read the message. "You must be off at once, Ranald Ingram, and save your house. Take this order from the king and pass it to the officer in charge."

Ranald, relief in his face, took the order and grasped the queen's hand warmly in his own. With a quick bow, he rushed out.

By the time he had passed through the Westport and into

the green fields, it was evening and he rode like he had never ridden before. He had the advantage of a firm track, where the holes had been filled not long before, for the passage of the bombards, and he rode fast, guiding the courser between the deep tracks that had been made by the wheels of the cradles.

At the junction at Gogarstane, where the track ran south-wards, the light was already fading. The horse panted and wheezed and Ranald felt the sweat on its neck. He had to stop or he would ride it into the ground. Further on, at the ford across the stream that flowed north to join the river Almond, he did stop.

As he rested the horse, Ranald knew that he could not hope to reach Strathalmond before dark. He was gripped by a numbing depression. Even now, his beloved Strathalmond would be toppling under the barrage of the great gun. And Marjorie? And his father? Were they safe? He must ride on.

He moved now at a steadier pace, nudging the horse along with a gentle heel and encouraging words. He passed the bridge over the Almond and the lighted windows of the cot-tages there, but it was already dark. Night had come down sud-denly in the end, like a black curtain. He could not see the track. It was too late.

He dismounted and led the tired horse, trying to feel his way along the level surface. Every few steps he meandered off the track, his feet slipping into the soft earth. Then he would feel his way back to the firm surface. But he was making no headway, and he finally stopped.

He put his head in his hands and cried, the horse's face nuzzling his elbow.

∾∾∾

Huw o' Nyddry felt the discomfort of a new sensation. It was if he was sick in his stomach, and yet it wasn't that. The pictures of the day flooded his mind: the women in the rain, the tall gables of the house with the sun shining through them, the lady in white, kneeling beside the old man on the ground, the hatred in the face of the officer.

He was only a workman, working for wages, for money that would keep his family. It wasn't for him to decide things. That was for officers and soldiers and others. Huw o' Nyddry just did what he was ordered to do, and now he was bringing up the bombard for it was to be fired before dark.

The oxen were hitched once more and the cannon was hauled through the gates into the drive. The tall officer was riding back and forth, shouting orders to the soldiers who were bringing up the gunstones. The three Flemish gunsmiths were fluttering around the bombard, feeling the huge barrel and bending down to look under the cradle.

Huw had marked the spot in the drive that would give a solid footing, and he crouched down to test it once more. Looking up, he caught sight of the lady in white and the old man. They were making their way along the edge of the trees towards the gates, the old man leaning on her slim shoulder. A streak of blood ran down the side of his face. They walked slowly, heads bowed, the lady staggering slightly as she supported him. As they were passing Huw, staying close to the trees that bordered the driveway, the lady looked towards him, her blue eyes vacant and staring, a long golden tress of hair hanging from under the cowl which was now pushed over at an angle.

Huw turned his face away and looked at the bombard.

Suddenly, Huw rose from his crouch and walked nearer to the edge of the drive. He waved his men to bring up the gun. The oxen strained in the yoke and the great wheels turned slowly. Huw pointed to a spot near the grassy border, and the man leading the oxen angled them to the right. The big hooves went onto the grass and Huw leapt in front of the beasts and tried to turn them back to the drive, but the momentum of the heavy load bore them forward. As the oxen turned, the right hand wheels of the cradle dropped off the drive into the soft earth and the determined pull of the animals caused them to stick. The cradle and the bombard tipped over sideways onto the grass, the weight of the long iron barrel pulling the far wheels into the air. The barrel leaned sideways in a slow pendulous arc, and the huge gun came to rest on its side, digging into the soft ground.

The team of oxen strained in vain, weaving from side to side, pulling the load further into the earth, as the men tried to calm them. The officer rode up and dismounted, eyes ablaze, shouting at the squad and the soldiers, while the men in the Flemish hats rushed to and fro babbling in a tongue Huw did not understand.

Finally the oxen were quieted and unhitched with some difficulty from the cradle. Men stood around in two and threes looking hopelessly at the bombard. The officer came up to Huw, waving his arms and cursing. Huw just stood there, eyes low.

"Get this gun righted!" the officer shouted. "Imbecile!" He raved for what seemed like an eternity as Huw made what he hoped looked like conscientious efforts, directing the squad to get the bombard and cradle lifted back onto the level. But Huw knew that this would not be possible before dark, and he smiled to himself.

∾∾∾

At the very first light of day, Ranald mounted up. He had walked most of the night, leading the horse, sometimes on the track but most often wandering off into the fields. Now he set off at a slow trot, for the track was still barely visible in the early dawn.

As he rode west from the river, branching north at the next fork in the track that would lead on to Myrestane, he cursed himself for coming too late. He should have departed for the city at the first rumour of the bombard. Why had it taken him so long to realise the danger? Now he was too late to save Strathalmond. It was his father's house and he could have saved it had he moved quicker. What of Marjorie? What of Thomas Ingram? Had they left the house? Surely Marjorie would have persuaded her father to get out. They, at least, would be all right.

Now the horse was galloping towards Myrestane in the bright light of the morning.

∿ ∿ ∿

As dawn came up, Huw was awakened by a rough kick in his side. He had slept the night under the trees near the bombard, covered by a thin blanket. The gun was still on its side. Opening his eyes, he saw the angry face of the officer.

"Get up, you scum!" the officer snarled. "Get up and right that cannon. The Frenchmen told me that last night you should have used the oxen. You've done it that way before. Why did you not do so last night?" He delivered a kick to Huw's leg.

Now Huw knew that his delaying tactics were discovered. The officer knew about the method of lifting the bombard. Thankfully, that was all he knew.

The soldiers were up and at the ready, rousing the squads of men. The oxen were being brought forward, and soon it would be light and the bombard would be pulled up and the cradle heaved to the firm ground of the drive.

Huw had done all he could to save the beautiful house. Now he must work, and work hard, if he was to save his job and be paid his money. He got to his feet, brushing the grass from his clothes, and began to direct the men.

As the midday sun permeated the woods and glinted from the windows of Strathalmond, the bombard, set in firing position in front of the pile of timber to absorb the recoil, sat on the drive facing the house. Four gunstones had been unloaded from the wagon, and they lay on the ground next to the gun.

"Myrestane Mary," Huw murmured, wondering why he would have given the name of the Blessed Mother to such an instrument of death and destruction. In the beginning, he had been excited by the bombard. He had given it his own private name, a woman's name like the other bombard, like Mons Meg, for guns were always given a female name. He had felt pride in moving it, in being the foreman and then the acting master of works. Even now there was a pride in knowing that he, and he alone, of all the men and soldiers, and even the officer, he, Huw o' Nyddry was the only man that could right the gun.

But now, seeing it lined up against the walls of this mansion, no fortified stronghold of war but a house, the lady's house, Huw was ashamed. Never again would he call it by a woman's name.

The soldiers on the sling had loaded the enormous gun-stone, and the Frenchman (as the soldiers called him) had opened the cask and was pouring the black powder into the hole. The officer sat erect in his saddle, chin up, like a champion on a battlefield. The fire bucket was being blown into life by the bellows in its side. All was ready.

Huw was sickened by the gun. He didn't want to hear any more of its thunder or witness any more of its cruel destruction. He turned his back on the house, looking back through the gates, as the Frenchman pushed the long handled torch into the fire bucket.

As he pressed his hands against his thighs, awaiting the horrible, evil explosion of the bombard, his eye caught the movement of a rider, approaching fast and calling something out as he waved a paper in his hand.

Huw turned back and shouted to the officer, stretching up his arms and bringing them together and apart in rapid movements. The Frenchman lifted the flaming torch from the bucket, looking in the direction of the shouts. The officer turned in his saddle.

When Huw o' Nyddry was an old man, and had told his tale a thousand times, he still thought, alone in his cottage at night, how long it took for these next few seconds to pass.

The rider, eyes aglow and teeth bared like a demon of the night, arrived at the spot where Huw stood. Huw waved him on to the mounted officer. The officer advanced to meet him. The Frenchman moved, with the flaming torch, towards the bombard. The rider thrust the paper into the officer's hands as he passed him, and then he dug in his spurs and bore down upon the Frenchman, thrusting the torch from his hands and throwing it wildly into the trees. It was a picture that Huw o' Nyddry would never forget.

ɶ ɶ ɶ

In the year 1455, at a place called Arkinholme, situated on the River Esk near the town of Langholm, James, ninth Earl of Douglas and his brothers were utterly defeated by the forces of King James II of Scotland. Archibald Douglas, Earl of Moray, was killed in the battle, and Hugh Douglas, Earl of Ormond, was wounded and taken prisoner. Later Hugh was executed and his severed head delivered to the king as a present.

James Douglas, the former cleric, fled to England. Years later, while leading a cattle-raid into Scotland, he was captured, and he ended his days in exile at the Abbey of Lindores. He was the last of the Black Douglases.

In the same year as the battle of Arkinholme, Richard Duke of York, at a village called St. Albans, gained the first victory in what would later be called the Wars of the Roses. Later, Richard fell in the Battle of Wakefield, and his head, adorned with a paper crown, was hung on the walls of the City of York.

Three years later, the Scottish Parliament reported of King James II of Scotland that, "God of His grace has sent our Sovereign Lord such progress and prosperity that all his rebels and breakers of his justice are removed out of his realm, and no masterful party remaining that may cause any breaking of his realm." Two years after that, King James, at the siege of Roxburgh Castle, stood, with his endless fascination for artillery, next to one of the siege cannon. It exploded on firing, killing him instantly.

Mary of Gueldres, whose son became King James III of Scotland, figured largely in politics and in her support of the Yorkists, but the scandal of her love affair with a young nobleman caused her fall from grace, and she died in 1463 at the age of thirty.

Mary's uncle, Philip of Burgundy, never did mount his crusade to the Holy Land. He lived to the ripe old age of seventy years, displaying a curious mixture of business acumen and obsession with ceremony, until he departed this life in Brugge in 1467, with the grandest funeral service ever seen in France.

Huw o' Nyddry's contribution to the saving of Strathalmond was never known to the Ingrams. On that final day, when the King's destruction order had been reversed, the men in the Flemish hats discovered a fine crack that ran along the under side of the barrel. The bombard was tipped from its cradle and left abandoned at the side of the drive, while Huw and his squad took the cradle and the wagon-load of gunstones and powder across the hills to Abercorn to join the other team that would return Mons Meg to Edinburgh Castle.

There, in Edinburgh Castle, Mons Meg still sits.

Ranald Ingram went on to build the greatest wine fleet ever to sail the North Sea. For his contribution to trade and commerce, he was knighted at a ceremony presided over by King James III of Scotland, the son of Mary of Gueldres, and there was no merchant, vintner or trader, in either Scotland, England or France, who did not know the name of Sir Ranald Ingram.

Thomas Ingram, in never-ending gratitude to his son for saving his grand mansion, retired from business and turned over the house of Strathalmond and the whole business enterprise to Ranald.

Strathalmond became reputed as a meeting place for merchants of all the nationalities that traded with Scotland. The quality of its hospitality, its food and its wines, the generosity of its hosts and the beauty and charm of its mistress, Lady Marjorie Ingram, became legend.

On a warm summer afternoon, long after the episode of the great gun had been relegated to memory, Ranald and Marjorie walked through the garden, along the yew tree hedge and past the walnut tree where their initials were still clear in the bark. They walked hand in hand, feeling the gentle breeze on their faces and listening to the cooing of the pigeons in the dovecote. Arriving at the spot where the bombard lay, half covered in the grasses that embraced the iron barrel, the pictures of the men and their machine of destruction flooded back to them.

"It should be removed, Ranald, and buried in some grave where it will never be seen again," Marjorie said.

"No, my dear. Here it sits, and here it shall remain, to

remind us of the evil of men and the deliverance of Strathalmond by the Grace of God. It shall remain here forever." Ranald said the words with powerful conviction, placing a foot on the gun.

But forever is a long time, and many years later, in a different time, another Ingram would dig up the bombard.

BOOK 2
PART 1

∽ 1912–1926 ∽

Chapter One

ᘛᘛᘛ

The year was nineteen hundred and twelve.

Peg Anderson shivered as she sat on a wooden bench at a table in the servants' dining room of Strathalmond House. She had been there for half an hour, looking around at the bare stone walls and floor and listening to occasional sounds that emanated from the kitchen through a partially open oak door. She drew her threadbare shawl closer round her shoulders, shifting the position of her legs under the long black dress. Her mother had obtained the dress from the Parochial Board as part of the annual clothing grant for Peg and her little brother. She hoped it would be all right. It was barely half a mile from here to her mother's little house in the place called the Randy Raws in Myrestane. How short a walk, Peg thought, to move from one world to another.

A tall stout woman had admitted her at the back door and led her through the pantry and the kitchen. "This is the servants' dining room," the woman had said. "Wait here for Mr. Makepeace."

If they asked her name, what would she say? Peg wondered. Would she say Margaret Anderson? Margaret was her real name. Her father used to call her Margaret. After he died and the family moved from Edinburgh to Myrestane, people started to call her Peg. She didn't mind that because the name Margaret seemed to maintain her bond with her father; conserve its privacy, its special nature. In the damp silence of the room, she started thinking about her father. He died two years earlier when she was twelve. That was when her happy life in the city with her mother and brother, Tommy, had been shattered in a single night. Her father had been killed by a runaway horse that pulled the milk cart. It was a freak accident. She was gazing blankly at the stone flags of the floor when the man swept in from the kitchen. He was tall and slim with refined features and silver grey hair combed back from the temples.

"I'm Mr. Makepeace," he said in a loud voice. She made to rise and he motioned with his hand. "Sit! Sit!" he said, raising the tails of his long black jacket and taking the single chair at the head of the table. He wore a waistcoat under the jacket and a black bow tie over a white dickey. Peg had seen men wearing outfits like this in newspaper pictures.

"I'm the butler here, and manservant to the Master, Mr. Sam Ingram. I hire the servants." With that he produced a letter from the pocket of the waistcoat. He studied it for a few seconds before looking up. "Your name is Peg Anderson?"

"Margaret," she said, her voice faltering. "My father called me Margaret. That's my real name."

"Peg is what it says here," Mr. Makepeace said, glancing at the letter. "This letter is from your aunt — your mother's sister, I believe. She worked here for a time some years ago and recommends you for the present position of general servant. Do you object to being called Peg?" Peg shook her head, and he went on.

"Your aunt says that when your father died your family fell upon hard times and moved to Myrestane. You have a younger brother and your mother gets Parish relief."

"She has two boarders," Peg said quickly, her cheeks reddening.

"Quite so," he replied with the merest flicker of a smile. "You have just completed your schooling at Myrestane Public School, I understand, and you can read and write."

Peg winced. She thought of all the stories and the poems she had read with her father. He had said that she would be a schoolteacher. Now that dream was gone.

"Yes sir," she said.

Mr. Makepeace got up from his chair, folding the letter and returning it to his pocket.

" I propose to give you a trial as a general servant. You will be replacing Hilda who is leaving in four weeks to be married, and she will show you your duties. You will be living in the house and you will have every fourth Sunday off when you may visit your family. You may go home now and collect your things and report for duty tomorrow at six in the morning. The general servants work under the supervision of Miss Hill, the housekeeper, while in the main house, and Mrs Woods, the cook, while in the kitchen and pantry. After you start, the Mistress, Mrs. Ingram, will want to see you. Make sure that you are clean and well presented. Off you go now and don't be late in the morning." Mr. Makepeace then straightened his jacket, pulling down on each lapel, and swept out of the room, head erect and shoulders back.

∾ ∾ ∾

In the week that followed, Peg Anderson cried herself to sleep almost every night in the tiny room at the top of Strathalmond that she shared with Hilda Chalmers. She cried softly and soundlessly into her pillow so that Hilda wouldn't hear her. She had never been away from home before and this house was like a prison from which she would never emerge. From her little window she could see Myrestane shale bing over the top of the trees and imagine her mother and brother in the Randy Raws that nestled below it.

Each morning she arose while it was still dark, made her ablutions and washed the redness from her eyes so that she could greet Hilda with a cheerful, carefree smile. Then the two began their labours: cleaning out fireplaces; opening shutters; lighting fires in half a dozen rooms; arranging breakfast dishes and setting tables; washing up breakfast pots and dishes; dusting furniture; all the endless repetitive tasks of a maid-of-all-work.

The house was larger than any Peg could have imagined: kitchen, pantry, servants' room and cellar on the lower level, half sunk into the earth; drawing-room, dining-room, morning-room and study on the ground level; four family bedchambers on the first level and five guest rooms on the second; the servants' rooms above that which housed Mr. Makepeace, Miss Hill, Mrs Woods, Hilda and herself. In the first week Peg had been in every room in the house, clearing ashes, laying fires, dusting and polishing. She had also seen the family members: the Master, Sam Ingram; the older son Peter Ingram and the younger son, the soldier William Ingram, who lived in India and who was here with his wife and son David for a vacation; all except the Mistress, Rachael Ingram. Attached behind the main building, with which they formed a quadrangle, were the stables and outhouses. That was where she met Sydney. Sydney was the gardener and odd-job man who lived in Myrestane and came in every day. Sydney seemed ancient to Peg though he was barely forty and smiled at her kindly through yellow teeth.

On the Monday of her second week, and with her morning smile in place, Peg shook Hilda awake. The latter yawned and screwed up her eyes, her bony white arms pulling the bed sheet up over her thin freckled face. She had brick red hair and tiny bird-like features and she wasn't a good riser. "Time to get up, Hilda," Peg insisted, pulling back the sheet. "I've filled the basin for you. Time to get washed."

Hilda was two years older than Peg but her slight build and little pug nose gave her the look of a little changeling, the kind that fairies left behind when they stole babies. Hilda gave a little groan and edged her feet towards the floor. Just then the bell rang above the door of their room.

"It's the Mistress," Hilda croaked, alerted into action, jumping to her feet and starting to pull the long nightgown up over her skinny body. "You go, Peg."

At 6.30am Peg knocked quietly on the door of Rachael Ingram's bedchamber. "Come!" returned the voice admitting her, and she moved nervously in.

Rachael Ingram was propped up in bed against a pile of pillows reading one of several papers that lay scattered on the quilt. She eyed Peg over the top of the half glasses that balanced on the end of her nose. She was pale and thin and looked all of her sixty-four years. Lying there, framed in the large four-poster bed against the heavy gilt-embossed wallpaper that decorated the room, Peg saw her as a relic of a different age, hiding from the present in this secret chamber of Strathalmond. She looked like an ancient version of Peg's mother. She had the same pallor, the same tired eyes. Peg had been told all about her by Hilda. Rachael Ingram was an invalid who rarely left her bed. The doctor visited her every week and sometimes Mr. Sam took her outside to sit in the garden in the summer.

"But don't let that fool you," Hilda had said. "She knows every move that goes on in this house and she checks up on all the servants. You see that little bell in our room. Well, she has one in all the servants' room — even Mr. Makepeace — and when she rings it you had better jump to it quickly and get up there. And call her Ma'm. Don't forget that!"

"Ah, you're the new girl. Peg, isn't it?" Peg nodded.

"Yes Ma'm," she said.

"Yes. I dare say that Hilda isn't up yet," the Mistress said, watching Peg carefully.

"Oh, she is Ma'm." Peg rushed the words. The old woman looked pleased.

"Then you must be a good influence on her," she said.

Rachael Ingram, notwithstanding her advancing years and her consumptive wasting frame, was a shrewd and clever household manager. She made it a point to know all the strengths and weaknesses of her servants and she measured these against the criteria for good domestics: honesty, industriousness, humility and loyalty. She had purposely rang the bell early, before Hilda was usually up, and she was pleased to note that Peg was loyal to Hilda. That meant that she would be loyal to her employer.

Rachael, contrary to the norm, never interviewed a servant until he or she had been there for a week. By that time her vigilant methods had already given her an assessment. She looked at the tall slim girl before her. Peg, in spite of her understandable trepidation, had a certain poise and a self-assurance not usually displayed by a fourteen year-old, snatched from the bosom of her family. She had a strong face — rather too big for beauty — and intelligent eyes. She would not be in service forever, Rachael thought.

"Are your duties, as explained by Miss Hill, clear to you?" Rachael said.

"Yes Ma'm," Peg replied.

"And you know that when you are in the kitchen, you take your orders from the cook?"

"Yes Ma'm."

"Good! You know that your wages will be sent each week to your mother?"

"Yes Ma'm," Peg said, the thought of that making her imprisonment tolerable.

"Then is there anything else you want to know about your service here?" Rachael asked.

"Just…Ma'm…just when I will be able to go home and see my mother?"

Rachael smiled. "Every fourth Sunday will be your day off. So, three weeks from now you will be able to see your family for the day."

"Yes Ma'm," Peg said, praying silently for the weeks to pass quickly.

And the weeks did pass quickly, aided by hard work and a variety of duties that took her mind off counting the days.

Hilda went on incessantly about her upcoming marriage to Joe McConnachie, a boy from Myrestane who delivered coal for the local coal merchant. Each week he came to Strathalmond, and once, Hilda dragged Peg out the kitchen door to meet him.

"This is Joe," Hilda said, her face beaming with pride. Joe had just slipped a hundredweight bag of coal off the leather pads that covered his back and shoulders into the chute that led to the coal cellar behind the kitchen. He smiled shyly at Peg and rubbed the back of his hand across his black brow.

"We have a room with Joe's parents for when we get married," Hilda went on. "They live at the Roman Camps. You can come and visit us Peg when it's your day off." Peg smiled as she looked at the huge coal man and tiny Hilda who barely reached his chest.

"That would be nice," she said.

It was at that moment that Peg realised that the only way out of domestic service was marriage. She stored this realisation in her mind, thinking that she might have to nurture it later.

Peg Anderson was a good worker. She was bright and pleasant and accommodating to family members and servants alike, and they all noticed it. Sam Ingram, the Master, took to calling for her each evening on his return from one of his shale mines or from the "Work" where they retorted the black shiny mineral called shale into oil. He would strip off his dirty shirt and get her to fill the big bathtub. Then, when he was in the tub, she would take him a glass of whisky on a silver tray. Sam was the owner of Strathalmond Oil Company where almost all the men in Myrestane worked. He had discovered the shale on Strathalmond Estate and he was a rich man. He referred to Peg as "the lassie".

"Get the lassie to bring me my dram," he would say to Makepeace, and Makepeace would call her. Peg sometimes had the feeling that Mr. Makepeace was none too pleased about something, but it didn't concern her and it certainly didn't concern Sam Ingram.

Miss Hill, the housekeeper, treated Peg as her protégé. She relished the notion that this new girl had the makings of a good housekeeper some day, and she made it her business to educate Peg in the skills of this honourable profession. Peg was aware of this, and she made every effort to comply with Miss Hill's directions and show her appreciation for her superior's interest in her. Mrs Woods, the cook, found Peg to be so capable in the duties of a kitchen maid that she began to impart to her some of the secrets of food preparation and storeage, and when Peg set off to Myrestane on her first Sunday off, Mrs. Woods wrapped a shank of mutton in brown paper and thrust it into Peg's bag to take to her mother. By the time Peg went home to see her family, she was already over the idea that Strathalmond was a prison. She had settled into her new environment and duties and would shed no tears when it was time to return. This was what Rachael Ingram had hoped for.

The only person in Strathalmond that Peg didn't like was Peter Ingram. It was the funny way that he looked at her sometimes. When she was dusting in the drawing-room and he was there, sitting in his usual chair by the window, she would catch his eye and he would leer at her. She would look away quickly, the blood rising in her cheeks as she felt him watching her. He never spoke to her. One day she mentioned Peter Ingram to Hilda.

"Oh, him," Hilda said. "You should hear the stories they tell about him."

"What stories?" Peg asked. Hilda leaned her little face closer, glancing quickly behind her.

"Was a bit of a lad, him. With women and the drink, they say. In one o' them foreign places. Old Sam had to bring him home." Hilda lifted her chin and gave a brief, confidential nod. "I'd steer well clear of him if I was you." Peg smiled at Hilda's moment of importance and wondered how much of the servants' gossip was true. Anyway, she thought, how can a servant in a house like Strathalmond steer clear of a member of the family?

∾∾∾

"How is your mother, Peg?" Rachael Ingram asked, the day after Peg's first visit home.

"Very well thank you, Ma'm," Peg replied.

Peg looked around the room: the rich wallpaper; the fine polished wood of the writing-desk and chair; the heavy velvet curtains in yellow brocade that dropped to the floor and were tied back by thick cords ending in silken tassels; the pale features of the Mistress resting back on the silk pillow-case. She pictured her mother's face, the deepening lines of worry exaggerated by the frequent hacking cough; her mother kneeling by the grate in the tiny sparse room in the Randy Raws shovelling ashes from the fireplace.

"Peg, there is a duty I want you to perform. Starting tomorrow morning, you will spend an hour each day with my grandson, David. He is twelve. As you know he is here with his parents from India. I want you to take him out each day. Take him for walks around Strathalmond and down into Myrestane. But keep him away from the shale bings. His mother and father want to visit friends in the district before they return and I'm sure David would rather spend some time with someone of about his own age than accompany them every day."

For the next two weeks, until Colonel Ingram returned to his regiment in India, Peg became David's companion in addition to all her other duties. David Ingram, though only two years her junior, seemed to her like a little boy. He was like her little brother Tommy, who was eight; talkative and trusting and quite often cheeky. Peg wished that it was Tommy that she was taking on walks, but that couldn't be.

The day before Colonel William and his family left for India, photographs were taken at the front door of Strathalmond by a little grey-haired man in a black suit who must have come, Peg thought, from the city. Peg watched from the edge of the garden, fascinated by the procedure, the man posing the family then getting under the black sheet to press the button that created the flash. The endless prattling of the man as he gave directions was interrupted only by long, statuesque silences terminated by the pop and burst of light: first the Colonel by himself, in full uniform; then he and his wife Nancy, a pretty woman, much younger than her husband, who had never spoken a word to Peg; then both parents with David.

Suddenly, as the photographer chattered and waved directions, David rushed over to Peg, grabbing her arm and pulling her into the picture. Pop went the flash from the bulb and Peg, overcome with embarrassment, rushed off round the side of the house burying her face in her chest, to the sounds of Nancy Ingram scolding her son.

By the time Peg was fifteen, she had come to treat Strathalmond as her home. She was allowed to go home every second Sunday and, much encouraged by Miss Hill, she was thinking that she might advance in domestic service to become a lady's maid or even, someday, a housekeeper.

All that came to an end one rainy afternoon.

Peg was alone in the kitchen cleaning the silverware, as directed by Mrs. Woods who had gone to Myrestane to order provisions. It was the job Peg liked most as it entailed no running up and down flights of stairs, or carrying heavy pots, or the back-breaking emptying of ashes. She mixed the paste of hartshorn powder and spirits of wine and applied it to the cutlery with a rag. When dry she brushed the items one by one with a plate-brush and polished them with a dry leather to a gleaming, satisfying finish. The rain pattered on the window as Peg admired her work, thinking how pleased the cook would be on her return. She wore an ankle-length black dress with a white collar, her long dark hair tucked up under her cap. She didn't hear the approach of the man at her back.

Suddenly an arm encircled her slim waist from behind and she felt his hot breath on her cheek. She dropped the cloth and the forks in her hand, and, with a little shriek, she tried to turn. The grip on her waist tightened and a hand seized the nape of her neck forcing her face towards his. It was Peter Ingram. Peg was transfixed with fright. For a few seconds she stood like a rabbit in the mesmerising glare of a stoat as the man's watery eyes and long jaws edged her closer. She could smell the drink on his breath. Then, with a strength born of terror, she pushed him back, hands against his shoulders, and ducked down and out of his grasp. She ran from the kitchen out the back door and down the drive, her cap hanging behind her head by a single hairpin and the rain plastering her hair and running down her face.

❧ ❧ ❧

Peg Anderson never went back to Strathalmond. When she told her mother what had happened, her mother just shook her head, hurt and sadness shadowing her face.

"Oh dearie me," she said, lowering her eyes to the floor. It was as if their change in fortune was too good to last; as if by a cruel joke the family had been lured into the hope that the injustices of loss and poverty had been overcome, only to be dashed down again into despair. Looking at her mother's face, Peg wished she had never told her. Then she felt a sudden surge of anger at having been denied her chance in service, her chance to aspire and be recognised.

"I'll go back and see the Mistress," Peg blurted out.

"No, lassie. Ye'll no' go back," her mother replied in a tired voice. "For there's nae justice fae these kind o' folk for the likes o' us." She moved to Peg and hugged her close.

"Put it oot o' yer mind, hen." The two stood in the small kitchen, joined together and gently rocking back and forth.

"Noo you go and make up yer bed in the room, and there'll be nae mair said aboot this."

∾∾∾

In the years prior to the Great War, the long summer evenings in Myrestane rang to the shouts and cheers that came from the quoiting green, a little level patch of field that lay behind the buildings on the main street and ended at the Beugh burn. Teams of miners met there to match their skill in quoiting. A quoit — that the men pronounced "kite" — was a metal ring about the diameter of a horseshoe and weighing five pounds or sometimes heavier. This was pitched, a distance of about twenty-five feet, towards an iron rod that was set into a circular mud bed so that four inches of the ring showed above the bed. The object was to land the quoit on, or closest to, the rod. It was a sport played by the Argonauts in their quest for the Golden Fleece, a game as old as time itself and the highlight of Myrestane nights. Teams of men milled around the green, making bets on their champions, while village girls sat on the wall and looked on, cheering and laughing to the young men.

The man who threw the heaviest quoit in the county was Tosh Douglas and the girl who came to see him every night was Peg Anderson. She watched as he took off his jacket and rolled up the sleeves of his shirt, a huge figure of a man with a shy, self-effacing manner that attracted Peg from the first. As the weeks passed, he would look over to her and smile, and that was the beginning of a slow and placid romance.

When they started to walk out together, Peg was sixteen and he was twelve years her senior, a shy, ambling giant whose arm around her shoulders brought protection from the world and its erratic ways. In the poems that Peg read there was much talk about love, notions that confused and perplexed her. She came to wish it for herself, and if the quiet attention of Tosh Douglas was not love, then Peg wondered what love could be.

The next summer, her mother took to her bed and it was clear to all that her struggle against poverty and adversity was nearly over. She died within a month. She had signed a paper giving her consent that Tommy be taken to a home for orphans for she wanted Peg to be free to have her own life.

Tosh stood on the path opposite the front doors of the little terraced row of miners' cottages. His hands were in his trouser pockets as he concentrated on one big heavy boot that nuzzled a stone. As she approached him, he looked up, concern in his face under the jaunty angle of his big cloth cap.

"He's away then, Peg?"

She stopped, a tall slim girl in a polka-dot dress and apron, her long dark hair pinned up tightly in a bun, her eyes red.

"Aye," was all she could sob.

He moved urgently towards her. "He'll be aw right. Dinnae greet." He reached out a hand in an uncertain gesture.

"You couldnae look efter him, lass. Quarrier's Homes are guid people. He'll get a guid hame. You'll see."

The softness of his words and the gentle strength of the man caused her to lose what little control she had and her grief poured out in great cries and sobs as she fell against him. He moved quickly and caught her in his arms. Her little

189

brother, Tommy, who had been the light of her eye, had been taken away — an orphan at eleven — taken to the Home.

"To be sent to Canada," they had said. "To get a good home in Canada," they had said.

That was the day that Peg lost a brother and gained a husband, the day that her love was born in the midst of her grief. That morning, she had seen Tommy washed and dressed in the little suit that she had bought for sixpence at the Parish Office, and his Sunday boots. She would never forget how his eyes had accused her when Mr. Forbes from the Home took his hand to lead him away.

She never saw her brother again, but she never forgot the look he gave her on that July morning in 1915.

Peg was seventeen when she married Tosh Douglas. He was twenty-nine. He was big, and quiet, and he said he loved her. She had no inkling of men or what they were, only of her father, but she knew that Tosh was a good man and it felt right for her to marry him. He never flew across the skies in his mind, nor sang songs, nor read poems, nor even laughed at foolish thoughts, but he worked hard and saved his money, and when they were married they moved into the Station Raw opposite Myrestane Station and he paid cash for new furniture at the Cooperative Store. For paying cash down, the store presented him with two ceramic lions, orange with white muzzles, that stared up from the floor on either side of the fireplace.

Chapter
Two

❧❧❧

The meeting of the owners of the independent shale oil companies was scheduled to be held at 2pm. on the 12th day of April, 1919 at Strathalmond House in the town of Myrestane, the home of Sam Ingram.

The industry, that had begun more than half a century earlier, the mining of shiny black oil shales from seven main seams within a seventy-five square mile area of the Lothians, was in trouble.

Thirty independent companies were now reduced to a handful. Oil that now flowed freely from the earth in America and elsewhere was predicting the shale oil industry's demise. Still, advances in technology had improved the efficiency of the huge retorts, designed to heat the oil shale and force it to give up its oil, and enabled its survival even in the face of unequal competition. And Strathalmond Oil Company stood at the forefront of the survivors.

Sam Ingram of Strathalmond was known to everyone in the oil field as "Old Sam". At an early age he'd waived his inheritance as a gentleman farmer on the substantial Strathalmond estate the day he discovered the shale seam near the gates of the family mansion. From that day in 1862, Sam had dedicated his life to the industry.

By 1902 Strathalmond Oil Company, known locally as "the Work", and covering over two hundred acres, was the largest single oil producer in the industry. Its two thousand oil workers and miners processed 1600 tons of shale every day in 500 Henderson Improved Patent retorts. Its refinery produced 13 million gallons of oil per year and its candle factory produced 20 tons of paraffin wax candles each day. The company's gas works supplied the town of Myrestane. Its profits exceeded £80,000.00 per annum, and Sam became richer than any previous Ingram of Strathalmond.

On the morning of the meeting, Sam sat in his big leather easy chair before the large open fireplace in the comfortable morning room of Strathalmond. He smiled at his old friend, Stewart Shaw, who sat opposite him at the other side of the glowing fire. The two men, well into their seventies though neither looked a day over sixty-five, sipped tea from china cups.

Stewart Shaw looked at the pattering rain from an April shower as it streaked the window panes. "It was a day just like this when it all began, Sam," he said, "a lifetime ago, yet it seems like yesterday."

Sam stretched his long frame, reaching over to put his cup and saucer back on a little mahogany table near his chair. He smiled his lantern-jawed smile, the little wrinkles bunching up at the corners of his eyes. "I remember it well, Stewart. The two of us with pick and shovel, the rain running off us, digging for that shale outcrop out there by the old gates of the house."

Stewart Shaw, short and sturdy with a ruddy complexion and thick mop of silver white hair, laughed. "And the roar that came out of us when your pick banged against what we thought was the seam."

"Aye," Sam chuckled, "the old rusty cannon. God knows how long that had been buried there. Took us another three months to find the shale. Aye, we weren't very happy that day. You remember we were so disgusted we just buried the gun back up."

The two old men leaned back in their chairs, silently nursing their reminiscences.

"A lot of water has flowed under the bridge since then,

Stewart," Sam said, getting out of his chair and walking over to the window.

He looked out over the trees that lined the driveway of Strathalmond to the huge orange bing of spent shale that dominated the Work. Smoke spiralled up from the four tall chimneys that rose above a maze of railway lines and groups of retorts, set together in clusters that the men called "the Benches". Sam could make out the hutches, small trucks that ran on rails and were drawn by a cable from the shale face in the mine up the incline to the surface, and thence up to the hoppers on top of the retorts, each carrying its one-ton load of shale. He could see the other hutches that hauled the spent shale, still burning, from the foot of the retorts on up the side of the great bing for dumping. He could see the tiny figures of the men on the bing who tipped the heavy hutches. He turned back to look at Stewart Shaw.

"We've come a long way since we dug up that old cannon, Stewart. The industry has been good to both of us. But you know as well as I that the golden years are past. We didn't know it then, but even before we dug up that old cannon, Colonel Edwin Drake of the Seneca Oil Company of America struck free flowing oil in Pennsylvania only seventy feet under the surface. Christ, think of it! Seventy feet! Oh, we're not finished yet, not by a long way, but that free flowing oil is already spelling the end of the shale oil business. American oil, Russian oil and now Iranian oil. You know it and I know it, Stewart. That is why this meeting of the owners has been called. We have to form a coalition of the shale oil companies; Strathalmond Oil Company, Stewart Shaw Oil Company and all the others, so that we can support each other in the marketplace, cut away the duplication of effort and work together."

Stewart Shaw's eyes narrowed. " You have a plan for that, Sam?" he said, watching his old friend closely.

Sam slowly shook his head. "Not my plan, Stewart, Peter's plan. I am, what you might call, semi-retired. Peter runs Strathalmond Oil now. He has a power of attorney to vote my shares."

As Stewart Shaw started up in his chair, his face filled with concern, Sam lifted a hand to hush him.

"I know, I know, Stewart. My son Peter has never been a favourite of yours, but there it is. I'm getting old and I'm getting tired, and Peter is all I have ever since . . ." Sam's voice faltered as his eyes flickered to the mantelpiece above the fire, "ever since poor Billy died."

Stewart followed Sam's gaze to the photograph in the silver frame — Colonel William Ingram, in the uniform of the Royal Scots Greys, stood tall and straight in the doorway of Strathalmond.

Stewart had been there the day it was taken, the day in 1912, the day before Sam's eldest son had returned to join his regiment in India. He remembered how these weeks with William and his family had been the happiest of Old Sam's life. He went to Sam and gently squeezed his shoulder.

Looking at the photograph, Stewart Shaw, a confirmed old bachelor, realised just how much the Ingrams had been his only family all these years. From the day Sam and he had uncovered the cannon, he had been a part of them.

He was best man when Sam married Rachael in St. Nicholas Church, and he was at her funeral after she died of consumption in 1913. He was godfather to both of Sam's sons, Peter and William. He had shared Sam's pride when William was commissioned in the Greys and went to India as a subaltern in 1894, and he had shared Sam's disappointment when Peter's gambling and womanising had squandered a small fortune. He had spent several days at Strathalmond when William came from India on a vacation, bringing his pretty young wife, Nancy, and his lively, talkative twelve-year-old son. He was there when Peter returned as a prodigal son in 1912, and Sam took him in to please his ailing wife, Rachael, and he was there when the telegram came in 1916 to say that Colonel William Ingram had died on the Somme.

Sam had never really recovered from that. The silver mounted photograph on the mantelpiece, that the two old friends now contemplated, was a constant reminder.

At the age of twenty-seven, while serving in India, William had married an English army nurse called Nancy Gray. Their son, David Ingram, was born in India in 1900. After William's death, David came to Strathalmond to continue his education in Edinburgh while Nancy Gray returned to her home in England. Two years later, Nancy remarried in England, and David stayed on at Strathalmond to study law. He was now apprenticed in Edinburgh with the firm of Cunningham and McCulloch, Solicitors and Writers to the Signet.

"You still have Davie, Sam. He looks just like his father."

"Aye, but he's just a laddie, Stewart. Just a wee laddie."

Old Sam wiped the tears that welled up in his eyes.

☙☙☙

The expansive drawing room of Strathalmond, where the shale company owners were meeting, was the outcome of extensive renovation and furnishing completed by Sam's grandfather in the 1840s. The original stone floor and walls were now concealed behind mahogany and rosewood wainscotting. The tall windows with their small panes and carved shutters looked over the lawns and gardens on the south and east sides of the mansion house. The room was elegantly furnished in the Victorian style and a fire blazed in the ornamental marble fireplace, its light reflecting from the dark polished wood of high-backed chairs and delicately carved side tables. The ceiling was of light oak inlaid with rosewood rose and fern patterns, and gilt-framed portraits of long-dead Ingrams graced the walls. Several leather easy chairs were arranged around the room and two large sofas, covered in heavy gold self-embossed brocade, flanked the fireplace.

Peter Ingram, tall and spare with thinning grey hair, a long straight nose and pronounced bags under his big sad eyes, stood with his back to the fire addressing the half dozen representatives of the remaining shale oil operators who sat around the room. He looked briefly at the group of owners, eyeing each one as a cat eyes pigeons.

"You all know why you are here," he began. "This industry of ours, and every man here, are facing ruin." A buzz ran around the room, feet quietly shuffling, faces perplexed and insulted.

"We are all busy men, so I'll waste no time. Cheaper oil from abroad is killing us. We've all known it for a long time. Now is the time to do something about it. That's why I called you all here." Again he paused.

Ernest Simpson of the neighbouring town of Oakbank, President of Oakbank Oils, raised his great florid face and growled in his gritty voice. "What can we do to stop the flow of foreign oil?" He looked around for support from the others.

"Nothing!" Peter shouted. "Not a damned thing! And it'll get worse."

Simpson sat back, momentarily intimidated by the unexpected vigour of the Ingram response.

"What we must do, Ernie, is unite. We must merge our operations to cut our costs. And we must improve our management. We can no longer sit on our fat behinds and draw money from a failing enterprise."

Some of the men made to speak and then thought better of it. Ingram's ability as a manager, bastard though he was, would not be disputed here. They looked on, and waited. Peter, now feeling the power of his control, smiled slyly.

"We merge all our companies into one enterprise. I propose that it be called Strathalmond Oils Ltd. and we will all hold shares in it on a pro rata basis dependent on the value of our present companies."

Ernest Simpson growled again. "How do we figure out the value of what we are putting in?"

"Accountants," Peter snapped. "We all have accountants, Ernie. They can get together and go over the assets and liabilities and profits of each of our companies and agree on the valuations. We have more important things to do."

"Where would this new company, this Strathalmond Oils Ltd., operate from?" Robert Mackie of Philpstoun asked.

"Here," Peter replied. "Here in Strathalmond. It will have

its Head Office upstairs that will be leased from Sam Ingram. Ours is the largest company in the merger and closest to the largest of the Works, so here is the obvious place. And it will be run by a Board of Directors made up those present at this meeting, and you will nominate me as President."

After about three seconds of silence everyone started to talk at once. Some leapt to their feet, waving their arms for attention, others stared wildly around their peers. Stewart Shaw leaned back in his chair. Peter's plan was no less than he had expected. Ernest Simpson took the lead once more.

"It doesn't sound very democratic to me, Peter," he said loudly. "Strathalmond Oil, Strathalmond House, Peter Ingram of Strathalmond as President. Looks like we are being asked to hand over our businesses to the Ingrams without even a 'by your leave.' "

A growing clamour of support followed his words.

Peter let the rumble of complaint die away before he continued.

"Do you want to be President, Ernie? Is that what you're saying?"

Peter was now giving a performance. He strode over to Ernie and looked him straight in the eye.

"Go ahead! You run the new company . . . or you, Robert Mackie of Philpstoun...or you, Sidney Black of Addiewell. Who do you all want to run it? Pick him now! We'll vote on it now!"

The men looked around the room, scared to catch the eye of Peter Ingram.

"But I'll tell you this," Ingram went on, his voice rising in anger. "Not one of you could run a soup kitchen, much less an oil company in hard times. And if you go with a President from among yourselves, you will be going without me. This proposal I am putting to you comes as a package. You take it all, or you take none of it!"

Peter's eyes glittered now, and his tall figure seemed to grow in the firelight. No one spoke.

"Good! Then it's settled. We form Strathalmond Oils Ltd. to operate from here in Strathalmond. We are all directors and I am president. Then, over the next two weeks we decide what Works will be closed and what retained, and what cuts will be made to wages so that we can survive."

The independent owners hated Peter Ingram more than ever. But he was right and they knew it. And they knew that, in the valuation, Peter Ingram would end up with close to half of the voting rights in the new company.

It was decided to incorporate Strathalmond Oils Limited without delay with those present as directors and Peter Ingram as president. The meeting was adjourned to a date that would allow time for the incorporation of the new company at which all appointments would be confirmed, the asset transfers put in hand, and decisions made on changes required in the industry.

Afternoon tea was served in the drawing room after the meeting. The owners sat around, most of them uncomfortable in the lavish surroundings, making small talk to conceal their feelings of having been steamrollered by the gentleman of the manor, Peter Ingram. At the earliest opportunity they took their leave in ones and twos until all that remained were Peter Ingram, Old Sam and Stewart Shaw.

"That went rather well Stewart, don't you think?" Peter began, a rather smug smile widening on his lips. "Even Ernie Simpson had nothing to say which rather surprised me. I suppose the mention of foreign oil was enough for them to see the sense of my proposal."

Stewart looked at Sam who was gazing into the fire, his face settled into a frown.

"The proposal is good, Peter, as far as it goes. The hard part is what comes next."

"Well," Peter retorted, "that will be up to you and me, won't it?"

Stewart knew exactly what Peter meant. On the formula agreed for the issue of shares in the new company, even if Peter would not control fifty per cent of the shares, Peter and Stewart Shaw together would control the majority of voting rights.

"Aye, I dare say it will, Peter. We'll control the company,

but that is not to say the decisions that must be made will be any easier. All these men that were here today put a life-time of effort into this industry and will need to be carefully consulted. Then there are the miners and the oil workers, not to mention the union."

"The union?" Peter said derisively. "Come on man. Don't talk to me about the union. Father there recognised the union in 1914 just after the strike in Strathalmond Oil. It was a bad mistake in my opinion, made before my time I might add." Sam continued to look into the fire and Stewart said nothing. Seeing the lack of reaction, Peter went on, suddenly animated.

"Now the oil is bubbling out of the ground in Persia needing only a pipe to carry it to the Abadan refineries in the Persian Gulf, while our shale has to be dug out, crushed and retorted to produce the same thing. How long can we compete with that? What does the union say? We've been paying the men good wages, housing them for low rents, even providing schools and shops and social clubs for them. How long can we continue to do that? What does the union say? What has the union, or that ragged-arsed mouthpiece of theirs, Shinwell, done for the ten thousand families supported by the oil companies around this country? No, Stewart. We've a lot to discuss and decide, but the considerations of the union will not be high on my agenda."

Old Sam raised himself up in his easy chair, briefly casting his eyes to the ceiling and sniffing loudly before settling back to stare again into the flames. Stewart felt sorry for him. Sam had been right. He was too old and too tired. It seemed that he was what the old miners called "done".

Peter was the man now, and Stewart had mixed feelings about Peter. He was bright, no doubt, and he had looked down the road and seen the writing on the wall for the shale and was trying to do something about it. But where was the compassion? Where was the feeling for the Work and the men? Maybe, Stewart thought, he also was too old. Maybe it was a time for the new men like Peter Ingram to make the decisions. Maybe growing up in the industry, working at the seam, firing the powder shots to make it give up its shale, hauling the hutches; maybe all that wasn't any good any more when it came to the boardroom and decision-making time.

Stewart got up to take his leave. "Well I hope Peter that we can work together," he said. "I have to be going, now." He leaned down and shook Sam's hand. "I'll be by in a day or two," he said.

As Sam got up to bid him goodbye, Stewart thought about William. He wondered what William would have done if he had held the future of Strathalmond Oil in his hands.

∾∾∾

About the time that Stewart Shaw left Strathalmond, David Ingram, Old Sam's grandson, was coming to the end of a long day in the Queen Street offices of Cunningham and McCulloch, Writers to the Signet. After only two weeks, having been enrolled as an apprentice solicitor he was finding all the days long.

He had started in the conveyancing department, and from 8.30 am to 6 pm every day, he had been engaged on the extremely tedious pursuit of noting titles. Whenever a piece of land changed hands, its title, usually consisting of a bundle of deeds, dispositions, mortgages and quit claims, sometimes going back four centuries, had to be sorted in order of date, and notes made detailing the progression of ownerships, beginning with the original Feudal Grant from the Crown. The notes on titles were painstakingly recorded in pen and ink in the Title Book.

Now and again David's keen interest in history was jogged by some old deed, inscribed on vellum and embossed with a little piece of silver that represented duties paid to the Register of Sasines. He liked to feel the smooth texture of the vellum and nurse the little shards of silver in his fingers, thinking back through the centuries. Who owned this land then? What kind of men and women were they?

But most of the time the job was a bore, and David looked forward to a change of department, where he might meet with some interesting case law.

The law had been Sam Ingram's idea of a career for his grandson. David wanted to be a soldier like his father but his grandfather wouldn't hear of it. It was the only time that he had seen Sam Ingram angry. His mother had visited Strathalmond several times after his father was killed. Now she had remarried and he never saw her.

In the last few years, the happy days in India with his parents had faded from David's mind, but his new life was just as happy, studying with his friends in Edinburgh and staying at Strathalmond with Grandfather Sam and Uncle Peter.

Sam Ingram had taken him through the Work, showing him every aspect of the process of retorting and distilling. He had ridden in the cage down the frightening incline of the shale mine and seen the miners firing the shots and the men and boys loading and drawing the hutches. He had smelled the dampness and felt the chill of the mine, and he was pleased to be making his living in the safe, comfortable offices of Cunningham and McCulloch, W.S., no matter how tiresome the present task might be.

The brass-faced grandfather clock that stood against the wall chimed six strokes, and Herbert McAllister, the Chief Conveyancing Clerk peered over wire glasses.

"Tidy up these titles before you go, my lad, and put the Title Book in the safe," he said in his gruff voice.

"Yes sir. Right away sir," David replied, busily complying with the order.

Bustling out the door and down the wide staircase to the entrance hall, satchel in hand and attempting to put on his coat as he went, David almost collided with Ewan Cameron Cunningham, the firm's octogenarian senior partner, who was making his way, leaning on his cane, across the chequered tiles of the hall.

David stopped short, his face flustered.

"Who are you, son?" the old man said.

"David Ingram, Sir," David spluttered. "A new apprentice."

"Have you had your holidays yet?" the old man said, his little blue eyes shining in his wrinkled face. Before David could reply, he continued.

"Make sure that they give you your holidays, son. Oh Aye. Don't let them forget your holidays."

While David stood puzzled, the elder partner disappeared into a room off the hall. He was still puzzled as he emerged into Queen Street and made his way over George Street and along Princes Street to Waverley Station.

The rain had stopped and the sky cleared, and the dying sun over the West Port cast a sheen across the face of the towering castle rock. David crossed the street and walked through the iron gates into Princes Street Gardens. Then he made his way eastward, smelling the grass and spring flowers, passing the statues and monuments to Scotland's literary heritage, towards the broad roof of Waverley where he would catch his train to Myrestane.

This was the best time of David's day in the most beautiful city in the world.

Chapter
Three

≈≈≈

There was a place, on the west side of Donegal, where a high and barren moor tips on its side and slopes down to the Atlantic Ocean. From that place, if a man had the vision, he could see the Americas.

It was a place marked by poverty and hard toil, religious obligations and family ties, singing and dancing and the love of hard liquor. It was a place that no longer exists, even in the minds of its people, for a living could no longer be had there and they moved away, some across the Atlantic and others to the cramped mining villages of Scotland.

That place was called Inishennan, and towards the end it was only a handful of whitewashed cottages cowering in the shadow of the hill that swept down to the sea.

Barney O'Shea was cutting turf on the high moor, sliding the two-sided spade into the bank and heaving the dark brown rectangles out of the earth to lay them side by side on the wet ground. It was warm work, and Barney had abandoned his shirt that lay crumpled where he had left it, beside his old haversack and his tin can of buttermilk, on the edge of the turf bank. Sweat glistened on his pinched, freckled face and left white streaks across the brown turf dust that covered his thin wiry body. His mop of red hair stuck out from his head at varying angles as if he had just fallen out of bed. Barney worked harder than usual, taking few breaks, for he wanted to stack the turf by nightfall. Tomorrow he would not be here for it was his wedding day.

He didn't see the figure that had emerged over the low rise further down the hill until it was quite close to him, and shouting out his name.

"Barney! Barney O'Shea! Is it yourself?"

The man approached him, stumbling in the soft earth as he came, all out of breath and peering down at his feet, lest he slip off a turf cut and land himself in the black water of the moss. Barney recognised him right away. It was Paddy Reilly, old Rosie Reilly's boy that she had late in her life, him that had upped and left the country ten years ago to go and work in the mines in Scotland. Barney was seventeen at the time and he could remember the wailing and crying that Rosie did to his mother at the loss of her only son. He stuck his spade in the cut and wiped his face with a rag as the visitor came up.

"God, it's yourself," Reilly said, catching his breath and smoothing the white shirt down over his stomach with a fat hand.

Barney could not see much difference in him, a bit heavier perhaps and a touch of grey creeping in around the temples. But it was the same Paddy, the big heavy cheeks on him and the little sharp nose, and the darting eyes that never seemed to look at you. He was wearing a hat. That was different. Not a cap that men wore around the country, but one of those square hats with a brim that you saw in shop windows in Donegal town. It sat back on his head at an angle, and there was a green feather sticking up from the band that ran around it.

Barney stuck out his hand. " Paddy! It's been a long time, boy," he said. He felt the strength in Paddy's grip and realised that it was no weakling that was inside the bulging suit.

The two men sat down on a bit of dry grass above the cut, and Barney took a swig of buttermilk from his tin and passed it to Paddy who waved it aside. "I've lost the taste for that stuff, boy. Tell me now, is it right what I'm hearing, that Barney O'Shea is getting wed in the morning to little Jeanie Byrne?"

"Tis so", Barney laughed, "if Barney O'Shea can get that turf up before tonight."

"Then, bi Jaysus I've come to the right man, so I have," Paddy said, grabbing Barney's hand again in his meaty fist and shaking it violently. "For you will be a family man now, and you will need work that will put more on the table than this diggin' in a bog for a few scraps of turf."

That was the beginning of it, and Barney needed little persuading to make his fortune in among the pagans in Scotland, for there was no hope that he would ever make enough here to take up a farm around Inishennan, and now he would have a wife and, God willing, the blessing of a family.

The wedding of Barney O'Shea and Jeanie Byrne took place in the little chapel in Inishennan in July 1919, and a few days later Barney and his bride resolved to go to Scotland where Paddy Reilly promised there would be a job in the Work.

"Sure aren't there plenty of Donegal men in the Work in Myrestane," said Paddy, and the word went around the countryside about "Paddy Reilly's Oil Works".

Old Mick O'Shea and his wife Gracie were not a bit happy at the prospect of losing their son and their new daughter-in-law, and they did a bit of crying and pleading for them to stay at home and not be going away among the heathens. But Barney's mind was made up for him by the contented look of Paddy, as he sat by the fire in Ned Byrne's house — Ned was Jeanie's father who made a drop of poteen now and then. With his fine hat on his head, Paddy kept pulling out the silver watch from his inside pocket to look at the time.

Paddy had done all right in Scotland right enough. Didn't he say that there was no more to the mining than digging a bit of shale out of the ground and trundling it up in a hutch to the surface? And was it not true that Barney's own sister, Martha, the one that had gone to America, had done so well that now she was writing home asking their sister Hannah to come out and she would be paying her passage?

The night before Barney and Jeanie left for Scotland, the whole of Inishennan was in Mick O'Shea's house. They crowded around the kitchen where a turf fire blazed in the hearth, the big black iron kettle hanging from its chain over the flame to provide a constant supply of boiling water for tea. They overflowed into the little bedroom where the bed had been stood up on end against the wall, and groups of them lined the lobby and stood along the wall outside. The table was laid with piles of soda bread that Gracie and her daughters, Hannah and Mary, had baked on the griddle all afternoon, and huge square blocks of newly churned butter with the knives sticking into them for people to help themselves. Mick had sent for Ned Byrne to bring with him a jug or two of poteen, for which he would be paid from the shilling each that had been collected from the men, and little Neilly had come up from Dunfanaghy with his fiddle as he always did when someone was leaving the country.

The singing and the dancing and the craic went on into the early hours. But for all the merriment of the night, there was the sadness that always came with the leaving of Inishennan. Mick O'Shea sang *Come Back to Erin* and *My Barque Leaves the Harbour Tomorrow*, and Barney's younger brother Sean, who had been blessed with the sweetest tenor voice that ever was heard around the country, sang *The Mountains of Mourne*. There was not a dry eye then, and Barney's father went outside so that the company would not be witnessing his grief at losing a son. Even Paddy Reilly, the successful emigrant, who had gone abroad to make his fortune and come back with a fancy hat and feather and a silver watch that hung on a chain, leaned against the mantel and cried openly as if it was he going all over again.

Such were the ties of Inishennan, that even those who had never ventured beyond their own kitchen could feel the pain of leaving.

The next day Barney and Jeanie O'Shea took the horse-drawn mail car over the moor to the station where they got the train to Derry. Most of the Inishennan crowd from the night before milled around the mail car, waving and crying and shouting their goodbyes, and it was only when the newly wed couple sat in the railway carriage, watching the last of Donegal flash by, that they could look into each other's eyes with the cold realisation that they had left their home. Jeanie opened her hand to look at the five silver shillings that her father had pressed into it as she boarded the mail car.

In the long shed that extended for more than a hundred yards along the Derry quay, Barney and Jeanie, struggling with their cloth bags that bulged with all that they owned, pushed their way through crowds of people. They dodged the porters' carts and the nags that were hauling in loads of rough wooden crates through the wide, sliding doors that led from the street. Further down the shed, cattle were being loaded onto the boat, and the whole place was filled with their lowing and their smell and the shouts of the men that were stick-handling them in ones and twos towards the gangway. Barney and Jeanie gave no thought to the beasts, for the smell of cattle was the smell of home.

They finally arrived in the long queue that snaked back from the little ramshackle of a ticket office that stood against the end wall of the shed. In the square aperture of the booth a little man in the uniform of the Laird Line, his sleeves rolled back over white cuffs and a round cap with a black skip protruding over his brow, peered over rimless glasses and issued tickets. When their turn came, Barney bought two steerage tickets for four shillings and sixpence apiece and they proceeded on up the gangway on to the boat.

The Derry boat left for Glasgow at 6.30pm and it would arrive at the Broomielaw, on the north bank of the River Clyde near the centre of the city, early the next morning. For twelve shillings and sixpence each, they could have had a cabin with a sink for washing and two narrow bunks, one above the other, and a steward who would fetch them a cup of tea whenever they felt like it. But twenty five shillings was more money than either of them was prepared to throw away on a bit of comfort, even if they could have spared it, and neither of them had any notion of being served by a steward for they were no better than he was. And they never even saw the lounges in the steerage, for whenever they emerged onto the first deck they came to, they took up a seat made of steel with long wooden slats than ran close together, and they settled themselves down there next to the rail with their baggage beside them and watched the ship loading.

It was a comfortable enough spot for there was no rain and little wind. Barney had on a thick shirt and his tweed jacket and big cloth cap while Jeanie had her long Galway shawl round her and up over her head. They sat and watched the ones that were coming up the gangway. Some were dressed like the gentry, with suits on and hats like the one Paddy Reilly had sported, and carrying suitcases made of leather and umbrellas for the rain. Others were just like themselves, looking haunted and scared, but putting on a brazen face for they wanted none to think that they were not seasoned travellers.

Soon the gangway was quiet, with only an odd straggler rushing up it as if he thought the boat might pull away from under him, and the great horn let forth a blast that made Barney and Jeanie jump with fright. They saw the sailors lifting the big loops of the hawsers up over the capstans on the pier, and tossing them off the quay where they were hauled into the boat by the lines attached to them. The engines churned up the water along the side and the people lining the quay started shouting their farewells to those at the rails, their voices rising here and there in echoes over the rumble of the boat. Many were wiping their tears with fluttering handkerchiefs, waving and holding up babies and small children, and the whole scene made Barney and Jeanie cry once again, thinking of Inishennan and those that they were leaving behind.

As the boat edged away from the land and out into the main channel of Lough Foyle, the calls and cries grew fainter but the handkerchiefs still fluttered for a long time.

Barney and Jeanie sat on the deck all night. It was still light when they passed through the narrow strait with its whitewashed lighthouse on Inishowen Head, but soon it grew dark and they settled down, a blanket from Jeanie's bag stretched over the two of them, and listened in silence to the monotonous drone of the engines. They were warm enough and happy in their own company, and they didn't want the talking with others in the steerage to despoil their leaving Ireland or the start of their new adventure. They held hands under the blanket and now and then they kissed and pulled up closer, for they were man and wife and they were going to a new life together.

Not long before dawn, the steamer passed the great rock of Ailsa Craig, and they could make out its dark triangle against the moonlit sky. It was called "Paddy's Mile Stone" for all the Irishmen that had passed this way in search of their fortunes in another land, and it was another silent reminder for the emigrants.

It was getting light when the boat pulled in at Gourock where the Firth of Clyde narrowed and turned eastward towards Glasgow. Barney went below decks and fetched two cups of hot tea, and the couple watched the passengers disembark at the coastal town. Soon they were underway again, and, refreshed and awake, Barney and Jeanie O'Shea, from the windswept solitude of the Townland of Inishennan, sailed into the second city of the British Empire.

They held hands and marvelled in silence at the great shipyards that ranged for miles along the bank on either side, yards where men had built half of all the seagoing tonnage in the world. The Derry Boat, that they had thought so big and so fine when it plied its way through Lough Foyle at the leaving of Ireland, was now dwarfed by ocean liners the likes of which the O'Sheas could never have imagined. They craned their necks looking up at these monsters as they passed. They could see sailors high above them on the decks, and some would wave to them as if they were old friends. They noted the names emblazoned on the prows, magical names that rang of strange women or far off lands and distant skies: *Lady Alicia, Tavania, The Southern Cross.*

Every now and then, as they slowly moved along the channel towards the heart of this enormous city, passing the parade of giants, some anchored and some towering high amidst the tall scaffolds on the bank, Barney tightened his grip on his wife's hand. "God save us. Would you look at that!" he whispered in sheer wonder.

It was still early in the day when the steamer pulled alongside the quay at the Broomielaw in the heart of Glasgow. Gathering up their bags the O'Sheas made their way down the gangway and out through the shed onto the cobbled street. Barney put down his belongings and consulted a piece of paper on which Paddy Reilly had marked out for him the way they must go to get to the Central Station. There they would get the train for Myrestane.

"Good morning to you, Paddy. If you tell me where you folks are headed, maybe I can show you the way." Barney looked up from Reilly's map into the smiling face of the little man who addressed him. He looked about sixty, with a long nose and tiny brown eyes twinkling under a large cap that sat at an angle on his head.

Without waiting for an answer, the man tipped the cap to Jeanie, reaching down to lift her bag. "To the train, is it?" he said. Barney nodded, and before he could say anything the little man took off across the wide street, holding the bag in front of him with two hands and dodging nimbly on little feet between people and carriages. Barney grabbed his bag in one hand and Jeanie's arm in the other and rushed off in pursuit. "Tis kind of the man to show us the way to the station," Jeanie gasped, as Barney caught a glimpse of their self-appointed guide disappearing into a street that ran away from the quay. They made their way with difficulty across the busy road to the street where Barney had last seen the little man, but now there was no sign of him. They walked on up the street, searching each street that ran off in either direction, and after fifteen minutes or so they realised that he was gone and so was Jeanie's bag. They stood against the wall of a large ornate building, no longer doubting that they had been tricked.

"My belongings are lost me, Barney," Jeanie cried. "Even the five shillin's I got from my Da. God forgive the little thief!" She burst into tears then and Barney held her close. They both wished at that moment that they had never left Inishennan to come among thieves and robbers in this heathen country.

They had tea and sandwiches at a booth in the Central Station and got tickets for Myrestane, and in the afternoon they sat in another train looking out at a different landscape.

"God, would you look at the size of the fields, Jeanie!" Barney said. "Sure there's more potatoes there in that one field than in the whole of Donegal. Would you look now! Jaysus, but it's a wealthy country right enough."

Jeanie was still sick at the loss of her bag that had contained her only two good frocks in the world, and her night gown and other things that she had got for her wedding, and the money from her father that had been all he had saved. She forced a casual glance out of the window, but what were fields to her if they weren't the fields of Ireland?

Barney turned towards her and took both her small hands in his own. "Come on now, m'darlin," he said gently. "Try and put that little robber from your mind. Sure we're goin' to Myrestane, to Mrs. McCormack's house in the Randy Raws, her that Paddy says will put us up 'till we get a place of our own. She's an Inishennan woman and we'll be right enough there, you'll see." Jeanie forced a little smile for she saw that her husband was trying to cheer her, God bless him, but she had an aching within her to be going home.

They left the train at Myrestane Station and passed under the railway bridge and down the hill, where the road ran along the base of a huge shale bing, an orange mountain basking in the evening sunlight.

The Randy Raws that lay directly in front of them were no more than five minutes walk from the station. They consisted of three terraced rows of houses, built, fifty years earlier, by Strathalmond Oil Company for miners and oil workers. There were fifty-two houses, a school and a shop. One row, longer than the others, stretched north along the Myrestane Road from a burn that flowed eastward. The other two shorter rows extended eastward from the long one and parallel to the burn. These shorter rows had names. The one nearest the burn was called the "Burn Raw", and the other was called the "School Raw".

211

The little burn was called the "Randy Burn" although at one time it had been known as the "Beugh Burn". On its way east to join the River Almond, it flowed through a large culvert under the great orange bing.

The houses in each row were all connected just as the people were connected that lived there, connected by the Work, connected by a level of subsistence, connected by survival and by hope.

On warm summer evenings like this, many people in these Randy Raws hauled out chairs and sometimes easy chairs to place them against the outer walls and sit in the sunshine talking to their neighbours. Mrs. McCormack was one who did this, and when she saw the young couple approaching down the hill from the station, the man stepping out boldly with a bag in one hand and his other arm around the girl, and she hanging back a bit with fear, Mrs. McCormack got up and waved to them, shouting a welcome in the Irish tongue. And when she heard it, Jeanie O'Shea's heart leapt in her breast for it was a call from her own country and her own people.

Chapter
Four

ௐ ௐ ௐ

The O'Sheas' first night in the Randy Raws was joyful. Mrs. McCormack made it so with her constant questions about Inishennan. Who was alive there and who had passed on? Where was this one now and how many of a family had she? Liam O'Neill, him that went to Americay, had anybody heard more of him?

Granny McCormack, for that was what they called her, made a pot of tea, and served up buttered bread and boiled eggs the way the Irish do it, and when Barney and Jeanie had eaten their fill she took them outside the little room and kitchen of a house to sit against the wall, and she introduced them to her neighbours in the Raw. There was a warm feeling that came from her. She was sixty something and big and stout, with a striped frock that was bursting at the seams and a big round potato of a face that was permanently creased in smiles. She told the O'Sheas that she had come to the Randy Raws twenty years ago with her husband, little Danny McCormack, who had lost his life in the mine five years later, "God rest his soul".

After Danny died, she took in lodgers, mostly Irishmen from Donegal or Mayo or Kerry, and here she had stayed. "Beef to the heels like a Mullingar heifer," she laughed.

They sat against the wall and laughed and talked and cracked on about Ireland as the sun went down. It was only then, as they were moving the chairs back inside, that Barney began to hear the clanking and rumbling of the Work and catch a sniff of tar in the air, and realize that he was in another country.

In each one of the fifty-two houses in the Randy Raws there were two rooms — a front room, that doubled as a kitchen, and a back room. There was a bed in the front room that was recessed into the wall with a curtain that drew across the front of it to hide the sleepers. It had the door that opened on to the street, an open fireplace, a table and chairs where meals were eaten, and a sink and a zinc bathtub for washing. When not in use, the bathtub was hung on a hook behind the door. Granny McCormack's back room contained two double beds. Water was carried from a pillar well at the end of the Raw, and the dry privies outside were emptied every week by a man with a horse and cart called Jock MacDonald.

Granny McCormack had eight lodgers, four on the night shift and four on the day shift, and they slept two to a bed in the back room. When the shifts changed, so did the occupants of the beds and it was said of the Randy Raws that the beds were never cold. Each lodger paid twelve shillings a week for full board and Granny McCormack, whose rent was three shillings a week, made a good, if cramped, living. Over the next few days Barney and Jeanie were to see how she did it.

Jeanie slept with the landlady in the kitchen and Barney slept in the back room on a shakedown bed on the floor. " Now you are welcome here," Granny McCormack said to them," 'till you find a place to rent and Barney gets taken on at the Work."

The O'Sheas were grateful though they longed to have their own place where they could be quiet and be together, especially at night. This little house was busier than the Llamas Horse Fair, with all its lodgers coming and going, stripping off their shirts in the kitchen to wash off the black dust of the mine, crowding around the table with their plates and mugs for their share of Granny McCormack's endless supply of meat and potatoes, bread and bacon and stewed tea. Some nights they returned from the Myrestane Hotel, noisy with the drink in them and singing about Ireland and talking in the back room to all hours.

Barney rose at dawn each day and went out with the day shift men to find work. On the fourth day there, he was hired on at the mine by a foreman who knew Paddy Reilly.

"So that's where the auld bugger is," the foreman said, "over in Ireland again recruitin' young fellahs like you. And did he tell ye how easy it was to mine shale? Just like cuttin' turf in a bog. Isn't that what he said?" The foreman laughed and the other men joined in.

"Well, son, now's yer chance to find out how truthful a man Reilly is. Ah'm giving you a start in the mine. Be here in the mornin' at six. You can draw for Tosh Douglas." Then, looking at Barney's puzzled expression, he added, "And if ye don't know what that means, son, Ah'm sure Tosh will put you right."

Barney was elated. He was getting a start in the mine they called Myrestane No. 4 as a drawer. He had no idea what that meant, but had been told that the pay would be based on the amount of shale mined, and should be in the region of four pounds a week for a good drawer. Four pounds for a week's work! He couldn't make four pounds in Inishennan in two months.

He marched from the foreman's office through the banging and clanging of the Work. He passed the huge retorts, breathing in with joy the pungent, unfamiliar smells of crude oil, ammonia and paraffin that filled his nose, and loving every sound and smell as he made his way along the base of the shale bing to the Randy Raws. It was a beautiful day and not yet noon, and he would take Jeanie out of the house. They would walk out like man and wife and make plans, for now they would have money enough for their own place and he would take away the furrow in her brow and her homesick cry for Inishennan.

And that was what he did. They walked hand in hand

beside the little burn, along the edges of fields of corn and potatoes, with the Work at their back and the smell of clover and wild flowers all around them. They passed by a great mansion that peeked out at them over the trees, and they looked up the hill behind it at the ruins of some ancient castle. Then, in a little hollow, hidden from all the world, they lay down on the rich grass and made love, and Jeanie O'Shea smiled for the first time since they had left Inishennan.

∽ ∽ ∽

The next morning Barney met Tosh Douglas at Myrestane No. 4, one of the two dozen shale mines that dotted the Lothian landscape south of the Forth estuary. Tosh was talking to the foreman when Barney approached.

"Here's your new drawer, Tosh," the foreman quipped. "Barney O'Shea from the Emerald Isle."

Tosh gave Barney an almost imperceptible nod and turned back to continue his conversation with the foreman. Barney stood back, watching the two and gripping his piece-box in his hand. It contained the thick slices of bread and bacon from Granny McCormack's kitchen.

Tosh Douglas was a giant of a man. He dwarfed the foreman and all the other men who were passing them to start their shift. Granny McCormack described him as a "big cannie man," explaining to Barney that it meant quiet and careful. But it meant more than that. The simple word "cannie" described some men, usually big men like Tosh, providing a whole picture of their character and demeanour. It related a kind of ease and confidence that needed no overt action to show their strength of purpose and command of life. You could tell a cannie man just by looking at him. Barney O'Shea felt relieved. Since he had to go into the bowels of the earth, he was glad to be going with this man.

"Can ye see in the dark, son?" Tosh addressed Barney, as he tapped a big index finger on the oil lamp that was fixed to the front of his cloth cap. A generous smile opened on his face.

"I have a lamp for him," the foreman said, disappearing into his office to reappear with the lamp. He showed Barney how to fix it to his cap.

"Now he's set," the foreman grinned. Then Tosh walked off with long strides towards the mine head with Barney, half running after him, gripping his piece-box and holding the lamp.

Myrestane No. 4 was an inclined mine. The road into it that carried two sets of rails, ran down at a forty-five degree angle twenty-five hundred feet into the darkness. Tosh and Barney climbed aboard the steel hutch that was hooked to a heavy cable driven by an electric motor. They sat on one of the two benches on the hutch and it took off down the incline, picking up speed as it went. Barney's hands tightened on the support rail in front of him as the red brick roof and walls on each side flashed past and the cool air gusted up from the depths into his face. Then the light from above died behind them and it was suddenly black. Barney shut his eyes and prayed as he hurtled into the night.

When he opened them they were rushing towards a brick wall that was lit up and rising to meet them, and Barney thought his end had come. As he frantically looked towards the dark shape of Tosh beside him, the great wheel at the minehead was braked and the hutch lurched slightly as the cable tightened. Then it slowed as quickly as it had begun, rolling forward gently to stop four feet from the wall. Barney gasped for air feeling that his stomach was left somewhere up the shaft behind him, then he felt Tosh's big hand on his arm pulling him out of the hutch.

"Christ! Are ye fallin' asleep there, son. Come on! It's only the first time ye get scared. Ye'll soon get used to it." Barney's legs were still shaking as he followed Tosh away from the hutch and into a wide roadway with rails running into the darkness. Tosh sat Barney down on a wooden seat against the wall and stood facing him.

"Now Ah'm goin' tae tell ye all aboot this mine and how it works, and Ah'm only tellin' ye the once for when Ah'm talkin' we're no' workin'. So don't forget any o' it." Then Tosh talked in a slow quiet voice and Barney listened, trying hard to take in everything.

Tosh began with an explanation of the terms used by the miners. The tunnels that criss-crossed the mine and were the means of accessing the shale faces were called roads or levels. They were six to ten feet high and twelve feet wide, and they had to be blasted out of the shale seam which was fourteen feet high in Myrestane No. 4. The pillars of shale that remained between these levels were sixty to two hundred feet square depending on the height of the shale seam. The shale face where the men worked was called the bench and the miner's spot at the bench was called his place. Barney looked around the dank cavern, his mind frantically trying to take all this information in as Tosh droned on.

"There's different ones workin' doon here," Tosh said. "There's the faceman, like me. He bores holes intae the seam and sets the powder charges." Tosh patted the wall with a big hand. "Shale has to be blasted fae the seam because it's too hard for coal-cuttin' machines. The faceman is self-employed, a contractor, if ye know what that means, and gets paid on the amount o' shale he blasts oot. He supplies his ain tools, called his "graith" — that's a drill, pick and shovel, and the gunpowder used for blasting. The drawer — that's you Barney — has the joab o' loading the shale that's been blasted oot o' the seam, into a hutch, and manhandling the hutch tae a central point — maybe a hundred feet away — tae be sent tae the surface. It was all sounding very complicated to Barney as Tosh went on.

"Then there's men that work direct fur the company. They're called oncost men. That's the roadsmen — the squad who check the levels, renewing auld or decaying timber supports and laying the rails for hutches — and the chainrunners, who attach the full hutches to the endless rope haulage system that takes them to the surface. These hutches weigh five hundredweight when they're empty — a quarter o' a ton — and each wan carries up to a ton of shale when loaded."

Tosh then explained that, to make their wages, he and Barney, his drawer, had to send up three tons of shale a day.

That was called the "darg" or daily output — three tons, or sometimes more for more money. Each faceman had a pin or label that was put on the hutch so that the surface man could allocate the load to that faceman and drawer. Tosh's pin was a bottle top. At the top of the mine there was an inspector who examined the load of shale for blaes. Blaes was non oil-bearing shale that lay just above or below the seam, and the inspector was called the "crow picker".

"There now," Tosh said, "that will give ye an idea who everybody is and what their jobs are. Now, put a light to that wick on yer oil lamp and Ah'll tell ye aboot safety doon here before we go any further, and this is the bit that ye must remember if ye want tae survive."

Barney was attentive and appreciative of the lecture so far, but the mention of safety and survival brought back his terror at the descent and his ears pricked up.

Tosh sat down beside Barney on the seat, his face grown stern in the half-light of the wall lamps. "There are three things that cause accidents in the mine," he continued. "Falls of ground — that's when the roof comes doon on ye — runaway hutches, and explosions from gas in the workings." He watched Barney's face for a moment to let his words sink in. "Noo there's little that ye can dae in your job aboot the first two except tae be aware o' them and watch yerself. Now the gas…Ah'm goin' tae tell ye aboot the gas." Barney's eyes were transfixed on Tosh's face as the big man went on.

He explained that the air in the mine was regularly checked, every two hours before and throughout the shifts, by the fireman. The mine had two inclined shafts; one, where they had descended, called the "downcast"; the other, where the shale was hauled out called the "upcast". Ventilation fans above circulated the air to keep it free of gas. The gas, that the miners called "fire-damp", was a mixture of methane and air and exploded violently on contact with an open flame. After an explosion a gas was produced called "after-damp". This was carbon monoxide, tasteless and odorless and deadly.

"Listen tae me now, son!" Tosh raised his voice for the first time. "Aboot ten years ago, when Ah wis your age, Ah wis a drawer, just like you, in a mine no' far fae here. Ah had some good pals there." He stopped for a moment, reminiscing.

"Well onywey, four o' the boys went for a shite in the auld workin's. Ye know there are no toilets doon the mine and ye have tae go where ye can. But there's rules, son. Ye're no' supposed tae go ootside the ventilated areas. They weren't thinkin'. Anyway four o' them went, Jimmie Toal, Wullie MacDonald and the two Wilson brothers, jist laddies they were, drawers jist like yersel'. There was fire-damp in these workings. It was an unventilated area ye see, and they should have kent that. Yin o' their lamps ignited the gas and they were a' killed. Every wan o' them, blown tae bits. Guid laddies tae, a' guid laddies."

Tosh sniffed loudly as his eyes looked briefly up at the roof then returned to fix on Barney's face. "Rules, son. Ye have tae know the rules and ye have tae follow them. If ye do that ye might survive in the mine, but ye'll never be totally safe. There's nae such thing as totally safe doon here."

Barney was silent. "God save us, what a place," he breathed.

"Come on now!" Tosh said, getting to his feet. "That's yer lesson for now. Come and Ah'll show ye how tae mine shale!"

They walked through the levels, keeping away from the rails where hutches full of shale trundled passed them, Tosh striding out in front and Barney tripping behind him, trying to see his footing and keep the other's broad back in view in the darkness. After what seemed to Barney like a very long time, they arrived at Tosh's place. There Tosh unshouldered his graith, the drill and tools and gunpowder, and picked up a long timber shaft, about nine inches thick, that lay against the wall of shale.

"This is what they call a "boring tree"," he said. "Ah'm goin' tae show ye how shale is blasted, then you'll understand how we make oor money."

He fixed one end of the boring tree under the roof and the other end onto the "pavement", which was what he called the floor, and tightened it into position so that became a long firm prop. Then he took the hand-operated boring machine from his bag and held it out for Barney to see it. "Ye see that this end o' the machine, the barrel, has a spike sticking out. Well that spike fits into the hole there in the tree." Reaching back into the bag, he extracted a drill and fixed it to the other end of the boring machine. "This is a one and three-eighths inch drill, a foot long, four threeds tae the inch, and turning this ratchet handle will drill a one foot hole. Then Ah'll change the drill to a two foot one, then three feet.That way Ah'll make a hole five feet deep. Ye get it? It'll take an hour to drill five feet. Ah'll start it and you can take over and dae some drillin', seein' that ye'll have nae drawin' tae dae yet."

Barney learned quickly how to handle the boring machine and was relieved to get working as it took his mind off the mine and it's lurking dangers. He bored for a while, then cleared out the dust and debris from the hole, then bored again, changing to a larger drill when required. In just over an hour the hole was completed and Tosh signalled to him to take a break. Barney sat down against the shale face, the sweat cooling quickly on his face and body in the cold dank air of the mine.

"Where are ye steyin, " Tosh said, and Barney told him. "Christ there isnae much room at Granny Mccormack's. If she had any more lodgers she could start a hotel," he laughed. "Are ye married, son?"

Barney explained that he and Jeanie were married in Ireland barely a week earlier. Tosh grunted, giving a little nod.

Then Tosh got up and took out his gunpowder. Barney took an involuntary step backward.

"Now Ah pit aboot three pounds o' this powder in the hole, like this," he said, talking as he went, "and Ah' press it right intae the back o' the hole wi' this tool. It's called a stemmer." He held it up to Barney. "Ye see that it has a copper end on it. That's so that there'll be nae spark if Ah happen to hit a steel brace or anything in the wall."

He removed the stemmer from the hole. "Rules, son. Remember? Ah knew a faceman that couldnae get the stemmer a' the wey in — the hole hadnae been drilled straight, ye see — and so he rammed the powder in wi' a steel pinch bar. Boom! The charge went aff and that wis the end o' him."

All Barney's terror came rushing back. Explosions, gas, fall-ins. God, why did he come here? He would never get out of here alive. Jaysus, what a place. Tosh's low, even voice came piercing back through his imaginings. "Rules, son, safety rules. Always go bi the rules and ye'll be awright. Ah'm puttin' the fear o' God in ye, Ah know that. But Ah'm tellin' ye how tae survive doon here, so that you and yer new wife can earn good money and get a good place to stey, and you can live tae enjoy it. Aye, this is an awfae place tae make a livin'; dark and dusty and hot; rats everywhere and hutches rushin' doon the rails ready tae flatten ye if yer no watchin'; roofs comin' doon on ye and gas explosions that'll suffocate ye or burn the skin clean aff yer body if they dinnae kill ye first. An awfae place. A' ye can dae is mind the rules."

Tosh gathered up his tools and led Barney out of the place and back along the level. "Now Ah'm goin' tae set the charge, so we'll get well away. And one final rule. If a charge disnae go aff, you never, never go back tae it. Never! Ah go back after an hour. You stay away!"

On this occasion the charge did go off and Barney was deafened by the blast. Down came the shale in great chunks and little ones and the blinding, choking dust filled the level as the droning ventilator fans worked to clear it. A hutch was delivered by some unseen hand into the place, and Barney, his schooling behind him, started the hardest day's work of his young life so far, lifting the shiny jagged lumps into the hutch.

After a few hours, he stopped and ate his piece, the two men sitting in silence now, no further lectures coming from Tosh. Then Barney was glad to be at it again for it was only by strenuous effort that he could exclude the surroundings and their dangers from his mind.

Tosh worked with pick and shovel, clearing the shale from the bench for his drawer to load and remove. He was beginning to take to the little Irishman. They were good workers, the

Irish. He was sorry that he had to frighten him so much on his first day, but if it would keep him safe, Tosh was glad. He had seen too much in his years down here. Too many friends had never made it. It was a matter of rules, he pondered. It was like working in Hell. All any of them had were the rules.

When the place was cleared Tosh set more shots to blast the shale, and when a hutch was filled Barney pushed it away to where it would be drawn up above and another hutch came in to be loaded. Tosh and Barney worked well together and a mutual respect flourished. How a man worked, his attitude and his application to work, this was how he measured up among his peers. Teamwork was everything at the face, and while nothing was said, each man made his own silent assessment of the others. It was a long shift and the sun was well down in the western sky when Tosh and Barney emerged into the daylight.

Barney breathed in the fresh evening air. As he made his way back to his lodgings, he was struck by the clarity of things, almost as if he had never seen them before: the bright blue of the sky; the green of the grass; the reddish orange of the bing.

New life emanated from these vivid, dazzling surroundings. It rolled over him like a great wave on a warm beach, enveloping his weary, dusty frame. It put a sudden energy in his step and a glowing smile on his face. He strode out along the little path that ran along the edge of the bing, buoyed up by the wave, eager to see Jeanie, to embrace her and kiss her sweet lips.

A long way behind him on the same path, Tosh Douglas trudged wearily home. He too would be reunited with his love. He would have a bowl or two of kail and she would lay out his bathtub in the kitchen and scrub his back. Then he would sit by the fire in clean vest and long underpants, what he called his "semmit and drawers", and he and Peg would talk about their day.

Theirs was another kind of love.

Chapter
Five

❧ ❧ ❧

Poems ran through the mind of Peg Douglas as she knelt down in front of the little fireplace at number 9 Station Raw, vigorously applying black lead to the grate; snippets of verses; long reams of verses; silent, uplifting music. Mostly there was a sadness in them that their long-dead singers had handed on to her, a parting from beauty.

I flew to the pleasant fields traversed so oft
In life's morning march, when my bosom was young;
I heard my own mountain goats bleating aloft,
And knew the sweet strain that the corn reapers sung.
                                        Thomas Campbell

He saw once more his dark-eyed queen
Among her children stand;
                                        H.W.Longfellow

No marvel that the Lady wept, — there was no land on earth
She loved like that dear land, although she owed it not her birth:
It was her mother's land, the land of childhood and of friends,
                                        H.G.Bell

These were her father's poems. They were all that he had left to her.

When the grate shone, the polished handles of its hot water tank bright against its black ribs, Peg rose from her knees, sweeping back the strands of dark hair that had escaped from the roughly tied bun on her crown, and wiping her hands on her apron. She sat down at the table by the window to look out at Myrestane Station. Tosh would be home soon and she would have to get the dinner on and fill the boiler for his bath water.

Peg Douglas ran her life to certain self-imposed routines. Her work, her recreation and her worship all fell into a seven-day cycle that never wavered. She did the washing on Monday, ironing on Tuesday, cleaning, polishing, and visiting on Wednesday, darning, sewing and reading on Thursday, and on Friday she made a huge pot of soup that lasted until Sunday, feeding family and visitor. It was a broth of kail, turnips and beef with a flavour that improved by the day. She called Sunday's soup "three day soup" and it had accumulated body and flavour that could not be matched. The rigid disciplines of Peg's life would become so instilled over the years that even occasions of great joy or of tragedy would be tailored and fitted into her days so that their impact would be tempered, and blended with normality.

Sitting at the window, she saw the Edinburgh train pull alongside the platform and the few passengers make their way down the long flight of wooden stairs that overlooked the Station Raw. Watching the train leave, Peg thought of the early days in Edinburgh and how happy they had all been then. Her father was a schoolteacher, and she remembered how she and little Tommy used to run outside and down the path of their front garden in Merchiston every day to welcome him home from work. He would gather up Tommy and take her by the hand and rush into the house amid giggling and laughing. Then he would kiss her mother. Every day he kissed her.

She had never known anyone so exciting as her father. He sang and played the piano. He read poems to her and showed her how to read them, how to stand and how to hold her hands. "Elocution" he called it. Following the motions and the inflexions of his voice, the readings would bear her away, out of the room and into some distant land or time, away to where her father was. When she was with him, the world opened up to her. There was no place she could not go and no one she couldn't meet in the flesh. It was as if she could hold onto her father's coat-tails and fly across space and time.

When her father died they were suddenly poor, but Peg discovered that the poems were still there and she could still hear the music.

When she married Tosh, she wondered if she loved him. Now, four years later, Peg knew that love was no mystery; not real love, not lasting love. Love was doing for each other, being good to each other, living out a life with each other. It was being friends and partners. And if her husband was a bit jealous at times with a drink in him, and if she could not share her poems or her songs with him, these things didn't matter because love was deeper than that, and stronger, and it wouldn't perish on a whim.

Peg was smiling, thinking about her husband's totally irrational jealousy of an accordion player called Wullie Begbie who lived with his mother in the Raws and talked like a woman, the kind of man that gave no husband reason for jealousy, when she saw Tosh turning into the end of the Raw, striding out, his graith bag slung over his shoulder and his bonnet slightly askew. Now she had a glowing fire of coals in the grate and the water simmering in the boiler. She had lifted down the tin bath from behind the door and placed it in front of the fire. Her man was coming home.

The Station Raw consisted of eight terraced houses with a shop at one end. Each house had a room and kitchen and a scullery with a sink and a boiler with a fire under it. Attached to the scullery was a tiny water closet. The house next door to Peg had become vacant. Tosh had contacted the rent man to put in a word for Barney O'Shea, his drawer at the mine, and the O'Sheas had moved in a week ago.

It was Saturday night and Peg had invited Barney and Jeanie to come next door for a cup of tea. She had made scones and would set out her linen tablecloth that her mother had embroidered when she was young, and they would have a fine time.

Peg loved to meet new people and talk and tell stories, and maybe sing a song or two if the company was right. She had a host of songs. In the circle of her friends, each was identified by their favourite song. The song gave each one of them dimension, and stamped their essence on her mind. Even when they had passed on, their song brought back the memory of them.

No day passed for Peg without the recollection of a song and its singer: *The March o' the Cameron Men* was her uncle John who had never returned from Flanders; *Afton Water* was Shug Cavanagh, a neighbour in the Raw; *Ae Fond Kiss* was Big Wally Simpson from the Randy Raws, and on and on it went.

Peg's own marker, of the many that she knew, was *Dark Lochnagar,* and she was a beautiful singer.

Other things too delighted Peg. She went once a week to the picture house in Myrestane, what they called the "geggie", to roar with laughter at the hilarious antics of Charlie Chaplin and Buster Keaton and to weep at the trials of the beautiful Mary Pickford. She followed the career of Jack Dempsey, heavyweight champion of the world, and faithfully pasted his news cuttings into her scrapbook. Celebrities fascinated Peg, as they fascinate all those who are dreamers and wishers, and for whom it would be unthinkable to merely live out the ordinary, humdrum days of their lives.

Poverty and hardship were hurdles to be conquered with the help of God, and God was never far from Peg's thoughts. She praised Him daily in her mind, and she met Him weekly in St. Nicholas Church. For her the words, "I am the resurrection and the life", were no mere cant. Loving her neighbour was a joyous privilege.

"God bless all here," Barney O'Shea said, as he came through the door, his cap in his hand and his face scrubbed red from his bath.

It was the Inishennan greeting and it flowed unconsciously from his lips. Peg's beaming smile answered it as she invited them to sit at the table.

"Sit yersel' doon son," Tosh said, rising from his chair by the fireside.

"Jeanie and I are much obliged to you, Mistress, for helping us to get the house next door. It's a great house altogether, isn't it Jeanie?" Barney said. Jeanie O'Shea nodded quietly, smiling to Peg.

"Well, you'll be glad to have your own place. Now, if there's anything you need, don't you be shy about telling us." Peg said, returning Jeanie's smile. "I'll put the kettle on for a mouthful o' tea."

Soon the young couple were at their ease, and the talk went from one thing to another, Peg making the conversation. She told them about the neighbours in the Raw, describing every one, what family they had, how long they had been there and where they were from. She asked them about Ireland, and whether they had been yet to the chapel and met Father Byrne, and she mentioned a host of the Irish ones she knew.

Peg had a secret admiration for the Catholic Church. Though proud of her Presbyterian roots, she still harboured a kind of longing to share in the strong and very visible ties of the Catholics.

After tea, Tosh suggested to Barney that they might go for a walk and see if they could pick up a rabbit or two. Barney readily accepted for the men in the Raws were not accustomed to long conversations with womenfolk. It was an understood thing that the sexes should maintain their own company, and Peg and Jeanie were just as happy to be left to themselves to discuss women's things.

It was a windy night with still an hour of daylight remaining as the men made their way out of the village and along the edge of the fields that bordered Houstoun Wood. A perfect night for setting snares, as Tosh explained it. Rabbits travelled further from their burrows when it was windy. Where faint tracks in the grass showed the rabbit runs, Tosh set his brass wire snares over the runs. Sometimes, where the run ran under a fence wire, he tied the long arm of the snare to that wire, arranging the noose to hang vertically below it in the path of the run. At other spots he staked the arm into the earth with a wooden stake.

"If we get a shower o' rain now, it'll take away the human scent," he said. "Aye, this is a perfect night for them. We'll come up first thing in the mornin' and see what we've got. Man, Ah think it will be rabbit stew the morn. Dae ye like rabbit stew?" When Barney said he had never had it, Tosh feigned a look of surprise.

"What! Never had it! Man ye've a treat waitin' for ye, son. My Peg'll show that wee lassie o' yours how tae make a rabbit stew, and once ye've tasted it, ye'll be up here every night when ye're no' workin'."

Barney laughed. The sun was nearly down now and he felt a spot of rain on the wind. They had emerged from the wood and he looked across the fields that sloped down to the burn where he had walked out with Jeanie. He could pick out the lights of Strathalmond below them, and hear the distant barking of a dog. There was a scent on the breeze and a soft feel of grass under his feet. He was seeing the world again for the first time, in the way that only miners saw it. He had a place of his own, and a friend, and the pangs of homesickness for Inishennan had all but faded from his mind.

"That's Strathalmond doon the hill there," Tosh said, striding on home now to beat the rain. "The Ingrams, them that own the Work, that's where they live."

Tosh chuckled. "Ah wonder whit new surprises they've got cooked up for us tonight."

"Surprises?" Barney said. Tosh looked back.

"Aye, son. Surprises. But no' really surprises, for we a' know whit's comin'. There's a merger o' the different Works. Aye, it'll be mair work for us, and less pay. Ye can bet on that. We'll hear a' aboot it. Jist wait and see. But come on, son! Get a move on, back tae the hoose before we get soaked."

When the men left, darkness fell on the valley of the Beugh

Burn. Not far from where Tosh and Barney walked, within view of Strathalmond, a boar hunt had once begun on the dark chilly dawn of a different time.

∽ ∽ ∽

In the months that followed the O'Sheas' visit to Tosh and Peg, the talk was all of the merger. Rumours buzzed around the Work like bees, becoming ever more laden wherever they alighted. A whispered five per cent wage reduction in the mine became seven per cent by the time it reached the retorts, and ten per cent at the top of the bing. There were no official announcements of changes to work or conditions, but the men knew that something was in the air.

Barney ignored their growing concerns. He and Jeanie had never been so well off. He had become a capable drawer, putting his back into the grinding work and always keeping his mind on the rules, prompted by Tosh's periodic reminders. Jeanie had her fine little house, which she kept as clean as a whistle, and her holy pictures on the walls. He and Jeanie never missed Mass on Sunday, and after it they stood around the gates of the chapel, mingling with their countrymen and talking in the Irish. They could afford to send a pound or two home every month, and Barney always had the price of a few pints for a Saturday night. Occasionally Tosh would go with him for a drink, though not regularly, for Tosh took a certain curious pride in declaring that he was "not a drinking man".

Late in September, the notice board at the Work carried a brief announcement about the merger, and a newspaper cutting that referred to the British Government's investment in the Anglo-Persian Oil Company that had been set up to exploit British oil discoveries in Persia. Tosh and Barney took a walk to the Myrestane Hotel. It was an old coaching inn, built before 1800, lying then on the Edinburgh-Glasgow Turnpike. Fifty years later, the advent of the railway link had snuffed out its original function in a few weeks. Now it was an informal, and frequently rowdy, meeting place for the men from the Work.

When they pushed their way up to the bar, the debate had already started. Wee Tammy Flynn, a cocky little man with a beak for a nose and a small head that bobbed up and down when he talked, was rattling on to George Crawford. They were both surface men. George worked on the retorts and Wee Tammy — well nobody in the work really knew what Wee Tammy did exactly. He moved about the Work like a little ghost, a long-handled brush in his hand, sometimes on the breaker where the shale was crushed for retorting, sometimes in the candle works, sometimes on the floor of the retorts.

What they did know was that Tammy was a part-time fiddler at dances, and a self-appointed union organiser.

"Ah tellt yez! Ah tellt yez!" Tammy was saying. "Yez should a' be in the union. Then the Ingrams will no' find it sae easy tae walk all over yez. But did yez listen? No! And noo yez are a' worried aboot yer jobs. But it's no' too late, George," now addressing his remarks to his one hopeful convert, "to join the union. Ah've got the papers right here in ma pocket."

George Crawford took a slow gulp of his pint of beer and turned his long sad face on Tammy. "Union, my arse Tammy," he said.

At that, a man standing further along the bar shouted over to Tammy.

"Tammy! What goes through the Work and through the Work, and never touches the work?"

Before Tammy could reply, the speaker shouted the answer. "Tammy Flynn's brush!" and the group nearest to him rocked with laughter.

Tammy, eyes shifting in his little head, ignored the joke made at his expense and concentrated on George Crawford as he tried a different tack.

"Ye're sayin' that because ye're controlled, George. And d'ye know what controls ye?" The men began to take an interest and Tammy paused to make his point to the gathering audience.

"Fear! That's what. Fear! The oldest weapon in the book."

Now Tammy had everyone's attention, and he forged on with his lecture.

"The managers ask ye if ye're a member o' the union, and ye're delighted tae tell 'im ye're not. They put a miner in places where the seam isnae regular, or there's bad clearment for shovellin', and he's too feared tae refuse." Tammy took a break for a mouthful of his pint, looking around his captive audience for support.

A voice from along the bar cut the long silence. "Whit the hell dae you know aboot miners?"

The speaker, a broad, barrel-chested man, pushed through the crowd to face Wee Tammy. It was Mooney who worked on the bing, the one everybody called Shine Mooney. He was the hardest man in Myrestane, and he was a bit the worse for drink.

Shine Mooney was a time bomb waiting to explode, and alcohol was the fuse. He did what was recognized as the hardest job in the Work. He collected the hutches from the chain at the very top of the bing, where they arrived overflowing with the fiery refuse from the retorts. With rags round his hands and his head bent over the hot shale, he pushed their ton weight, still smoking and burning, to the very edge, heaving the box of the hutch upwards with his head against its hot steel, to deliver the contents over the side in a slide of fumes and smoke. He did this for eight hours at a time, six days a week, summer and winter, so that the rigid repetition of it burned into his nature and set there as hard as the steel he pushed.

Shine was a different kind of man, revered by some and avoided by most. Every man at the bar had seen him lift a fifty-six pound weight on each pinkie and clap them together above his head, eyeing onlookers with bold, challenging eyes. Some had seen him in a fight, pounding an unsuspecting adversary in a vicious, drunken rage. Now the bar cleared like magic around Shine and Wee Tammy Flynn.

"Ye know, Ah'm getting' sick o' listenin' tae you and yer bloody union," Shine growled, his eyes widening with a growing rage. "See you!" he went on, prodding a fat finger into Tammy's chest that rocked him back on his heels. "You're nothin' but an agitatin' wee bastard." Tammy's face went white and his head bobbed with involuntary jerks like a puppet on a string. The bar went quiet.

"Ah'm gonnae fix you once and for all, yah wee bastard that ye are. There'll be nae mair talk aboot unions when Ah'm done wi' ye."

As Shine advanced on him, Tammy staggered back until he was against the bar. He had nowhere to turn. The faces of the men around him turned away from his pleading eyes, trying to hide their own shame.

"Jist a minute, Sir!" Shine heard the low steady voice behind him just as he felt a huge hand clamp down on his shoulder. "There's nae need for that".

Shine turned his head to look up at the stern, towering shape of Tosh Douglas. In the seconds of total silence that followed, Wee Tammy sidled his way along the bar and into the crowd. Shine turned fully around, eyes blazing with anger.

Tosh's hand adjusted its grip and his calm, unflinching stare fixed on Shine's face. "You're done here, Shine," he said quietly. "Finish yer drink now and go hame tae yer wife."

Shine tried to shake loose from the hand that held him, but it merely tightened on his shoulder. He looked frantically around the bar but could catch no eye. The silence dragged on. Then it was broken by the scuffling of feet and low whispered voices, almost imperceptible at first, then growing, getting louder, a mix of relief and courage being resurrected.

Tosh released his hold, his stare still level and unblinking. After a long moment, Shine shrugged his shoulders and, with no word spoken, turned back to the bar.

"Give us anither drink!" he shouted to the barman. "Whit are ye waitin' fur? Christmas?"

The Myrestane Inn was back in business. "Ah've got the papers in ma pocket, George," Wee Tammy shouted to George Crawford.

Chapter Six

ососо

On the same night that David Ingram ran all the way from the train and up the long driveway of Strathalmond to announce to Old Sam that he was now a fully-fledged solicitor, Peg Douglas carefully pasted into her scrapbook the cutting of Jack Dempsey's knockout victory over the Frenchman, Georges Carpentier, in Jersey City.

It was 1921 and Rudolph Valentino had just tangoed his way into Peg's other life.

ососо

That afternoon, when the marks had been announced, David was called into the presence of the partners, who sat, in a semicircle, on leather upholstered chairs, backed by a high rise of library shelves close packed from floor to ceiling with leather-backed volumes of Session Cases.

They were all there: Ewan Cameron Cunningham, ancient but unchanged, as if he had somehow got stuck in time; his sons, Andrew and Edward Cunningham, referred to as "Mr. Andrew" and "Mr. Edward", short in stature and like their father but without his spark, and Angus McCulloch, the pale pinched-faced son of Ewan's long deceased partner and co-founder of the firm, Eugene Bracken McCulloch.

Even the newly qualified apprentice, David Ingram, could see that Andrew was the leader. And now he spoke to David.

"Firstly, Mr. Ingram, my partners and I congratulate you on your success in the final examinations of the Law Society. We are impressed by your application and attention to duty in the time that you have been with us." He looked around the table and received some decrepit nods of approval before continuing. "The partners are prepared to offer you a post of assistant solicitor with the firm, which we trust that you will be disposed to accept."

It briefly occurred to David that the offer was put in such a way that refusal was not contemplated. In the eyes of Andrew Cunningham, an offer made to an apprentice to join the firm of Cunningham and McCulloch W.S., was an undoubted privilege made available to few. David knew, of course, that the firm handled the legal affairs of Sam Ingram as well as Strathalmond Oil Company and the newly incorporated Strathalmond Oils Limited, and this fact had no small influence on his new appointment. Nevertheless he was delighted and it showed in his face and his ready acceptance.

"Thank you, Mr. Andrew," he said. Perhaps, at last, he would be given access to some real legal work, and escape from the stern command of Herbert McAllister and the endless conveyancing.

"Good. Then that is settled," Andrew Cunningham said brusquely. "From Monday you will be in the trust department where you will work under the guidance of our trust clerk, Miss Violet Walker. Be good enough to report to her when you leave us, and advise her of that."

After a few moments of silence, during which Andrew studied papers in front of him and the others chatted to each other, David realised that the interview was concluded and he turned to leave. As he opened the door, Andrew looked up.

"Mr Ingram, I do not believe that I have dismissed you, sir." As David mumbled a flustered apology, the partner went on.

"You may go. But in future, be kind enough to wait until you have permission to do so."

David turned to the door once more and Mr. Andrew added, " By the way, as from Monday you will take your morning tea break with the assistants on the second floor. Please now report to Miss Walker."

David was glad to be out in the corridor. He must remind himself, he thought, about the morning break. Ten-minute tea breaks were taken by partners on the third floor, assistants on the second floor, Mr. McAllister and Miss Walker in their own little lounge off the conveyancing room, and secretaries and others on the ground floor. The location of tea breaks expressed itself as a daily reminder of the pecking order in Cunningham and McCulloch, Writers to the Signet.

☙ ☙ ☙

There are some who take genuine pleasure from the success of others. They harbour no concealed envy, nor sentiments of grudge nor meanness of spirit. They are happy for the other person. Old Sam Ingram was one; Peter Ingram was not.

When David announced his news, Sam's old face lit up and he stepped forward to envelope his grandson in a powerful, bone-crushing hug. Peter smiled thinly and proffered his hand, as if he were welcoming a newcomer to the Linlithgow and Stirlingshire Hunt. After a few minutes of congratulatory chat, David took his leave and descended to the kitchen to lord it among the servants. Sam and Peter returned to their discussion.

"There is no other solution, father," Peter went on, standing by the table and poring over the spread of documents and accounting records. "The workforce will have to be cut by twenty per cent across the industry, and the wages of the men who remain will be down at least ten per cent in addition to the recent cuts. I have listed here the mines to be closed and the retorts and candle factories." He reached out the list to Sam who ignored it, and, shaking his head, walked to the fireplace.

"If there is an alternative, I would be happy to hear it," Peter continued.

Sam Ingram's face set in a frown. "There'll be a strike, Peter, if the wages go down again. Then what happens to production?"

"Production, father, isn't the issue," Peter said, his voice growing with his frustration. "It's profit that's the issue!"

It was always the same, Peter thought. The old man was impossible to talk to about cuts. He had never stopped living in the good old days of the shale, the golden years before the war when annual shale production reached over three million tons. Then there were big profits, big dividends for shareholders, and fat wage packets and inexpensive houses for the workers. Peter tried again.

"Father, look at the Raeburn works. Three hundred workers are producing over eight hundred tons of shale each day. It has three hundred and fifty-two retorts arranged in six benches, a naptha recovery plant, a sulphate of ammonia house and a power station. It used to be the only crude works to treat and produce its own petroleum. Production is not its problem, father. There is no limit to the shale that it could produce over the next fifty years. Its men work hard, and I don't doubt its efficiency. But, father, it is losing money. Every day that it continues to operate, it is costing the company money because we can't get a decent price for the output. If a strike closed that place tomorrow, we would be better off for it would cut our losses."

"And would the miners be better off, or the retort men?" Sam said sharply. "What about these three hundred workers and their families? They rely on us Peter. They draw our wages and they live in our houses. What do we tell them, eh? Do we show them that piece of paper you have there in your hand? Eh?"

Sam was getting worked up. It was always thus when Peter tried to explain his decisions to his father. It was useless, Peter thought. Old Sam didn't see figures any more, only people for whom he felt responsible. Why did he keep trying to explain things to Sam? He had power of attorney. In future he would just get on with what had to be done and say nothing to his father. Then Peter realised that he wouldn't do that. He would likely always try to argue the right in his decisions, justify them to his father, and likely he would always fail.

Peter gathered up the papers from the desk. "Well, Father, I think we have exhausted the topic. I have to go now and see the accountants. I'll be back later." With that, Peter left and Sam sank into his chair by the fire.

Sam was sick over the whole business. He wished things could be as they had been before, when Sam Ingram could walk into the Myrestane Inn at lunchtime for a pint of beer, and have a drink with a miner without the knowledge that the man was going to be jobless and homeless and that he, Old Sam, was the cause of it. He began to wish that Peter would make his decisions without consulting him. Then he wouldn't know about them. It would be better if he didn't know.

Peter, with profit still on his mind, rang for his manservant to pack his overnight bag, telling him to advise the Master, Sam Ingram, that he would be spending the night at the George Hotel in Edinburgh. Then he made his way out the front door to his Rolls Royce Silver Ghost, one of the two joys of his life. It was the only one of its kind in the county, 7.428cc and 50hp., the choice of the late Russian Tsar and of Peter Ingram of Strathalmond. He allowed nobody else to drive it, for only he, of the inhabitants of Strathalmond, had attended the Rolls-Royce driving school. It was there that he had engaged the services of a travelling Rolls-Royce mechanic who came to Strathalmond to carry out regular maintenance.

A Rolls-Royce Silver Ghost, of course, never broke down. Although Peter had heard that on occasion one might "fail to proceed," he had never had that experience himself. It moved down the driveway with the almost inaudible purr that Peter Ingram had grown to accept as the measure of his success in life. It cruised down through Myrestane and past the Myrestane Inn where a few of the locals regarded it with wonder, and on towards the capital.

Tomorrow Peter would visit the accountant. Tonight he had other plans.

◈◈◈

Violet Walker, bookkeeper and trust clerk in the firm of Cunningham and McCulloch W.S., had lived in the same house for all of her forty-two years. It was a tall, narrow, two-storey villa in a quiet cul-de-sac on the edge of Morningside where former grandeur had been overtaken by the years.

Her father had been an insurance man six days a week and a lay preacher in the Church of God on Sundays, and her mother, one of his flock. Every Sabbath, when Violet was growing up, her parents kept an open house for serving girls of the district to whom they would serve tea and scones and read stories from the Bible. It was an unbridled sharing of the affection that should have been hers.

When her parents died, just before the war, the endless sermons died with them, and Violet inherited the house and a sizeable annuity, laid in by her father years before, and she had devoted her life to Jane Austin and to Cunningham and McCulloch where she had been for the last twenty-four years. It was only in the last ten of these years that a new devotion had grown.

In the firm where being qualified in the law was the yardstick by which Mr. Andrew and Mr. David measured human attributes, Violet's position was unique.

She handled the funds and prepared the accounts for a host of family trusts; she attended the annual meetings of their trustees to whom she was known personally and by whom she was considered the prime guardian of their respective accumulations of wealth. Partners and clients alike deferred to her accounting skills, and she had inveigled her way into their families through the black and white columns of her ledgers. She knew them all: grandfathers and grandchildren; wives and sweethearts; white sheep and black sheep; all the private beneficiaries of the rich.

She knew David Ingram long before he had ever set foot in Scotland. She knew his father and his grandfather, his mother and his uncle, for she had handled the Ingram trusts for twenty years. Now he was here in her office, a handsome young replica of his father and a most fortunate ward of his grandfather.

David was learning about trusts and accounts from the best of teachers and after a few weeks he began to understand something of Miss Walker's passion for balancing and presentation. He performed well and showed a genuine interest, and she became less distant. She began to laugh and recount anecdotes from her past. She took to appearing in the mornings more colourfully dressed, and sometimes sat on the desk and swung her legs. David blushed with embarrassment, not knowing exactly why.

When his time in the trust department came to an end, he was moved upstairs to assist Mr. Angus McCulloch whose area of law was litigation. David would spend the next year or so researching legal points and trudging back and forth to the Parliament House, delivering briefs to the black boxes that were maintained by the Faculty of Advocates in the long lobby of that ancient building.

Violet Walker went back to the drab tweeds of her former existence, taking her excitement on weekdays from the surrogate acquaintances that dwelt in her ledgers.

Saturdays were the thrilling days for her. On Saturdays she left work at noon, and made her way home by way of the library where she picked out her favourite novels. In the afternoon she would prepare the table for her weekly visitor, and take a leisurely bath. Then, clad only in her bathrobe, she would stretch by the fire and wallow in the daydreams of Jane Austin or the Bronte sisters.

Her visitor arrived, always on time, at eight o'clock in the evening. To herself, and to none other, she called him the "Captain", a name she had stolen from Jane Austin's Captain Wentworth, a name that illuminated Violet Walker's existence.

At seven forty-five on the dot, Violet put on a black negligee with a low neckline that showed the swell of her ample breasts, and a hem, taken up by her own hand to cut across the highest part of her white thighs. She applied the faintest touch of rouge to her pallid cheeks and lavender to her throat, and when the bell rang, she opened the door to admit her Captain.

In he came, tall and handsome in his long dark cape, Violet Walker's reason for being: Peter Ingram of Strathalmond.

ରେ ରେ ରେ

When Peter Ingram's wage cuts were announced, yet another meeting was held in the Myrestane Inn. So many came that the bar was soon packed to overflowing and the meeting was adjourned to the adjoining building that had once been the stables.

While man after man came to the front to reiterate the extent of the cuts to the others who were well aware of them, and disgruntled voices rent the air but suggested no solutions, Wee Tammy Flynn worked like a beaver, handing out his "papers" in every direction for men to join the union.

After a lot of talk and a lot of shouting, during which the blame for the current plight had been laid on the Americans, the Russians, the Persians, the government and mostly on that bastard Peter Ingram who drove the fancy car and didn't give a toss for the men that paid for it, Barney O'Shea came forward, his tousled red hair standing up like a beacon and his face still black from his shift.

"Boys! " he began. "I have a suggestion to make." A few shouts of "Order" ran round the room, and the noise died down to a murmur.

"As you all know, I have not been here very long, but there is one man I have heard no word said against." The crowd quietened. " That man is Old Sam Ingram."

At the sound of the name, there were nods and low noises of approval.

"Now it seems to me, boys," Barney continued, looking around the men, "and as I say I have not been here too long, that maybe, if a man could go and see Old Sam, there might be something that could be done about this trouble we are havin'."

A general note of approval sounded from the assembly.

"Now I've been thinkin'," Barney went on, "that whoever would go and see Sam — to speak up, you understand, for the workers — would need to have piles of education."

At that remark several loud guffaws echoed from the crowd.

"Piles o' education! Christ Barney, the half o' us can hardly read or write. Jist march." The voice came from Wull Aicheson and it was drowned with resounding laughter.

"Auld Findlater saw tae that!" The laughter surged once more.

Barney saw at once that this was some kind of local joke, and he allowed the laughter to subside before pressing on.

"Well, there is wan person who could speak for us, wan that has the education to go up there to Strathalmond and put forward our case to Old Sam Ingram." The room became quiet.

"Peg Douglas," Barney said, with deliberate finality. "Mrs. Tosh Douglas should talk to Sam Ingram. That's all I have to say."

"But it's not right for a woman to represent us," Tammy Flynn interjected. "This is a matter for the union. A union representative should be going." He looked around for support.

"You go then, Tammy," a voice shouted out. "And take yer brush wi' ye. Maybe ye can clean up the mess the Ingrams are makin'." Loud laughter ensued.

"Tammy, we need education here . . . no speechification." More laughter, and Tammy skulked back to the bar. It was a thankless job, the union.

It took no time at all for Barney O'Shea's suggestion to be heartily endorsed, and only Wee Tammy Flynn complained that she was not a member of the union, and, what was worse, she was a woman.

On the way back up the dark road to Myrestane Station, Tosh plodded along in silence as Barney jogged here and there to keep up.

"What do you think Peg will say?' Barney asked, breath-lessly.

"How the hell would Ah know?" Tosh retorted, secretly buoyed up with pride for his Peg.

When they got back to 9 Station Raw, and Peg Douglas had put on the kettle and invited Jeanie next door for a cup of tea, the events of the meeting were recounted by Tosh. At the phrase "piles of education" Peg laughed so much that she took a coughing turn and Tosh had to clap her on the back. She was still laughing when Barney interjected.

"Will you go then, Peg? Will you go and see Old Sam?"

Peg hesitated. She thought about Peter Ingram and the day she ran away from Strathalmond. She had kept in touch with Hilda over the years. Hilda was in Myrestane now, with her coalman husband and four children, and from her Peg had learned of the death of Rachael Ingram and the changes in the household. Only Sam, Peter and young David lived there now. Mr. Makepiece had gone and the only servants left were Miss Hill, the housekeeper and Mrs. Woods, the cook. Peg's short stay in Strathalmond now seemed so long ago.

"Will ye go, Peg?" Barney repeated. Peg shook the memories from her head.

"Of course I'll go," she replied, smiling at the earnest look on Barney's face. Barney slurped his tea in relief.

"Great!" he exclaimed. "That would be great altogether." Then, looking at Tosh, he added, "What was that thing about education, about marchin?"

Tosh laughed and then explained to the Irishman.

"Every man in that pub tonight was at Myrestane High School, some longer than others." He smiled at Peg. "It was run by two men: Findlater, Major J.P. Findlater, the headmaster, and Smith, the janitor. Now Smith was an auld pig. He was an ex-sodger — an auld sergeant. You could hear the shouts fae him away up here at Myrestane Station when he was drillin' the laddies. He drilled the bairns wi' widden guns and some-times wi' dumbells, and he widnae think twice aboot drawin' the strap across their bare legs. It was seen as part o' their

education, drillin' them wi' guns in the front playground. Then
there was his partner, Findlater the heidmaister, a big fat man
wi' a waxed moustache. He wis in the Territorial Army. It was
Major J.P. Findlater. If anything went wrong in any o' the classes, it wis: 'Send for Major Findlater!' and he wid gie ye a wallop
wi' a leather strap as long as yer airm." Tosh reflected for a
moment. "Aye, many a one Ah got," he chuckled. "So ye see,
Barney, there wisnae much in the way o' education. Unless ye
were joinin' the army, that is."

Then, looking again at Peg, Tosh continued. "But ye were
right, son. Peg there got plenty o' education. She once went tae
a fancy school in Edinburgh. Her faither wis a teacher, ye
know."

"That'll do now, Tosh," Peg said, smoothing her pinafore
with the flat of her hand and pouring the tea. She was embarrassed, not by the fact of her early education but by the self-
effacing reference to it by her partner. She was ashamed that
she had taken a benefit that wasn't available to Tosh and the
others. She knew that the people in the Raws never, not even
for a moment, grudged her the legacy from her father, but she
felt a sadness for them, a heart-rending regret that so many
good men and women had to look to the likes of her for their
own missed opportunity.

Peg was honoured to be selected to speak to Sam Ingram.
She didn't know if it would make a difference. She only knew
that she would do her best for the men and women that she
admired.

Chapter
Seven

ॐॐॐ

Peg Douglas thought it an amazing thing that the men in the Work, with few exceptions, had chosen her as their spokesman. What was she, after all, but a twenty-three year-old housewife, and yet it was only Tammy Flynn and a few of his union converts that had opposed the idea, and that was only because Tammy thought that any talking should be done by the union.

It was even more amazing to her that not a one wanted to accompany her. They were happy for her to go on her own in the knowledge that she would do what she could. They were also under no illusions as to the chances of success, and, whatever the outcome, no blame would attach to her. Of all of this, Peg had been assured by the men and women of Myrestane.

A meeting was requested for Peg with Sam Ingram, and shortly thereafter she received an invitation, in Old Sam's flowing hand, to come to tea. Tea would be at five, and she was invited to come early, at four o'clock, so that they would have time to talk.

Peg walked alone between the big stone pillars at the end of the drive and along the avenue of trees that led to Strathalmond. Tall and erect, she wore the fitted suit that was her Sunday best and showed the slim line of her body. Her hair was strained into a bun beneath a large circular straw hat, lacquered and shiny black, that was fixed in place by a single silver-mounted pin. Around her shoulders hung a red fox fur fastened at the front with a tiny imitation gold chain.

The sun, glinting through the tall trees, dappled the drive in front of her and the towering, shimmering mansion thrust its history into Peg's poetic mind.

But hark ! the tramp of armed men ! The Douglas battle-cry!
They come — they come ! — and lo ! the scowl of Ruthven's
hollow eye !

A horn sounded behind her, and Peg jumped from her reverie as the silent Silver Ghost swept past. She caught a glimpse of Peter Ingram in the driver's seat and the long floppy face of his bloodhound that sat beside him. The dog reflected the preponderance of a pet to look like its master, and Peg's annoyance at her scare vanished into a smile as she thought about Wull Aicheson's remark on Peter and his travelling companion.

"Peter is the one with the hat on," Wull once said to his companions outside the Myrestane Inn, touching his cap to his benefactor as the Rolls-Royce passed by.

Peg reflected for a few seconds on the wild, glaring eyes of Peter Ingram as he pushed his face into hers, the smell of his breath and the grip of his hands. Then she gritted her teeth, the anger of the moment changing to resolve, and strode on along the drive. As she approached the house, the huge door swung open and Sam Ingram stepped out to greet her.

Peg Douglas had shared many a flickering moment in the company of the gentlemen of her books, but this was the first time, as an adult, that she had met one in the flesh. She had read enough to know a gentleman when she met one, and Sam Ingram did not come lacking. He led her into the morning room where a fire burned brightly in the hearth, and relieved her of the fox fur which she delicately proffered. She kept her hat on for she knew, from her father, that ladies did not take off their hats. She also knew intuitively that a woman in a hat is a more formidable creature than one without, and she was here for a purpose.

Sam talked incessantly to put her at her ease and he offered her a sherry which she politely declined. He felt as old men feel towards young women, protective and attracted, the one complimenting the other. He told her to call him Sam and he would call her Peg. Then he looked closely at her face. "You look familiar, Peg," he said. "Have we met before?"

Peg smiled. "Maybe it was when I brought you your dram in the bathtub," she said.

"Bathtub ... dram . . ." Sam mouthed the words as realisation dawned in his face. "The lassie! The servant lassie. Peg! Well, well!" He sat back in his chair, gazing at her in silence.

"I sometimes wondered what happened to you. You were here one day and gone the next. Did you have a falling out with Makepeace?"

Peg shifted uncomfortably in her seat. "No," she said. "Nothing like that. I was just needed at home, that's all," she said, maintaining a calm exterior.

"Well, well!" Sam repeated, shaking his head. "But tell me now, how is Tosh? You know, that man of yours is one of the best miners I ever knew. I wish we had a hundred like him." Peg didn't know how well he knew Tosh but she inclined her head graciously.

"He's fine, thank you, but like all the others he's worried, Sam," she said quietly.

"Aye," Sam breathed. He got up and walked to the fireplace where his glance fell briefly on the photograph of William. Peg followed his eyes. "That's Colonel Ingram," she said. Their eyes met and Sam Ingram could feel the sympathy that flowed from this young woman, this wee lassie that sat in front of him. She understood him. She felt his grief, this bit of a girl from the miners' rows.

"It's an awful thing to lose a son, Peg," he said.

A picture flashed into Peg's mind.

She was propped up in bed, white and spotless; white sheets at her chin, white pillows one on one; white night gown tied at the neck with a white bow. Red coals glowed in the grate opposite. She could see them round the edge of the curtain that screened the bed. A thick odour of disinfectant hung in the air of the little kitchen.

Then Doctor Rennie stood in front of her holding a small bundle wrapped in a white shawl. He was shaking his head slowly from side to side.

"He was perfect, Peg. Not a mark on him." He looked down at the tiny face. "Just no life — that's all. It wasn't to be, my dear."

Everything was white. White was no colour. It was the colour of no life.

Peg was going to call him Christopher.

It was her second tragic loss in two years; her brother first, and now her baby.

She remembered going later to a young mother in the Raw who had just been delivered of twins, and asking her for one of the twins. That was five years ago, about the same time that William Ingram died in that hellish war. The time that God had come into Peg's life.

"It's an awful thing to lose a son," Peg repeated Sam's words in a whisper.

∞ ∞ ∞

Tea was served in the resplendent drawing room.

Old Sam had gone out of his way to give it a feel of informality, having it laid out on a small table that was placed between them. It had been a long time since Peg had eaten scrambled eggs on toast with silver cutlery, or drunk tea from a delicate china cup on which the thin lined figures of mandarins leaned from the balconies of exotic bowers.

"I know fine why you're here, Peg," Sam said, touching the corner of his mouth with a linen napkin. "This is a terrible time for the industry."

"A strike will be a worse time, Mr. Ingram. Is there nothing you can do to avert it?" When Sam made no reply, she continued. "The men sent me here because they trust you." Peg's eyes wandered round the room. "Even though you come from all this, they look at you as one of them, someone who cares about what happens to them, someone who began in the Work and wrought on the shale face, just like them."

The hurt that creased Sam Ingram's old face at that moment made Peg wish that she had swallowed her words. She was ashamed, ashamed of her cruelty to the old man, ashamed of her cutting accusation. This was a man that had built an industry that had fed and housed thousands of people, and she had just used the comforts of his retirement against him. She thought of what Tosh once said when he looked out the window from Station Raw onto the bing.

"Ah can see mah whole life fae this windae, Peg. Blood, sweat and tears. There it is, up on that bing."

She suddenly realised that Sam Ingram was no different. He too saw the bing every day from the wide, shuttered windows of Strathalmond.

It was clear to Peg that Peter Ingram made the decisions now, and she resolved to shame Old Sam no longer. "Do you think I might talk to Peter Ingram?" she said. Sam looked relieved.

"Of course, my dear," he said. "I'll just go and see if he is available." With that, Old Sam left the room.

Peg had resolved to put her first encounter with Peter Ingram out of her mind. He had no place in the life of Peg Douglas, nor would she give him any. She sat upright in a chair that had been designed for relaxation but could only serve that purpose to those whose style of life took it for granted. Looking around her, she felt elated to be a part of something that her early dreams had pictured for her. The silent elegance of the room enveloped her, uplifting her spirit as her chin tilted upward and her shoulders pressed back. She turned her head only slightly as Peter Ingram entered the room followed by Old Sam. Peter walked purposely towards her extending his hand.

"Mrs. Douglas," he said, giving her hand an almost imperceptible shake. "Father tells me that you want to speak to me."

He took a seat opposite her and she could feel his eyes running over her, lingering here and there. Old Sam stood by the window. In the first few moments of silence, Peg realised that Peter Ingram didn't know her. He never had known her. To him she wasn't a person. She was just a vulnerable girl that had floated into his path.

"I was nominated by the men in the Work, Mr. Ingram, to come here." Peg's voice was clear and firm.

"Oh yes?" Peter intoned, the semblance of a smile appearing at the corners of his large mouth.

"Yes," Peg repeated, maintaining her calm demeanour. "They are concerned about the wage cuts and the possible closures." When Peter Ingram made no move to reply, she continued. "These wage cuts will have a dire affect on hundreds of hard-working families, sir, and there will be a strike that will benefit nobody. Perhaps you might reconsider your decisions."

Peter Ingram sat silent for a long time. He glanced at Sam who looked down at the carpet, then looked back at Peg, the proud tilt of her head, the long slim neck and the steady grey eyes that fixed on his own. His irritation at being once more put in the position of the profit-seeking ogre riding down the crops of the struggling poor, mingled with his admiration for this young woman.

"Mrs. Douglas, what you are asking is not possible. My father, there, has already asked it. If it were in my power to cancel the wage cuts and still make a profit, I would do it. But it is not. I am not going to go into all the reasons for this, Mrs. Douglas. I can tell you that foreign competition and lower oil prices will eventually finish this industry. I am doing everything I can to extend that eventuality as far as possible into the future. A fortune has already been spent on technical improvements to retorts and mining methods so that your hundreds of families still have work. If there is a strike, so be it. You are correct. It would help nobody and I can assure you that it would only hasten the evil day. If you can give me an alternative solution, I will be happy to listen to it."

"Profit would seem to be the key to the problem," Peg said. "A cut in profit might be preferable to a cut in wages," she continued, her eyes once more taking in the luxurious surroundings.

Peter caught the meaning in her look. "I can see that you have been listening to Mr. Flynn and his union friends," he smirked. "Profit, my dear, is an essential part of the continuation of the Work. Without profit for the investors, we may as well close the doors right now. It is profit, as you so correctly point out, that is the key. It is also the solution. Mr. Flynn, I'm afraid will never understand that. There might have been a time when profits could be cut; that was when dividends were soaring over fifty per cent; that was when people like us were able to accumulate all the trappings that you see around you. But that time has gone, my dear. If Sam Ingram discovered oil shale in his backyard today, he couldn't build an industry. There are too many places in the world where oil is running out of the ground."

Peter stood up. "Really, Mrs Douglas, I wish I could help. I have the feeling that you can understand me even if the men can't, or won't. It was very nice to meet you, but now I must go. I'm sure that my father will see you out."

With that Peter nodded stiffly to Peg and left the room with a glance at Sam.

Peg felt a sudden emptiness. The visit was all for nothing. She understood what Peter Ingram had told her, that the Work would come to an end and there was nothing that the Ingrams or the workers could do about it. She didn't care for Peter Ingram, for his emotionless assessment that excluded the plight of the people she was a part of, but she knew he was being honest. She also knew that she could not go back and explain any of it to the men. How do you tell people that their livelihood is in peril and fighting the fact is useless? She looked at Sam Ingram who saw the realisation in her face.

"I'm bound to think he is right, Peg. There will be hard times coming, but there must always be hope. We can't take away a man's hope."

∾ ∾ ∾

Walking down the long driveway, Peg thought hard about what she would say. Sam Ingram was a gentle old man who was full of sympathy for the workers but could do nothing. Peter was without sympathy but equally ineffectual. If she had achieved nothing, she had at least learned a great deal. But what she now knew could not be revealed, and she resolved to keep the inevitability of eventual closure to herself and her husband. If there was more to be told, she would leave Tosh to tell it.

As she emerged from the driveway, she was hailed by a man who sat on the low wall that separated Strathalmond land from the main road.

"Hey, Miss!" he called, rising to his feet and lifting a bag from the ground.

Peg could see that it was a soldier's kitbag, worn and dirty with faded white letters near one end.

"Hey, Miss!" The soldier approached her.

He was shorter than Peg and wore an ill-fitting blue suit of the kind that she remembered soldiers wearing when they returned from the war. "Demob suits" they called them. He had a strong good-looking face and brown curly hair, and Peg's attention was drawn to the light blue eyes that engaged her with a merry smile. She estimated that he was about her own age and she tried, without success, to recognise him.

"Excuse me, Miss, but could you tell me where I might find a Colonel Ingram, Colonel William Ingram? He told me that he lived in a house called Strathalmond in the village of Myrestane." His eyes continued to smile and she noticed a pallor on his face that made the eyes even more alluring.

"This is Strathalmond", she said, stretching out her arm to point back up the driveway. "Did....do you know William Ingram?"

"Deed I do, Miss," he countered, his smile growing broader. "He was my C.O. in France. Oh, my name's Jack, Jack Armstrong", he said, putting out his hand. Peg felt the strong handshake and saw how his broad shoulders strained the thin material of the suit.

"'Look me up when you get home, Jackie,' the Colonel said. 'Strathalmond in Myrestane, that's where I'll be.' Jackie was what he called me, never Private Armstrong. Very informal, the Colonel. You just came from the house, then, Miss. Can you tell me if he's at home?"

"Mr. Armstrong," Peg began, as she tried to think what to say next. She moved to the wall and sat down. "Sit down for a minute." She watched his face as he sat next to her, laying down the kitbag.

"My name is Peg Douglas. When did you last see Colonel Ingram?" The soldier looked at her closely, the beginnings of a frown forming on his brow.

"A few years back, Miss, during the war. 1916 it was, during the battle of the Somme. Is there something…?"

"Mr. Armstrong….Jack", Peg interrupted, "Colonel Ingram never came back from the war."

Peg said the words softly, seeing the shock in his face. Without thinking she put a hand on his shoulder. Jack Anderson closed his eyes tightly and bowed his head, as he sat perfectly still, the slight breeze shaking his thick brown curls. After a few moments he looked up into her eyes. "Are you a member of his family, Miss?"

"Peg," she said. "Call me Peg. No, I am not related. I was at Strathalmond on business."

He nodded his head, turning his face towards the driveway, the cheerful smile now swept away by the sudden burden of his grief. Peg slowly withdrew her hand from his shoulder, feeling an overpowering urge to embrace him. Her heart filled up with all the grief and crying that that war had brought, with the tears of fathers and mothers, wives and sweethearts and fatherless children, Old Sam Ingram and the thousands like him whose smiles would never come back again.

"Jack", she said, as he stared vacantly into the trees. "Jack!" He looked at her and forced a little smile.

"I'm so sorry", she said. He took her hand in his and gave

it a gentle squeeze. "Thank you for telling me," he said. "Poor Colonel Ingram".

"Do you have a place to live?" Peg asked. He shook his head and continued.

"I just got back to Scotland and I thought I would look up the Colonel. I made no plans beyond that, I suppose."

Peg was puzzled. "But the war has been over for nearly two years now. You've just returned?"

Part of his old smile came back. "Well it took me longer than some. I was a prisoner, you see and....ah, it's a long story, Peg. Can I call you Peg?"

"Yes," she said. "I think you could say we have been introduced." They both laughed.

Sitting on the wall beside a young soldier, opposite the old mill outside the gates of Strathalmond, the "Miller's Wall" they called it, on a warm summer evening, Peg was transported into her dream world, away from the Raw, away from the daily routine of Mrs.Tosh Douglas, away from the bings and the blackened hearth and the soup pots and clothes on the line, away even from the camphor smelling pew of St. Nicholas Church.

She was flying, soaring somewhere where her poets went, and she didn't want this moment to end.

"Should I go up to the house, do you think?" Jack's words brought her back to earth.

"Yes, oh yes," she said. "Go up and ask to speak to Sam Ingram. Tell him why you came. I have no doubt that he will be happy to meet a comrade of his son."

Jack got up and swung the kitbag over his shoulder. "Will I see you again?" he said. "Do you live in Myrestane?"

Peg hesitated, not knowing what to say, afraid of what she might say if she tried to speak.

"Tell you what," he said, quickly. "I'll see you here, at this wall, next week — same time, same place, as they say. If you can't make it I'll understand. Goodbye Peg Douglas." He flashed his smile at her and took off up the drive without looking back.

Chapter
Eight

ल ल ल

The strike started a month later and lasted for six months, carrying through one of the severest winters in living memory.

When news of Peg's complete lack of success in her appeal to the owners was relayed to the men, Wee Tammy Flynn got busy signing up members and was soon able to count George Crawford and even the unpredictable Shine Mooney among the growing ranks of the union. Tosh, to whom Peg had explained the economics of the industry as described to her by Peter Ingram, tried to make reason prevail over sentiment, but his efforts, notwithstanding his own reputation among the men, were to no avail. It was "us against them", the downtrodden against the privileged, the ancient battle cry of the working man.

Peg never did go to the Miller's Wall to see her soldier.

When she got back home from Strathalmond she was thrust back into the real world. But she didn't forget him. She just relegated him to her thoughts, somewhere below the urgent requirements of her daily existence but above Rudolph Valentino and Jack Dempsey. She had the ability to justify all the things that happened to her in her life as what was meant to be. Notions of guilt or betrayal never entered her mind, and when she was with Tosh, nothing had changed, for the soldier was not part of that world.

She knew that she would see Jack Armstrong again, just as she would go and see Valentino again, and she looked forward to it because it was one of the pleasures of her life, and God brought pleasures to every life. Peg didn't believe in original sin, and that, more than anything, put qualifications on her adherence to the preachings of the Christian Church.

Her inner sense of righteousness was shored up by Robert Burns, another one of her heroes,

> *If I'm designed yon lordling's slave —*
> *By nature's laws designed —*
> *Why was an independent wish,*
> *E'er planted in my mind?*

It was a hard winter for the families of Myrestane.

Peg started up a soup kitchen using the boilers in an old washhouse to make soup and sometimes cloutie dumplings. She and Jeanie scrounged bones for soup, ham bones and beef bones, from the local butchers in Myrestane and other nearby villages, and dug cabbages and leeks from the frozen earth of their own and their neighbours' gardens.

As the weeks passed, many of the single men who had lodgings in Myrestane and no ties there to home or family, returned home or went to the Fife coal field for work, leaving the beds of countless landladies untenanted and the bar at the Myrestane Inn quieter than it had ever been. The union held meetings of the executive to count and distribute strike pay, a few pennies a week, to the members, and to organise expeditions of men to attend football games and travel outside the area, begging cans round their necks, to ask for relief for the strikers from those who could or would give it.

"Ah joined the union, for ah think it wis time tae dae it," Tosh proclaimed, sitting in his fireside chair and staring over to Peg and the O'Sheas who sipped tea at the kitchen table."But Ah'll be damned if Ah'll carry a can like a beggar."

"Nor me neither," Barney piped up.

"Well, that's a fine sentiment, Tosh," Peg said, rising and wiping her hands on her apron. "But you'll have to carry something, the pair of you, for this is going to be a long winter."

"We'll shaw neeps, that's what we'll dae. Auld Murray up at the ferm has a field aboot ready tae work. Ah'll go up there in the mornin'. Barney and me both." Barney nodded vigorously, then looked perplexed. "What does it mean, neeps?" he said.

"Christ, turnips man!" Tosh retorted with annoyance. "Can ye no' speak bloody English?" Peg and Jeanie burst into laughter.

"Shawing neeps, Barney, means pulling up turnips and cutting off the shaw, that's the stem, with a knife," Peg explained, still laughing. "It isn't too difficult to do, they say". She winked to Jeanie.

"No' difficult!" Tosh roared, his eyebrows rising in disbelief. He looked from the women to Barney. "Listen son! Some o' these neeps are as big as fitba's, and they're frozen solid intae the grund. Ye hiv' tae pull them oot wi' wan hand and swipe the shaw aff wi' the other. And it's no' a wee knife ye'll be usin'. It's wan o' they big long-bladed buggers like ye' see darkies usin' in they foreign countries for cuttin' their wey through the jungle."

Tosh went through the motions of pulling up a turnip and swinging the blade, while Peg and Jeanie tried to keep straight faces.

"That's whit ye dae . . . like that!" he exclaimed.

"Well the trick is to get Farmer Murray to hire you," Peg said. "You know he has the ones he hires and them he wouldn't see on his land, never mind employ them."

"Listen Mistress Douglas! Never you worry yer' wee heid aboot that. He'll hire me. Ah shawed neeps wi' ma faither many a winter, aye for better men than Andrew Murray." He paused, nodding to himself. "Mind ye, ah dinnae ken aboot Barney here."

"Now what would you mean by that?" Barney said. "Sure'n there is no work done on a farm anywhere that Barney O'Shea couldn't do. This shawing of the neepers, sure I'll have half the field done before you get right started."

"Neeps! yah silly bugger," Tosh replied, lifting his newspaper and burying his face in it.

ດາ ດາ ດາ

The Myrestane Institute, a single storey edifice with the arched windows of a church and a steep, slated roof, had been erected by Strathalmond Oil Company for the benefit and recreation of its workers. Behind it lay the bowling green where bowlers demonstrated the ancient skill of lawn bowling on summer evenings. Inside, two tables for billiards and snooker sat in the centre of a large, pipe-smelling room, surrounded by long oak benches punctuated by brass spittoons. Through the wall was the meeting room, and it was here that Tammy Flynn and the union executive counted the proceeds of collection boxes and allocated strike pay to the union members.

Tammy's face was a picture. "Ah cannae make head nor tail o' this, ye know, " he mumbled to himself as he peered over the columns of names and figures before him. He looked up at the men sitting round the table. "George, whit's this payment here to Henry Rae? Three shillin's on the twentieth."

George Crawford got up from his chair and bent down to look over Tammy's shoulder, pushing his wire-framed glasses up onto his forehead. "Cannae be him," he intoned. "Henry Rae from the Station Raw?" Tammy looked up.

" There's only one Henry Rae, George," he said. " Station Raw Henry."

"Aye, that's whit ah mean Tammy. Cannae be him. He died aboot six months ago. Christ, Peter here and I were at his funeral." Peter Small grunted in agreement from the end of the table.

George pulled down the glasses over his eyes and inspected the list closer. "Christ there's Big Jimsey Johnston — one shilling and threepence. He emigrated tae Canada last year wi' his wife and a' they screaming weans o' his. How can he be drawin' strike pay?"

Wee Tammy snorted and drew himself up to his full height,

like Napoleon addressing his lieutenants. "This is a serious matter, boys. It looks like there has been a fraud committed here wi' union funds. Until this matter is investigated, no word of it must leave this room. Who was in charge o' the collection tins at the game today?"

"Shug Anderson," George replied. "That should be a big draw. All that Glasgow crowd here tae see their Glasgow Rangers getting' their arses kicked by Myrestane United." He laughed to the others.

"Aye, Shug will need to get their contributions before the whistle blaws," another added.

"Order!" Tammy banged the table to arrest the hilarity. "Before Shug brings any contributions, Ah want these lists checked and a' these ones that are deid or moved away scored aff. Here! Take a page each and let's get on wi' it. Ah'll look into this further tae establish where these contributions went tae. This a serious matter. A very serious matter."

The laughter died and those present got busy with the lists while Tammy got up from his seat and walked up and down the room with his brows knit and his hands behind his back.

ରଉ ରଉ ରଉ

Myrestane Athletic didn't beat the Rangers, but they were only down one goal at the final whistle, a very credible performance for a bunch of amateurs against a professional side. It put the thousands of Rangers supporters, who had travelled by train from Glasgow to Myrstane Station, in a very happy mood, happy enough to fill the strikers' contribution tins as a consolation prize. It also filled the Myrestane Inn with rowdy Orangemen, singing the bellicose airs for which they were notorious, and cursing the Pope. Shug and his collectors followed them to the pub, where they extracted even more donations before the fights started with the Irish immigrants, unhappy, out of work and intoxicated.

Shug Anderson was a long time union man, a friend of Wee

Tammy Flynn, and a supporter of the war against alcohol. He was in the Temperance Society, joined at an early age by his mother shortly after his father choked to death on his own vomit after a thousand drunken nights in the Myrestane Inn. Shug's active participation in the Society made Tammy select him to head up the collections. Being in the Myrestane Inn was, for him, a labour of duty. He sat back in a corner, wincing at the revelry, while his collectors went around with their tins.

"Shug!" A voice beside him caused him to start like a peeping-tom caught in the act.

"Fancy seeing you here. I thought you never went near pubs. What'll yer mother say tae this, eh?" It was Sandy McLaughlin, who worked in the candle works and spent all his wages on the horses.

"Ah'm jist.... Ah'm overseeing the collection tins," Shug stuttered. "We're collectin' fur the strike fund."

"Oh aye," Sandy said, sounding not quite convinced. "Ye'll do well here right enough. A' they Glasgow guys, the drunker they get the mair they'll gie ye. Good idea, Shug. Wis that wee Tammy that thought o' that wan?"

"It was my own idea," Shug said angrily.

"Awright, awright, keep yer hair on," Sandy replied, smiling happily. "Ah nivver saw ye here, awright?" Then, almost as an afterthought, he added, "Ah bet ye'll have a pile o' money when these tins come in, eh?"

Shug nodded. "We should do awright," he said, keeping his eyes on the collectors as they mingled among the drinkers.

"Are ye still runnin', Shug?" Sandy said, changing the subject.

Shug Anderson was a runner. Well he was a sprinter, really. But when you were training, running around the Albyn Park, or out along Greendykes Raws towards the next village of Winchburgh, you were a runner. You were only a sprinter when you competed.

The hundred was Shug's distance, that and the two-twenty. One hundred yards in even time, ten seconds, that was his dream. His best was ten point four, but it was good enough for him to take all the cups that were on offer at the Myrestane sports, and he had taken them, year after year for the last three years.

"Aye," he told Sandy. "Ah'm still runnin'."

Sandy took a gulp of beer and wiped his mouth. "Ye know, that Thomson laddie is doin' well in the hundred these days. Did you ever meet him?"

Shug had met Thomson for the first time that past summer. Thomson had pipped him at the post in the hundred yards, the first time Shug had lost in three years. Thomson was a new contender, barely seventeen, and Shug did not look forward to meeting him next year. "Aye," he said ruefully. "Ah've met him."

Sandy hunched his shoulders and looked around furtively as he pulled his chair nearer to Shug.

"He's running at Powderhall on New Year's day," he said under his breath. "Ah got it straight from his faither. There's a lot of money goin' on him. He's gettin' ten yards aff Perrin"

Shug was suddenly alert. "Ten yards!" he exclaimed.

"Shhh…," Sandy rejoined,"keep yer voice doon, man," looking around for eavesdroppers. "Thomson is gettin' ten yards and we can get odds of 10/1 aboot 'im. He's a sure fire certainty his faither says. What dae you think? You ran against 'im."

Shug's mind was racing. Nobody could afford to give Thomson ten yards in the hundred. At 10/1 a man could pick up a roll of notes, if he had a decent stake that is. Then he caught sight of one of the collectors moving along the bar, and an idea formed in his head.

∾ ∾ ∾

Powderhall, lying on the south side of Edinburgh, was a training ground for generations of runners. The great Eric Liddell began his running career there that led him to an Olympic gold. But each New Year's day fielded a different breed, the professional sprinters, the men who ran not for medals or fame, not even for God, but only for cash.

Sydney Perrin was one of these, and at the advanced age of twenty-nine he was still the man to beat.

The bookmakers started to arrive around eight, erecting their boards and marking up the odds with white chalk. The morning was clear and bright and the ground hard, a white carpet of hoar frost clinging to the grass. Shug edged his way towards the front of the assembled men, his collar up and his cap pulled down low over his forehead. He saw Thomson, slight and fidgety in a white vest and shorts, rolling his shoulders as his father and a few others talked in his ear and rubbed the back of his neck. Then he saw Sydney Perrin, wide shoulders spreading the blue wool of his track suit as he ambled forward from the crowd smiling to his supporters.

Shug felt the money in his jacket. Five pounds, all in change, that he had quietly and purposefully separated out from the union takings, leaving the balance to be handed in to Wee Tammy Flynn. What little conscience he had was readily dispersed by the fact of certainty. Nobody could give Thomson ten yards. Of that he was sure, and anyway it wasn't an evil thing he was doing, not like spending the money on drink, as Shug suspected some of his collectors did. Running was a wholesome thing, and this was a certainty. One thing did niggle Shug, however, as he stood in front of the bookie, looking at the 10/1 scrawled in chalk on the blackboard. It wasn't the odds, or the big dumpling face of the man in the pin-striped suit, or the eagerness with which he snatched the bet and handed it to his clerk to count. It was the placid, joking figure of Perrin that emanated an impression that he had already won.

But he couldn't win, thought Shug; not giving away ten yards he couldn't.

They were down at their marks now, Thomson lithe, and looking sideways at his master, like a greyhound at a strange track; Perrin, ten yards back, easy, and staring straight ahead with the hint of a smile lingering on his lips.

At the sound of the pistol, both men shot forward and Shug bit at his bottom lip, squeezing the betting ticket in his hand.

The sprint is no spectator sport. It is over in seconds. Thomson ran like a gazelle, maintaining his lead past the half way point. Then Sydney Perrin eased into a long stride, shortening the gap at every second until he stretched his head into the tape just as his rival went to breast it. A roar went up from all sides of Shug and the fat-faced bookie smiled a big smile.

ॐ ॐ ॐ

About the same time as Shug Anderson was making his way back to Myrestane, Barney O'Shea was walking out of the turnip field, his hands pushed deep down into the pockets of his long jacket, and tears from cold and frustration collecting in his eyes. Fifteen minutes later he pushed his way through the sagging door of the old washhouse where Peg and Jeanie were making a new boiler-full of soup.

"That man of yours isn't human, Peg," he said, his hands still delved down in his coat.

"Holy Saint Catherine, he's standin' up there in that field shawin' them turnips as if it was a summer day, and the cold drivin' right through him. I nearly froze to death, standin' there along with 'im. I can't feel my hands even yet. It's the devil that's in him for sure, for there is no ordinary man could stand that. I'll go back to Donegal first, before I would work for the likes of Murray."

The women worked on at the soup without reply for they could think of nothing to say that would not sound like pity, and they knew that pity was the hardest thing to bear for a man who had tried and failed.

"I'll go now up to the Institute. Maybe there is a beggin' bowl they could give me."

After he left, Jeanie burst into tears and Peg hugged her in her arms.

∾ ∾ ∾

There were only two men working in Murray's turnip field that morning, two from the ten that had been hired, and Murray was the kind of man who made a careful mental note of that, no matter how bone-chilling the morning.

They moved slowly along the rows, pulling the turnips out of the hard earth and swinging their long blades to separate the shaws, dropping the turnips at their feet and tossing the cuttings to the other side of the row.

Around noon, Tosh stuck his knife in the ground and walked up the field to the fence where his knapsack hung on a post. After a few minutes, the other man did likewise, pulling his lunch from the torn pocket of his ancient jacket as he came up to Tosh. He held out his hand in greeting.

"Jack Armstrong," he said. "Looks like we're the only two left on the job this morning." Tosh took the other's hand and slightly inclined his head, his mouth trying to cope with a great wedge of bread and cheese which he eventually managed to swallow.

"Ah'm no' surprised, son. It's a wonder Ah'm still here. But it's either this or beggin' for money at fitba' matches."

He looked the youngster over, the powerful shoulders and strong hands, the striking blue eyes and the ragged suit that looked like it had fallen off a tinker's cart.

"Ah hivnae seen you around. Ye're no' a local laddie, then?"

"Just back from the War," Armstrong said, sitting down on the frost covered grass. "I'm from the Calders, but I had some business here, and then when this job came up with Murray I thought I might stay on. Murray hired me and I've got the ploughman's cottage."

"Ye're a brave man son, workin' for Auld Murray. He's a crabbit auld bastard. But, mind you, he'll pay ye well enough if ye can stick the work. Mornin's like this, Ah mean."

The other laughed. "I've been in colder places," he said.

After a short break they returned to the field, for Murray paid by turnips, not by time.

In the afternoon Tosh brought up the question that puzzled him. "How did it take ye sae long tae get back fae the War? If ye dinnae mind me askin', son."

"Ah, it's a long story," Jack Armstrong replied. "You wouldn't be interested."

Tosh had known enough heroes, as he called them, returned from France, desperate to tell their tall tales to anybody who would listen. This was a different kind of man. If he had a story he didn't want to tell it, and that made Tosh all the keener to hear it. Besides he admired anyone who could shaw turnips on that particular morning, and a thought suddenly came to him.

"Listen, son! Seein' that ye're new in the district and have the misfortune tae be workin' for Andra Murray, why don't ye come ower tae the hoose on Saturday night fur a bite o' dinner wi' the wife and me? Then ye can tell us yer long story, eh?"

Jack Armstrong was as impressed with this new met giant of a man as Tosh was with him. "Aye, sure," he said quickly. "That would be very nice. I'll tell you the story if you insist, and I'll try not to bore you."

"That's fine Jack," Tosh replied. "And wan mair thing ye could mibbae tell me noo. How is that ye talk sae different fae the folk roond here. Wis yer faither a doctor or somethin'?"

Jack's happy laugh echoed across the field. "No. I was brought up in England, that's all."

Tosh was bewildered. He had never met anyone from England; Ireland, yes, but never England.

"England, ye say. Christ, England!" That was all Tosh could say.

Chapter
Nine

ᴕᴕᴕ

Jack Armstrong had a faded photograph of his parents in a small cardboard frame. He had carried it in his breast pocket ever since his elderly aunt had given it to him when he left West Calder to join the army in 1912. His mother, for that was who his aunt had said she was, sat, all in black, in a stiff pose beside a stuffed studio donkey. His father stood behind her with a hand upon her shoulder. At the foot of the picture was the word 'Blackpool'. The photograph stood on a chest of drawers next to a cap badge of the Royal Scots Greys, an eagle with open wings perched above the word "Waterloo". These were the only ornaments in the sparsely furnished single room of the ploughman's cottage. His kit bag lay on the floor beside the crumpled bed.

Jack rocked gently on an ancient wooden rocker by the fire, glad to be alive and thankful for the comforts of his present home. He might have thanked God, had he believed in such an entity. As it was, he thanked the farmer's wife for his regular hearty meals at the main house, and the farmer for the work and the cottage. He grinned as the thought struck him that old Murray would have him work in the dark as well as the light if he could figure out a way that it could be done.

For some men, this would be enough, Jack thought. This,

and perhaps a wife and some children to liven up the evenings, and the nights. Sometimes he wished that he could be one of these men, but he knew that he could not. For that he blamed his father.

There was a time, not so long ago, when he had blamed the army. Being a soldier excluded family life. But later he had come to realise that soldiering wasn't a life, it was an episode in a man's life, an adventure, and for some, a snuffing out of life.

With the wind rattling the door of the little cottage and the cold draught sneaking in at the window frames, Jack sat gazing into the fire, his mind going back to those first months in India with the Greys. That was when it was fun to be a soldier; when it seemed to be all play in a world of mystery.

He was standing in the crowd of natives with Mickey Beezley from Newcastle watching the little fakir spreading six eggs on the dry ground in front of him. The little man was hunkered down, his brown stick like legs protruding from the white bedsheet that was gathered round his middle. Now and then he would look up at the onlookers and smile, revealing ivory white teeth in his dark face.

"What's he goin' to do, Jock?" Beezley said, keeping his eyes on the eggs and the little man's circling hands.

"Don't know," Jack replied. "Some kind of trick I suppose. Just keep watching him."

The fakir turned to one side and withdrew a white sheet from a leather pouch that lay beside him on the ground. Then, with a silent grin to the crowd and a deft movement of his hands, he swirled the sheet in front of him and it fluttered slowly to the earth, covering the eggs. The two young soldiers and the locals looked on in silent expectation. The sheet just lay there and the little man looked around the crowd, smiling his white-toothed smile and lifting his dark eyebrows. The buzz of conversation faded into silence as all eyes stared at the sheet.

With a rapid movement of one bony hand, the magician whipped away the sheet. There, before their eyes, six tiny yellow chickens tottered and wavered on shaky legs, wandering off in all directions.

"Jesus, Jock! That's fuckin' magic. Jesus!" Mick breathed, rubbing his eyes. And it was magic, Jack recalled — no eggs, no egg-shells, no clue as to how it was done. It puzzled Jack Armstrong for many a day. It was a mystery in a land of mysteries.

But wandering among these strange sights, or galloping along tracks on warm Indian evenings, or going into the edge of the jungle to hunt game, with a Martini Henry rifle and a bandolier of rounds, had only been the lure in a greater game. And when that game was played out in France — mud, mud, mud everywhere, and rats as big as terriers, and the constant, deafening shelling — that was when Jack discovered the essence of a soldier's life.

On the Somme, when he had wakened up in a shell hole, lying next to what was left of a comrade, the Germans above him pointing their rifles down into the hole, and later leading him away to end his war in prison camps, he was no longer a soldier. He was a chess piece that had been moved, played, lost, then laid aside. The army was not to blame for anything that a man became. The army was an interlude, a test that you either survived or didn't.

His father, on the other hand, was a real and lasting influence. He was a hotel chef that worked the winter season in London and, in the summers, took positions in different tourist towns like Harrogate, Bath, Brighton, or Keswick in the Lake District. He was a good chef, well paid and well reputed, and he brought Jack up after his wife left him when the boy was six years old. Jack recalled a series of different schools and different hotel rooms. The most pleasant memories of his youth were his friendships with hotel porters, waitresses and chambermaids across the country.

Whatever was lacking in formal education, Jack made up in the skills of cooking and serving meals, telling hotel guests what they wanted to hear, and in hearing the stories of these men and women of the world who were travelled and experienced in the ways of people. This boyhood gave him a taste for travel, and when his father died and he was sent north to live with a maiden aunt, he started to plan for an army life.

The aunt was kind enough, but she lived in a rural backwater among people to whom Jack would always be a strange boy, and whose dialect they couldn't understand. The army promised him the world as a setting for his life, and the Greys the chance to ride horses.

And now the ploughman's cottage was a temporary haven, a port in which to shelter for a while from the storm while he considered his next move in the world.

He was thankful to Sam Ingram for securing the job for him with the old farmer. He was sorry for Sam, sorrier than he had been for the men that never survived the harsh conditions of the German prison camps, because for Sam the Great War would never end as long as Colonel Ingram looked down from the mantlepiece.

He thought at first that his visit to Strathalmond had helped the old man who had seemed to come alive on hearing stories of his son, how cheerful and how brave he was, and how courageous at the end. Later Jack realised that it merely brought more pain by resurrecting a life that was gone.

Jack would erase his memories of that time and get on with his life. Sam Ingram's life had ended on the Somme, as did the lives of so many others who had never even been there.

Thinking about that day with Sam brought his thoughts back to his meeting with Peg at the Miller's Wall. He had returned the following week. He had even bought a new shirt and a tie from a store in Myrestane and practised what he would say, but she never appeared. He had waited around for hours, sitting on the wall and then rising to look along the road, until the sun finally dropped down behind the trees and he couldn't see the road any more.

He looked around the little room of the cottage. If a girl like that was here, he thought, here with him, permanently here, what kind of a man would Jack Armstrong be then? Then he discarded the thought and poked the fire with the iron poker.

෨෨෨

The strike brought to the O'Sheas their first setback since arriving in Scotland.

Until the Work closed down, all their prayers in the new country had been answered and all its promise realised. Barney blessed the day that he had met Paddy Reilly in the bog in Innishennan, and Jeanie's face was bright and cheerful, the pinched tear-stroked features of a homesick waif long forgotten.

Since moving to Myrestane Station, they had housed four lodgers in the back room, young Irishmen from home. The twelve shillings a week that they each paid for full board, covered the running costs of the house and allowed Barney to send money home and still save the bulk of his wages.

On Saturday nights he could put his hand in his pocket for the two shilling piece that would buy a gallon of beer for the table at the Myrestane Inn, and on Sunday morning he and Jeanie would walk the mile and a half to the chapel and thank God for their good fortune.

Then they would stand outside the chapel after Mass, and laugh and talk in the Irish with the crowd of young men in moleskin trousers, and long shapeless jackets made with the wool spun by their mothers' hands on the little farms of their home.

The people of Myrestane Station were welcoming enough, except for its few Protestant bigots that everyone knew, and though they didn't show the warmth or the open trust of the people of Innishennan, Barney and Jeanie were well pleased with the place they had chosen. Having the Douglases for friends made a great difference to them both, but mainly to Jeanie, for the need of a true friend is greater for a woman than for a man. At least, that's what Barney believed.

Peg Douglas was closer to Jeanie than her own sisters. She sometimes felt as she did towards her own mother, and that was a strange feeling, for Peg was little older than herself.

At the beginning it was the way Peg had taken her into the Raw, almost as if Jeanie were a long lost sibling returned from a far journey. Later it was the easy way Peg had with her, making silent inroads into Jeanie's deepest thoughts and concerns without the need of questions or demands. Peg Douglas had a gift for understanding people and gaining their trust, and when Jeanie discovered that Christmas that she was pregnant, Peg was the first one she told.

Jeanie remembered how Peg had smiled and said what a wonderful gift God had given her.

After Barney's bitter experience in the turnip field, and the departure of their lodgers in a quest for work outside of the shale field, Barney and Jeanie began to take stock of their finances, estimating how long they could survive on their savings. It was then that the first of the letters came from Ireland.

> *Inishennan*
> *2nd January 1922*

Dear Jeanie,

> *Praise be to God for the news of the baby coming. I went to the chapel and prayed for you, and I say the rosary every night for the both of you. Mother wants you to come home Jeanie. Do come now and don't be refusing your mother. Barney should come too for the poor man must be killed working. My father will give him some of the land. Sure you have plenty of money. Come both of you home now in God's name.*

> *We are well here. The crop was very good last year, thank God.*

> *Your loving sister*
> *Bridget.*

As Barney and Jeanie pondered this, another followed on its tail.

Inishennan
7th January 1922

My dear Barney,

I heard the good news, now you both must come home, you know you never intended to live long in Scotland, your child must be Irish not Scotch. We will all be waiting. I am going out up the hill tonight with the good news. I think I see your father singing and dancing. Heavens, but they will be glad.

I have no time to tell you any news, it is mail time. Come home and don't disappoint us.

Your sister
Hannah.

Jeanie did a lot of crying in the days that followed, and Barney was of little help to her for he had only to look at the letters and the tears ran down his cheeks also. But for all that, the decision to return home was not an easy one. When the strike finished, the Work would open again, and the wages, though likely not what they had been, would still be better than the profits of a farm at home.

On the Saturday, Peg came in to find Jeanie weeping by the fire.

"Sure I was happy here, Peg," she sniffed. "But what should I do now? My mother and sister want me to come home. They want my baby to be born in Ireland."

"And what do you want?" Peg said softly.

Jeanie looked up at her friend, her cheeks red and wet in the light from the fire.

"I would go tomorrow, only it is a poor life in Donegal and our savings would be spent in no time."

"Then you have answered yourself," Peg replied. "You would go tomorrow. That is what your heart is telling you. Never mind about money, for neither money nor the lack of it were ever good reasons for ignoring what the heart says."

"And Barney?" Jeanie began.

"Barney will do what he must do," Peg said firmly. "That

will be for him to say. But he's not the man I think he is if he doesn't join his wife and baby whenever the time is right for it."

Peg reached for the kettle on the stove. "Now," she said, "we will have a cup of tea. Then you will dry these eyes and come in next door when Barney gets home. I am making a dinner for Tosh and me and a man he met at the farm, and there will be enough for two more. It will take you out of yourselves for a while."

After Peg left, Jeanie felt better, and when Barney came in she met him at the door. She had on her best frock and her eyes were smiling once more.

"Get ready to come next door for a bite of dinner," she said. "Peg is after inviting us. And by the way, I have decided. We are going home to Ireland!"

❧ ❧ ❧

Peg made Tosh put on his suit and his white shirt and tie. He thought this entirely unnecessary for the only ones coming were the O'Sheas, and a laddie that worked on the farm, and this was his own house after all, but he saw the deliberate look on his wife's face and he complied without comment.

Peg herself was dressed in a white blouse and long black skirt with a belt that emphasised the slimness of her waist. Her hair was set up in the usual bun, held in place by a wide, curved tortoiseshell clip. Wisps of dark hair had escaped this stringent arrangement to fall lightly on her temple. Her face had the shine that a vigorous application of soap and water creates on young skin, and Tosh caught the faint, elusive odour of Lily of the Valley. It was the only cosmetic application that Peg had ever contemplated, not for the effect but rather for the connotation.

Consider the lilies of the field...

The chairs, including two brought from the room, were arranged around the kitchen in a rough semi-circle facing the fire, for Peg did not believe that people should sit around the table except when the meal was served. That made for too stiff a gathering, and when she had company she wanted fun. Tosh, of course would retain the master's seat at the fire. Tosh got dressed up as ordered, minus the jacket, for the absence of which he gave Peg a challenging look before relaxing into his chair, reaching for his paper and lighting his pipe.

There was a knock at the door.

"That'll be the wee sodger noo," Tosh said, making no move to rise from his chair. Peg straightened up from setting the table and went to the door. "Soldier?" she said, glancing back.

Jack Armstrong stood on the doorstep.

The two simply stared at each other, their prepared smiles dissolving from their faces. Neither one moved. Then they looked each other up and down.

Jack made as if to speak when Peg called out.

"Tosh! Your friend's here,"she called, her eyes still fixed on Jack's. Then she pulled her face away and brushed her palms down the front of her skirt.

"Aye, ye made it then," Tosh's voice lumbered up behind her. "Come in, man! Come away in!" he exclaimed "Come on mistress. Are ye gonnae keep the man standin' there a' night?" The three moved into the kitchen.

"Jack Armstrong, ma'am," Jack said, putting out his hand.

Peg smiled at the purposeful introduction made in front of Tosh. It crossed her mind that that is what a gentleman would do. "I'm pleased to meet you, Mr. Armstrong," she replied. Then, after a few seconds, she added, "But haven't we met before?"

Seeing the perplexed look on Jack's face, Peg continued before he could answer. "At the Miller's Wall, that day. Don't you remember?" She looked at Tosh who had settled back into his chair.

"I met Mr. Armstrong, Tosh, that day I went up to Strathalmond. He was looking for the Ingram house." Then back to Jack, "did you find the Ingrams, then? Sit down, sit down. Take the weight of your feet."

Jack was happy to comply, taking a chair opposite Tosh. Peg noticed the relief on his face. She also noticed the new shirt and tie and the restored colour in his cheeks under the bright blue eyes. "Yes," he said. "I visited Sam Ingram."

Just then the O'Sheas came to the door. Jeanie, her face glowing with her news, mouthed an aside to Peg. "Going home".

"You mean that you are workin' in that turnip field every day?" Barney surveyed Jack with a mix of incredulity and wonder. Jack laughed.

"I am," he said.

"Aye, and this laddie can work," Tosh joined in. "He wis a sodger, ye know. Jist back. He's goin' tae tell us the story aboot how it took 'im sae long tae get back fae France. That right Jack?" Jack's embarrassment went unnoticed by all but Peg.

"Oh, your friends wouldn't want to hear that," he muttered, looking down at the carpet.

As Tosh began to respond, Peg cut him off. "Later Tosh. We'll hear Jack's story in a bit. Right now I think Jeanie has something to tell us." Jack threw Peg a grateful look.

"Come on Jeanie!" Peg said. Jeanie looked quickly at Barney, her eyes shining with anticipation.

"We're going home," she announced. "Back home to Donegal".

In the moment of silence that followed, Jeanie cast her eyes round the small audience like an actor whose best line had fallen on deaf ears. The English soldier didn't look up, while Tosh and Barney could think of nothing to say. Peg rushed to Jeanie's aid, embracing her in a bear hug. "That's wonderful, Jeanie. I'm so happy for you."

"When is this goin' tae happen?" Tosh said, addressing his question to Barney, his tone not exactly rejoicing. Barney shrugged his shoulders.

"Well, I don't know. We haven't made any plans yet." He paused, under Tosh's gaze. "But the wife here wants to go back," he added, sheepishly.

"Tosh! This is an occasion for celebration. Go and get that New Year bottle of whisky from below the bed. There's a few bottles of stout there too. Go and get them!" Peg ordered, still hugging Jeanie.

The bottles came out and Peg, the self-appointed Master of Proceedings, attended to pouring drams of whisky for everyone, except herself who never drank, filling the little nip glasses right to the brim as was the custom. The men had a bottle of stout along with their nips, and soon Jeanie's announcement brought the reaction that she had hoped for. The talk went from going home, to babies, to the strike, and back to going home. The dinner was served and the dishes washed by Peg and Jeanie in the little scullery at the back, while Tosh poured more drinks and asked Barney what the hell he was going to do in Ireland where there was no shale to draw.

Peg came back and sang *The Homes of Donegal* and Barney and Jeanie said how much they would miss the Douglases, the best friends they ever had. Barney then sang a song about an Irish beggar man that made everyone tap their feet, while the carpet was hastily rolled back and Jeanie danced a jig. At the end of it they all sat back, replete with Peg's stew and warmed with the liquor.

"Noo, son. Ah'm still waitin' tae hear that story o' yours," Tosh said, turning to Jack Armstrong. Jack, seeing that it would be useless to deny his host further, took a swig of stout from his bottle, and began.

The memories flooded back, raising vivid pictures in his mind, and the listeners seemed to dissolve into the misty background of the little kitchen.

∾ ∾ ∾

The mud was the worst thing. Sucking yellow mud, a sea of mud that had been churned up out of the bowels of the earth by the constant, thundering shelling. It was as if a giant spade had turned over the landscape and patted it down, burying everything that was there a moment earlier.

Jack Armstrong opened his eyes. He could see nothing but the mud. The guns had stopped. He thought that maybe he was dead. He shouldn't move. If he was dead something would happen. He sat there a long time, half-propped up against the remains of a barbed-wire fence, waiting.

Where was Josh? His memory was coming back to him. He and Josh had been together, climbing over the top of the trench and advancing. The "Big Push on the Somme" the Colonel called it.

Where was Josh? Where were the others? He looked across the desolate plain of mud. Josh wasn't his real name. His real name was Richard. Richard Reynolds. He came from Wishaw. He and Jack came to France together in 1914. That was two years ago when Colonel Ingram had transferred to the Royal Scots and Jack Armstrong did the same. Because Richard Reynolds was always drawing pictures on an artist's pad, they called him Josh; short for Joshua, as in Joshua Reynolds. Where the hell was Josh?

He was a good artist too. All the men said so. Even Colonel Ingram came by all the time in the trenches asking to look at Josh's drawings. They were drawings of men, and tanks and horses and broken, exploded barbed wire. One was of a horse pulling a water wagon. The horse had sunk into the mud. You could only see its head and neck and flailing front hoofs.

"You should save these, Corporal Reynolds, the Colonel said. They'll be worth something someday. People will want to see these." That's what the Colonel said.

A shell exploded somewhere off to his right; then another and another. They were coming closer. Jack pulled himself upright, looking around for his rifle. The earth shook to the sound of another shell. He got to his knees and scrambled forward looking for a hole, somewhere to hide from the bombardment. His hands and knees sank into the mud as he crawled forward, his eyes peering through the smoke that now drifted over him. Then he saw the shell hole and lurched headfirst into it, rolling onto his side and sliding down into the yellow water. He thrust out a hand to stop his decline and it fell on the rough surface of a battle dress jacket. He gripped the jacket and the thing slid with him into the water. He turned himself over on top of it. "Josh!" he breathed.

Josh stared at him with wide eyes. He grabbed the jacket by the lapels, pulling Josh up out of the water. There was no weight. The face and the jacket rose clear of the water like a doll. Jack looked down. There was nothing below them. He dropped the thing back into the water. The smell made him gag.

A long time later Jack Armstrong gazed up from the hole at the two dark shapes of his captors, invincible in black helmets, blocking out the sky. He remembered what he said. He lifted his arms. "It's a fair cop." That was all he said. It would sound funny if he told it later.

He was on a train. He could hear the engine and the beat of iron wheels on the rails. They were all crammed together on the hard wooden floor of the wagon. The man next to him had a bandage around his head and it had come loose over one ear and an end of it hung down his cheek. Someone handed Jack a piece of black bread. He ate it then dozed off again. He had a dream about a soldier lying in a shell hole, his bandage all unravelled and floating in the water. Germans stood in a ring all around the top of the hole, laughing down at the soldier.

He didn't remember how long he was on that train. Maybe it was days; maybe a week. At the end of it there was a circle of broken down shacks in the middle of a bleak, darkening landscape. They were hustled off the train and put into a long line. Then they were marched towards the shacks, some helping others that were too weak to walk; a long trailing line of misery.

Someone said the camp was near the Eastern Front and that the Germans were getting ready to make a big push on the Eastern Front. Jack had returned to the land of the living and he laughed at them. Rumours ran around the men even in this God-forsaken hole. How the hell would they know about a German push? How would they even know where they were? The guards, mostly old men, relics of some earlier war, said nothing. They just delivered a scant ration of black bread and water, grimacing now and then and looking fierce. Jack knew they would think nothing of shooting a man. He turned on his side on the narrow mattress that covered the iron cot and pulled the two threadbare blankets up over his face. Eyes closed, he heard the constant shuffling of men going to the single latrine bucket at one end of the hut.

Jack thought that nothing could be worse than the trenches. He tried to hang on to that thought in the weeks and months that followed, during the endless hours and days in the salt mine at Beienrode. He had stopped trying to count time. If the shifts in the mine had a finite length, he had no way to measure it. His life had become a ritual of intrusions on the senses: the sickening smell of the latrines; the taste of rotting cabbage and sour soup; the cutting edges of jagged salt crystals on his bare hands as he loaded them into carts; the freezing hut; the suppurating salt sores on his limbs and in his armpits.

He dragged on, day after day, in his private world of hurt. He saw men's faces come and go, blank, gaunt, lifeless faces. Sometimes the pain of an engorged boil would become unbearable, causing him to stop and lean on the cart. Then a guard would club the boil, its poison squirting out, and the salt was waiting to invade the open wound.

He thought that he might turn and run and a guard would shoot him. Then he thought the guard might not shoot him. He might be made to walk between the lines and be struck with pick handles and rifle butts. He had seen them do that to others when the quota was not made. The face was blasted again and the surge of ragged salt crystals flowed from it to rise up again in front of him.

Jack was what they later called a "behind the lines" prisoner, lost and forgotten, unacknowledged by the enemy and unknown to those who sent mail and food parcels to others. He was all alone and not alone in a camp of dying men that had once been soldiers.

The saving of Jack Armstrong came in the shape of a small,

wizened man who could neither hear nor speak. He was a miner, a German civilian worker, who advanced to Jack at his pile, backed by two guards. He pointed at Jack and moved on towards the shaft, the guards pushing Jack along behind him. At the surface, the group, led by the little man, went into a large shed where trucks had pulled up alongside smoking heaps of cooling coke. The guards moved off and the civilian lifted two shovels that stood against the wall and stretched one out to Jack with a sign indicating that the coke was to be filled into the truck, then he started shovelling.

Jack watched him. He had a slow, rhythmic action, like a little machine, delving the shovel into the pile and swinging it up in a wide arc, tipping the end of it to deposit the load as it returned to the pile. The guards were standing at the door of the shed, talking between themselves and looking their way now and then. Jack started to shovel. At first it was hard, the boils under his arms giving tight, stinging pain on every lift. Later it became easier and Jack started to appreciate the drier air of the shed and the daylight coming in through the door.

The little man stopped and pointed to the tip of the pile of coke that had emerged above the truck box at his end. There was no sign of Jack's pile appearing, and the little man smiled at Jack, showing a single big yellow tooth in his elfin face. Then he held up five fingers and walked over to take a seat against the wall. Jack understood what it meant. "Take five!" That night, in the hut, a prisoner spoke to Jack.

"I saw you going up in the shaft with the dummy. You're a lucky devil, Jack."

"Yeah," said another. "If he likes you, he'll keep you out of the mine."

Each time Jack looked at the man they called "the dummy", something changed inside him, something that gave him the determination to survive this place. The little old man with no voice, who stood no higher than the shovel he wielded and whom Jack never did out-shovel, became a picture in Jack Armstrong's mind of survival. And the picture remained with him after he was moved on yet another train, this time to a camp near the Eastern Front, away from the mine, into the chilling never-ending cold of a winter forest.

ఴ ఴ ఴ

"It was on the Baltic Sea, somewhere near Riga," Jack said, returning to the pleasant warmth of the room. "We were there for a year, digging up roots in the surrounding forest and catching rats at night with homemade traps." He paused. "You can eat a rat raw, you know," he added in a matter of fact tone, looking around in a serious attempt to convince.

"Holy Mother of God," Jeanie whispered, making the sign of the cross with a rapid movement.

"And the Germans, Tosh said. "Whit were they like?"

"Oh, they were all right, mostly, except for one or two bastards like you see everywhere, I suppose. Older men, retired from the front. They were just as keen to go home as we were." Then he pulled his bottom lip down and back into his cheek to reveal a space in his teeth. "You see that?" he said. The others peered into his mouth. "I got that tooth out in that camp. I was murdered with toothache for two weeks, and after I complained about it, a day or two later, these two guards marched into the hut one morning with another man in civies. The guards held me down on the table and the other man stuck these pliers into my mouth and pulled the tooth right out. Christ, I never felt pain like it." Then he smiled at the horrified faces. "But that got rid of the toothache."

Peg could see Tosh's admiration for Jack Armstrong grow by the minute. For her own part, she felt seized by an unwelcome but persistent attraction. The low key description of his horrendous experiences, the devil-may-care attitude that exuded from the mesmerising eyes and the flippant curl of the hair, the set of the powerful shoulders and the strong, unyielding line of the jaw; all merged into a magnet that was drawing her out of her world to some other place where she had never ventured.

"The worst time came when the Germans left," Jack continued. "The war was finished, you see, but none of us knew that. One morning we got up and they were gone; no guards, no trucks, nothing. We ran about the camp cheering and raking in the cookhouse for food, but there was nothing there. Then it dawned on us. Here we were, in a forest in the middle of nowhere, not even knowing what country we were in. No food, buggerall. And winter had begun. It was snowing and bloody freezing. We made fires with bits of wood stripped off the huts and sat round them, wrapped in whatever rags we could find. That was the worst time."

He looked around at the others. They sat in total silence now, hanging on every word.

"At first we waited, sure that somebody would know where we were and come for us. After three weeks, most of us gave up on that idea. That was when the panic set in. A couple of men died in the huts, died of cold you know. Some went crazy and started fighting among themselves. I knew it was useless to stay there, with the snow coming every day now and it getting colder all the time, so I took off and started walking. I walked south, going by the sun. I was on my last legs when I found a shack. There was nobody in it but there was a field of turnips growing next to it. I stayed in the shack and made a fire, and I ate turnips, bashing the skin off them against a rock. Didn't bother shawing them." He winked at Tosh.

"I was there for a few days and then I set off again south, always heading south. I don't know how long I walked but I finally got to a farmhouse and they took me in. I was warm for the first time for ages. There was the farmer and his wife. She was called Olga, I think. I couldn't understand what they said but I ended up working for my keep and I ate with them and slept with them around the stove at night. I was there for nearly four months when an official of some kind arrived who spoke English. At last they had discovered the missing prisoners it seems. You know, one prisoner from that camp, one of the Russians, had walked home. All the way across Russia to the Ukraine. Walked it!"

Jack looked at Tosh. "So there's your story, Tosh. Except

to say that I'll never work in a mine again." I spent over a year in a veterans' hospital after returning to England. He smiled, then pulled a folded paper from his pocket. He opened it up and showed it to the others. It was a faded drawing of a horse sinking in the mud and an officer aiming a pistol at its head.

"Jesus Christ!" Tosh said.

"Holy Saints preserve us!" enjoined Barney O'Shea.

Chapter
Ten

~ ~ ~

The strike ended two months later and the line of men trudged through the gates of the Work as March went out like a lion. Fine powdery snow pirouetted in sporadic gusts of wind, settling briefly in corners of scrap metal and derelict masonry before whirling up to attack the procession. It danced around eyes and noses and funnelled into warm places through shirt collars. The line plodded on in silence.

Nothing had been achieved. The wage cuts stood unchanged.

Tammy Flynn's new union members had drifted away as quickly as they had joined. They had no interest any more. When Shug Anderson's escapade at the Powderhall races had been discovered, and Tammy had hauled Shug before the committee and extracted his agreement to pay back the money by instalments, no one really cared, except perhaps to reflect on how good a time Shug must have had, at least for a little while.

Tosh had shawed enough turnips to last him a lifetime. He walked on, eager to be back in his place at the shale face where he could exercise his own particular skills and see the results. Barney, walking by his side, was going home to join his wife whenever he had amassed enough to buy a farm in the Townships. He would work extra shifts to shorten the wait.

The two climbed onto the hutch and descended into the mine.

❧ ❧ ❧

With the men's return to work, a wave of relief flooded through the Raws of Myrestane and the minds of its women. No longer would they have to trip around the big feet of husbands and sons in their little kitchens, bearing up under their tantrums and their hopeless self pity, doing their housework each day in frantic fear of finding a letter at the door demanding the keys for non payment of rent.

For Peg, the routine of life came back, but her world was no longer the same. Jeanie had returned to Ireland in February, taking a final farewell of her friend in the early morning rain on the railway platform. There would be letters, of course, for Peg was a great correspondent, but both women knew that they might not see each other again. Peg sang *Galway Bay* that last night with Jeanie. It became Jeanie's song.

Jack Armstrong had dropped in several times at Tosh's invitation, and Peg had taken to filling a can of her broth each Sunday morning and going up to the farm after church to hand it in to Jack at his cottage.

The road to the farm was a narrow, gravelled track that ran westward from the Station alongside the railway. The plough-man's cottage was the first building you came to, about a half mile from the village, and lay just beyond a wide five-barred gate that gave access across the railway line to the fields on the other side. On the third Sunday, Jack came out to the gate to meet her and collect the soup, and each Sunday after that she looked for him at the gate when she got close to the farm. He was always there. He always waved as she came up.

Then they would sit down on the grass, she in her Sunday best and he, always in a shirt and tie and a checked waistcoat. Peg would hand over the soup can and he would ask her about her week and how Tosh was doing. They talked about their lives before Myrestane, their dreams and ambitions, even plans that had not panned out. They talked about people that they knew, the Ingrams, the O'Sheas and the characters in the Work that Jack had met in the Myrestane Inn.

When Peg asked him about the hotels his father had worked in and the towns where he had lived with his father, Jack would launch gaily into some tale or another. At the end of it she always noticed a wistful expression come over his face, and he would look away from her across the field.

Jack had grown a small moustache, a thin neat toothbrush type, across his upper lip. It made him look older, and when he was dressed, as he was on Sundays to meet Peg, he was dapper. He looked different from the crowd, like a man who was going somewhere and had not yet arrived; like Marco Polo browsing in a Persian bazaar.

For Peg, coming up the farm road on a Sunday was like taking a break from the world. It was if she were going on a journey to a foreign land where the sun always shone. It was vitalising. It was like taking the hand of a stranger and walking from a tunnel into bright daylight.

Then Jack would take the soup can into the cottage, transfer the contents to a bowl and rinse out the can to return it. She would take it by the wire handle and swing off down the track, head up and holding her hat in her hand. Jack would watch her go, the long slender shape carrying away on the breeze like a tall ship on a tropic sea.

ॐ ॐ ॐ

Tosh Douglas was a fearless man. He was not just a man who was unafraid of other men; for his size alone saw to the fact that he was never challenged. But fear was just not in Tosh's makeup.

Every day he fired his shots in the shale face, in dark holes two thousand feet under the ground. He bought gunpowder, twenty pounds at a time, and kept it under his bed until it was needed. Unlike Barney O'Shea, he was not haunted by the ghosts that religion puts upon men. Unlike Peg, he was immune to the temptations of dreams.

For all these reasons he was chosen to investigate the complaints of certain housewives arising from some incidents that had taken place on the canal banks near Myrestane.

The canal, constructed a century earlier, ran between Edinburgh and Falkirk, and its horse drawn barges moved coal, bricks and other heavy goods between these centres. It's level towpath, where the horses walked, also served the women of rural settlements as a route into Myrestane on Saturday shopping trips.

On several occasions of late, several women had been frightened by a tall man who seemed to suddenly appear by their side, always on the canal side of the path. The tall man walked along beside them, never speaking nor looking in their direction. He just walked along for a time and then was gone. He came without a warning and at different times of day. After several occurrences, no woman would walk the canal banks to Myrestane.

The descriptions of the man were somewhat vague and confused, but generally confirmed that he was thin and very tall, and not a local man. Those who alleged to have seen him said that he wore no hat, but they were unsure of his dress for their fear prevented them from looking at him.

When Tosh's own sister Nellie had a visitation from the stranger, he took the complaints seriously and set out on several Saturdays, when he was not on shift, to walk along the canal.

Barney O'Shea said that it wasn't a natural thing at all, and that, if he were Tosh, he wouldn't be going anywhere near the place. Peg, on the other hand, was sceptical, inclined to think that the reports were no more than yarns, spun by the residents of the Ryall cottages where the complainants lived. She could think of nothing that would alarm Nellie McBurny.

Peg's recollection of Nellie, whom she had not seen for years, was of a visit she had made to the Ryall shortly after her marriage. Nellie, then Nellie Douglas, and her old mother, Peg's new mother-in-law, had grudgingly asked Peg into their dark parlour. As they sat there in the half-light, by a polished oak table, both women regarded Peg with grim-faced assessment. She saw what they were thinking. This was the young hussy that had stolen Tosh away and deprived their household of his wages. Peg knew they were old-fashioned Scots, with little to say and never a smile. They didn't even offer to make a cup of tea, and when Peg rose to leave, the old mother pressed a six-pence into her hand, implying to Peg that this was why she had come. Now, to Peg, it seemed that this tale of a tall, silent man had been concocted to get Tosh back out to the Ryall. Of course, she said nothing of this to her husband, and Tosh went faithfully on his weekly vigils to the canal.

Some weeks later, on a bright, sunny afternoon, with Tosh ambling along twenty yards or so behind his sister and her neighbour, the long man appeared.

By this time Tosh was bored with the duty, and grasping absent-mindedly at waist-high grasses that grew along the tow-path. Suddenly Nellie screamed out his name. Looking up he saw the back of the tall figure walking close to the water and away from the women. They'd stopped and were frantically summoning Tosh. The anger rising in him, Tosh overtook the man and turned to bar his way.

"Whit are ye daein', yah big lang hoor, ye?"

The man stopped short. He was fully four inches taller than Tosh, perhaps six feet eight or nine, and thin to the point of being emaciated. Two clumps of long grey hair flopped down to frame a pale, gaunt face. He had a long straight nose and tiny eyes that might have been green or hazel. At Tosh's angry words, the thin lips slowly widened into a queer little smile that reflected mild but good-natured amusement at the challenge.

"Ye're frightenin' these bloody weemen," Tosh went on, glaring at the strange face, but seeing neither fear nor threat in it.

As Tosh's anger abated, the man brought a little book from behind his back and held it up to Tosh, a long-nailed thumb holding it open at a page. The little eyes motioned Tosh to regard it and the other hand pointed, in a spreading gesture, at the canal. Tosh looked briefly at the page and read the line marked by a pencil cross:

The waters wild went o'er his child,
And he was left lamenting.

Tosh looked up from the book at the figure before him. Now he took notice of the ancient threadbare suit of black cloth and the tightly fitted waistcoat with its line of pearl-coloured buttons. It was like an undertaker's suit, long since discarded by the undertaker. Tosh looked again at the face that was still smiling, and at the book which was being withdrawn to its place behind the man's back. The long arm moved out once more to indicate the water, and the figure moved forward.

With an involuntary movement, Tosh felt himself step to one side to let the man walk past him and on along the bank. Tosh turned back towards his sister who waved and pointed behind him.

Turning, Tosh saw that the stranger was gone. He guessed that the man must have left the towpath somewhere and made off across the fields. There was no sign of anyone on the long straight path that passed before him under two bridges on its way to Myrestane.

∾∾∾

"So, what did he say?" Peg persisted, as Tosh sat at the table, spooning his soup. Barney looked on with wide eyes.

"Not a thing," Tosh replied, between mouthfuls. "It wis jist like Ah tellt ye. He showed me the wee book wi' the words aboot waters goin' ower a child — Ah mind that bit — then he jist pointed at the canal. Like that." Tosh demonstrated the movement.

" 'Twas the devil, sure enough," Barney whispered, crossing himself.

"Devil, my arse!" Tosh mumbled through a mouthful of bread. "It wis jist a big hungry lookin' man wi' a long white

289

face; big hermless soul he wis, if ye ask me."

"And he walked through you," said Barney, crossing himself again.

"Naw, naw," Tosh cut in. "Ah moved aside and he walked past me, yah silly bugger."

"Why then did you move aside? Why did you not stop him?" Barney replied with a look of triumph. Tosh got back to his soup and said nothing. "Well, why?" Barney repeated.

"Listen!" Tosh exclaimed, his voice a bit too loud. "Let that be an end o' it. Ah don't want tae hear ony mair aboot it, ye hear! It wis jist a big man on the canal bank wi' a book and wearin' funny claes. Maybe he wis a wee bit touched in the heid. Hoo the hell wid Ah ken? Noo, forget aboot it. He'll no' be back."

Peg, who had gone through to the room, returned at that point reading from one of her own books.

"The waters wild went o'er his child
And he was left lamenting."

"Was that it, Tosh?"

Tosh looked up in surprise. "Aye, the very words," he said. "Whit is that?"

"It's from a poem called "Lord Ullin's Daughter". It's a favourite of mine. It's about Lord Ullin's daughter eloping with a Highland chieftain. Her father and his men were chasing them and they tried to cross the ferry in a storm. The two lovers were drowned and Lord Ullin was grief-stricken." Peg looked at Tosh and Barney. "You see what it means. That man on the canal bank must have had a child drowned there, and he walks the banks to protect people."

"Saints preserve us!" Barney said, his face ashen.

Tosh slurped the remainder of his soup straight from the plate. "Aye," he said.

"Anyway, Ah better go and get ma powder ready for the moarnin'."

After that, Tosh would meet the tall man again, from time

to time. Tosh gave him a name, for he thought that every man needed a name. He would call him Drumshorling Davie because he usually met him on the moor called Drumshorling Moor. While Drumshorling Davie would never talk, Tosh would get to know him in some strange way, but he would never again say a word to a living soul about their meetings.

෨෨෨

It seemed that no crisis ever occurred in the lives of the residents of the Station Raw that was not brought to the door of number nine. Peg was always there, and always available.

The night that Podge Docherty, two days out of Barlinnie prison, came home and beat up his wife, their two little girls ran screaming along the Raw to Peg. She took them in and washed their faces and sat them down at the table for milk and scones with jam. Then she went along to number five and barged her way in. Podge met her in the doorway, his hands clutching his forehead, where Rosie had hit him with the fireside poker. The blood cascaded down his face onto his shirt. Rosie sat by the fire, looking dreamily at the handle of the bread knife that stuck out from her beefy thigh. Peg tore up sheets and cleaned their wounds. Later she brought back the girls and put them to bed in their own house.

The next day she watched Podge and Rosie walk along the Raw, arm in arm, all smiles and bandages, off to the Myrestane Inn.

"Never come between a man and his wife," Peg used to say.

When Barney O'Shea came in, his face fraught with worry concerning the fact that he had, entirely inadvertently, eaten a slice of toast before communion, and what could he tell Father Byrne about that, Peg told him that God would surely forgive him for such a small sin. "We are all only mortal, Barney," she said, "and the things we do are human. As a priest once said, Barney, 'Sure if it wasn't a sin we'd all be doin' it!'" Barney looked at her with a vacant expression, and Peg scolded herself inwardly for having been unable to resist the joke.

For her own sin, Peg had no confidant. And, notwithstanding her usual powerful ability to justify her own actions as she did the actions of others, there was a niggling feeling inside her that refused to go away. The English soldier was emerging from the fiction of his earlier classification and pushing his flashing eyes into her real world.

One Sunday morning, as she dressed for church, Tosh looked up from his paper.

"Whae is this Wullie Begbie?" he asked, with more animation in his voice than he normally expressed in matters of people.

"Wullie Begbie?" Peg repeated the question, buttoning her coat. "He's that man who plays at the dancing. You must know him. Stays with his mother in the top Raw. Why are you asking?"

Tosh returned to the paper. "Oh, Ah jist heard somethin' aboot 'im last night in the pub. Likes the married weemin they say." Then, looking up, he added with a note of censure. "Jist you watch yersel at these dances wi' men like him."

"Och," Peg shook her head. "What a lot of nonsense. Wullie Begbie indeed!"

"Aye, jist watch yersel' onywey!" Tosh called after her as she went out the door.

∾ ∾ ∾

In August of that year Jeanie had her baby in her father's house in Inishennan, Michael Patrick Sean O'Shea.

Barney had gone over to be with her, and a month later he and Jeanie and their Irish son returned to their house in the Raw to the great pleasure of Peg Douglas.

The long summer nights saw the sofas and chairs dragged outdoors once more, and wee Sean rocked and mollycoddled by Peg, Granny Mooney and Rosie Docherty from tea-time to dark every night.

The Work was back in full swing, the lodgers had returned to their nests, and Jeanie O'Shea's heart was back once more in Scotland where a pound or two could be put by quicker than it would take to milk a cow in the old country.

The Gala Day came and went, with the dancing round the maypole and the children's races, and Wee Tammy Flynn handing out milk and cakes and cash prizes, his "wee refreshment" hidden among the milk bottles.

Peg never missed her church on Sunday nor her weekly errand of mercy with the can of soup to the farm. Jeanie thought it funny that, on the one or two occasions that she'd offered to put the baby in the pram and accompany her, Peg had put her off, saying that it was a rough old track for the pram or that it looked like it might rain.

In September, Jack Armstrong announced that he was leaving old Murray at the end of the week and going off to London for the winter. Some friend of his father's had a job for him in a hotel there, and it would be a warm change from the turnip field.

"And when will you be coming back?" Peg asked, with a sudden quiver in her lip, her hand tightening on the handle of the soup can.

Jack looked at her with a level gaze, as if he were seeing her face for the first time. "March," he said. "March or April, maybe." He held her eyes as she proffered the can at her side. He took it and laid it down on the grass by the gate.

"So we should say so long now, I think. And I'll see you when I get back."

All this time their eyes never moved. It was as if they were drinking each other in like some new nectar discovered in a hidden cellar, some numbing anaesthetic that they couldn't shake off.

Then, both in the same second, they grasped each other and their mouths met in a violent passionate kiss that joined their bodies and their souls, as a red dawn ensnares the treetops.

Chapter
Eleven

∾∾∾

The year 1925 was not a memorable year from the historical aspect. A pact was signed whereby Germany would never again make war against France or Belgium, but Peg Douglas found nothing to cut and paste into her scrapbook of heroes. There was another strike in the shale industry, this time extending over the whole shalefield. Wee Tammy Flynn and his union cohorts met Emanuel Shinwell at a political meeting in Myrestane, and elevated him in their minds to the status of champion of the working class after listening to his tirade against the House of Lords.

Many, including Tammy, lived on to realise the value of the promises of Germany and of the later Lord Shinwell. They were all lies.

But for David Ingram, who had no great interest in any of this, the year was memorable. It was the year in which he became the youngest ever partner of Cunningham and McCulloch, now Cunningham, McCulloch and Ingram W.S. Moreover it was the year in which he first clapped eyes on Eleanor Ross.

He met her at that little square in front of St. Giles Cathedral, as he was coming from the Parliament House and she was walking down the Lawnmarket with her father. The father hailed David and quickly crossed the street with his daughter in tow.

Herbert Ross was the manager of a small branch of a bank situated in the district called Blackhall on the western edge of the city. He had met David once or twice in relation to certain foreclosures that David's firm were handling. He was a short fat man in his fifties, with a florid face and a tricky expression that told David that his notion of doing business was to put one over on those he perceived to be his adversaries. David hadn't liked him from the first, and would happily have pretended not to see him on the street and made off in the opposite direction, were it not for the girl who followed along behind him. David wanted to see more of her, and closer up, so he waved back to the banker and waited for them to approach.

David saw at once that Eleanor Ross was a beauty. Up to now he had taken no great interest in girls mainly because he hadn't met any that showed the slightest bit of interest in him. His days had been filled with studies, the preparation for a career in the law, and his extra-curricular passions for gardening and astronomy. It wasn't that he hadn't noticed attractive girls. It was just that no opportunities to meet them had presented themselves.

Herbert Ross wasted no time in pushing Eleanor forward, much in the way that a winning sportsman might hold up a trophy to an admiring crowd. The effect on David Ingram was even more than Ross had hoped for, which brought a cunning little grin to the banker's lips.

She had fair hair. No, not fair. Golden hair, golden with the merest touch of red that sucked in the ordinary daylight from the street and whirled it around in its strands before blasting it out, new and regenerated, right into the eyes of the watcher. The face was masterfully formed with a pallor of perfection, and the eyes ... the eyes shone out like emeralds, bright green emeralds, turned up on the sand on a white tropical beach.

She was slim, but not too slim; tall, but not too tall; straight but not stiff. When she said "Good afternoon", her voice was soft, but not too soft, and her smile was exquisite.

That, in any event, is what David Ingram saw, and he just stood there, gazing, not even hearing the prattling little banker beside him.

Within a very few minutes he had been invited out to Blackhall for Sunday tea, had accepted, and still stood vacantly beside the cobblestone marker of the Heart of Midlothian as the Rosses moved out of his sight along the High Street.

On Sunday, in the parlour of the Ross house, Herbert Ross stood like a captain on the bridge, while Mrs. Ross, a small mousy shadow, flitted silently around with cups and spoons and napkins. David sat opposite his angel, oblivious to the wheeling-dealing of the master of the house.

Eleanor had had many admirers, of course, a long string of them, ever since her days at St. Ophelia's School and on through her life as a clerkess in the George Street insurance offices where she put in her days. But none had survived the testing assessment of Herbert Ross. None, until now, had been a partner in a prestigious firm of solicitors and an heir to a mansion like Strathalmond. None had taken Sunday tea at Blackhall.

Herbert's long wait had finally paid off. Now his gorgeous daughter would do the rest, and Herbert could relax from his searches in the knowledge that an acceptable suitor had been netted.

The daughter, for her part, was not slow to realise the power of her charms. She just had to flick the shining hair and flare the green eyes, and the young eligible bachelor before her would turn to mush.

And she did — that day and on every day thereafter that David could arrange to be around — and that was very many days indeed.

ᗯᗯᗯ

When Stewart Shaw received the request from Sam Ingram to come to Strathalmond, he had the feeling that something of importance was about to take place. Sam Ingram rarely summoned people, especially his friends, for they were free to visit any time and Sam would always be pleased to see them. The sending of the note by the hand of a servant implied a duty to be performed.

When Stewart stepped through the door into the drawing room, Sam was sitting in his usual fireside chair. He looked old and frail and had a blanket over his knees. Peter and David, the length of a sofa between them, sat opposite him. Sam waved Stewart Shaw to a seat.

"Thank you for coming, Stewart," Sam began. "I want you to be a witness to a document I have had drawn up. But first I want to explain what's in it and why." He looked toward the others and smiled. "That is so that my decisions are clear to everyone here, and nobody will later accuse me of being senile or not in my right mind."

David started up in his chair. "Grandfather . . ." but Sam raised a hand to silence him. Peter looked down the long length of his legs at the carpet, a bored look on his face, as Sam continued.

"I've had my three score and ten and a bit more. They say that when you get to my age you start thinking about all the things you might have done and didn't, and regret all the things you have left undone. Well, that might be the way of it for some, but not for me. For all the things I was able to do, I thank God for them. I have no regrets, not a damn one. I would do it all again tomorrow." He paused and looked round before going on.

"Now there only remains one thing, and that is to make my will, and it will be my last will. And that's what I have done, and I'm going to tell you what's in it, and then I'm going to sign it and get two servants in to witness it, and that will be the end of it. I'm doing it now, before I get too decrepit to do it, and if there is to be any argument about it, I want to hear it now."

The room was silent. At that point Sam removed the papers from under the shawl and carefully smoothed them out in his old hands. Then he produced a set of rimless glasses, attached by spindly wire legs, and hooked them over his ears.

"I'm not going to read all this, not all the lawyer talk," smiling at David, "just give you the gist of it.

"To my friend and partner, Stewart Ross, the sum of ten thousand pounds and my collection of old tools that I keep out in the garden shed." He looked up at Stewart. "You didn't know I had these Stewart. These are the first picks and shovels and long chains we bought when we started. Fifteen pounds. Remember them? You argued the toss with Tommy Simpson for about three weeks over the price." Stewart laughed.

"Then there are some legacies to the servants, some who are still with us and some who are retired. You will not be interested in these. I am leaving fifteen thousand to your mother, David. She was a good woman, and a good wife to Billy." At that, Peter looked up quickly as if to speak, then settled back, just as quickly, to his former disinterested composure.

"There's some money here for St. Nicholas Church, and one or two charities, and the workers' Friendly Societies that provide for them in hard times. Oh . . . before that bit, there are some gifts of paintings and furniture and things to different ones who have admired them." He looked up. "I might say that anything of that kind that's left will go with the house, and if there is anything here that any of you want to have, just tell me and I'll add it at the end and sign it. That's what's called a codicil." He winked at David.

"And now for the rest of it," Sam said, now peering at the will. "The house of Strathalmond, and everything in it, barring these items that are already excluded, is left to my son Peter Ingram and my grandson David Ingram, equally between them, and to the survivor of them." Sam paused before going on. "You know what that means. Peter and David will own it jointly, and when one dies the other takes it all."

Peter and David looked at each other like gladiators before a contest.

"All cash, bank accounts, bonds, stocks and shares belonging to me at the time of my death, save and except any shares referred to specifically in the next following clause hereof, to my said son Peter Ingram for his own use absolutely, provided that, should the said Peter Ingram fail to survive me for a period of fifteen days, the said cash, bank accounts etc. etc. to go to the said David Ingram."

Peter relaxed, the smile inside him never reaching his face. Sam raised his eyes from the will and took a sip from a glass of water on the table by his chair.

"Then there's this," he said, looking down again at the paper. "All my shares in Stathalmond Oils Limited to my said grandson, David Ingram."

Sam stopped talking but didn't look up from the paper in front of him. The others looked round the room, then at each other, eyes questioning. The seconds passed in deadly hush.

Suddenly Peter Ingram leapt to his feet, his face drained of all colour, his hands screwed into fists. He stood there for what seemed like forever, transfixed like a mammoth trapped in a coffin of ice, looking but not seeing, in a world it can't believe. Then, turning his back on the room, he strode out.

The others listened in silence as the Silver Ghost purred into life and swept off down the driveway.

David voiced the question that had immediately sprung to his mind at Sam's pronouncement.

"Grandfather, why are you doing this? I think Uncle Peter expected to get your shares in Strathalmond Oils. He has been running the business for years and I must say that I don't understand your decision. I am a solicitor, grandfather, not an oil man."

The old man laid the will papers on the little table. "David, I want you to run the company the way I would run it, with the interests of the men foremost in your mind. I know that times are hard in the industry, and likely they will get harder with the imports of foreign oil. I know all that. And your uncle is a capable manager. I know that too. But oh dear, he has no thought for the workers. Everything is figures and accounts, profits and losses. That might be the new way, but it never was my way, and if I have one last contribution to make to this business, it's to put some soul back into it. And I'm betting on you to do that, and I hope I'm not wrong." He looked at Stewart. "And you have an oil man here that will guide you right when you take over my holdings. Now away you go, the two of you, and talk about it, for I am going to get this thing signed and that will be an end of it for me. Never worry about Peter. There'll be enough for him to keep him in style for the rest of his days. He's angry now, but I'm sure he'll get over it. I don't think his heart was ever really in the business anyway."

∾ ∾ ∾

But a father can be entirely wrong in his perception of a son, and the bitter blow that was dealt that day to Peter Ingram was all the more grievous because it came from one he loved and who loved him.

He ran like a wounded fox to its den, the powerful Silver Ghost consuming the miles to Edinburgh and Peter, looking straight ahead, hands gripping the wheel and eyes blinking to clear the tears of rage and rejection. He had nowhere to go except to the house where his lover lived. Once there, he would curl up on her couch and lick his wounds.

Peter remained there in Morningside, closeted with Violet Walker to forget his hurt, leaving the running of the company to Stewart Ross and the other directors and spending his afternoons in the cocktail bar of the North British Hotel. When Old Sam died, a few months later, Peter returned to Strathalmond for the funeral, but the house held nothing for him any more and he stayed there only as long as it took him to arrange for the transfer of his things to the city, telling David that he would not return.

Notwithstanding the terms of the will, David had hoped that Peter would go on directing the daily affairs of the company. He even offered to transfer half of his shares to Peter, retaining the remainder out of deference to the wishes of his grandfather, but Peter would have none of it. He had no wish to take charity from his nephew.

He had spent his adult life trying to prove himself to an old man whose love had died with Billy on the Somme, and it had all been for nothing. What did he care now if the company prospered or foundered? What did he care now if the Anglo Persian company refused to take over the shale fields to shore up the local industry, and thereby drove another nail into the coffin of Strathalmond Oils? He would take what his father had left him, every penny to which he was entitled, and leave Strathalmond for good. David could have it. He could have it all, the house, the company and all the bleeding hearts that went with it, their whining and their crying, their cringing wives and their numberless empty-headed children.

All that he had done was done for that old man in the cemetery. He had made an industry work long beyond the time when it would have foundered but for him. He had listened to Sam's self-directed remorse for the treatment of workers, and closed his ears and his mind to all the sentimental clap-trap that would have impeded his efforts to keep the company going. He had worked, every hour of every day — aye, harder than any of them, harder than miners or surface men or any of them — to make it survive; to prove to Sam that he could do it; that he could do it better than Billy would have done it. And for what?

David could keep Strathalmond and all that came with it. Peter Ingram was leaving to pick up what was left of his life, to live it for Peter Ingram.

When he drove out through the gates after the funeral, Violet Walker was there, her ample figure straining in the tight black skirt and low cut fur top, waiting at the Miller's Wall where he had left her on the way in.

That was the nearest that she would ever get to Strathalmond.

∾ ∾ ∾

They say that when an old face leaves the world, a new one arrives, and that seems always to be the case.

About the time that Old Sam Ingram left on his final journey up the hill to St. Nicholas Church, Peg Douglas was delivered of a baby girl in the kitchen at 9 Station Raw. She called her Sandra, for no particular reason other than that she liked the ring of the name, and she loved her from the first second of her arrival.

Tosh, when he had returned from the mine to find that the baby was on its way, turned around and went back to do another shift. In 1925, men kept well clear of the birthing of babies.

Peg had ordered new sheets from the Cooperative, blue sheets and floral pillowcases. She would have no white around her. When her time came, Jeanie O'Shea sat with her, and made cups of tea on the stove, while Barney went to the chapel to say a prayer or two.

Jeanie, of course, being by now something of an expert in the raising of babies, talked non-stop about feeding times and changing nappies and what a great gift God was bringing to number 9. Listening to the soft Irish brogue, Peg let her mind wander. She was happy and she was unafraid, for everything felt right to her. She thought about Tosh and how pleased he would be in the morning when he came in to see his new family. She thought briefly about Jack Armstrong who had never returned, wondering where he was at that moment. When Doctor Rennie's car pulled up outside the door, Peg put all these vague musings from her mind and began to concentrate on her work and her immediate duty.

By the time the nights had drawn out again, and the late evening sun turned the bing outside their window into the fiery red mountain of a story book, Peg was walking out through Myrestane Station, pushing her pram and stopping a hundred times through the Raws to show off the new arrival.

Tosh turned over his garden, lifting cabbages and sprouts, nipping the weeds on the path, bursting with the inmost pride of fatherhood.

Chapter
Twelve

∾ ∾ ∾

On the last day of February in the following year there was a blizzard. The snow began early in the day and came down thicker all through the afternoon, the wind whipping it into a frenzy. By nightfall, nothing could move.

That was the night that Shine Mooney, the hardest man in Myrestane, went over the bing.

He was heaving up on the smoking hutch, hands gripping the steel and head down against the trams — the heavy metal frame — when the whole thing slid forward and tipped over the edge. Shine, trying to hold it back, was jerked forward by a ton of steel and burning refuse and dragged down the steep side of the bing before his frozen hands could release the load.

The chainrunner was the first to realise that something was wrong when the next two hutches were not taken off the chain, and the two men who arrived at the top of the bing to investigate, peered down through the dark swirling snow. They could see nothing of the missing hutch, nor of Shine.

It was around midnight by the time the nightshift had formed themselves into groups and set out along the foot of the bing to look for the missing man. The word got to the houses in the Randy Raws and men leapt out of warm beds, throwing on shirts, trousers and coats, and setting out to join in the search.

They looked all night, constantly relighting lamps blown out in the wind, feeling their way along the base of the bing and up its sloping side, lurching and sliding on snow and loose shale. They found the hutch, lying on its side fifty yards from the bing, but there was no sign of Shine.

When daylight came, Tosh and Barney joined the search, and made their way right up the face of the bing before they were summoned back down by shouts from those below.

"He's OK," Tammy Flynn said, when Tosh and Barney finally joined the men.

"He went doon the bing right enough, but then it looks like he got up and went hame tae his bed."

"Whit?" Tosh said, his eyebrows rising.

"Aye," Tammy said. "Big George went ower tae the hoose tae tell his wife, and she said that Shine had fallen doon the bing and came hame in the middle o' the night and went tae his bed."

"Jesus Christ!" Tosh exclaimed. "And aw they men oot lookin' fur 'im aw bloody night in the bloody snaw. Jesus Christ! Went tae his bloody bed! Christ, that'll dae!"

The relief that Shine was all right was quickly swamped by the groaning disbelief of the searchers which in its turn changed to smiles and the shaking of heads. But they later found out that Shine hadn't escaped the episode scot-free. He had a compound fracture of one wrist, and a face, black-eyed and swollen, like a cloutie-dumplin' put out on a window ledge to cool. At least, that was what Tammy Flynn said, and he had been round at Shine's house to see about a claim for compensation, Shine being a valued member of the union.

"That's a dangerous bloody job," Tammy said, "and the company will need to do something for this man. You don't see the Ingrams standing on the bing in the middle of a snow storm." Everyone knew that when Tammy began to talk "proper", this was a serious union matter.

Shine got compensation right enough. He got six hundred pounds for the time lost off his work — for you can't shove hutches with a broken wrist — and for what Tammy called "the grievous pain and extreme suffering".

Over the next few weeks, while Tammy strode around the Work with his head up and a triumphant smirk on his little face, Shine bought a greyhound for a hundred and fifty pounds and spent the rest in the Myrestane Inn from which he was oxtered home every night by the new friends he had suddenly made.

And that greyhound was going to bring a pile of trouble to the Station Raw.

∾∾∾

About the time that Shine Mooney's compensation ran out, Jack Armstrong returned to Myrestane and got himself a job in the brickwork, that tall metal shed at one end of the Work where the spent shale from the bing was crushed and compounded into red bricks.

Jack had read somewhere that a person learned more about the human condition by reading fiction of quality than he ever learned from living. That was when he had started reading, filling his leisure hours that fell between his stints of carrying luggage to hotel rooms, firing the boilers or serving drinks in plush lounges. After two or three seasons of acquainting himself with books, he began to think that what he needed most was some place that he could identify as home, just as all the heroes of his stories did. Myrestane was the only place that jumped to mind.

That was part of it anyway. The rest of it was that he was thirty-three and had little to show for it. He had no home, no bit of garden where he could grow a row or two of lettuces or sprouts or a few rows of potatoes of his own, no girl that would look out for him coming round the corner. His romances were all quick captures of transient waitresses in dark outfits with white frilly caps pinned to their hair. No real women, like the women in the books; women like Peg Douglas for example.

So when the time came for chefs and porters, waiters and

barmen, receptionists and chambermaids, to leave the warrens of London in the Spring and head out for Bath, or Harrogate or the Lake District, Jack just stayed on the train going north.

He moved into the Myrestane Inn for a few days while he looked around for suitable digs, for he had no notion of lodging in the Raws with a bunch of Irishmen, and he soon found accommodation in the house of an elderly widow called Mrs. McElvie. One large bed-sitting room and the use of the parlour, to entertain any guests.

Mrs McElvie referred to her house as her "establishment" and Jack, in this Victorian setting of dark oak and thick velvet curtains down to the floor, began to feel established. He set his books in the glass-fronted bookcase and paid a month's rent in advance, assuring the widow that her rules — no alcohol and no women after 10p.m. — were entirely satisfactory to him. Not that she had ever doubted it.

Nobody came or went from the Work in secret, and in no time at all Tosh had Jack Armstrong — "the sodger" as Tosh called him — over at Station Raw to hear all about his travels.

Tosh could sit for hours listening to Jack's tales of England: the grand hotels with indoor spas; the well-to-do gentlemen who arrived in carriages and drank brandy in lounges late at night, sharing their foibles with Jack as he helped them up to bed.

Tosh lay back in his chair, puffing his pipe and staring up at the chimney breast, stretched out in his salmon combinations-his semmit and drawers — for he didn't need to dress up for the sodger coming. He listened just as children listen to fairy stories, giving a little chuckle of disbelief now and then and winking to Peg.

Peg busied herself with her knitting or crocheting, looking up on occasion to catch Jack's eyes, then quickly away again. Sometimes little Sandra came toddling in from the room, demanding to say goodnight to "Uncle Jack" before being whisked off by her mother.

For Jack it was far from ideal but it was better than anything he had had before. It was being in a family, and while it was not his family and never could be, he bore no grudge. Tosh Douglas was a man's man and that was how Jack saw him. The baby was the first baby he had met and she called him Uncle Jack. When his eyes met Peg's, and he saw her blush and look away, he shivered inside. She was another man's wife and he had to stop his imaginings about her.

He thought that maybe he could invite her to call on him at Mrs. McKelvie's and sit in the parlour, and maybe take a cup of tea. She could bring a can of soup perhaps.

Tosh's voice boomed in his ear. "So what happened then wi' the auld Major? Come oan! Get oan wi' it man!"

ɔ∾ɔ∾ɔ∾

Many miners kept animals and birds. It was a well known fact. It had something to do with what these creatures represented to them; life and daylight and open space.

George Crawford had homing pigeons, his "doos" he called them. They were sometimes sent in large square baskets on the train south and shipped across the Channel to Reims to fly back over the North Sea right to the roof of George's doocot in Myrestane.

Walter Donaldson kept canaries in a small hut at the foot of his garden. Ferrets and rabbits abounded, and Jimmy Low took lifelong pride in the show prizes of his Kerry Blue terriers.

When miners got the one week annual holiday, the ponies that pulled hutches in the mine were brought up to the surface and tarted up to be shown by their handlers at the annual Agricultural Show at Linlithgow.

Below ground they wore harnesses called thwates — chains hooked to the collar and then to the swingle tree — and from that came a gabby that was attached to the front of the hutch. Then the pony pulled six hutches out of the miner's place to a point where the chain runner attached them to the chain to take them up the mine.

One particular pony waited until the hutch was loaded, then kicked off the safety catch and trotted freely off through the mine workings and back to its stall for a sleep.

For their savvy, and their efforts, mine ponies and miners shared a mutual affection, and on the day of the show, a mutual pride.

Now Shine Mooney, who had never previously shown any great interest in animals, or even in men come to that, had bought an Irish greyhound, and he gave Barney O'Shea the boat fare to go over to Ireland and collect it, as Shine had never been out of Myrestane.

Shine called the dog "Booey", for it was very light tan in colour, almost yellow, and some Highlander fellow in the pub said that "booey" was how you said yellow in the Gaelic. Shine had a notion in his head that, if he had nothing else, he would have this greyhound that cost more than a miner earned in four months. He bought a leash for it with brass studs, and walked it down to the Myrestane Inn, where it sprawled at his feet and guzzled the odd pint of beer that anyone would put down for it. It had a pedigree, written down on paper, that Shine drew from his jacket pocket a hundred times a night to show the admiring crowd. It listed names of sire, dame, grandsire and so on, going away back.

Tammy Flynn said one night, scanning the list, "Christ Shine, if that dug could talk, it widnae talk tae the likes of us." The dog looked up at Tammy as if in agreement.

Another night, Jack Armstrong was admiring the dog in the bar. "Have you ever had it at the track?" Jack said casually.

The question caught Shine by surprise, presenting, as it did, an idea that had never occurred to him. In Shine's mind, Booey wasn't the kind of dog that you take to a dog track as if it was just an ordinary old greyhound. He was happy for it to lie on the floor at his feet while he read out its filial commendations, or sleep on the end of the bed at night. Barney joined in.

"I was thinkin' that meself, Shine. Sure a dog like that would be bound to have the breedin' to whip anything around here, being an Irish pedigree an' all. You should give him a run some time to see what he can do."

As murmurs of approval went round the bar, Shine began

to feel oppressed by the suggestion that his dog had to perform, but it was a feeling that he would not convey.

"Well, ye know, Ah wis jist thinkin' masel' that that might be an idea," Shine said, taking a long swig from his pint and wiping thick fingers across his lips. "Aye, maybe Ah could see aboot that."

While the men stood around, wondering when Shine had ever seen about anything and what exactly did it mean, Sandy McLaughlin elbowed his way through to Shine. "Ah'll take him," Sandy said quickly. Shine turned his head to the new voice, his eyes now bleary with the beer.

"Ah'll take him," Sandy repeated, "tae Lithgie. Next Tuesday, if ye like. Enter 'im in the second race." He looked around for support. "That's the best race. The punters are a' there by then. Last race is nae good when they a' start leavin'. Ah'll enter 'im and walk 'im roond, Shine. Pit 'im in the traps. You dinnae need tae dae anythin'." Then he smiled and added, with a wink to the men, "Jist pit yer money oan."

And so, by common consent, it was settled. On the following Tuesday, Booey would run in the second race at Linlithgow Greyhound Racing Stadium, know locally as "Lithgie" to the dog betting fraternity.

Shine stood at the bar with an alcoholic grin on his still swollen face, accepting pats on the back, while Sandy ran around with his usual furtive look, telling everyone to keep it quiet.

"He's a new dug. Say nothin' tae anybody. They don't know 'im at the track. We'll get twenty-five tae wan aboot 'im. And Christ! Whatever ye dae, say nothin' aboot his Irish pedigree!" Sandy McLaughlin knew a thing or two about dogs and how the betting worked.

And so did Jack Armstrong.

∾ ∾ ∾

When the traps snapped open in the second race the following Tuesday night, Booey came out like a bullet. It was in the blood, you see. You don't pay a hundred and fifty pounds for a sleeper.

Of course it was helped by the fact that Sandy McLaughlin walked him around the fields twice a day and persuaded Shine to stop taking him to the pub for slops of beer.

When the cloth rabbit lolloped past the gate, whishing along on its wire, Booey was after it, a light fawn streak of bone and muscle, and the Myrestane men thought they had died and gone to Heaven. They got odds of 28/1, and while Jack Armstrong was quietly pocketing one hundred and forty pounds, the bookies were buzzing around like disturbed bees intent on identifying the invader of their hive.

Booey did the same at Armadale track before the forces of right could assemble themselves, and then again at Powderhall in Edinburgh, in front of the biggest crowd of greyhound aficionados north of London.

And that was it. Booey was known.

The story went around that he was a distant relation of the great Master McGrath himself, and Shine who had acquired him, and Barney, who had gone for him, graciously accepted the gratitude of the thankful punters. But taking him to the track now was a fruitless exercise, for you were lucky if you could get 2/1 on, and there was no money in it any more.

That is, until Jack came up with a new idea.

"Sure'n it was great while it lasted," Barney said, when he and Tosh had caught up with Jack on their way to the Work. "Everybody made a few quid, right enough. Sure'n we know Tosh here doesn't gamble, but I wouldn't mind bettin' that Peg had a bob or two on Booey." Tosh didn't reply.

Jack nodded. He had been pondering this whole matter for some time.

"Of course, it doesn't need to be finished," Jack said, carefully assessing the reaction of the others.

"He could be entered again at Linlithgow. Suppose he was a different dog this time?"

That was when the plan was hatched, and there were only the five of them in on it: Jack Armstrong, Barney, Tosh and Peg and, of course, Shine, whose only involvement was to lend the dog. Barney kept it quiet at first from Jeanie, for he knew that she interpreted the tenets of her church a bit differently from himself, but she later got to know.

A week later, in Peg Douglas' kitchen, Booey, the yellow tan champion of the local tracks, became Mr. Abe, the all black new contender. The transformation was effected by the application of a dye, a concoction of Peg's, made in a big pot on the stove. The dog kept looking round as Barney held him and Jack put the stuff on with a paint brush, the drips spattering on the newspapers laid out for the purpose.

Tosh, who was not a gambling man, merely looked on the scene over his paper, with the odd comment, "Silly buggers", before returning to his reading.

None of them, as they conspired to bend the odds, thought of this as anything more than a clever trick, a "great tear" as Barney called it. Jack saw it merely as a way to even the odds against bookmakers who had been robbing the punters for years, while Peg, for whom the Bible said nothing about painting dogs, and who would all her life enjoy a flutter or two on dogs or horses, had no difficulty justifying it. Anyway it was Jack's idea, she thought. A bit of excitement. Jeanie was not invited for she would call it a sin. Mr. Abe was none the worse of it except that he found the smell of the dye overpowering.

But to the practised eye of the track officials, not to mention the bookies, Mr. Abe had a familiar look about him as he romped home in front of the pack.

Jack, Barney and Peg picked up their winnings all right, but it wasn't too long before Sergeant Webster, the guardian of the law in Myrestane, called on Shine Mooney and later found his way to the Station Raw.

Whenever "Big Webster", in his long black raincoat and diced cap, parked his bicycle against the garden fence and made his way purposefully along the Raw, the neighbours were at the windows or squinting out through the cracks of partially opened doors.

A visit from Webster had a strange affect, especially when he passed right by Podge and Rosie Docherty's, his usual port of call. It was almost as if everyone suddenly became criminals, as if the only things they had that were unassailable, their honesty and their self respect — for they saw themselves as having little else — were suddenly being challenged, and there was a collective fear of losing even them. The guilty party — and there always was a guilty party when Webster came calling — felt the worst of all for bringing down shame on the Raw.

When Sergeant Webster knocked his big policeman's knock on the door of number nine, the neighbours were what the women of Myrestane called "black affronted", the shame of the offense stripping them of their honour and their name.

Later, being fined three pounds each — all five of them — and seeing their names in the local paper under "Sheriff Court News," was decimating to all except Shine who looked on it as an item of praise for his fine animal, rather than a conviction for fraud.

Jack hoped that his landlady wouldn't see it because she lived far enough from Myrestane Station not to learn about it otherwise. Tosh ranted and raved for weeks about it, and about Armstrong and O'Shea who got his house involved in it. Peg, after the initial blow to her status, bore up and resolved to put it from her mind which she was quite capable of doing. Jeanie O'Shea made frequent trips to the chapel to pray for all of them, and especially for Barney.

Later, when she was on her own, Peg smiled about it, and she added it to her list of tales, suitably edited, of course, to leave her name out.

Mr. Abe returned to his old lifestyle, lapping up beer slops in the Myrestane Inn, the light streaks of yellow appearing through the black.

He was the hero of the piece and well he knew it.

BOOK 2

PART 2

～ 1927–1972 ～

Chapter
Thirteen

ᖫᖫᖫ

I n the twenty or so years that followed, it would be untrue to
say that nothing happened, but the place was the same and
the Work was the same, and if Rip Van Winkle had drunk his
potion and gone to sleep in Myrestane instead of the Kaatskill
Mountains, he could have returned and been recognised in
just the same way.

Peg Douglas grew, almost imperceptibly, into a woman.

Tosh remained Tosh, and Jack Armstrong made a habit of
taking off every two or three years to England, or sometimes
the North of Scotland, for months at a time, before returning to
his home base at Mrs. McElvie's. The Douglases would get
postcards from places like the Ben Wyvis Hotel in Strathpeffer
— exotic mountain vistas. When Mrs. McElvie died in 1935,
Jack bought a little one-roomed house in the town called "Brig
Cottage", and continued in the same way.

Shine Mooney was killed in the first year of the war, and
George Crawford, who had joined up with Shine, was reported
missing in action until the truth about him was discovered a
long time later.

David Ingram married the beautiful Eleanor Ross one year
to the day after Old Sam died.

After one of the biggest affairs of a wedding ever seen at

St. Nicholas Church, to which the whole of the county set was invited, and at which Peter Ingram was conspicuous by his absence, they moved into Strathalmond.

Eleanor threw invitations to luncheon parties, dinner parties, coffee mornings and afternoon teas to a select, though voluminous, guest list. The banker, Herbert Ross, and his mousy wife frequently turned up. David took to disappearing into his greenhouse whenever the first guest appeared in the driveway and remaining there until they had all departed. No amount of remonstration by Eleanor could change this, and after a while the invitations ceased. She had to resort, for company, to the four high walls and the lavish décor of Strathalmond, for she had no use for walking in its grounds. When the influential visitors stopped arriving, so did Herbert Ross.

Barney and Jeanie O'Shea had four more babies, two boys and two girls, much to their delight and to the delight of Father Byrne. While these four were not born in Donegal, they were never allowed to think they were anything other than Irish. They were raised on a diet of stories and pictures of the Townships around Inishennan, and would travel there someday whenever the money and the time became available. But for now, growing up, Auntie Peg next door was the harbinger of songs and tales of Ireland and wasn't that the greatest thing?

Whenever Jack Armstrong was at home in Brig Cottage, back from his roaming and once again ensconced in the Work or back with Farmer Murray on the land, Peg took to walking down the road to Myrestane with a can of soup or a home-made pie, still warm from the oven.

She would go once a week, on afternoons when Jack was not on shift or when he was rained out at the farm, spend an hour or so, and then leave to collect Sandra from Myrestane Primary School at five minutes to four when the children got out.

It became so regular a thing, and Jack had grown to be such an addendum to their small family, that neither Tosh nor anyone else gave any thought to it other than that it was it a nice gesture to a single man fending for himself in that wee house.

When she started to make these trips, neither she nor Jack allowed themselves to recall that parting kiss from before. They talked together, just as they had always talked, about people and things, and the places Jack had been; and Jack lent her books from his new and growing collection lined behind the glass of the bookcase that Mrs. McElvie had left to him in her will. With time, each visit became more and more anticipated, and all the rules of conduct and morality, instilled in their generation, began to crack and crumble like the walls of a great dam, constantly pummeled by a raging river.

They both knew it. They both felt it. And neither one of them could do a thing to stop it.

∽∽∽

One bright Saturday afternoon, when David and Eleanor had been in Strathalmond for five years, a tall man in a long shabby overcoat made his way up the drive towards the house.

David was out in his greenhouse, his favourite place in all the world, and Eleanor, prettily attired in a light green pinny with large sunflowers embroidered across its surface, her golden hair swept back under a spotted kerchief, was dusting the window ledges with light, frolicking strokes of a feather duster. She saw the man approach, noting at once the poor quality of his clothing and the bald, hatless head. He approached with long uncertain steps constantly looking around at the trees as if he were in some strange forest.

Another tramp, she thought, as she downed her duster and whisked off to the kitchen for some piece of bread or cake to offer him.

Eleanor Ingram was good to tramps. It was a fact well known to the ones who called on her once or twice a year. She thought it funny that she did not recognise this one; funnier still that she heard the knock on the front door for her "regulars" knew to come to the back. With this censure in her mind, so that he might remember it the next time, she hastened across the wide hall to the door.

He stood on the top step, slightly swaying, the ragged coat hanging on his emaciated frame. At once, Eleanor smelled the rotten odour of bad alcohol. When he raised his large head, which he had difficulty in keeping steady, she felt a sudden rush of sympathy that came from the sad drooping eyes and gaunt cheeks.

She forgot her prepared remarks.

"Please," she began, "if you will just wait there a moment."

As she turned to fetch the food, the sad figure spoke. "You must be Eleanor," he said, smiling to reveal a few large yellow teeth. The smell of drink overpowered her. "Might I. . . . speak to David?" Then, seeing the perplexed look on her face, he added, "Tell him it's Uncle Peter." With that, he staggered and reached out a skeletal hand to catch the door frame.

Arrested by surprise and disbelief, Eleanor tightened her lips and motioned him in. She glanced at the door to the lounge, briefly discounting it, and led him into the kitchen where he thankfully plunked himself down on a wooden chair at the table while Eleanor hurried off to fetch her husband.

Peter Ingram sat there, head back, his watery eyes roving around plate racks and brightly papered walls. This was the place he had abandoned, given up to his nephew in a fit of rage. Now look at him. He was a hopeless drunk and had lost everything.

His confused mind pondered dreamily over the interval of years. When was it that Violet had left him? It was after the time he had been found lying in a close off the Grassmarket. Or was it before then? Which time? When he'd lost his car? Where was his car? When he vomited over her bed, she said he wasn't her Captain any more. Or was that later? He was trying to remember when David entered.

"Uncle Peter!"

It's funny how grown men still say "Uncle". It must come from their childhood training that won't go away, even after they have grown up, even when the uncle is a drunken old wreck of a man, smelling of cheap wine and urine, swaying in the chair and gripping the table with black talon nails.

"I' don't . . . wan . . . t' trouble you. Jus . . . came t' see how you . . . are." That was as much as Peter could say. His head flopped down onto his chest and he went into a snuffling, snoring sleep.

David and Eleanor helped him to a bed in the guest room and later cleaned him up.

The next day at lunch Peter Ingram had recovered his sobriety and some of his old self as he sat down at the table, cleaned and brushed and wearing some of David's clothes. His own rags had already been burned by Eleanor in the garden incinerator. It was clear that he wanted no talk of the day before, or where he now lived or what he did. Why had he come?

He talked about the Work, as if he had never been away. He was genuinely horrified to discover that David had seen fit to use a major part of the company's capital reserves to avoid further cuts and closures, and had even granted a substantial mortgage on Strathalmond in favour of the bank.

David was not sure why he told Peter this, except perhaps because it had become a constant concern for him, and Peter — the old Peter anyway — had a good business head. But he winced inwardly at Peter's animated criticism of his nephew's decisions. Was this not a drunk that he and his wife had just taken in and cleaned up and given the hospitality of their house?

After lunch, Peter stood up, thanking them for their time and trouble and announcing that he must be on his way. Eleanor, whose tramp had turned into a prince — Peter Ingram of Strathalmond, former Chairman of the Board of Strathalmond Oil Company — made delaying gestures. Meanwhile David made a serious effort to get Peter to stay. Perhaps they could discuss the Work.

Peter smiled as one might smile at a lost chance. Suddenly he looked every day of his sixty-two years: the deeply lined face, the tired eyes and the slumped, narrow shoulders.

"No nephew. It's too late for me now. I'm going back where I came from, so I'll be saying goodbye. I just came to say goodbye."

Two months later, Peter Ingram died in a model lodging-house in the Grassmarket. He had apparently choked on the cork of a wine bottle. Found in his pocket was an old crumpled photograph of Old Sam Ingram and Stewart Shaw, posing with their shovels beside the old cannon at the gates of Strathalmond.

❧ ❧ ❧

Peg had decided that there would be one time for her and Jack. She came to that conclusion in St. Nicholas Church just as the minister looked hopefully for a message in the Song of Solomon.

> *The voice of my beloved! Behold he cometh leaping upon the mountains, skipping upon the hills.*

One time, for there could only be one time. She knew that now. It had become very clear in her mind, and the very next afternoon she went to Jack Armstrong. The minister's words still rang in her head, as they lay down on the bed in his cottage, clutching, grasping, enveloping each other, the blood surging up in them as if to consume them.

Afterwards she lay against him, her head nestling into the pillow, and he leaning on one elbow looking into her face, and their eyes said that it was finished. She cried then.

Jack left again in the Spring.

All that summer Peg set her heart, her happy, rejoicing fulfilled heart, on pleasing her husband in every little way that she could dream up. In the day she cleaned and cooked with a renewed vigour, and at night she lay beside him, feeling the warmth of his long shape through the cotton of her night dress. She would suddenly turn and kiss him. And Tosh would hold her then and they would make gentle, leisurely love.

In the year that the war broke out, they had a son whom they called Ian, and every Sunday in church from then on, while the service ground along, Peg said her own prayer thanking God for him.

When Ian was two, he learned that stamping on his father's corn, as Tosh reclined with his paper, produced a lively reaction. When Peg rushed forward to deliver the required doze of discipline for the offense, Tosh rose right up to meet her.

"Don't you touch that laddie!"

Then he would rest back again with a well-contented look.

∽∾∽

The cough came on Tosh all of a sudden, the night he was standing in the Myrestane Inn listening to Wullie Robinson, the new union man for the Work, telling about Tammy Flynn's trip to London to see Manny Shinwell. Tammy had survived the Work, but the killing silicosis that it spawned in its dust-filled chambers was now sucking away his life. He had kept himself alive for one final union duty — one last visit to see Mr. Shinwell, on behalf of the members.

It was nineteen forty-five.

"We went tae see him," Wullie went on. "It was the cruellest visitation Ah've ever been on." Wullie laughed ironically. "We sat ootside his office, and the agent, Bert Logan, was on two sticks with athritis. Wee Tammy was the organiser and he was pumped fu' o' morphine, to keep him living, to get to London. The doctor says: 'You'll never make it Flynn!'

" 'Aye well,' says Tammy, 'I'll die on the road doon, then.'

"They took us into the office down there, and we weren't half an hour in the place — no' even a cup o' tea — when Shinwell told us there was no hope for the industry, and it was antiquated ... Aye, it was a cruel blow. Logan says to me, 'D'you know, Wullie, that's the worst treatment Ah've ever had. Ah never got worse treatment fae a Tory minister, than what we got fae that man the day.'

"This was a cripple on two sticks, and Flynn fu' o' morphine ... no' half an hour in the place ... after travellin' all night tae.

"And coming home," Wullie went into a laughing fit, "coming home the army and the sailors were all coming back fae the war. Logan says tae me: 'Listen Wullie. We'll get doon a while before the train's due, and we'll be sure of gettin' a seat.' Him wi' athritis, and the other wi' the silicosis. Some bloody hope!

"Well, we went doon about an hour afore the train was due, and you know, there wasn't a soul on the platform. *But*, afore the train come in, there was a queue aboot half a mile long and Logan and us, we never got on the bloody train. . . . a great rush. . . . sailors, sodgers, everythin' comin' back fae the war. Logan says: 'Christ almighty, Wullie, away you go hame yersel' . . . Ah'll get hame some time . . . *Ah'll never be back tae this bloody London ever again!'*

"We got the next one, and we were lookin' for tae grab the hud o' a door, ye know. . . . get the hud o' a door. One stopped right opposite. . . . a mad rush. . . . Logan and Flynn and me landed right across the other side o' the bloody carriage; *Aw Christ Lads . . . Bloody London..Ah help ma Christ!"*

Wullie Robinson took a swig from his pint in the silence that ensued.

When Tosh got home that night, the cough grew worse, and in the morning a large circle of blood stained pillow and sheets. A few days later, Peg raised him in the bed to fix his pillows and saw the great lump of blood and tissue disgorged on to the bed in front of him. Doctor Rennie ordered the ambulance and told her that Tosh had to go to a city hospital for it looked bad.

It was cancer. Peg knew that although the word itself was never uttered, only mouthed in silent fear. That particular ward in the Southern General Hospital was the end of the road.

They prayed, of course, Peg in her church and the O'Sheas in the chapel. Even Father Byrne called on Peg, though she was not one of his flock, and prayed with her.

They went to see him, every Saturday, Peg and Ian, for Sandra had been married the year before to Eddie McLean and had her own house in another town. They took a bus to

Edinburgh, then a tram down Leith and along the sea front, summer and winter for nearly a year. That was how long Tosh lasted. That was how long it took to reduce a man from twenty stone to six.

The ward was a long room with twelve beds spaced along each side. It had double entrance doors at one end, and two toilets and an emergency exit at the other.

Ruined men lay in each bed.

Nurses would move the beds so that sometimes when Peg and Ian went, Tosh was closer to the entrance; sometimes further away. Tosh had a theory that a move away from the entrance meant improvement.

Peg asked him on one occasion why a certain patient, formerly in the next bed, was now up near the door. Tosh leaned up with an earnest, pained expression.

"Because he's packin' in," he said in a whisper.

Ian looked along the ward at the man in question, and wondered what it meant.

For Tosh Douglas, it was a year of agonies, with operations to remove part of a lung, then more of it, then all of it.

After he died, the doctor told Peg that he was riddled with cancer, and Peg walked out of the hospital door, taking Ian by the hand, and stood looking across the road at the grey waters of the Forth. The words bored into her mind; "riddled with cancer". After all the operations, the pain, the cutting, the endless praying, the hope in Tosh's face one week, the despair the next. All the months of hope and the tears of her beloved husband were reduced to folly in that phrase "riddled with cancer". They had known it from the beginning. It was the cruellest thing that she could imagine. Done to the finest man.

In that drafty porch of the large hospital, Peg Douglas cried as she had never cried before, as Ian held her hand tightly, his eyes gazing straight out across the estuary.

The day she buried her husband Peg sat in her usual pew in St. Nicholas Church, straight-backed and black, like a great witch of old. Her eyes moved from the coffin to the gold-lettered message above the pulpit.

IN THIS HOUSE WILL I GIVE PEACE

She looked back to the coffin. It was the first time that Tosh had been in a church since their wedding day, thirty-two years before.

"Pie in the sky when ye die, Peg," he used to laugh, as she dressed for church on Sunday morning. But she went and he didn't and somehow that had never mattered to either of them.

Snatches of Reverend Thomson's words, distant and frail, pierced her reverie as she cut away the years, bringing pictures of her husband so fixed and clear into her mind that he was there beside her.

"....a man so well liked by all who knew him...", the minister paused, looking at his notes. "....a good man, a temperate man..."

The words triggered a thought in Peg's mind that brought the merest smile to her lips.

"A temperate man! Tosh?"

She thought how strange it was that the wildest nature of a man could be lost forever in the equalising cant of a eulogy. No man was kinder, no man more gentle, no man more intemperate on occasion than Tosh Douglas.

For weeks, Tosh Douglas, the gentle giant of Myrestane, would trim the privet hedge at the bottom of the little garden that he had claimed from the mineral railway siding and nurtured over the years, or sit on the front steps on long summer nights puffing his pipe and puzzling at the world. Then he would rise, feel in his overalls for the pound or two that he had secreted there and go off to the Myrestane Hotel, returning later, much later, eyes wild with drink.

Tosh Douglas, whisky taken, was a jealous man, jealous of Wullie Begbie. It was as if all his calm deliberations during weeks of sobriety had been merely the concealment of a basic dread.

ᨦ ᨦ ᨦ

"And where are ye aff to tonight?"

Tosh swayed in the doorway as he asked the question. Peg didn't look at him as she reached for her shawl and purse. "The dance."

Tosh didn't dance, but it had long been an agreement that Peg could attend the local dances on her own, or with a girl-friend, as dancing was one of her great loves.

"Is Begbie goin'?"

"What Wullie Begbie does or doesn't do is no concern of mine," Peg said, in that polite English way she adopted when she was becoming annoyed.

"Oh is that so now?" Tosh returned, getting set for a long argument.

"Yes that's so. And don't start the old story of Begbie again. I have to go. I'm meeting Jeanie at seven."

"Ye're sure it's no' Wullie ye're meetin'?"

Peg pushed past him out the door. "I'll be back when the dance finishes. Mind and keep that fire going. I'll need hot water in the morning."

"Tell Wullie Begbie Ah'm askin' fur'im. Tell 'im Ah'll be comin' tae see 'im wan o' these nights," Tosh shouted after her, staggering in the doorway.

The monthly dance in Myrestane school hall was the clos-est that Peg Douglas ever came to a county ball. She used to dream of officers in white gloves and scarlet uniforms and her-self in crinoline, hair up in a chignon, floating across the floor in some palatial setting. That was the dream with her father in it. The dream of what might have been.

But when the music started, wee Tammy Flynn striking up the *Gay Gordons* on the fiddle, Peg's dreams faded into the happy, noisy, here-and-now of the evening. All her friends were there, sitting along the benches by the wall, chatting and laughing amid reel and hornpipe.

Peg was a good dancer and she would be asked up often by Angus Stark or his brother Matt, and sometimes she would dance with Jeanie and they would whirl and stomp to the *Dashing White Sergeant* and laugh their way back to their seats, hanging on to each other like the old friends that they were. Come midnight there was tea and sandwiches, and the musicians slipped through to the kitchen for what Tammy called his "wee refreshment".

Wullie Begbie extracted himself from his accordion and came over to plunk himself down next to Peg, his fat face red with effort and his big dimpled knees pushing out beneath the kilt like two Druid burial mounds.

"How are you tonight Peg?" he asked breathlessly in his soft girlish voice.

"Oh, grand Wullie, grand."

Jeanie giggled and nudged Peg with her elbow. Peg strove to keep a straight face.

"How's your mother Wullie?" she asked, knowing that his mother was Wullie's favourite subject.

"Couldn't be better, m'dear. Couldn't be better. She was up the town yesterday and got a new dress. My, it looks lovely on her."

Jeanie burst into laughter and Peg struggled, purse-lipped, to stay serious. She looked away from Wullie, trying to maintain control.

It was then that she saw Tosh. He was standing in the lobby peering into the hall. A fear rose in her, putting flight to her laughter, and she jumped up quickly and made her way along the benches to the door.

"Did you come to see me home?" she said as she drew near to him.

Tosh seemed non-plussed by that. "Ah . . . er . . . Aye," he mumbled.

"Well I'll just get my coat and I'll be right there," she said.

Tosh shuffled backward into the lobby, looking at his feet. "Aye," he said.

Outside the night was black. Peg walked ahead with Tosh following, entirely unaccustomed to the notion of seeing someone home from a dance. After a while he spoke. "Who was that ye were sittin' wi'?"

Peg felt her heart give a leap. "Who?" she said, walking on in the darkness.

"That big wummin wi' the big knees," Tosh said.

Peg's mind fluttered for a moment, then grasped it. He thought Wullie Begbie was a woman. Of course..the kilt. Peg could hardly restrain the laughter.

"Oh, just a friend of Angus Stark's; a woman that's visitin' them", she said.

"Oh Aye," Tosh replied, resigning himself again to silence.

They walked on in the black quiet of the night, Tosh's befuddled brain looking for a peg to hang its hat on. Nearing home she passed the long fence by the road with a big anchor post at its end.

"Ye see that!" Tosh shouted from behind her. Peg looked round.

"Ye see that!" His anxious cry split the darkness.

He was standing before the post, staring at it in a growing rage. "That's Wullie Begbie!" he shouted, looking up briefly to Peg then back to the post.

She made a move towards him and suddenly he drew back his arm and plunged his fist into the post with such a force that Peg just halted there in the darkness, riveted by his madness. She heard the crunch of his breaking knuckles and felt the cold sweat opening on her brow.

"Oh my God," she breathed as she stood fixed to the spot, unable to move to him.

Tosh turned slightly towards her, his useless hand hanging by his side, a look of hopelessness on his face.

"Oh God," she said. She went to him, putting her arms around him, covering his face with kisses.

"There's no Wullie Begbie, Tosh," she said. "There's no Wullie Begbie."

Tears burned down her cheeks as she stood there, crying in the dark night, holding that big man.

∾ ∾ ∾

But there was a Wullie Begbie. Not Tosh's Wullie Begbie, but her own. The one that had been her own secret over all these years, the one that had never gone away, the one that could still leap into her consciousness even now, even in this place.

Peg wondered, sitting there in the pew, how a man's life could be summed up and ended in a single sermon. She looked again at the coffin and she heard the sniffles of mourners in the hollowness of the church.

She suddenly thought of her father and the poems he had read to her. Christina Rossetti was his favourite.

When I am dead my dearest,
Sing no sad songs for me.

She took strength from the thought.

The minister was coming to a close as Ian nudged his mother. "Are you all right, Ma?" he whispered.

Peg squeezed the hand of her eight-year-old son, the little dark-haired Douglas with the same proud tilt of the head that her husband had. "Fine, Ian," she nodded. This was Tosh's legacy, she thought. When all the memories faded of the life that was gone, this boy would remain. The thought consoled her as she cast a last long look at the coffin.

"Pie in the sky when ye die, Peg." She smiled a farewell to Tosh Douglas, her husband and her friend.

Outside the church Peg kindly accepted the handshakes and embraces and the soft spoken condolences of the multitude of mourners. They trooped past her: Barney O'shea, her husband's great friend and drinking crony; neighbours from the Randy Raws, and from the Station Raw where she had lived a lifetime with Tosh; relatives and friends; men from the Work; and even the owner of the Work himself, David Ingram.

As he approached her through the crowd, tall and stooping, prematurely bald with the long face of the Ingrams, Peg was struck by his resemblance to his grandfather, Old Sam Ingram. She remembered her visit to Strathalmond twenty years earlier as spokesperson for the men. She remembered when she had gone there as a girl and served drams of whisky to Old Sam who called her "the lassie", and she remembered the day she left, running through the rain. Old Sam Ingram was like Tosh, she thought, "fondly remembered and sadly missed."

David Ingram shook her hand. "Your husband was a fine man, Peg." He covered her hand with his own in a brief expression of warmth. "A fine man." He turned and walked off through the mourners, inclining his head here and there to men that he knew.

Peg watched him go. The last of the Ingrams of Strathalmond, she wondered. The end of an era for the Douglases and the Ingrams?

Later, at the graveside, on the cold windswept side of the hill that overlooks Myrestane, Ian Douglas, now the man of the family, let the cord run through his hand as the coffin tilted into the black earth. Only men attended the cemetery. They crowded around the grave, six or eight deep, in their black ill-fitting suits and big polished boots. Men from the Work. Ian could see Wull Aicheson, Mathie Thompson, George O'Neill, Wee Tammy Flynn and a host of others that trudged between the miners' rows and the Work every day.

Ian looked around the men. Back from the crowd, under a big elm by the pathway, he saw a long erect figure in a black funeral suit, holding a bonnet in his hands as the wind blew up his great white head of hair. It was Davie.

Drumshorling Davie was what Tosh had called him on that fine September day the year before.

∾ ∾ ∾

Fifteen minutes walk from the Randy Raws in Myrestane, along the Beugh Burn and south past Strathalmond House, the ruined shell of Houstoun Castle groaned with age. Sheep grazed in the dry hollow around its walls and wood pigeons nestled among it's crumbling stones. A lark sang itself into oblivion in the cloudless sky as Ian searched through the grass around the thick bare roots of the ancient tree. He could smell the clover and feel the sun on his back.

"Ah've found one, Faither!" he shouted, lifting the walnut, extricated from its outer shell, and squeezing it between his fingers as he examined the perfect seam that joined its two halves.

"Aye, that's a guid yin son," said Tosh, taking it and turning it in his big hand.

"Ye see that tree?" Ian looked at the broad gnarled trunk, split down its length to the ground by some invisible giant axe. He squinted up at the sparse craggy branches, eyes blinking in the sun.

"That was here when yon castle wis new. And the folk that steyed there got walnuts aff that tree." Tosh put his hand on some ridged scars on the bark. "Ye see that risen up bit there? Somebody's carved something there a long time ago. Yin o' these folk likely."

"Who stayed in it, Faither?"

"Some say the Black Douglases," Tosh said, smiling at the boy. "Same name as us. Ye've heard o' them in your school lessons, haven't ye?"

Ian knew the name from somewhere, not from school but . . .

"Ah heard Mrs. McGrath singing to her baby something about Black Douglas, Faither. Wis that them?"

"Aye son." Tosh laughed and sang the words.

Hush ye, hush ye, little pet ye,
Hush ye, hush ye, dinna fret ye,
The Black Douglas shall no' get ye.

Ian looked fearfully at the ruin. "Did they get people, Faither? What did they dae tae them?"

"Oh, it's jist an auld sang, son. Nothing for you tae worry aboot".

Tosh looked over to the castle, rubbing the walnut in his hand.

"Here's a man comin', Faither", Ian said, moving closer to Tosh.

The man who approached was tall and spare. He walked erect with long steps, holding one arm behind him while the other swung freely. He wore funny clothes and a big bonnet and he smiled at Ian, a funny little smile. Ian pressed against Tosh, not sure why he was scared.

"Just stand there a meenit, son", Tosh said, setting the boy by the shoulders against the trunk of the walnut tree and then moving off towards the stranger.

Ian stood under the tree watching the two men. He heard his father say something. The other man produced the hidden hand from behind his back, holding up a small book. He couldn't believe his eyes, seeing that the man was three or four inches taller than Tosh. He was the tallest man that Ian had ever seen.

The man opened the book and seemed to show it to Tosh. Tosh nodded his head. They stood for a long time, gesticulating with their hands, and now and then the boy could see the book being held up as if it were the final word in a discussion.

Then the tall man turned and walked away with the same long stride, reassuming the posture with the book clutched high up behind him. Tosh returned to Ian, a happy smile lingering on his face.

"Whae wis that, Faither?" Ian asked.

"Oh him. He's Davie," Tosh smiled, looking back at the departing figure. "Drumshorling Davie."

"Where's he from?"

"Oh he's. . . . fae here, son. Well. . . . nobody really knows where he's fae . . . but he comes here fae yon moor. Well, it used to be a moor. It was called Drumshorling at wan time."

Tosh continued to stare absently after the stranger.

"What's his book aboot, Faither?" Tosh, turning round,

smiled and then knelt down in front of Ian, taking the boy's shoulders in his hands.

"It's a book o' writin', son. Writin' o' great men."

Ian was puzzled. Tosh continued. "And Davie meets folk here sometimes and shows bits o' things tae them oot o' his book."

"Have you met him before, Faither?" Ian questioned.

"Aye," Tosh replied. "Maybe if you come here when you're a big man, you'll meet him. But he disnae come tae everybody. Only some."

"Is he. . . . a ghost then, Faither?" Ian's eyes were wide with a mixture of awe and fear.

Tosh turned away his head, looking at the empty fields and the old castle then returning to his son. He laughed. "Naw son. Not a ghost. He's jist a man." Then he arose. "Come on. Your mother'll hiv the tea ready."

The man and the boy silently made their way down across the fields to Myrestane.

∿ ∿ ∿

The biting cold wind that whirled around the mourners in St. Nicholas cemetery made Ian's eyes water, and he cleared them with his fingers. Men brushed past him, mumbling their respects. "Sorry for yer trouble, lad."

He looked over again at the elm tree but there was no sign of Davie. He was gone just as Tosh was gone; as if neither of them had ever been. Not real, but only pictures that flickered on and off in the minds of the living.

That's what men became, Ian thought. They became ghosts. Maybe that's all they ever were. And all the things they did, and all their laughter, their jokes, their tears and their songs, and all the folk they touched, lingered for a while in folk's memories and then faded away.

The handful of dirt that Reverend Thomson tossed down into the grave bounced across the polished surface of the coffin.

"Dust to dust and ashes to ashes. . . ." His voice trailed away on the wind.

Following the church service and the cold, miserable graveside ceremony for which Scottish Presbyterians are noted, Peg gave Tosh a send off that was talked about for years. She rented the Institute Hall and laid on tea, cold meat sandwiches, scones and cakes from Burns the baker, and drams of whisky enough to go around all the men from the Work who attended. And they all came. And they talked about Tosh, reminiscing all through the afternoon and long into the evening, a continuing interactive eulogy that Peg Douglas interpreted as a collective thank you for the pleasure of having known him.

∾ ∾ ∾

Barney O'Shea became faceman at Tosh's place in the mine, and while he missed his friend for a long time, he continuously felt his presence on the descending hutch and as he walked through the roadways to the bench; Tosh with his cannie ways and his constant reminders of the rules.

But even the rules could not make this place safe. Two years after Tosh died the disaster that lurked in the darkness of every mine, waiting to happen, happened in Myrestane No.4.

Barney had two drawers, just boys really, and they had all stopped to eat their pieces. Then Barney went back to the workplace to check for gas. This was one of the rules following a break. One of the boys followed him, a naked acetylene lamp on his cap. As Barney turned to shout a warning, the explosion came. A wall of fire ran through the roadways.

When Barney came to, he felt the pain in his face and hands and could smell the burning flesh as he groped around for the boys. Later he discovered that one of them had been killed outright, thrown against the wall by the force of the explosion.

The fire spread out of control through the mine. Part of the roof caved in and fourteen men were trapped behind a hundred feet of waste and a wall of fire. The fire raged all weekend and on Wednesday the fourteen bodies were brought to the surface.

Rescuers told about it. "The explosion . . . couldnae recognise any o' them . . . like scalded cats, running around trying to get out . . . you could see their 'Glenny' lamps, powder cans, coats and jackets hanging on the "trees" where they were aw straggled thegither. Bodies ta'en tae lie at the baths tae be identified. My . . . dear . . . what a death."

Barney was two months in the local hospital, the Burns Unit that had been set up to treat victims of the war. Jeanie and Peg went to see him several times a week, and there was a constant flow of men from the Work. David Ingram visited him twice.

Barney's burns healed. He was one of the lucky ones.

Chapter
Fourteen

∾ ∾ ∾

Myrestane High School stood on a small rise, grey and
squat and challenging. Not far away the Work puffed and
blew in mechanical rhythm, grinding its message into the
hearts and souls of Myrestane, as it had now done for over half
a century, its black smoke darkening the sky.

In the grey school, in classroom four on the second level,
Mr. Cook, English master, moved at his own pace; a shade
slower than the Work but just as relentlessly.

> *On either side the river lie*
> *Long fields of barley and of rye*
> *That clothe the wold and meet the sky. . . .*

Mr. Cook delivered Tennyson's lines in a monotonous,
nasal voice, head slightly bowed and face almost hidden
behind thick, shiny black hair.

> *And thro' the fields the road runs by*
> *To many-towered Camelot.*

His students watched his eyes, weak squinting eyes
behind heavy black-framed lenses, eyes that darted from

side to side to catch the inattentive.

"You boy!" The devastating nasal command issued through a sneer. A podgy white index finger singled out a victim on his left while the eyes still looked right.

The class of twelve year-olds stiffened.

"You! . . . Simpson! Recite!"

Ian Douglas, who sat behind the ill-fated Simpson, leaned forward at his desk with a show of attentiveness that he hoped Cookie would notice. A victim had been selected, and Ian was ready to cheer inwardly with the others as a Christian entered the arena. The heart-pounding gave way to immense relief, and now they were ready to throw Simpson to the lions.

Simpson rose shakily to his feet with a hopeless glance at the class. He was a tall, freckled boy with the fine features of a girl, smartly turned out in the school uniform by a doting widowed mother who believed that Myrestane High would help her son.

Simpson knew that Cookie would select him. He should have been resigned to it by now, but he wasn't. He began with faltering words.

"On either side the river lie. . . ."

His voice quivered in high-pitched terror. The classroom was silent.

Mr. Cook's sneer softened to a kind of smirk, through his thin lips, beneath the still indecipherable squint.

". . . . the many towered Cam..el..ot," Simpson quivered.

The final syllable rose in pitch. It always did. Simpson knew it would, and the class fretted.

In three steps, Cook, an animated tailor's dummy in grey suit and laundered shirt, was beside Simpson.

"Cam..el..ot?" he screamed, imitating Simpson. "Cam..el..ot? "Get out to the floor!"

He seized Simpson by the ear and hauled him half around and half across his desk to the front of the class. The freckled boy was crying. He was a long way from home. The others shuddered with fear.

Ian tried to reason that Simpson was a deserving fool. He

was angry at Simpson and at Cook at the same time. He was angry at his own cowardice.

"Cam..el..ot," Cook reiterated, now dropping the last syllable of the word to a baritone.

"Cam..el..ot. Say it, boy!"

He had, by now, forced Simpson against the blackboard by repeated blows to the chest with his fat palm. The boy's arms rose involuntarily to fend off the blows as he staggered back on spindly legs.

"Cam..el..ot," he sobbed, the 'ot' still perceptibly higher than the rest.

Ian winced. He felt hot tears welling up in his eyes. Simpson was his friend. He was the poorest kind of boy, a victim of school bullies, pupil and teacher alike.

No father, no grime-faced muscled miner would come to the aid of David Simpson. He wasn't Wullie Bell.

Wullie Bell, who sat in the back row last year, used to be Cook's victim. That was until the day when he had wiped a torn sleeve across his face, smearing tears and saliva, and shouted, "Ah'll get ma faither!" After Big Puncher Bell had arrived at the school the next day and almost broken Cookie's jaw, everyone thought there would be no more bullying.

They were wrong.

"Cam..el..ot, Cam..el..ot," Cook droned.

Simpson leaned against the blackboard like a boxer on the ropes, sobbing and running a hand across his eyes. The bell sounded for the end of the period.

In relief the class rustled bags and books. Ian packed Simpson's bag and his own and moved to the blackboard. Cook was already preparing for the next class, unperturbed and unemotional.

Simpson shamefacedly took the bag from Ian, and, rubbing his eyes, left the room. Ian followed him, not knowing what to say, not saying anything. The ordeal was over for today.

The next period was music with Mrs. Taylor, "Squeak", as she was called by consecutive years of unsympathetic pupils who had never failed to note the exact point at which her soprano began to shake. Squeak was kind, and she suffered for that in Myrestane High.

Thirty-five first years, escaping from Cook, descended the stone stairway to the music room, Genghis Khan' hordes. Tackety boots sparked on grey granite and girls, gripping briefcases, were jostled along the handrail by apprentice ruffians.

Angus Knight, the brainy one, Cook's pet, was kicked on the shin on the way to music. Simpson kicked him, but nobody noticed. Knight was in tears when he arrived at Mrs. Taylor's room.

They pushed and shoved their way into their seats, ignoring the massive back and rear-end of the long-suffering Squeak who was writing on the newly cleaned blackboard.

She formed in large letters, "George VI".

At length she turned to face the class, her eyes red and moist.

"Class. . . . I'm afraid I have bad news for you today."

She paused, taking a little frilly handkerchief from a huge sleeve and dabbing daintily at her eyes. An expectant hush settled over the room.

"The king is dead."

She said the words in a whispered kind of finality, looking around her charges for some rapport. Angus Knight was still tearful as he rubbed his bruised shin, and Squeak gave him a painful little smile. Class 1A began to react, heads turning and questions arising on their lips.

"Whit king?"

"Ah dunno. Ah think she means Archie King, the janitor."

"Naw, he's no deid. Ah saw him this moarnin' "

"The king o' England, that's whae she means."

"Whit's she greetin' fur, onyway . . . wis she related tae 'im?"

"Ma faither kens the king o' England."

"He dis not!"

Class 1A didn't know that Mrs. Taylor had once met the king. That was when she had sung *Cherry Ripe* at the Young Musicians Concert in the Usher Hall, and after the performance the king had shaken her hand and said that she was a fine example of the young musical talent of Scotland and that she could look forward to a glorious career in music. Mrs. Taylor's tears were real.

School closed early because of the death of George VI and Ian walked home to Myrestane Station with big Hugh Donaldson. Big Hugh lived in the Raws behind Ian. The boys walked along the railway line that branched from the main line in a long gradual sweep into the Work. Big Hugh stepped out easily from one railway sleeper to the next, Ian breaking into an occasional trot to keep up.

"Want tae go oot tonight?" Ian asked, concentrating on the slippery wood under his feet. "We could get Simpson and Podge and go up the bing. Look for rabbits."

"Awright," Hugh grunted.

There was a single wagon on the line where it passed their houses, and the boys jointly lifted the heavy brake lever and were straining to push the wagon when a black-faced man in a cloth cap shouted from across the track.

"Get tae hell oot o' there!"

Hugh made a face at him and both boys ran down the embankment and through the vegetable patch to their respective doors. Peg was down on her knees, doing the step with red stone, when Ian reached the house.

"We got out early, for the king's deid," he smiled as he sallied past her into the house.

"Wipe your feet!" she shouted after him. She looked back to her work with a little grin.

Jack came home from the Work at six. He threw his piece box in the corner and tousled Ian's hair with a strong, calloused hand.

"Give Uncle Jack his chair," Peg said.

Ian readily jumped from the fireside chair. Uncle Jack smelled of sweat and of the Work, a unique smell, a smell that Ian loved. He could stand big-eyed and smell his uncle all night.

Afterwards, he watched Jack strip off his shirt in the

scullery, and pour the big kettle of hot water into the tiny sink.

Ian wondered if he would ever have muscles like that . . . these little ones behind the upper arm that most men never had, but his uncle had. Ian didn't have them. It scared him to think he might never get muscles like that.

"What's doing tonight then?" Jack spat through the soap, leaning his powerful frame further over the sink.

"Goin' out wi' Big Hugh," Ian replied, ogling at every ripple of Jack's back.

"The king's deid, Uncle Jack." Ian was suddenly elated to have something new to tell Jack. It made him feel worthy.

"Oh aye," Jack keeked around at Ian under a raised arm. "When did that happen?"

"Today. The teacher told us. We got off school early for it."

"Aye it's an ill wind," Jack smiled, turning his middle finger in his ear. Ian didn't understand.

"What's that, Uncle Jack. . . . an ill wind?"

"Oh, it's just a saying, son. It means there's always something good comes out of everything. The king died and you got a holiday." Jack sloshed water over his face and reached for the towel. Ian watched him for a minute, still wondering about the ill wind.

"Jean Maxwell at the school says that her faither knew the king. Is that right?"

"Not likely, son. Folk like us don't move in those circles," Jack laughed.

Ian felt deflated. He was sure that Uncle Jack would have known the king. He returned to the kitchen where Peg was setting the table for tea, and sat on Jack's chair looking into the glowing red fire in the polished grate.

"Ma. . . . do you think that the king would have had muscles?"

Peg looked up, a handful of cutlery in one hand, the other pushing the long black hair back from her face. She burst into laughter.

"Muscles? Heavens, what made you think of that?"

∾ ∾ ∾

In the next Raw, in an identical living space, Walter Donaldson sat in his chair looking vacantly into the fire for a face to appear there. He had begun to do that after his wife died, and it had become a habit, a daily ritual.

Walter tended the breaker at the Work on a permanent six to two shift. Then he came home to his untidy house, lit the fire and just sat there watching it, looking every day for its secret faces.

His wife Rosie had gone out one day, no coat, no purse . . . just walked out the door and never came back. Weeks later they found her, round behind the bing, lying in the long grass. An open bottle of household bleach lay beside her body and her frock was torn apart at the neck where she had clawed at it in her final agony.

In those days, these tragedies fell on Myrestane like the plagues of Egypt, and men had to harden themselves, at least on the surface, and face up to the living. But on the inside the toll was often too great, the cost too dear, and the life that should have been sufferable became a daily purgatory.

Hugh burst through the door into the middle of the little kitchen, big and loud and tousle-haired, with all the strength and energy of youth that should have raised Walter Donaldson from his lethargy. Instead, it only pressed him deeper into his dark solitude.

"Ye'll need tae feed these birds," Walter said, hardly looking up at the vibrant youth. "And then cut some sticks for the fire in the mornin'." The boy swung his school bag over a chair and, without comment, made his way through the house and out into the back green.

In the ten by four hut, heated by a paraffin lamp and sealed with bits of cloth and newspaper against draughts, Walter Donaldson's fifteen prize canaries swung on spars, or sat on eggs, or preened their feathers behind the close mesh of the cages.

It was no chore to Hugh, feeding the canaries. He liked the

warm smell of the hut. Inside, with the door shut, it was like another world, a fluttering chirping world of birds where little things were done: nests made, eggs laid and hatched, tiny beaks groping wildly in the blind act of survival. Now and then he would lift a bird, holding it gently as his father had shown him, with the first two fingers behind the wings and the thumb resting against a yellow beating breast. He felt the life between his fingers and admired the roundness and hues that won prizes. Walter came into the hut behind him as he transferred a hen from one cage to another.

"Watch her now! She's a wee bit nervous," he said quietly, opening the cage and guiding Hugh's hand with his own. The wings fluttered briefly, and Hugh brushed the tips of his fingers against the soft feathers.

"Sh-sh," he whispered.

The bird relaxed, letting itself be set down on the straw.

"Ye see how she's a prizer, eh?" Walter said, watching the bird.

"Aye, it's her shape faither . . . an' her stance."

"That's right, son," Walter said, closing the cage door. "She got it fae her mother. Her mother wis a champion, ye ken."

Hugh looked briefly at his father, then back at the cage. "Aye," he said.

The two stood for a while in silence, looking around at the birds. Hugh could feel the warm nearness of his father and smell the pipe tobacco from his jacket, the strong and sickly sweet "Old Bruno".

"Mrs. Toal wants a bird for the hoose, and she wis doon yesterday and says she likes him the best." He pointed to a white canary on a perch.

"Shows ye how much she kens aboot canaries, eh?"

His father laughed, and Hugh wished that they could stay in the hut forever. Then his father wouldn't go away and leave him as his mother had done.

Peg was happy. Jack was a good man. He was good to Ian and Ian needed him.

The way that Jack had come to be living in Peg's house after Tosh died would not have been believable to the residents of Myrestane, especially if they had had any inkling as to Peg's earlier passion. But the fact of the matter, and how it began, was that Peg was afraid to live alone. She was afraid of ghosts.

She told the O'Sheas about her fear because of the way the thing transpired.

Some weeks after Tosh's funeral, Peg was awakened in the night to a knocking on her front window. It was about 2am and her first thought was that perhaps someone needed her assistance and had knocked on the window, rather than on the door, to attract her attention quietly and quickly. She got out of bed and went to the window, asking who was there. There was no reply, just more tapping on the glass.

For most imaginative people, and particularly those for whom religion plays a major role in their lives, the supernatural is never far from their thoughts. It comes from their notions of mortality and their already ingrained belief in a controlling entity that lies just outside their own existence. Peg Douglas fell into this category. While she was no coward in the normal sense, the continual tapping from an unknown source, elevated by the lack of response to her questions through the glass, began to conjure up phantoms in her mind. As she stood there, shivering in the cold of the kitchen, the tapping ceased. She gathered up the courage to open the door and look out. In the dull moonlight, the Raw was empty.

Peg barred the door, but as she returned to bed the tapping began again, this time at the back, on the bedroom window. She moved from her bed past that of Ian, who was sleeping soundly, and through the open door to the room. She called out again, her voice breaking now with a growing fear. The tapping continued.

She could only stand there, terrorised, wishing that Tosh was still with her. Her mind raced in pictures, trying to grasp reasons, real and unreal. Was it Barney O'shea playing a prank? But why would he do that? Who was it? Why didn't they answer? But there was no-one outside? Was the knocking real? Was someone making it . . . or something?

The knocking went on, then it stopped. She heard it again at the front. She thought of going next door to the O'shea's but she was too terrified to go out. Crawling back under the blankets of her bed, she lay there trembling with cold and fear. She shut her eyes tightly, trying to force it away. A spirit? Someone trying to contact her from the spirit world? Was it Tosh? No! No! She knew that Tosh wouldn't do this. Not Tosh. He knew how much it would frighten her. Then she thought about the man on the canal banks, Drumshorling Davie. Ian had told her that his father met him frequently and he had been at the funeral. Was he a ghost? Was it him?

She lay awake until morning.

In the daylight, she tried to reason once more. She went next door and asked Barney if he had knocked on her windows in the middle of the night. She almost blamed him, for she didn't want to countenance the alternatives that the darkness had raised in her head.

Barney denied it. More than that, he was hurt that Peg should think he would do such a thing. Peg listened to him, stubbornly refusing to believe him, though she knew all the time that she did believe him. Jeanie wanted to send for Father Byrne, because for her it was unnatural and only the priest could resolve it.

Peg knew one thing. That she could not stay another night alone in that house. In the afternoon, she walked down to Brig Cottage and asked Jack Armstrong if he would stay in her house that night. She told him of the knocking, and of her fear, and he agreed. She made up the bed for him in the room, and he came and stayed that night. And every night thereafter.

If there was any talk around Myrestane about Peg Douglas, a very recent widow, and the sodger, Jack Armstrong, it never fell on Peg's ears. Jack was her lodger, and that was all he was. Somehow, between themselves, this relationship suited them exactly. The notion of marriage never entered Peg's head, because of Tosh and because she had Ian, Tosh's son, and that was enough for her. Jack had what he dreamed about — a home — and he got even more than that, a boy to whom he could be a father.

He was Uncle Jack, but somehow he was more than that, much more. He knew it and Peg knew it, and most of all, Ian knew it.

Chapter
Fifteen

∽∽∽

David Ingram and Eleanor had few arguments.

They had their own separate areas of responsibilty and involvement that rarely overlapped. His were the offices of Cunningham McCulloch and Ingram in Edinburgh, the meetings of the board of Strathalmond Oils Limited, which still took place in the head office in Strathalmond, and his garden; hers were the keeping of their home and the raising of their two children, Jonathon and Ann. But on the odd occasion something would crop up which involved them both, and on which they did not see eye to eye.

One such issue raised its head when Jonathon was ten, and finishing Primary 6 at Myrestane Primary School. That was the age when children were admitted to private schools in Edinburgh, or to the Edinburgh Merchant Schools.

The difference is not a matter on which it is essential to linger. It is enough to say that there were Merchant Schools where education was thought to be good, where children could go if their parents had gone, or to which they could win scholarships if they had enough grey matter to do so. Then there were other schools which were not so good, but which would take those who failed the entrance examinations for the Merchant Schools.

All of these schools charged fees. All of them gave some guarantee that their pupils would have any vestige of the Myrestane vernacular excised in favour of the English language. All of them sought to create, at least in the minds of parents, some notion that their children, either through education or proper speech or mixing with "their own kind", would have an enhanced opportunity to succeed in the world.

David Ingram did not subscribe to these claims. Eleanor, who had herself attended St. Ophelia's School for Young Ladies, one of the private schools in the "stupid but saveable" category, as David later put it, could not imagine her offspring continuing for a moment longer than was necessary in the State schools of Myrestane.

It is notable indeed that Eleanor had not been academically distinguished, but she had never needed the nurture of any particular institute of learning to arrive at her chosen goal. Her looks alone had served the purpose very nicely.

"I don't want to argue about this any further, Eleanor. Jonathon will continue his schooling in Myrestane and that's all there is about it," David concluded.

Eleanor's green eyes flashed. "Oh but I think not," she retorted. "The well-being of our children is as much my concern as yours, and I will not permit them to grow up among a tribe of hooligans just because you have some misguided ideas about the benefits of State education."

David, who wasn't given to outbursts of emotion, shook his head. "State education is every bit as good as what they dish up in these fee-paying places. Look at the records. What school in Scotland do you think produces the greatest percentage of university entrance pupils? A State run school. And it does it year after year."

"I'm not talking about university entrance, I'm talking about upbringing. I'm talking about language and manners and the people they will be mixing with." When she got no reply, Eleanor continued. "What about George Usher? Eh? What about him? One of your own under-managers. He didn't send his boy to Myrestane. Oh no. George Heriot's, that's where he went.

What are people to think if Jonathon ends up in that . . . that jail-house of a school in Myrestane? The son of the chairman of Strathalmond Oils. A partner in a law firm. What will your partners think?"

And so Eleanor went on. She stopped to serve up tea, which they ate in silence, then she started again. But she knew that, as in all major decisions, she would have to give way to David, though, for the life of her, she couldn't understand his thinking on this occasion.

David didn't tell his wife, but the reason for his decision was entirely financial. They had two children and that meant two sets of school fees. Nor was the practice of law as lucrative as many thought. David's moves to refinance the oil company were now causing him great anxiety. There was a mortgage on Strathalmond and a less-than-healthy cash reserve. And the industry continued to slump. There had been a revival during the war, when oil was in big demand, but cheaper oil from elsewhere was gaining ground and the mining and retorting of shale had a limited future. David had listened too much to Old Sam, and not enough to Peter, and now he would pay for it.

Jonathon continued his schooling in Myrestane, and Eleanor, whenever she had occasion to walk into Myrestane for shopping, spent much of her time trying to avoid Mrs. Usher and her constant harangue on the subject of Heriot's school.

"You know, Mrs. Ingram, Robbie is doing so well in French and German. Of course the fees have gone up again this year, but I was just saying to George, one gets what one pays for. They don't do languages in Primary 7 at the local school, do they? Such a pity I always think. Languages are so useful, wouldn't you agree? And Robbie is doing so well, and you know, just the other day........"

Robbie Usher was Bob when he was at Myrestane Primary, "Boab" in fact. What a marvellous thing...fee-paying schools. Eleanor still thought so, anyway, and she hated to be reminded of it.

∾∾∾

Jonathon Ingram, without the aid of a Merchant School, and in fact without the aid of the Myrestane schools, turned out to be quite brilliant all on his own.

He had, in abundance, two of the three ingredients for success in life, intelligence and the power of concentration. He lacked the third, sociability.

At twelve, he built an adding machine that worked. At fifteen, he discovered a series of numbers which he sent off to a university in Manchester or somewhere, only to be advised that it was called the Fibonacci Series and had been discovered by an Italian mathematician called Fibonacci in the twelfth century. After that disappointing news, Jonathon set himself the tasks of designing a perpetual motion machine, and of discovering the formula for the nth prime number. These two problems took up thousands of hours of Jonathon Ingram's time, nor were they ever resolved, either by him or by anyone else.

But Jonathon hid his light, as they say, under a bushel, saying nothing of his deliberations to either parents or teachers, and the only three people who ever saw that light were his sister Ann, Ian Douglas, and Hugh Donaldson.

While Jonathon pondered upon the mysteries of mathematics, Ian and Hugh were catching trout in the Beugh Burn — Hugh being possessed of an amazing ability to "guddle" them, catch them with his hands and pull them out from beneath rocks to throw them up on the bank. They were also learning to snare rabbits, or walking through the woods looking for the former site of the fish pools of Houstoun Castle or the odd, tentative contact with two rather special girls from that area whose morality left something to be desired.

Alone, Jonathon ploughed his solitary way through his books at the long oak table in the study of Strathalmond. In Myrestane High School, he gave the impression that he was putting up with a bothersome obligation that wasted his time, and he gave that institution no more than minimum attention. As a result, his marks were maintained at no higher a grade than was needed to keep David and Eleanor marginally satisfied, for he knew that marks were of the utmost importance to them.

After a while, Ian took to visiting Jonathon in his cloistered study of Strathalmond, and Jonathon was glad enough of the visits, as indeed was Eleanor. By now she realised that Jonathon needed the company of a boy his own age, albeit of a less than ideal background. Besides, Ian Douglas had consistently high marks in school and Eleanor thought that perhaps some of this ability might rub off on her own son.

Over their final years at Myrestane High School the friendship between the boys matured, although it was always circumscribed by their respective perceptions of the human condition. Ian, whose interest in mathematics was active enough, but far from intense, did not achieve the status of kindred spirit, something Jonathon craved. Jonathon's lack of feeling for his fellow man, as Ian saw it, put a certain distance between them.

Jonathon's books, which were many and supplied for him without reservation by his father, all in the good cause of education, would be lent to Ian without hesitation. Two weeks later, Ian would receive a letter in the post, phrased exactly like a library reminder, saying that the books were overdue now and should be returned. Ian would take umbrage at this and miss a visit or two. Jonathon would have been sorry, had he been able to understand what he was to be sorry about.

David Ingram rarely emerged from his garden, and Ian saw little of him. Nor did Jonathon. Eleanor delivered tea and cakes to the study for her son and his rather dour, unsmiling friend, and regulated the time and termination of their meetings. Sometimes Ann would appear — "my little sister" Jonathon called her — two years their junior, a freckled-faced, bubbly girl with chestnut hair and a rather well developed figure. Neither boy really noticed her as they engaged themselves on some earth-shattering mystery.

Jonathon's interests extended to music and collecting records, everything from classical to popular with the exception of folk-singing which was Ian's favourite. David and Eleanor didn't have a note of music in their respective bodies.

Jonathon was one of these people who love music, can hear it in their heads, but are unable to reproduce it in any recognisable form. Ian, who had been raised on music, the music of words and voice and instrument, could not understand this; that Jonathon could not even hum "O can you wash a sailor's shirt?" Nor could Ian understand what Jonathon saw in the record sleeve photographs of Virginia Mayo that he had plastered around his study as if she were some kind of goddess.

Ian's interest in the opposite sex had not progressed beyond the two woodland nymphs who would sometimes let him and Hugh put a hand up their skirts, but who would have to be chased off when they threatened to follow the boys home to the Station Raws.

ოს ოს ოს

Ian's early association with Jonathon ended at the age of sixteen when Ian, Hugh and Jonathon had a party in Strathalmond.

It was Jonathon's idea. He somehow got it into his head that it would be good to have a party for himself, Ian and Hugh. Ian never understood the reason for the party. There was no special occasion to celebrate, but it sounded like a good idea to himself and Hugh.

Eleanor also thought it a good idea. She was concerned about Jonathon's fairly solitary existence and lack of friends. Anything that would reverse this situation had her approval. She was convinced that, had her son gone to a proper school, things would have been different. The other local boys, who attended Merchant Schools, would have included him in their circle. As it was, he had two visitors, Ian Douglas and Hugh Donaldson from Myrestane Station Raws, and although they were not an ideal choice of companions, they were all Jonathon seemed to have. As his mother, Eleanor would not discourage them from coming to Strathalmond.

The party fell under Eleanor's category of good housekeeping. Because boys had big appetites, she would bake

350

cakes and scones, shortbread and biscuits, and her own very special gingerbread. She would clean and tidy the study and lay out a table for these goodies, and she would buy in a selection of lemonade and fruit juices. And she would talk to David about letting Jonathon have his party on the night of the Strathalmond Oils Annual Ball.

David and Eleanor rarely went out. There was no function or performance that other people attended which could attract David away from his greenhouse or garden, or that he considered as anything other than a waste of time. Eleanor was generally happy enough with this. With her reading, sewing, crafts and baking she had plenty to do. Besides, she did not care to be thrown into the midst of these wives whose children attended school in the city. But Eleanor and David had decided that the company ball might merit their attendance this year, particularly since they had not attended it before and some people were asking questions about the repeated absence of the chairman.

And so it was decided. They would attend the ball, and Jonathon could invite his friends and have his party on the same night. Eleanor was happy about the arrangement and pleased that David didn't object to the plan.

Things would have been different had they known that Jonathon had laid in certain supplies of his own — six Babychams and two cases of VP wine.

On the night in question, Jonathon's sister, Ann, had her first ever date. He was a pupil at Myrestane High called Joseph Condy. They were off to the cinema and Condy promised to bring her home by ten o'clock.

Ian and Hugh arrived at the house with a couple of bottles of cheap wine of their own, and the boys had Strathalmond to themselves.

It was the greatest party.

Discussion ranged from prime numbers, to the Rubiyat of Omar Khayam, to the climbing of Everest, to Jack Kerouac; wise, serious, erudite discussions. Toasts were made to the picture of Virginia Mayo, to Joseph Stalin, to Wolfgang

Amadeus Mozart, to Brendan Behan, and to the budgerigar in its cage, which was invited to join in the celebrations by having its water container filled up with wine.

Records were played by needles held in the hand; girls were phoned with befuddled, amorous suggestions; wine was poured across rows of glasses in a single flourish.

When the wine ran out, Jonathon made his way to the kitchen, returning with a three-quarters full bottle of Cherry Heering, a bottle that had lasted his teetotal parents through half a dozen New Years, by being produced only when necessary for the odd imbibing guest.

As Scotland's national bard once wrote: *the night drave on wi' sangs and clatter; and ay the ale was growin better . . .*

"You've got to meet these girls, Jonathon," Ian said, lifting a shaky glass to his lips. "Up at Houstoun Wood. Eh Hugh! Tell him about the turnips. Eh!" Hugh just laughed and poured himself another glass of wine. The South African VP, that, at the beginning of the night, had tasted like paraffin, had now matured to a very acceptable vintage.

Jonathon stared glassy-eyed at Hugh. "What turnips?" he slurred. Ian answered.

"Well, the fat one . . . with the big arse and the pink knickers . . . she threatened to follow me and Hugh home, you see. And she started after us. I think she was in love with Hugh here." He started to giggle. "Anyway, Hugh pulled up a big turnip out of the field and he fired it at her. Bounced right on her head . . . that right Hugh? Bounce! Just like that! Christ I thought he had killed her." Hugh took up the story.

"Aye, then the other one. . . . what's her name? . . . the skinny one . . . your one, Ian . . . well she grabbed Ian's shirt and wouldn't let go."

"Aye," Ian said. "Ah put ma hand in her blouse and grabbed her tits. . . . they were like wee hard oranges. . . . but she still held on to my shirt. What a bloody night, eh Hugh? Jonathon, you'll have tae come wi' us up there. We have the new mating ritual. . . . throwing turnips at them. They love it!"

The three collapsed with laughter into chairs, wine spilling across the carpet.

"Hugh!" Ian said, "give that budgie anither drink, will ye! It's gone awful bloody quiet." More laughter resounded through the house. It was the greatest party.

When Joseph Condy brought Ann Ingram home at ten, as promised, they met Hugh Donaldson and Ian Douglas steering an uncertain course down the driveway, Hugh supporting Ian who was speechless as well as legless.

"Ann!" Hugh exclaimed, his head swaying in front of her face, "Jonathon's drunk!"

Surprise, turning to curiosity, turning to panic projected her steps towards the house, Condy following along behind like a lost sheep.

The great oak door was wide open. As the two passed through it, the smell of vomit and putrid alcohol made them gag. The hall table was overturned, its vase of flowers smashed and strewn across the tiles. A trail of regurgitated wine and cake led across the floor to the door of the study. Ann forced herself forward, petrified at what awaited her there.

She had never seen such a mess. Pools of wine and vomit stained the carpet and dripped off the edges of the table. Newspapers, originally designed to cover the table, now lay crumpled and torn all round the room. Empty and partially empty wine bottles lay everywhere, fragments of broken wine glasses were strewn across the fireplace and the remnants of half-eaten cakes were ground into the Persian rugs.

Her brother, collapsed on a sofa, looking for his missing spectacles among the ruins of the evening, raised his head and peered at Ann through the fog.

"Don't tell mum'n dad I've been drinking!" The effort of saying it exhausted him. He could say no more.

All Ann could think about was cleaning the place up, and she immediately set about the hopeless task with the help of Joseph Condy. Condy took Jonathon upstairs and put him to bed, while she worked feverishly on the wreck of the study. But she hardly knew where to start. There was devastation everywhere she looked. Mum and Dad would be home soon. What would they say? What would they do? The budgie looked on from the floor of its cage, its feathers all fluffed up the way budgies go when they're drunk.

When David and Eleanor returned, happy from their evening out, Eleanor was anxious to find that Jonathon's party had been a success. They stood in the doorway to the study as if struck by a thunderbolt. Their eyes travelled around the room that Ann had had no time to restore. Eleanor cried, a little sobbing cry, while David, his face clouded in anger, turned on his heel and took the stairs two at a time to his son's bedroom.

That night Jonathon Ingram got the thrashing of his life. He was dragged from his bed and down to the study where his nose was pushed into the vomit and the pools of wine, He was whipped through his pyjamas with the belt that hung behind the kitchen door.

Ann had never seen her father so animated nor heard him shout so loudly. Eleanor stood transfixed, staring at the room in disbelief, seeing nothing, hearing nothing. Joseph Condy had made his exit, resolving never to ask Ann Ingram out again, while Jonathon felt nothing through the haze of booze.

But next day he could hardly lift his head. While he was nursing this strange new affliction, Eleanor took him by the shirt collar out of the back door and made him put thirty-two wine bottles into a wheelbarrow and wheel them away from her house, well away, digging a hole in the woods and burying them, so that the refuse collectors would never find them.

Then she barred Ian Douglas forever from Strathalmond.

ை ை ை

It was the saddest story that Peg Douglas had ever heard.

Barney O'Shea told it to her when he came out of hospital, and she resolved at once to do what she could for the poor soul who had told it to Barney.

The Burns Unit in Bangour, the local hospital was known

country-wide for its work with soldiers and airman who had suffered horrendous injuries in burning tanks and planes. Many of them spent months there. Others, a few others, were there for years. One of these was a man who had no face and no name. The staff merely called him Tommy, for, on arriving there, he had been unable to communicate, and later he was thought to have lost his memory.

Barney, during his period of recuperation from the mine explosion, met Tommy every day in the patients' lounge, or walking in the grounds. Even after all the reconstruction and the efforts of some of the finest surgeons in the field, Tommy's face was a mask with no lips and no nose. The eyes were sunk into a pancake of unbaked dough, wrinkled and swollen and traversed in every angle by deep scars.

Tommy talked in a kind of whistling monotone. He had been a driver in the army. He told Barney how he had driven a flame-thrower truck, seated on its single seat mounted on top of tanks of petroleum, sent in to clear the ground wherever nests of enemy soldiers threatened the advance. A mobile death trap, it had been so easily ignited by a random bullet.

Tommy was accounted missing in action. It had been a wonder that he had survived.

Eventually, as their friendship grew and Barney could look at the face without revulsion, Tommy confided that he had suffered no loss of memory. He had a wife and three children who thought he was dead. He had never returned to them, and had feigned loss of memory to avoid any pressure to do so from medical staff or do-gooders.

"So they'll never have to look at this," Tommy explained, jabbing the burned stumps of his fingers against his destroyed cheek.

Tommy and Barney took long walks across the Bathgate Hills, and, over time, Barney persuaded Tommy to walk with him down to the Myrestane Inn for an afternoon pint. Eventually the locals became used to the sight of Tommy's face and life for Tommy began to return.

After his release from hospital, Barney brought Tommy

home for tea and introduced him to Jeanie, and to Peg and Jack. When they first saw him, Jeanie mouthed a silent prayer to St. Catherine. Jack was reminded of the horror of war, and Peg's heart went out to the family somewhere, forced to carry on in their grief; the wife and the little children without husband and father. For Peg, it was not right. It was not fair.

Tommy returned many times to the Station Raw. He had a new family, people that could look at him without horror on their faces. And how it came about, no one, to this day, can recall, but Tommy finally revealed himself, as if his secret had become just too onerous to bear any longer.

He was George Crawford, back from the war.

And what had been for Peg Douglas the saddest of stories, was made sadder yet through her own act. She told George Crawford's wife, thinking to right a great wrong and relieve the distress of that family.

The next day, when Tommy got news that a woman called Mrs. Crawford was in the hospital reception asking to see him, he walked out the rear entrance of that hospital, across the fields and into the low hills, and was never heard from again.

かかか

The party at Strathalmond was only the first of Jonathon Ingram's troubles at home.

While his sister Ann was discovering her passion for French, which was being nurtured and extended by a new French teacher who had had the misfortune to join the staff of Myrestane High School, Jonathon discovered the mathematical fascinations of games of chance and the opportunities for their application.

In the summer term, behind the main school building where a grassy extension of the playground sloped down to the canal, Jonathon produced, before the mesmerised eyes of the fifth year boys, a roulette board. He set it on two blocks of wood, demonstrated the simple application of its rules, and began to take bets.

Two weeks later, the Bank, which was Jonathon, had accumulated a sizeable part of the allowances of his fellow pupils. One week after that, he was rearranging the odds on each number of the wheel — which he did whenever the Bank was losing more than what he considered a fair percentage — when he felt the fat fingers of Mr. Cook squeezing his ear. He was dragged off to the headmaster's study.

At home, he got another thrashing. David Ingram could not understand how any son of his could feel that he had to acquire money dishonestly. Eleanor, for her part, considered gambling a pursuit of the lower classes. Both parents were generous in their allowances to their children. All these things were part of the post-thrashing lecture.

Jonathon, of course, hadn't done it for money, at least not only for the money. It was merely an exercise in probabilities, permutations and combinations and he loved to see how these could dazzle and dumbfound his peers.

Not long after that, George Usher, the father of the Merchant schoolboy, called at Strathalmond to say that he thought Mr. Ingram should know that Jonathon had been seen leaving a bookmaker's office in the town. He thought Mr. Ingram should know that.

David Ingram chased Usher off the premises. Then he called Jonathon from the study again for another session of retribution.

All the while, Ann was a model pupil whose French essays were the subect of display by the new French teacher to every other class in the school.

When the school trip to France was announced, her heart leapt with joy, and she rushed home, grasping the information pamphlet on the trip with the form to be signed by a parent authorising his child to go.

France! Paris! She couldn't wait to get before the mirror in her room, practising her phrases, her verbs, her intonation. France!

Ann stood by the kitchen table, the permission form gripped in her hand, her face shining with glee. Eleanor sat by the fire, embroidering a tablecloth.

"It's Paris, Mum, and Provins where Monique lives! You know Monique, my pen-pal Mum. Oh, it's going to be fabulous. I'll write to Monique and tell her I'm coming. I bet she'll take me to their house at the seaside, in La Rochelle. Did I tell you that they had a house in La Rochelle? Do you think I could get away from the trip to go there? Just for a day or two? I'm sure the teacher wouldn't mind. He knows about Monique. He knows her parents." Ann jumped up and down with joy. "France! Mum, I'm going to France!"

Eleanor looked up and smiled. She had never seen her daughter so happy. "Let's see what your father says," she said, thinking that it could only be good. "He'll be here in a minute."

When David came in from the garden Ann grew quiet, biting her bottom lip in anticipation. He looked at his daughter and then at Eleanor, his face weary and worried. "Would you excuse us for a minute, Ann? I want to talk to your mother."

Ann Ingram read his face and her world collapsed. She laid the papers on the table and left the room without a word, making her way to the study where Jonathon sat in a fog of smoke from his "Passing Cloud" cigarettes, concentrating on a book.

"He's not going to let me go!" she cried, staring wildly at her brother. After a few seconds, Jonathon looked up.

"Go where?" he said, vacantly.

"To France! On the school trip."

"Oh, that," Jonathon replied, showing little interest as he returned to his book.

Ann could see Jonathon's school trip form on the edge of the table. It was already half covered by a mathematics book. "If father doesn't let me go, will you talk to him?" Ann said, almost crying. Jonathon looked up, sympathy growing in his face.

"Sure, but I don't know what good that will do," he said.

It was another one of those occasions when David came in from the garden to discuss and then decide. It was not possible for Ann to go on the trip. Eleanor said little, for wasn't the French trip a desirable thing for a daughter to embark upon?

Wasn't Ann the best French pupil in the school and wouldn't that be a smack in the face for Evelyn Usher?

But this time David made no secret of the fact that his reason for refusal was financial. If Ann got to go, Jonathon would have to go, and that would be two expenditures. After all they had two children. And so it was settled and David went back to his plants.

When Eleanor called Ann from the study, she came quietly in followed by Jonathon, and the two children stood by the table, silently awaiting the decision.

"I'm sorry, Ann, but your father says that you can't go on the trip. It's a matter of the expense. There are two of you and if one goes . . ."

"It's not fair, Ann shouted, cutting her mother off. "It's just not fair. Jonathon doesn't want to go. Tell her, Jonathon!"

"Don't you raise your voice to me, young lady!" Eleanor responded. "What Jonathon wants or doesn't want has nothing to do with it. Your father has decided and that's an end of it." Ann threw herself down into a chair.

"It's not fair," she repeated. "I never get to do anything."

This last remark seemed to enrage Eleanor who came and stood over her.

"Never get to . . . What! You, Miss, get everything from your father and me. Who do you think pays your allowance? Who paid for your dancing lessons? Who bought you that French dictionary that you had your heart set on? Don't you dare to tell me that you never get anything. You get everything that money can buy, and don't you forget it!"

"Ann really wants to go to France, Mum," Jonathon piped up. "And I'm not going, so there would only be one cost."

"You go to your study, Jonathon. This has nothing to do with you. Your father has decided the matter and I don't want to hear any more about it." At that, Jonathon turned and left the room and Ann got up quickly and rushed out after him.

Ann cried herself to sleep, that night and many other nights. Nobody could know just how much that trip meant to her. She lived for French, she corresponded with French pen-pals, spent all her allowance on French papers and magazines and dreamed of the day she would get to go to France. She thought of how Mary Pierce was going, who could not speak a word of French and whose father was just the gravedigger at the cemetery. And Jonathon! Jonathon had no more interest in going to France than flying to the moon.

The French teacher called to see David to make a plea for Ann to be allowed to go on the trip, but he received the same short shrift as had George Usher when he had reported on Jonathon's gambling. To David, there was no difference. He needed nobody to tell him how he should be raising his children.

There are things that happen in your youth that you remember for the rest of your days. For Ann Ingram, not being on the French trip was one of them.

Chapter
Sixteen

ରେ ରେ ରେ

Ian Douglas and Hugh Donaldson were of the first generation
from Myrestane to see the inside of the lecture halls of the
city; the generation that nurtured all the hopes and dreams of
those who had trudged out their lifetimes between the Raws
and the Work.

Following their first year at the University of Edinburgh,
both of them got summer jobs in the Work. They had been
there for six weeks, and this was their last day.

When Ian walked through the iron gates, smells took him
by the nose and dragged him among the maze of pipes and
girders and broken down brickwork; oil smells; smells of old
decaying mechanical things; ammonia smells from the sulphate plant. Pipes, leading nowhere, hung at angles from tanks
or the tops of sheds down to face level and ended there, issuing wisps of steam or white smoke. Iron bars, rusty tin barrels
and bits of corrugated steel littered the ground and men
stepped over them with dirty boots.

That summer Ian had a recurring dream about people in
the Work, faces he seemed to know, disappearing forever
among the steel foliage. That's what had happened to the
Sweeney twins when he was at school. They were in the class
below him. He had a vivid memory of two identical little boys

with black curly hair and podgy red faces, dressed old-fashioned by their granny. People said they had gone onto Work property and a hole opened up in the ground and swallowed them. People said they found a school cap near a path ... all that was left.

Uncle Jack said it was the underground workings. Around Myrestane it was all burning underground. Ian dreamt about Hell burning and the Work and the men that went there every day, and his Uncle Jack, all coming and going and sometime maybe not returning.

He kept his fears silent, walking behind Hugh who carried his haversack like the men, swung on a long strap right back over the hip. On that last day, they stopped at the office and punched their cards in turn just as the long wail of the whistle started the shift.

For Ian, noise suddenly blotted out the outside world. Retorts hissed like great fiery serpents risen up skyward. The breaker churned out its rhythmic crushing of black glistening slabs of shale. Squat heavy bogeys trundled on steel rails merging all the sounds into a deafening relentless hum. They reached the bothy, a dilapidated shack that was the home of the railway squad for breaks and for sitting around when it rained. The railway squad couldn't work when it rained and today it was raining.

There were six on the railway squad, including Ian and Hugh, five workers and a foreman called George O'Neill. They called O'Neill the "polite Irishman" because he spoke quite proper English and found it more rewarding to request that things be done than to order them. Then there was Wull Aichieson who seemed old enough to have been in the Work from its beginning; Mathie Thompson whose comments on life seemed to Ian to be the irrefutable words of a philosopher; and Wee Tam McEwan, a diminutive silent stick of a man, like a porridge stirrer. In some distant time this had led to his nickname, "the Spurkle".

As the boys entered the bothy, Wull Aicheson was peering at a newspaper through ancient spectacles that had one leg fixed to the frame with a plaster.

"I see they're jailin' Peter Burns for assault," Wull commented. There was a moment of silence.

"Jailin's too good fur 'im", Mathie retorted. "Whit he needs is a good hard kick up the arse."

Ian's sudden laugh was silenced by a newspaper-rustling glare from Wull. Looking away, he realised that Mathie's comment wasn't a joke but merely a statement of appropriate punishment.

Wull sucked thoughtfully on his pipe. Ian reckoned he must have been about seventy-five. How long could a man keep coming to the Work, day after day? He wondered. The Spurkle gave Ian a watery stare from black eyes in a little fox face as he rocked quietly on his seat.

"Christ are yez goin' to let that fire go oot?" George O'Neill's gruff voice bellowed as he waved a beefy finger at the old stove in the middle of the hut. Then, almost as an afterthought, "It would be a considerable favour to myself if it could be revived." Hugh jumped to get a shovelfull of coal and O'Neill relaxed back against the wall, his big stomach settling over his belt.

The morning passed, rain pelting on the tin roof. Wull commented on the day's news with Mathie adding approval or rebuke and the odd phrase of explanation.

"So this is yer big day boys, the day for yer test?" George smiled as he said it, looking round the others.

"Aye Mr. O'Neill", Hugh beamed.

Just then the door opened and Smith, the "go-for", forced his way in past the heaped coats bulging from the pegs. A tall skinny youth with a shock of black hair, his thick, heavy-rimmed glasses enlarged his weak eyes.

Winston Churchill Smith, named after his father's hero, was what folk called a "daftie". While he would never be fit for a real job, he was happy doing all the errands for the population of Myrestane and the men in the Work. Myrestane was kind to Winston. It let him stand on the platforms of its buses, sit in its barbershops directing hairstyles and lead the public band around its streets on gala days. Winston was a catalyst that merged the better natures of the Myrestane people, bringing smiles from despair and laughter from fatigue. Winston would never know the value of his contribution to the community.

"How's the boys these days?" Winston squeaked his favourite phrase, his hair all flattened by the rain, as he rubbed at his glasses with a dirty cuff.

"Winston!" Wull shouted, looking up from his paper. "Whit the hell are ye daein' walkin' aboot in this weather? Ye'll get yer death o' cauld man."

"Ah dinnae feel the cauld Mr. Aicheson," Winston sniffed.

Mathie looked up. "The laddie's tough Wull. A wee bit o' rain disnae worry him."

Winston beamed and straightened up his skinny frame to prove the point.

Ian liked it when it rained. He quietly prayed that it would rain until five o'clock, so that he could stay in the bothy, in the smell of old clothes and coal, away from the Work, hidden from it, in the heart of it, with these old philosophers.

He thought about the university and Professor Sims who lit one cigarette off the other and could talk, without notes or trappings, about the sixteenth century price rise in Europe, or banking in the eighteenth century, or the Corn laws. Sims had so impressed Ian Douglas.

But at the Work, here in the bothy, O'Neill and old Wull and Mathie and the silent Spurkle didn't talk about these things. Here there was a different kind of truth, a truth of existence, of survival that was tied somehow to poverty and hardship and the noise and smell of the Work and the rain on the bothy roof. A truth of knowing the other men intimately and merging with them in mutual support and caring. It was not the truth that strangers talked in unfamiliar lecture halls to other strangers.

Ian and Hugh knew they were part of this. When Mathie spoke to them they were accepted. They were real because he made them real in his very acknowledgement of their existence.

"Ah came tae see the test Mr. Aichieson. Ma mother said Ah could come and see the test."

"There ye go boys", Mathie smiled. "Winston's here to see yer test. I hope yez don't disappoint him." The men in the hut laughed and the Spurkle rocked back and forward, his hands clasped against his chest.

Mathie's words jolted Ian's thoughts back to the test. He looked over at Hugh who returned the urgent question in his stare with a sheepish grin.

"Och aye", Wull joined in, folding his paper and laying it on the bench. "This is the day the university boys are goin' tae lift the Bucket. Watch yersel', Tam. Ye might soon be redundant!" Tam rocked and screeched.

Ian looked again at Hugh, remembering the challenge he made some weeks earlier that they would lift the Bucket on their last day here, remove it from its place and empty it just like Baldy and the Spurkle did. "Aye, that wid be a real test for yez, right enough…see if yez are any guid as workers." Wull had said.

Ian thought about the Bucket. He and Hugh had been to see it several times and had even watched it being lifted by Wee Tam, the Spurkle, and a huge bald giant of a man called Baldy Johnston. It was a big steel container, maybe fifteen gallons in capacity, located in a hole at the base of the retorts to catch the residue of matter reduced and distilled by searing temperatures. What flowed into the Bucket was a sludge of thick black tar that was removed and dumped every Friday. There was no mechanical device to remove it. Two men placed a thick steel bar through the handle and heaved it out of the hole into the daylight.

Baldy and the Spurkle were the Bucket men. It was said that no other men could lift it. In their first days at the Work, Ian and Hugh, fresh from the halls of learning and sceptical of these working men's myths, seized upon the challenge. Mathie had said it would be a test. Surely students were used to tests. Well this was a test. It was a test from the Work set for four o'clock on the boys' last day.

Now that day had arrived.

At the appointed hour Ian and Hugh left the bothy and

made their way through the rain to the retorts. Minutes earlier Mathie had slapped two half-crowns on the table.

"Ah have five shillins says yez can't lift it!" he said.

That was the beginning of Ian's fears but he said nothing to Hugh. He depended on Hugh. Hugh was taller than Baldy and younger, if not so heavy, and Ian had no doubt of his own ability to match the tiny Spurkle. But it was the bet that concerned him because it was Mathie's bet and Mathie was never wrong...was he? All Ian had to do was get into the hole and steady it, just as the Spurkle did, and Hugh, like Baldy, could heave it out. It was an easy five shillings. Yet something gnawed at Ian because Mathie had laid it down.

He thought briefly about Professor Sims and the kind of knowledge that a few short weeks ago had been so important, so triumphant. He wondered if Sims would have laid a bet on this test.

At the hole, the men had gathered, from the retorts and the brickwork and the ammonia plant. The bothy men appeared, George and Wull and Mathie. The Spurkle rubbed his hands and nodded to the men who clapped him on the back, and whispered quiet words in his ear.

Ian took his stance in the narrow confine of the hole where the Spurkle had stood. Hugh grabbed the bar on each side of the Bucket and Ian the base.

"After three", Hugh said. "One . . two . . three . . . up!"

Hugh strained on the bar and the Bucket moved up a foot from the ground. Ian reached under it and heaved, but it hung there refusing to rise further.

"Are ye liftin'?" Hugh grunted through his teeth.

"Of course I'm bloody liftin", Ian panted in reply, glancing up towards the giggles and chuckles of the faces peering down.

Hugh heaved again and the Bucket shuddered up a few inches more, but Ian knew it was useless and Hugh, cursing, let it sink back to the earth.

They tried it again with the same result. They could move it a few inches from its resting spot in the hole, but then it just hung there. No amount of straining or heaving could raise it further. Ian climbed wearily out of the hole.

"It can't be done", he said to Hugh who stood with a look of puzzlement on his red face.

The Spurkle came over. "I think ye'll have tae eat yer porridge laddies," he whispered.

"Balls!" Ian retorted and strode off towards the bothy. He could hear the laughter behind him and feel the heat of frustration on his cheeks. He would get his stuff and go home and to hell with them all and to hell with the Work. It ground down human effort and took these men year after year and sucked their energies and made them old and done. And he failed its test — but he was gone. It wouldn't drag him down like the others.

The boys were getting ready to leave when the bothy men returned.

"So yez are finished now. Back tae school for yez." Mathie's voice was kind.

Hugh looked up with his puzzled look. "That Baldy must be a strong man," he said.

Wull prodded Mathie with his pipe stem. "Ah believe he's got it, Mathie." He looked from Hugh to Ian. "That's right boys. A strong man. Did yez never hear o' the Myrestane Strongman?"

The boys were silent.

"Well, well!" Wull continued. "What dae ye think o' that Mathie? They've never heard o' the Myrestane Strongman. Well, well!"

The foreman, George O'Neill took up the story. "It was twenty years ago now that I first saw him, at a fair, writing his name with a fifty-six pound weight hanging on his wee finger over the edge of a table."

"Aye," went on Wull, "and he lifted three hundredweight o' corn. And I've seen him bend pennies double between his fingers."

Ian saw a smile growing on Hugh's face. So that was it. Baldy was a strongman. That's how he could heave the Bucket out.

Hugh was laughing now as the bothy men recounted more

tales of the strongman, O'Neill talking his best English, Wull taking prodigious sucks on his pipe and the Spurkle rocking on the bench, hands between his knees, cackling like an agitated chicken.

The bothy quietened down to the rain pattering on the roof.

"So there you are," Mathie said quietly."It wasn't your fault at all. There's nobody can lift the Bucket — nobody except big Baldy Thompson and the Myrestane Strongman."

It took a few moments for the words to sink in. Hugh looked at Ian then back at Mathie. "How do you mean?" he began. "I thought that Baldy was . . ."

Mathie fished a big copper penny from his waistcoat pocket. "No son. It wasn't Baldy," he said. He tossed the penny to Wee Tam who caught it, and with a lightening movement of one little hand bent it double and threw it on the bothy floor where it came to rest, folded over in half, two ends touching. The Spurkle screeched with laughter and rocked back and forward. Hugh and Ian stared from the penny to Wee Tam in disbelief.

"Aye," said Mathie. "There he is! Wee Tam McEwan, the Spurkle — who used to be known as the Myrestane Strongman!"

Leaving the Work at the end of that summer, Ian looked at the bent penny in his hand. Maybe the Work didn't always win. Maybe there were men that never gave it everything, men that could pass its tests, men that could beat it.

He could still see the Spurkle rocking on the bench, laughing.

∾ ∾ ∾

Eddie McLean, who had married Peg's daughter, Sandra, was what Peg called a good husband.

"He's a good man, Eddie McLean," she would say, and the single reservation that she had on this point, she kept to herself — Eddie's total aversion to the Roman Catholic faith and all its devotees. He was born with it, just as some people are born left-handed.

When Eddie was courting Sandra Douglas, and started to come around the Raw with a view to impressing Tosh, he got off to a bad start. He had always been a bit of a smart guy, making out that he knew a lot, coming up with these "Did you know this?" or "Have you ever seen that?" openers. The first time he met his intended father-in-law was in 9 Station Raw. Tosh sat in his usual chair, in his usual laundered salmon pink combinations, in front of a heaped fire that glowed red in the grate.

"Did you ever see water boiling in a paper bag?" Eddie quipped.

Tosh put down his paper and gave Eddie one of his "Are ye talkin' tae me?" looks.

"You might not believe me, but I could take a paper bag and fill it with water at the sink, and I bet you if I put it on top of that fire there . . . What do you think would happen?"

Tosh turned his head to look at the fire, then turned it back ever so slowly towards Eddie. Peg's eyes smiled and a little laugh burst from her lips. Sandra's face lit up with wonder at Eddie's latest pronouncement.

"It wouldn't burn," Eddie said. "The water would boil inside the bag. It's scientific, you see." He sat back with a knowing nod. The others looked at him in total silence.

"Watch this!" Eddie said, getting up and going to the room door. "Have you got a paper bag, Mrs. Douglas? Is your sink through here?" Peg followed him.

Inside a few minutes Eddie came back holding a brown paper bag, roughly tied with twine at the neck. He had filled it with water and it was starting to drip on the rug.

"There!" he said, as he planted the bag right on top of the glowing coals.

Tosh raised himself up, his big elbows pushing against the arms of the chair. He regarded Eddie under knitted eyebrows as if he had just become aware of his presence. The bag sizzled on the glowing coals and a look of disbelief appeared on Tosh's face as his mind grappled with the younger man's intention. He had just begun to lean forward in his chair to witness this scientific miracle, when the bag exploded with a loud bang. A deluge of soot plummeted down the chimney and enveloped Tosh in a black, swirling cloud.

Eddie McLean was up and out the front door in a flash. He ran for his life, along the Raw to the main road then down through the railway-bridge towards Myrestane.

Tosh chased him, in bare feet and black face and combinations, like an enraged Masai warrior in pursuit of a jungle trophy.

∾ ∾ ∾

There is a bit in the Bible about growing up that Peg was forever quoting to Ian.

When I was a child, I spake as a child, I understood as a child, I thought as a child: but when I became a man, I put away childish things.

Ian sometimes wondered about this, and how it applied to Peg and Jack when they were having one of their many silly arguments.

A week earlier, Jack was laughing at an item in the *News of the World* that said that a man's wife threw a lump of custard at him.

"What's so funny about that?" Peg cut in.

"Well," said Jack, "a lump of custard. There's no such thing, woman. Custard is a sauce. You pour it from a sauce-boat. You can't have a lump of custard."

Jack Armstrong knew very well that Peg's custard came in lumps, and that's how the argument started. It was such a childish thing, Ian thought.

But when it came to Eddie McLean, Peg's quotation made sense.

Ian's sister, Sandra, was more in the nature of an aunt to him, having married and moved to another town long before

Ian was born. Eddie and Sandra had a girl called Shona who was only a few years younger than Ian. They had a nice house with fitted carpets, nice furniture that was all paid for, nice friends who neither drank nor swore, and they took pride in the fact that they had never had an argument in all their married life.

Eddie was storekeeper in a small engineering works. He worked hard and made sure that his wife stayed home, except for her weekly visit to her mother. He went to see Glasgow Rangers play soccer every Saturday, rain hail or shine. He walked in the hills around his home —"no better scenery anywhere," he said — and did his bit to warn the world about the insidious conspiracy of the Roman Catholic Church.

When Ian was young, Eddie was fun to be with. While Uncle Jack seemed satisfied with Myrestane United, Eddie took Ian to Rangers games. Eddie liked to take Ian to the games. After all he had no father. And you couldn't take girls to football matches. Eddie was good to Peg too, the widow woman, but he kept a wary distance from Jack Armstrong, an unknown quantity to Eddie, a bit of a drinker and gambler. What would a poor widow woman see in a lodger like that, Eddie thought, when he gave it any thought at all.

And the O'Sheas; Peg should watch them. Eddie knew what they were.

It was when Ian was talking about going to university that Eddie's protective conscience kicked in on behalf of the widow woman and her son. He felt an obligation to his young brother-in-law. He liked him and he would do what he could to help his career. He went to see his manager at the engineering shop where he worked, and that was when he found out about the Sandwich Courses.

"A Sandwich Course, Ian. That's what you should be looking at, son," Eddie said, taking a short stop on their walk to light a cigarette. "I was talking to Mr. Bell at the shop. He's an engineer, you know. Can make anything, read plans and everything. He says to tell you to take a Sandwich Course. You go to school and then learn on the job — turn about — six months at school then six months in the workshop, for two years.

Then you're an engineer. Better than these university guys that come out not knowing anything. And you get paid all the time, even when you're in school. You'll have a pay every week to hand in to your mother. And Mr. Bell says you should just go and see him. We're pretty close, me and Mr. Bell. And I told him you've got the brains for it. Tell you what! I'll go and see Mr. Bell and arrange an appointment for you for next Monday."

"But I have school on Monday," Ian began.

"School!" Eddie said. "Take a day off school. This is more important than school. This is your career, son. What can you learn in school, anyway? I left school when I was fourteen. Never did me any harm. Next Monday. I'll arrange it."

The last thing Ian wanted was to hurt Eddie's feelings. He wanted to go to university but he didn't know how to say it. He liked Eddie, and he liked going to the matches and the walks in the hills. He liked Eddie's nice house and the radiogram player, and Sandra and Shona. He liked it so much he sometimes took his friends there on the bus to show off to them, and Sandra always served tea and chocolate biscuits and the boys sat on the sofa and looked around, suitably impressed.

Ian did what he always did when he had a problem. He told his mother. That was when she came away again with that Bible quote. She explained that the Rangers matches and the walks in the hills were childish things, and the decision about university was for a man to make.

The outcome was that Ian didn't go to see Mr. Bell at the appointed time, and Eddie didn't say any more to him about school, or university or anything much else.

Chapter
Seventeen

∽∽∽

The shale industry declined quickly in the end. Strathalmond Oils Ltd. could no longer subsidise the rents of its workers and work began on the demolition of the Raws. Some of the residents, including Peg and Jack and the O'Sheas, were re-housed in modern council houses only a few hundred yards away.

Peg's council house was more than she had ever dreamed she would have. It had a living room, two bedrooms, a real kitchen and a bathroom with a bath. Her living room had a little tiled fireplace that served no other purpose than to heat the room, for there was now an electric cooker in the kitchen, and a hot water tank. The bedrooms were large and airy and there was no need to sprinkle DDT in bed recesses to kill fleas, for there were no more bed recesses. The bathroom was a dream. She bought a television set with a nine-inch screen and she planted a rose bush by the front door.

When they knocked down Station Raw, she and Jack walked down to watch the breaker's ball being swung into the old soot-blackened bricks. She smiled when she saw a pyramid of bricks still sticking up from the ruin, single bricks being held up by a six inch thick spear of wallpaper to which they adhered. How many times had she papered that wall, applying the new layer on top of the old? How many years? How often had Tosh complained about her papering obsession? So many layers were moulded together that it supported the bricks. So many layers of her life.

She smiled and looked at Jack, nodding silently towards the pyramid of bricks. He smiled back and squeezed her hand in his. That was the first time he had done that in years.

They turned and walked back to the new house. Ian would be home for his tea.

❧ ❧ ❧

Ian met Jonathon Ingram in Princess Street Gardens. He was sitting on a park bench reading a book and eating sandwiches from a paper bag. He wore a long raincoat that was entirely superfluous in the warm sunlight. It was open, revealing the old tweed jacket that Ian immediately recognised.

"Long time no see," Ian said, taking a seat next to him on the bench. Jonathon looked up, his face brightening into a smile. "Hello Ian," he said.

Ian leaned over, looking at the book. "History of Mathematics, eh? Still on the prime number thing, are you? What are you doing with yourself these days?"

"Oh, not much," Jonathon said, closing the book. "I'm a lab technician in a place over in Granton. This is my day off."

"Christ, what a waste," Ian thought, but he didn't say it. "Are you still living at home?" he asked.

"No. I have a room." He mentioned an address that was on a street of decrepit tenement buildings up near the university, Edinburgh's student ghetto.

Ian felt the wave of sympathy that Jonathon had always incited in him. It was always the worse for being concealed. He could never express it. Sometimes he didn't rightly understand it. He knew that Jonathon would never have understood it. Jonathon's grey intelligent eyes never left Ian's face as Ian floundered with the conversation.

"I visit my folks once a month," Jonathon said, as if coming to Ian's aid. It was like saying "I go to the pictures once a month". It was a mere observation that bespoke of neither enthusiasm nor pleasure.

"How is your little sister?" Ian said. Then he laughed. "I suppose she's not little any more."

Jonathon's eyes lit up. "She's doing fine. She's at Moray House doing Teacher Training. I'm meeting her here for lunch. She'll be along any minute." After a few seconds he added, "why don't you join us? Do you have a girlfriend right now?"

Ian felt sudden relief. This was the old Jonathon. Everything matter of fact, no subtlety, no hidden meanings, everything mathematical and precise and spoken straight out.

"No girlfriend," he replied. "You?"

The smile faded from Jonathon's face and he turned his head away to look across the cropped grass and tailored flower beds towards the gentle slope that led down to the foot of the castle. Dotted across the lawns, individuals and groups, white-shirted office workers, old men in baggy trousers and bonnets, widows in black dresses and big hats, took their ease in the sun. Boys spoke earnestly to girls over brown lunch bags. A middle-aged man in shirt and shorts went puffing by, dragged relentlessly by an Irish wolfhound on a steel chain.

"I would like to have a girlfriend," he said with a longing gaze.

Ian wasn't listening. He was watching the girl who walked towards them along the concrete path that ran the length of the gardens. She was wearing a light coloured trench coat, belted at the waist, and her hair fell in long thick tresses to her shoulders. She wore high-heeled shoes and walked like a model, placing her feet as if on a chalk-line and holding up her head, the chestnut hair bouncing ever so slightly with each step. She carried a tan leather briefcase, which she swung with a certain gaiety, so that the whole picture seemed to Ian to have been staged by a film director for a love story; *Breakfast at Tiffany's*.

Ian was a sucker for love stories in films. His mother had immersed him in them, taking him in tow to Myrestane Cinema for all the years he could remember, to see her heroes and heroines. There they had sat in the dark and sucked chocolate eclairs or squares of that toffee with the picture of a cow on the wrapper, transported to the world of dashing men and beautiful women in grand hotel lounges or on the windswept decks of pirate ships.

The girl walked up to them. She had large brown eyes that seemed to grow wider when she smiled at them. Jonathon got up and she kissed him on the cheek.

"You remember Ian Douglas," he said to her. "Ian, this is my little sister."

Ian remembered Ann Ingram as a short, plump, freckly thing that used to hover, now and then, on the fringes of the conversations in the study at Strathalmond. This wasn't her. It couldn't be her.

She sat down on the bench and the calf length skirt rode up slightly to reveal the most shapely legs Ian had ever seen, or maybe he had never noticed legs before. He pulled his eyes back to her face, wondering what was wrong with him, trying not to stare at her, but desperate to look.

"Hello Ian," she said, her smile growing bigger. She held out her hand.

For Ian Douglas it was love at first sight. Ann Ingram was his own personal movie queen, springing to life in three dimensions, life-size before his eyes in the middle of Princes Street Gardens. The movement and chattering noises of the gardens faded into the background as he stood there, dumbstruck, gazing at the smile and the long sweep of the hair and the smiling eyes. He tried somehow to look gallant, like Flynn on the deck of his ship, but he knew it wasn't working. He croaked a response and felt awkward, more like Lou Costello, and he looked away to hide a blush. She laughed.

"Where will we go for lunch?" she said. "Will you join us, Ian?"

The three walked past the Scott Monument, where noisy schoolchildren hung over the parapets at different levels of its towering pinnacle, shouting squeaky calls to those below. Minutes later they were squeezed around a corner table at that place half-way down the Waverley steps that did a three-course lunch for three shillings and sixpence. Ann and Jonathon were talking about their week and Ian was still staring, reluctant to talk unless he should suddenly wake up.

When the pudding came — the pudding was the best thing about that place, steamed treacle pudding covered with thin custard — Ian found his voice and asked Ann if she would like to go to the Plaza with him on Saturday night. The Plaza was a kind of up-market dance hall where students and office workers took nice girls; it wasn't like the Palais where the riff-raff went and fights ensued. When she agreed without hesitation, his spoon slipped along the edge of the steam pudding and sent a spray of custard across the white table cloth.

Jonathon looked happy for the first time.

ↄↄↄ

The romance of Ian Douglas and Ann Ingram, like all good movie romances, was played out to music. *Moon River*, the song from *Breakfast at Tiffany's,* that was their song. Ian played it all the time on the piano.

Peg Douglas had seen to it that her son took piano lessons from a very early age, and by the time that a succession of piano teachers had given up on the idea that this boy could be the next Paderewski, Peg had spent a shameful amount of money on lessons and Ian had emerged with the ability to play most things, not well, but good enough for the non-playing listener. A piano-player, he called himself, never a pianist, for Ian had learned enough to know the difference. It was certainly good enough for Ann Ingram who came from Strathalmond where no kind of music was ever played or listened to.

Ann remembered a visitor to the house, one of her father's foremen in the Work, Tom Naysmith, a part-time Baptist minister. Ann was about ten at the time. They all sat around the kitchen table after tea and Mr. Naysmith announced that he was a singer and would they like to hear him sing? Then, in the dumbfounded silence that followed, he launched forth into the *Wee Cooper of Fife.*

The picture of his face, as he poked it forward in every verse, shaping a prissy smile to the words *nickety, nackety, noo noo noo,* and of her mother's totally perplexed expression, stuck in Ann's memory for years. Music of any kind, in the presence of David and Eleanor Ingram, was snuffed out at the moment of its birth, as would Tom Nasmyth's comic song have been had it not been so unexpectedly delivered.

Ann fell in love with Ian's music, and the sporadic and pervasive nature of its delivery. It was new to her and it threw open a door into a world that excited and intrigued her. She had had no shortage of dates with boyfriends, many of them resulting in awkward, sloppy goodnight kisses at the gates of Strathalmond, and she had formed a strong attachment to a particular boy from her college whom she sometimes thought she loved but wasn't sure. She had strong notions of good behaviour and manners, instilled by her parents, and Ian Douglas was less of a gentleman than the others. At times he was moody and quick-tempered; at other times he was loving and caring. But he was never boring to be with, and that and the music won her heart in the end.

When Ian, prompted, as he was in most things, by his mother, gave Ann a present of a second-hand piano for her twenty-first birthday, so that she might take piano lessons and indulge her great enjoyment of music even in the tuneless bastion of Strathalmond, it was admitted into the mansion by David and Eleanor with the same bewildered frowns that had greeted the *Wee Cooper of Fife.*

The occasion of its arrival was made the worse by the piano, a tall upright that was as heavy as it was ugly in the eyes of Eleanor, being delivered on the flat bed of a George Wimpey low-loader, driven up the drive and manoevered around the entrance by a loud, jocular cousin of the Douglases.

"Where dae ye want it Missus?" the cousin shouted, as he and his co-driver man-handled the brute through the front entrance. Eleanor threw a hopeless look at Ann who took over the direction of the struggling men, her eyes shining with happiness. When the instrument was established against one wall of the study and the puffing labourers had left, Eleanor flopped onto a chair feeling positively unwell.

That was the way that Peg Douglas did things. Ann was such a nice girl and was it not a pity that she loved music so much and had no piano to take lessons on? Whatever could the Ingrams be thinking of? It wasn't as if they had no room for it. Anyway Ian and Ann were very sweet on each other. She was Ian's girlfriend so she would get a piano and the Wimpey truck could deliver it.

It never occurred to Peg Douglas that the Ingrams' dislike of music was only outstripped by their abhorrence of Ian Douglas and his association with their daughter. Had it occurred to her, it would not have made a blind bit of difference. The piano was got and delivered, and that was that.

ᴥ ᴥ ᴥ

Whatever reservations David and Eleanor had about the piano and about Ann's early, plodding, practice pieces, they said nothing to their daughter. When Eleanor saw that her attempts to dissuade Ann from seeing Ian Douglas were futile, she and David relented in that matter also, and Ian was finally admitted to Strathalmond to pick up Ann instead of having to wait for her at the Miller's Wall by the main gates. Whenever Ian did call at the house, he sat with the dourest of expressions, making no conversation whatever with the Ingrams, and Eleanor referred to him as Ann's "poker-faced friend". It was still the hope of Eleanor and David that the romance would cool and Ann would find a more suitable boy — one of her own class.

Peg Douglas, on the other hand, was delighted that her son was courting the daughter of Strathalmond. "She's training for a teacher, you know," Peg said to Eddie McLean and Sandra who had arrived on a Saturday afternoon with their own daughter, Shona, to see Peg's new house. Peg was putting on a tea and had invited the O'Sheas, and, of course, Ian would be there and his new girlfriend. Jack Armstrong came and went between the living room and the back garden, where he had planted all kinds of vegetables, taking a limited interest in the conversation and passing the odd remark with Eddie about the standings in the football league; more than a lodger and less than family.

"Yes, a very clever girl, and pretty too," Peg went on, as she laid the table for tea. "Looks a bit like her grandfather, Old Sam Ingram. Same eyes and cast of features. Aye, Old Sam was a real gentleman you know. He started Strathalmond Oil. Now Ann's father runs it."

Sitting behind Peg, Sandra tightened her lips and cast her eyes up to the ceiling. Eddie McLean's normally cheerful face twisted itself into a scowl.

"And how about you, Shona?" Peg said, laying out cups next to her granddaughter. Any boyfriends yet?"

"Oh, Shona's all right," Eddie piped up. "She's going with an under-manager at the new tyre factory, Jim Fraser. Oh, she'll be all right. He's a real up-and-comer, Jim. He has a company car. They send him down to England all the time. Gets his expenses paid, hotels and everything."

"And how is school, Shona?" Peg went on, seeming to ignore Eddie.

"I'm at Merciston Street, Nana," Shona said. "The secretarial college."

"Aye, she'll get all the education she needs there," Eddie cut in. "Typing and things for a good office job. All a lassie needs. All this university and all that, just a waste of time for a lassie."

Peg pondered briefly on the fact that her granddaughter had come first in the qualifying class years before, and had shown great promise then, but she said nothing.

"Aye, Jim Fraser's an under-manager at Wilson's Tyres. You know Wilson's, Jack?" Eddie said to Jack Armstrong who had just then plodded in from the garden. "Good company, eh?" Jack nodded in agreement.

"Oh aye," Jack said.

As Ian and Ann walked hand in hand up the road from Strathalmond to Myrestane Station for Peg's tea, Ann glowed with the anticipation of joining a real family. She had been to Peg's several times and she liked everything about it. She liked the way that nobody knocked on the door — they just walked in. She liked the way that Ian called his mother "Peg", how he played the piano and she sang and how Peg made her feel welcome as one of the family. She liked Jack Armstrong and his welcoming smile, and the way he would come in from the kitchen offering a plate of roasted cheese on toast, his own mouth stuffed with the first slice out of the grill. She liked the O'Sheas, whom she had met once at the house, and the talk about Ireland. She liked the whole easy, relaxed atmosphere where she had to do nothing to please, but just be there and be happy.

She reflected on Strathalmond, where no such ease or informality existed. Everything there, her own life included, was ordered in a certain way under certain rules of the house. Ordered mainly by her mother, for her father seemed to merge into the background, and if he was the guiding hand he never seemed to show it. He came and went from his Edinburgh office or his meetings of the oil company, sat at the table for meals, snoozed and read the paper then disappeared into his garden or greenhouse until dark.

Eleanor fluttered through household chores, said that she needed no help, then invariably bemoaned Ann's lack of help when the chore was done. Her flighty, nervous disposition that ranged continuously from tearful despair over little things, when Ann's heart went out to her, to sharp-tongued rebuke that made Ann wish that she lived a thousand miles away, was wearing the girl down. More and more she tried to be out of the house. She loved her mother but she couldn't live with her. An invitation to tea with the Douglases, this perfect family to which she might some day belong, offered an escape into another world.

Ian strode out eagerly, grasping the hand of this prize creature that he still couldn't believe was his, desperate to arrive home and show her off to his sister and her family who would be so good to her and so glad for him.

That was the way they thought. That was the innocence of youth.

Ian Douglas had some other good news for Peg that he had saved for this house-warming occasion. He had passed his final exams. He was a Bachelor of Laws, and under his arm he carried a parcel that contained the graduation robe, rented for the occasion of his formal graduation in a few weeks time. He had the idea to put the robe on for the benefit of those at his house who would not be at that ceremony, and they could see the first law graduate in the family, the first from the Raws in fact. He and Ann had concocted the surprise, and the prospect of it hurried their steps.

When they got to Peg's house, the O'Sheas had arrived and everyone sat around carrying on rather stiff conversations — all except Jack, that is, who continued to dodder in and out from the garden in wellington boots and an oversized cap that had paper wrapped around the inside of it to keep its shape.

Eddie McLean had nothing to say to Barney O'Shea, him being a Catholic, and not only that, an Irish Catholic. Sandra talked freely enough to Jeanie O'Shea, whom she had known all her life, but occasionally threw an odd, apologetic look to Eddie.

Peg introduced Ann to the McLeans, and Sandra and Eddie each attempted a very tight smile. Shona, about Ann's age and just as pretty, looked glumly at the carpet.

"And how are your parents, Ann?" Peg said, as if she had known them all her days.

"Fine, Mrs. Douglas," Ann replied.

Ian and Ann found chairs and Peg began to dish up the tea. Jack smiled warmly to Ann as he wandered through from the back. Barney started talking to Jack about the latest Derby winner, "the Horses" being one of Jack's favourite subjects. Eddie sulked, having no interest in horse racing. Ann tried to start a conversation with Shona, but the other girl answered briefly and looked away.

"I have something to show you, Peg," Ian said, getting up

and reaching for the parcel. "I just need to go upstairs for a minute."

When he returned to the room he was wearing the graduation robe with the crimson-edged white collar piece of the Faculty of Law. He smiled broadly at the others. "I made it Peg! Bachelor of Laws!"

Peg's sharp inhalation of breath was accompanied by her clasping her hands together, then she bit her bottom lip as her pride and endless love flowed through her gaze.

"Well, would ye look at that!" Barney O'Shea whispered in awe.

"Holy Saints preserve us!" said Jeanie.

"Well done, son," Jack said, moving forward to shake Ian's hand.

At that point Eddie got up. Without a word, he walked through the open door into the kitchen and on out into the garden. Shona looked back at the carpet that she had studied all afternoon, and Sandra just sat rigidly in her chair with a face like fizz, as was the expression around Myrestane.

Peg only briefly glanced at Eddie McLean leaving the room before she enveloped her son in a big hug, tears of pure joy running down her cheeks.

Chapter
Eighteen

ͼͽ ͼͽ ͼͽ

When Jack Armstrong was younger, and the men of the Work toiled in their dark roadways far below the green summer fields around Myrestane, the gentlemen and ladies of the Linlithgow and Stirlingshire Hunt galloped over these fields, behind their baying hounds, in pursuit of crafty little foxes.

Jack would anticipate their routes and open gates for them, gates in the corners of fields that were painted white so that these intrepid hunters might see them. Then they would toss Jack a florin or a half-crown, and he would have doffed his cap to them if he had worn one then.

As a boy, Ian witnessed this, and whenever he did, feelings of shame and resentment rose up sharply inside him. He couldn't explain the feelings but they were powerful and they never did go away.

In the mid 1940s, when he used to go with Jack to Myrestane Races, an annual steeplechase, he saw these people again.

They wore trench coats and tweed caps and sat on these walking sticks that had a leather part that spread open into a seat. The men all had the same haircuts, fairly long with wedges of hair that stuck out under their caps. Ian used to wonder who gave them these haircuts. Jimmy Sweeney, the local barber, never cut anyone's hair that way.

The women had long faces, not unlike their horses, and woollen stockings and flat leather shoes. There was a lot of leather around these people. They smiled and laughed a lot, but only to each other. They didn't seem to notice the locals at all.

If you could meet them as they came from the car park, and you happened to pass a race card to them, they might give you a shilling or two. That's what Jack said.

When Ian got older, he would sometimes fantasise about the Russian revolution, this "county set", as they were called, huddled in a compound and shaking with fear, now at last giving their captors their undivided attention. Why did Jack Armstrong, a hero of the Somme, a survivor of the notorious salt mine, bow and scrape to these parasites?

But what Ian hadn't guessed was that Jack had been a professional servant most of his life. He had come to be unable to separate the cap-doffing from the shilling that it brought. For him there could never be the one without the other. That is what Jack thought anyway, if he ever thought about it at all.

Peg was the same of course. So were the McLeans. So were the O'Sheas. The whole body of Ian's people made him cringe when he saw them fawn to what they perceived to be the upper class. The men in the Work, who had spent years killing themselves in dark holes in the ground or in the stinking guts of the retorts, came up to the surface at Myrestane Races, to rejoice at the merest acknowledgement of their existence by people that valued their dumb, sweaty horses more than their fellow man.

It was no accident that the poet, Robert Burns, was one of Ian's heroes.

What made it worse was that Jack and Peg and all the others drew their own levels of class. They would repeatedly intone that the true upper class — by which they meant these leather people at the races — were real gentry. You could always tell. They weren't mean-spirited or jumped-up snobs like the others. The others were an indeterminate crowd that seemed to include those who were successful but had worked for their money; those, in fact, whom they perceived to be no better than themselves, only luckier; those whom they knew.

What a load of shite, Ian thought. There were people with money and people without it. That was the only truth so far as he was concerned. And he viewed them all in a certain way, and not necessarily as equals. His own half-formed notions of class, and who to hate and who to like, were already being influenced by Ann Ingram. She seemed to be unaffected by all the bitterness of this internal war. But then she was from those who had. Ian was from the have-nots. For a young man with a law degree and a Myrestane up-bringing, the whole thing was very confusing.

However, Peg and Jack liked Ann, and Ian loved her. He knew that, because when he was not with her he was counting the days until he would be. So he would ask her to marry him and they would plan a great wedding.

∾ ∾ ∾

In 1962, at the end of the summer, Ian was taken on as a law apprentice with the firm of Mason & Jardine, Solicitors in Edinburgh. Peg bought him a car, a new Mini, which she paid up over thirty-six months from her widow's pension. Nobody quite knew how she could afford it. They imagined that she had some secret stash of money hidden away. Peg took delight in letting them think that, although it wasn't true.

The car, shiny blue and with its new car smell, was acquired and delivered to the door in inimitable Peg style. Ian was overwhelmed. When he passed his driving test, he drove it to Strathalmond and he and Ann went in it to the shore of the Forth near South Queensferry and made love in it.

They sat in the little car, its windows fogged up by the heat of their passionate petting that had finally gone beyond its earlier bounds. Ian, fully gratified as only a new lover can be, smiled at Ann. She looked away. "What's wrong?" he asked.

"This is wrong," Ann replied. "I wanted to be married

before . . . I . . He took her in his arms and kissed her gently.

"Is that all?" he said. "Then let's get married. We love each other. Why wait?"

Ann was elated. It wasn't the way she had thought it would be, not exactly a romantic proposal, but it was what she wanted to hear and it made everything all right.

"I would rather be in a bed than in an Austin Mini," Ian went on. "See! The handbrake is all bent over". Then they both laughed and decided to get married, for, in these days, at least for Ian and Ann, making love sealed the promise.

Shona McLean had just declared her engagement to Jim Fraser, her tyre man, and they had set a date for the wedding a year away. That was the way it was done in Ian's family. There was this long lead-up to a wedding while the couple put their name down for a council house and saved like mad for fitted carpets and three-piece suites and spanking new appliances. Ian hated the idea. He couldn't run the risk of cooling passions, and he couldn't wait. He would soon be a solicitor and Ann would be a teacher, and fitted carpets didn't seem all that important anyway.

∿∿∿

In the same year the shale mines shut down. The long struggle to compete with foreign oil was finally over. It was the year of the "big scatter", men trying to find other jobs.

Some stayed on, dismantling the Work. It was a hard job, handling heavy metal and loading it up for the scrap dealers. It was a sad time for Myrestane.

It was a sad time too for David Ingram. The demise of the Work brought to light the fact that he couldn't earn enough in his law practice to redeem the mortgage that he had placed on Strathalmond.

Sitting in his greenhouse, looking through the open door across the flower beds, that were now less than tidy since he could no longer purloin men from the Strathalmond Oils Limited to tend them, he reflected on his meeting with his partners. Angus McCulloch had come straight to the point as usual.

"You have to see our concern, David. These loans that you took out to shore up Strathalmond Oils, although they are secured on your house, were negotiated for a client of the firm. Should there be any difficulty now in repaying them, it could be argued that we, as your partners, are jointly liable." The Cunninghams, Mr. Andrew and Mr. Edward, nodded their assent as the little man continued.

"I take it that you are prepared to put Strathalmond on the market to satisfy the current debts of the company. It seems to us that there is no other solution. In the meantime we would require you to sign a dissolution of our partnership, just for our protection. I'm sure you understand. You would go on the notepaper as a consultant and continue here with the firm in that capacity. It would mean a drop in income of course, but I'm sure that you would manage adequately, especially if your household expenses were reduced by your moving to a more modest residence."

David gazed over the garden. How could this have happened? How could he tell Eleanor that she had to give up her beautiful house?

But he knew how it had happened. Now, after all these years, he knew that Peter had been right. Strathalmond Oils Limited had been fighting for its very life from the first day that it had been formed. There had been no room for sentiment for the sake of satisfying Old Sam's generous gestures to his workers. The times had overtaken Old Sam. Peter knew it and he was thrown out for saying it. Poor Peter.

Now the Ingrams were about to lose Strathalmond thanks to David's own folly in trying to please his grandfather.

He sat in the greenhouse until it got dark, all these thoughts running around in his head. And he did the same the next night. And the next.

∾ ∾ ∾

In October, Ann and Ian went to a wedding reception in Myrestane Cooperative Hall. A cousin of Ian's, a daughter of the Wimpey driver who had delivered the piano, had been "married onto" — as they termed it — a fellow called Charlie Rae, a butcher's apprentice from somewhere up in the Calders. It was a Registry Office arrangement, and had they waited any longer, the "wean" would have been at the wedding. But the Registrar, old Paterson, rhymed off the ceremony with his usual bored demeanour to the next of kin only, and half of Myrestane turned up at the hall in the evening.

They had an accordion band and a group of wee lassies with fat knees who did Highland dances, and the long trellis tables were lined with fish suppers, black pudding suppers and white pudding and haggis suppers, and no end of bottles and cans of beer and drams of whisky. It was a night to remember.

"Let's have a do like that," Ian said, as he and Ann left the hall close to midnight, the band still beating out the *Gay Gordons* and a lone voice by the exit weepily singing *The Auld Hoose*, each syllable drawn out ad infinitum.

"But I want to be married in a church," Ann said, and as she said it she tried to imagine her relations eating fish suppers in the Cooperative Hall to the accompaniment of accordions and liquor, both of which were taboo in her family. She winced briefly at the thought.

Driving back to Strathalmond in the Mini, they both realised that the kind of reception they had just attended was out of the question. They explored the possibilities and agreed that they both wanted to get married now, not a year from now. Ann wanted a church wedding and Ian was happy with that, but they couldn't plan beyond that when they pondered on their respective families.

"Tell you what," Ian said. "Let's get engaged. We don't need money for that. We'll shop for a ring tomorrow, then we'll tell our folks, put an announcement of the engagement in the paper and go from there. But let's keep it simple."

Ann wasn't sure about the idea of getting engaged to Ian

Douglas without telling her parents. They didn't like him. She knew that. But maybe it was the thing to do, then David and Eleanor would just have to accept it. She looked at Ian's happy face as he drove along in the dark. He was impulsive, just like his mother. Decide on a thing and do it. That was the Douglas way; so far removed from the carefully thought out decisions of the Ingrams. Then the car radio played *Moon River* telling her that the plan was good.

They bought a ring for Ann from a secondhand jeweller's called Harry Chernak's in Rose Street in Edinburgh. It was in the shape of a fastened belt, with a row of garnets and one tiny diamond, and it cost six pounds. Then they walked up South Bridge and put the announcement of their engagement in the *Scotsman*. That afternoon they told Peg and Jack who wished them well. Ian could see how pleased his mother was that the commitment had been made. He knew that she suspected that he and Ann were beyond the petting stage from a recent remark she had made to him. "Remember son, a new coat makes a new man. It doesn't make a new woman." She had said no more than that, but he knew what was expected of him and he was delighted that she approved of his choice of a wife. From Peg's they went to Strathalmond.

Ann knew that there was only one way to tell Eleanor, and that was straight out and quickly, for if there was any doubt about a wedding, if Eleanor got room to manoevre in even the slightest degree, their plans would be altered, or perhaps shelved altogether.

They went in the back door and through the kitchen, Ann leading Ian by the hand. Ian suddenly felt like a naughty boy being hauled along to the headmaster's study. "They'll be in the drawing room," Ann said, almost in a whisper, as if they were burglars.

Ever since he had been allowed access to Strathalmond again, after the night of Jonathon's party, Ian's normally buoyant personality flattened into a scowl whenever he crossed its threshold. Now he and Ann were about to announce their engagement, and he was plain scared. He had always been somewhat intimidated, much against his will, by the splendour of the house and gardens and the elevated social position of the Ingrams. On this occasion he felt like an urchin, caught stealing apples from the manor house orchard.

"Hello Mum, hello Dad," Ann announced, as she entered the drawing room. She sat down on a couch, pulling Ian down beside her.

Eleanor sat in the big soft armchair by the fireplace, studying her menus. Every meal she had ever made had its recipe included in a thick hard-covered notebook which she pored over constantly. She smiled briefly at Ann and then glared at Ian who slouched, poker-faced, as usual. David Ingram's newspaper rustled in the silence as he lowered it to peer over at Ann.

"Will you stay for tea, Ian?" Eleanor said, forcing herself to be nice.

"I would like that, Mrs. Ingram," Ian replied, brightening up. Ian Douglas didn't know when an offer was not entirely genuine. He was used to people who said what they meant rather than what good manners dictated. What he did know, however, was that Eleanor was a fantastic cook and served sizable dinners which she called "tea". In his experience, only his mother, Peg Douglas, could cook a dinner like Eleanor Ingram.

"Mother, Ian and I got engaged today. We have decided to get married." Ann said the words quickly, looking expectantly from one parent to the other.

In the oppressive silence that followed, Ian could hear the ticking of the grandfather clock in the hall. Eleanor sat upright in her chair, laying down the menus and David lowered his newspaper. "This is a bit sudden, Ann," he said, frowning at Ian.

Eleanor looked at the ring on Ann's finger. "You're not . . . in any trouble, I hope," she said.

Ann's face flushed with anger. "No, mother!" she retorted.

"Well, we can talk about this later," David said ponderously, beginning to raise his newspaper.

"No, dad!" Ann said angrily. "There's nothing to talk about. Ian and I are engaged to be married. Are you not happy for us?"

All the while Ian felt like an interloper, eavesdropping on a family conversation. His admiration for Ann Ingram had just leapt a hundred points and he felt acutely embarrassed by his own inability to come to her aid.

To Eleanor, it was if a bomb had dropped into her domain. All she could do was look to her husband.

David Ingram wrestled with the entirely foreign proposition that his daughter was suddenly an adult, and refused to be excluded any more from the Ingram decisions. He was being forced to countenance her, and this boy that was with her, as a trial that wouldn't go away, and he didn't like the feeling. Then he looked at Ann and saw the earnest expectation in her face.

"Your mother and I are happy for you Ann," he said at length, in his soft baritone voice. "Happy for both of you," he added, looking at Ian. Ann squeezed Ian's hand and smiled. Eleanor moved to embrace Ann and then Ian, giving him a peck on the cheek. Eleanor always knew when to do the proper thing.

Later that evening, when on their own, David Ingram explained to Eleanor their current financial predicament.

"You mean we have to leave Strathalmond?" she said, her voice quivering.

David couldn't bear seeing the pain in her still beautiful face. He went to her and put an arm around her shoulders. "That's not certain," he said. "We don't have the final figures on Strathalmond Oils Limited. Much of the dismantling of the Work is still in progress. It will be months before any final decision has to be made. It's just that my partners want to be sure that my debts are covered and will not involve the firm. You know what lawyers are like."

He spoke quietly in his low voice, hugging her and watching the anxiety in her face, wishing now that he had never confided in her. But he had to make a decision about Ann's wedding and he didn't want Eleanor making big plans that might compound his problems.

"Look dear," he said finally, "don't worry about it. We'll be in Strathalmond for the rest of our days. All it means is that Ann may need to wait a year or so if we are to give her a big wedding. I'll talk to her about that. I don't want you worrying about a thing."

Eleanor searched his face, desperate to believe him. She had never had a day's worry about money in her life. David had never discussed financial things. He had always attended to the major expenses and placed a regular monthly sum in her account for the running of the house. The idea of having to move was unthinkable. It terrified her. She wanted him to tell her that it wasn't so, and to keep telling her.

David, now certain that he should never have raised the matter at all, persisted in his quiet reassurances and eventually she calmed down and relaxed against him.

He went on to talk about the wedding, changing the subject, as it were, to something less devastating for Eleanor. Bit by bit he succeeded. They sat up way beyond their normal bedtime, and Eleanor was relieved to get onto the wedding of Ann, a subject that, though it had been a major catastrophe before, now seemed of little importance to her.

In the morning, Eleanor told Ann that her father wanted to talk to her on his return from the office.

It was only the second serious talk that David Ingram had had with his daughter in all of her twenty-three years. The first had been about her going to Moray House College to train for a teacher. That had seemed to David an entirely appropriate career for Ann, and her pleas that what she really wanted to be was a nurse had been summarily ignored for reasons that Ann never to this day understood.

On the present occasion, her father looked serious. More than that, Ann detected a sadness in his face which she couldn't understand. She was well aware that her parents were less than enamoured to the idea of her marrying Ian Douglas, but she thought that that issue had been resolved and that they were now resigned to accept it. She sat at the kitchen table, her mother silently embroidering a tablecloth in the background, and listened anxiously for her father's address.

"You know, Ann, that Ian Douglas wouldn't have been our choice of a husband for you, but he is your choice and we hope you have made the right choice."

A smile crossed his lips and Ann felt a wave of relief.

"Your mother and I have discussed the matter of your wedding, and for reasons that needn't concern you, I want to tell you that, if you can wait a year, we will be in a position to give you a proper wedding."

He regarded Ann's puzzled look and quickly went on. "This is an awkward time for us Ann, with the Work closing and such. In a year all that will be resolved and we will be in a better position to deal with a wedding."

Ann knew at once that there was something wrong, something that she was not being told about. It had always been like this in her family. She and Jonathon had never been included in major decisions. The reasons for decisions had never been imparted to the children. What was the problem now? What would change in a year? A year!

Then it began to dawn on her that her parents' idea of a proper wedding meant a grand affair befitting the Ingrams of Strathalmond and, therefore, that money must be the issue.

But it was no issue for her.

"A simple wedding, father." She blurted out the words. "All we want is a simple ceremony in the church, just immediate family members, just you and mother and Jonathon, and Ian's mother and his sister. That's all I want. That's all Ian wants."

Of course it wasn't all Ann wanted. It had never been all that any girl wanted since the beginning of time. But a year! A year was unthinkable.

Ann's eyes filled with tears, and David Ingram's heart was wrenched with anguish though it never showed in his face. He moved over and put a hand on her shoulder. "All right, my dear," he said softly. "Whatever you wish, that's what we'll do." He looked sternly at Eleanor who gave a slight nod.

∿ ∿ ∿

Ann Ingram, and Ian Douglas too for that matter, were inno-
cents when it came to arranging a wedding. Once the decision
was made for the simple wedding to proceed without delay,
David Ingram blended once more into the background, leaving
the matter to Eleanor.

A day was fixed, a Saturday a sufficient number of weeks
away to allow the banns to be called in St. Nicholas Church.
While everyone, Ingrams and Douglases included, quietly pondered upon how far advanced was the pregnancy of Ann
Ingram, the couple rushed gleefully around their friends
announcing their happy news. At the same time these friends
wouldn't be invited. This, Ian and Ann hadn't considered, and
there was worse to come.

It would be a long time later before Ann Ingram would
realise that her mother should have guided her and corrected
her rash decision on the subject of the simple wedding.
Eleanor let her go and invite Peg Douglas, but not Jack
Armstrong; Sandra McLean, but not Eddie McLean.

For Jack Armstrong, it mattered not. Jack didn't care for
churches or ceremonies and would always be delighted to see
Ann at any time. For the McLeans, it was a slight that would
never be forgiven. Rectified or not, it would cause a rift that
would widen the already open chasm.

For Ann Ingram, the idyllic family, whose doors were
always open and into which she had hoped to throw herself
from the rigid fortress of Strathalmond, would topple like a
sand-castle in the tide.

Chapter Nineteen

❧❧❧

"**M**other," Ian said. Now and then he would call Peg "mother" when the talk was on something serious. "Mother, what are we supposed to do about these wedding arrangements? Sandra's got her knickers in a twist about Eddie not being invited, so we've said we'll invite him. Now Ann's mother has a whole list of Ingram relations that are coming. It's going to be a bloody disaster. And all we wanted was a simple ceremony."

Peg poured tea from a brown china teapot into three mugs. Then she placed one in front of Ian and one in front of Jack Armstrong as they all sat around the table.

"Don't worry about Eddie. I'll invite him. I'll just say there was a mix up with the invitations and the Ingrams are very sorry that he didn't get his. And it doesn't matter who Eleanor Ingram is inviting. Does it?"

She slurped her tea and looked up at Jack who was looking over the top of his glasses at the *Daily Record* racing page. "Your Uncle Jack has no notion of going anyway. He doesn't go to things like that." Jack didn't look up but continued to study the paper.

"Maybe he'll come along and have a drink at the reception," Peg continued.

"Good luck!" Ian said with a sigh.

For the first time in the conversation Peg looked alarmed. "They are planning a reception, I hope. I expect that your friends would be going to that. Wullie Kerr and the Patersons and your friends from the university. And I think you should be asking the O'Sheas, and some from the Station Raw. I'm sure Ann will have her college friends there."

Ian said nothing but just turned the teaspoon around in his mug. He knew what Peg had in mind — the Cooperative Hall. Receptions were his mother's speciality. After Tosh's funeral everyone was invited back to the Institute in Myrestane where Peg had arranged a boiled ham tea and set out bottles of whisky and cases of beer. Tosh Douglas' send-off was still talked about in Myrestane.

Now Ian had come to the difficult part.

"I think, mother, that the plan is to have a sit down tea at Nicholson's Restaurant after the ceremony. For those who attended the church, that is." Ian looked back into his mug, wishing that he could have crawled into it and hidden there.

All expression vanished from Peg's face and she stared at Ian with wide, unblinking eyes. "Nicholson's Restaurant?" She spat out the words as if they made a foul taste in her mouth. "That's yon temperance place next to the Baptist Hall. And only for the church guests?"

"None of the Ingrams drink, mother," Ian began, then, catching the look on Peg's face, he gave up and went back to concentrating on his mug.

Peg's jaw tightened and she sniffed her nose. "Jack, do you hear this? A temperance wedding!"

It was one of the strangest things about Peg Douglas, her attitude to drink. Like so many women of her generation, she had seen too much of it and the disastrous effects of it. She was teetotal and always ready to declare that fact. Yet, for some reason, she was never without a bottle of whisky in the house for those who enjoyed a snifter. She would ply them with it generously. Eddie McLean, funnily enough, was the same. Each Hogmanay Eddie would run around the houses with his half bottle and his little nip glass seeking out the drinkers. And he didn't have far to look. Then he would top the little glass to overflowing and force it into their hands, watching with relish as they emptied it.

It was as if Peg and Eddie took some gratification from being immune to the temptations of John Barlycorn, a gratification that was fed from witnessing the weakness of the imbibers. For Peg, the idea of a wedding reception without drink was unthinkable — criminal, in fact.

"Oh dear," Peg said, getting no response from Jack Armstrong. "My, my! This will be some wedding. And it the first wedding between a Douglas and an Ingram of Strathalmond." She shook her head and tidied away the mugs and teapot.

The truth, though Peg didn't know it, was that it was not the first wedding of a Douglas and an Ingram of Strathalmond. That had occurred centuries ago.

ᐁ ᐁ ᐁ

There was a joke about a father slipping his future son-in-law a handful of cash to elope, the father even throwing in the ladder, and if David Ingram had listened to jokes he might have paid some attention to that one. As it was, he had become weary of listening to Eleanor at the kitchen table, checking and cross-checking her list of guests, and had escaped to the lounge with *Amateur Gardener*.

But the peace was not to last. Eleanor followed him, list in hand, reading out the names to ensure, as she said, that they had not missed anyone important. Her father, the little banker from Blackhall and his long-suffering wife; her brothers, Tom and Robert, who had both followed their father into the bank, and their wives; several assorted cousins whom David had never met since his own wedding; an estranged uncle who had apparently made a fortune in the scrap business, and a distant cousin of David's from Ayrshire whom he had never liked.

"Who among them was important?" David mused. Then he banished the thought quickly lest it showed on his face.

"And guess what," Eleanor added, her eyes shining with glee. "Uncle Charlie and Vi will be here from America. Isn't that wonderful?"

Charlie was her father's brother who had gone to Detroit in the twenties to work in the car industry. Every Christmas he sent polished postcards to Eleanor and David and pictures of well-fed American children sitting around barbecues; his off-spring, with names like Eugene and Mary Lou and Elroy. One of them was now in the F.B.I. for God's sake!

But David was happy enough that Eleanor had something to excite her and that she seemed to have forgotten the catastrophe of losing Strathalmond.

"And by the way, Peg Douglas is coming to tea this evening. I asked Ann to invite her. It's only right that she be included in the arrangements," Eleanor said.

David groaned.

"Ann and Poker-Face will be coming, and I asked Jonathon to come too, and stay for the weekend." David groaned again, this time more audibly.

∽∽∽

As Ian turned the Mini into the driveway of Strathalmond, Peg glanced at the Miller's Wall where she had first met the young soldier, Jack Armstrong, so many years earlier. The late sun filtered down through the high branches of the trees and the place looked not a day older. She reminisced on the tall figure of a girl stepping out up the drive towards the great doors, and the welcoming face of Old Sam Ingram who had greeted her. She thought of the urgency of her visit then, and the earnest faces of the miners on that long ago day.

Now, like Old Sam himself, most of them had passed on. And there were no mines any more, no jutting, smoking retorts; only the great orange heaps their lives had created and left behind, like pyramids in the land of Egypt. Shelley jumped to her mind.

My name is Ozymandias, king of kings:
Look on my works, ye mighty, and despair!

Thirty feet inside the old gates of Strathalmond, they passed a verdant spot not far to their right where Sam Ingram had dug up the rusty barrel of the ancient canon, and later reburied it in the ground. Moving up the driveway, Peg looked up at the high south-facing window that looked over the lawns and gardens towards Houstoun Wood. That was Rachael Ingram's room, the room that Peg would have chosen had she been born with a silver spoon in her mouth.

Inside, the house was just as Peg remembered it; magnificent. She sat in the same room where she had talked with Sam and Peter Ingram. William Ingram no longer looked down from the mantlepiece. Some changes had been made to walls and furnishings, but it was the same room, though somewhat the better for the delicate, feminine touches of Eleanor Ingram, and there was a distinct perfume of flowers in the air.

Eleanor smiled graciously to Peg as she flitted around the gorgeous setting, preparing the tea. Ian sat huffily in a corner, and Ann smiled at Peg and glanced at her mother from time to time with a hint of wonder in her look, as if she couldn't quite believe what she was seeing.

David Ingram, who had come in from the garden, welcomed Peg with the same old-fashioned charm that Old Sam once displayed, and they talked about the old days in the Work and some of the men whom they both remembered. He didn't recognise Peg as the girl who had taken him for walks when he was a boy.

"Aye, your grandfather was a good man to the miners, Mr. Ingram," Peg said.

"David, please!" Eleanor interjected. "It's David and Eleanor. And we'll just call you Peg. After all, we'll soon be related." Eleanor smiled at Ann and Ian and Ann thought that wonders would never cease.

"Did you ever see David's medal, Peg?" Eleanor went on, walking to a large three-sided china cabinet set into a corner of the room.

"Eleanor!" David said, gruffly, shaking his head and making a sign to her with his eyes.

"Oh, don't you be so modest," Eleanor quipped, as she withdrew from the cabinet a large bronze medal, mounted on a mahogany base and proffered it to Peg. "He got that from the R.S.P.C.A.you know. For saving the sheep."

Peg turned the artifact in her hands, reading the inscription. She remembered the incident, as Tosh had described it. It happened in 1941. A German bomber, passing over Myrestane, returning from a raid on the sugar refineries at Clydebank, had jettisoned a bomb which landed in a field just outside the Work. It had made a crater forty feet wide, and the next day most of the field caved into the underground workings taking a dozen sheep with it. David Ingram, who toured the mine in the early hours of most mornings, had been first on the scene and had apparently climbed into the hole, at no small risk to himself, and pulled eleven sheep to safety. It was talked about in the days that followed.

"Do you know, Peg, that we never knew anything about that rescue until the R.S.P.C.A. officer came to the door with this award?" Eleanor said looking at David with obvious pride, while he took the medal from Peg and returned it to the cabinet, mumbling under his breath. Peg was impressed, more by his modesty than his heroism, and Ian sat up, suddenly taking a new interest in his future father-in-law.

During the meal, the small talk continued. Peg was aware that only brief references were made to the wedding arrangements. It was evident that these were already in place and the object of this meeting was not to discuss them or change them, but merely to establish that they were a *fait accomplis*. Eleanor made a quick reference to the misunderstanding that resulted in Eddie McLean's omission from the invitations, and hoped that he had not been offended. Peg just smiled politely. Ann noticed that no reference was made to Eleanor's extended guest list, and she was relieved at that since it was the kind of sore point that could have made a problem.

Towards the end of the meal, Jonathon Ingram burst into

the room, mumbling apologies for being late and stripping off the long drab raincoat which he casually threw over one of Eleanor's antique chairs. He was cheerful, and to Peg's practised eye he had had a drink or two. He looked around the room with a ponderous gaze, identifying the company one by one, like one who had just slid down a laundry shoot into the middle of a party. Then he came over to Peg with his hand outstretched.

"You must be Ian's mother. I'm very pleased to meet you. So old Ian here is finally going to make an honest woman out of my little sister. Marvellous! Marvellous!" He shook Peg's hand warmly and tilted his head to wink to Ann.

Eleanor approached him, gathering up and folding the coat as she came.

"I've laid out your tea in the kitchen, dear," she said, giving Peg a little hurt smile as she led Jonathon firmly by the shoulders towards the door. "You must be hungry after your journey."

Jonathon half turned to say something to Peg, when David's deep voice stopped him.

"Go into the kitchen with your mother, Jonathon. Perhaps you can join us later. And wash and brush up before you have tea."

Jonathon's buoyant manner folded like a poor kite in a high wind as he stared at his father for a long second before letting himself be led away.

"Youngsters!" David said, turning back to Peg. "Who would have them?" He smirked briefly but Peg caught the sadness in his eyes.

Chapter
Twenty

ᏔᏔᏔ

The wedding, when it came, was every bit the disaster Ian had anticipated.

The pews up each side of the central aisle of St. Nicholas Church reflected the huge imbalance that resulted from the efforts of Eleanor Ingram. In the front pew on the groom's side sat Peg Douglas, in one of the big cartwheel hats that she favoured. Next to her, Eddie McLean and Sandra fidgeted and threw long-faced looks across the aisle at the bride's side, three full rows of Ingrams and Rosses with tilted up chins and attentive faces, looking straight ahead. Jonathon slouched, all by himself, in the fourth pew back, a dreamy smile on his face.

Big Hugh was the best man. He dropped the ring while they awaited the arrival of the bride. It bounced off a step and rolled under the first row of Ingram pews, and little Herbert Ross, Eleanor's father, split the trousers of his hired suit as he bent quickly to retrieve it.

The organist had failed to turn up and the young minister, ever inventive as young ministers are, played the *Wedding March* on a little cassette player that he had recovered from the vestry. To its somewhat crackling refrain, David Ingram marched down the aisle with his big splay-footed strides, his daughter dancing in and out between his feet to avoid a permanent injury.

But it was in the singing — and singing there would be for this was something that Peg Douglas had insisted upon — that's where things really came apart.

Ann Ingram had conspired with her future mother-in-law to include a selection of hymns, and these were contained on single sheets of paper that were pushed into the hands of the guests as they entered the church. Eleanor stared at hers as if it was a blueprint for World War 111.

On a difficulty scale of one to ten, for a group of untutored and unrehearsed singers, the hymn, *O Perfect Love,* is a ten. For the Douglases and the Ingrams, without an organist, it was a twelve. Peg Douglas fired right into the hymn with gusto, as if she had paced herself for a lifetime just waiting for this moment. On the third line, Sandra attempted a descant, with a cocky sneer at those across the aisle, and Eddie joined in with his Bing Crosby croon. The in-laws, what Tosh used to call the "outlaws", were left in hopeless disarray. David Ingram's baritone, and some totally surprising deep base conjunctions that issued from the fresh-faced young minister, joined in to dig the hymn's final grave.

Ian and Ann smiled into each other's eyes. It was unforgettable, anyway, the smiles said.

Outside the church, their friends sat along the wall, some with cameras, some with cans of beer. They weren't invited but they came anyway, and they gave a rousing cheer as Ian and Ann emerged. As the guests piled into cars that would take them to Nicholson's Restaurant, Ian and Ann talked and shook hands with their friends, acutely embarrassed that they would not be joining the wedding party, while Jonathon stood off by himself, taking a few swigs from his hip flask.

Later, at the restaurant, some stiff speeches followed the boiled ham and chips. Peg Douglas, in her long navy dress and great targe of a hat, laughed and chatted with Ingrams and Rosses as if she had known them all her life. She held the floor, with the same supreme confidence that had led off the hymns, and the guests were relieved for they had no great deal to say to one another.

Eleanor eyed Peg as a bull eyes a capering bull-fighter, while David, fortunate enough to find a rose grower in the group, conducted a gardening conversation in a corner.

Eddie and Sandra sat in silence, making polite, but not quite successful faces when addressed in the foreign accents of the Edinburgh toffs, Sandra trying to assess the cost of the outfits around her. Jonathon, who had little time for anyone, disappeared at regular intervals to the Gents, from which he returned ever the more fortified.

When the wedding couple were making ready to leave in the Mini for a two day honeymoon in the Lake District, Eddie caught Ian in the Gents, produced his bottle and nip glass, and insisted that his brother-in-law celebrate with a drink. Ian was wise enough not to refuse the fiery, overflowing gift, and he struggled it down. Then Eddie gripped his hand in a vigorous handshake.

"Here's the best tae ye, son," he said, capping his dram bottle and secreting it back into his jacket.

Right at that moment Ian felt sorry for Eddie. It was as if he had abandoned Eddie somehow.

"Thanks, Eddie," he said, squeezing past him to return to the crowd.

As the Mini left the car park, Ian saw the guests in the rear window. Peg was out in front, tearfully waving her handkerchief. Jonathon, off to the side, waved his flask which he no longer bothered to hide, while David Ingram and Eddie McLean watched him in disgust.

Ian glanced at Ann, then changed gear and headed south to another country.

∾∾∾

The party that never occurred at her son's wedding, would occur if Peg Douglas had anything to do with it. And she had everything to do with it.

Peg had a relation in Edinburgh by the name of Auntie Liz. She was a widow who lived in the top floor of a tenement in

Lothian Road in Edinburgh and had worked for years as a chambermaid in one of the big hotels on Princes Street. She had a pension from her late husband's employer and owned a one-bedroom flat in Myrestane which she rented out. Jack Armstrong called her "Mrs. Hunky-Dory".

Ian could recall visiting Auntie Liz with his mother when he was a boy. They had climbed five flights of stone stairs in the half dark to find the door locked, and as they turned to go back down, they heard her coming up. They could see her down the stairwell, a small ageing woman, bent down with a large bag in each hand, and wearing a black hat with a bunch of red, plastic grapes jiggling on its rim. She was singing as she ascended, and the song grew louder at every level, wafting up the inside of the building.

For these are my mountains, and these are my glens . . . . .

Ian and Ann rented Auntie Liz' flat as their first home, and Peg Douglas was the instigator of their first house-warming party.

The flat was on the upper level of a two-storey terrace on a street called Holmes Road that had existed since the beginning of the shale industry. The terrace would be pulled down five years later, before it fell down all on its own.

The entrance to the flat was through a close — a narrow pend — from the main street that led to a small courtyard, and from there by an outside stairway with iron railings. In all the little houses accessed from this courtyard lived the families of men from the Work, most of them now retired, but all of them shaleworkers.

Ann Ingram loved her little house. She and Ian had wall-papered the ancient walls of its room and kitchen and cleaned its cooking stove. They had laid linoleum where the floor-boards showed, and scattered some colourful rugs on its uneven floor.

On the afternoon of the house-warming, Ann hung up curtains on the single window that overlooked Holmes Road, white ones with a bold red design, and was taking a final walk around her domain with a duster when two men arrived in a van. They had a delivery, they said, a three-piece suite from Myrestane Cooperative, courtesy of Mrs. Peg Douglas. They carried the sofa and two armchairs up the stair and stripped off the wrappings.

Ann surveyed the brown tweed of the seats and the vinyl armrests. She hated them. Then she was overcome with guilt, for they were a gift, and an expensive one. She said nothing to Ian. When Peg arrived in the evening, she would thank her profusely and Peg would nod and say that they were the best in the store.

After the Randy Raws, where the Osheas had first stayed when they came from Donegal, and the Raws in Myrestane Station, where Peg Douglas and Tosh had spent a lifetime; after these had gone and their residents departed, Holmes Road stood as one of the few remaining testaments to an industry and to a time. To have a party here, a last fling, as it were, to commemorate old times, was Peg Douglas' secret motivation.

Some wouldn't come here: the Ingrams for one; Eddie McLean and Sandra for another; and some of the new couple's student friends who had graduated to better things and wouldn't be seen dead in this decrepit slum, this reminder of their origins.

But others would come: Peg and Jack; Barney and Jeanie O'Shea; the cousin who drove the Wimpey lorry and sang *Phil the Fluter's Ball* whenever there was an occasion. And Hugh Donaldson would come; and Tammy Flynn with his fiddle; and the railway squad that used to be, George O'Neill and Wull, and Mathie Thompson.

Maybe even Wee Tam McEwen, the Spurkle, would come and bend some pennies for the crowd.

∾ ∾ ∾

It was a great night. It was one of the last great parties of an era that was passing, in a place that would soon be no more.

They sang and they danced until four in the morning.

When Constable Ritchie, "Big Pundy Ritchie" to the locals, called in to quell the noise, he was whisked off, by the Wimpey cousin into the kitchen for a drink.

Around ten o'clock, when the celebrations were at their height, Ann led Ian outside and down the back steps to the courtyard, out of earshot of the revellers who had spilled out onto the stairhead.

"Jonathon didn't come," she said, and Ian saw the concern in her eyes. "I'm worried about him, Ian." She paused, as if unsure how to go on. "When I dropped in at his flat this week, he was. . . . painting things again." She anxiously searched Ian's face. "All over his furniture — these strange shapes."

"Oh, it's just this latest craze he has about Salvador Dali," Ian smiled. "All these melting clock faces and things hanging on forked sticks in deserts. You know Jonathon. I wouldn't worry about it."

"But he's got the wardrobe and his bedside table covered with funny looking designs, painted with thick black lines. And he has pictures, hanging on his walls, of gruesome faces that he makes himself with a charcoal pencil held between elastic bands. They're horrible!"

Ian looked away from Ann's glaring eyes. This was something new to him, the pictures and the furniture painting. He recalled the last time he had seen Jonathon. It was a week earlier, and he had gone to the flat on his way home from work to see if Jonathon fancied a pint at the pub round the corner. When he got no answer at the door, he went to the pub.

∽ ∽ ∽

Jonathon was sitting in a corner of the lounge bar, nursing a pint glass. It was one of these old Edinburgh lounges, with dark mahogany veneer and bench seating around the walls, upholstered in red velvet. Everything about it was designed to give the impression of discreet and hushed luxury, even the lighting — especially the lighting.

Jonathon was leaning across the table talking to a peroxide blond whose back was to Ian. As Ian approached, the blond got up with a raucous laugh. "Ah'm no that desperate, son. Make it a tenner and yerr on." Jonathon waved her away, reaching for his glass with the other hand.

When she turned to leave, Ian saw that she was about fifty, caked in makeup, big breasts bulging over the top of a low cut, over-tight dress. She puckered her fat lips in a silent kiss to Ian as she pushed past him in a cloud of choking perfume.

As Ian took her chair, Jonathon looked up. He gave a little smirk. "I can't even get the likes of that any more," he said.

"Come on, man! You're not serious. Finish up your drink, and then you're coming back with me to Myrestane for your tea. What do you say?"

Jonathon swayed in the seat, bringing up his head to give Ian a bleary stare.

"Back with Ian, good old Ian. Back to Myrestane . . . arsehole of the world . . . back to the happy home." His voice was slurred with booze and his chin dropped on to his chest. "How's the happy home? How's my little sister? How's the Ingrams of Strathalmond? Eh? How are they? Eh?" He was mumbling to the floor and drooling down his shirt.

Ian rose and took him by the arm.

"Come on Jonathon! I think you've had enough. Come on! Let's get out of here."

Jonathon wrestled free, lifting his head with a start and suddenly becoming aggressive.

"How's Mrs. Douglas? . . . and how's your old man? Eh? Little Jack Armstrong. Eh?"

"What?" Ian said, his mind trying to grasp what he was hearing.

"Your father, my dear Ian." Jonathon opened his arms in an expansive gesture. "Or maybe not. Eh? Maybe you're not sure. Eh?" Ian was stunned into silence as Jonathon raved on drunkenly.

He leaned over and whispered in Ian's face. "My father's a bastard, you know. You know that. Eh?" Then, flopping back on the seat, "but at least I know who my father is!"

Ian Douglas, neither before nor since, had ever felt such anger. It rose in him like a great red wave, burning him, and blinding him to everything except the dishevelled drunk sprawling there in front of him. His hands seized Jonathon's jacket by its lapels and he lifted him bodily out of the seat, heaving him against the wall. "Bastard! Fuckin' bastard!" he shouted. Jonathon hung in the air, the stupid grin fading from his face. "Ah'll kill ye, yah bastard!"

Ian had no clear recollection of leaving the pub. He had the picture of a rotund little barman rushing over shouting. "Order there! Order!" Then Jonathon, sitting back in the seat, trying to straighten his collar.

He didn't think of driving. He walked aimlessly down South Bridge, his rage turning to disbelief. How could Jonathon, his friend Jonathon, have said it? Why?

Ian Douglas had little or no thought for any plight Jonathon may have been in. When you are in your twenties, it is only actions that matter, not reasons. How could his former friend have accused Peg Douglas of that . . . that thing? Did other people think it?

Ian's mind filled with pictures of his mother, and Tosh, and Uncle Jack. He turned into another pub and ordered a double whisky, and stared at himself in the bar mirror.

∾∾∾

"Ian! Ian!" Ann's voice broke into his thoughts. "We should go and visit him tomorrow."

Hugh Donaldson had come down the stairs to join them.

"Tomorrow, Ian! I'm afraid for him. I'm afraid he might . . . do . . . something.." Her voice trailed off.

"Do what?" Ian said, coming back from his reverie.

A shadow crossed Big Hugh's face, and his haunted look moved from one to the other as the tinny strains of a fiddle rollicked above their heads.

∾ ∾ ∾

There were only the two of them in Strathalmond now, and the old house was quieter than it had ever been.

They rarely saw or heard from Jonathon, whose performance at the wedding, in front of Eleanor's invited guests, and particularly in front of those awful Douglases, had caused David Ingram to send him out of his sight once again. He was a great disappointment to his father. Every opportunity had been afforded him to make something of himself and he had ignored them all. Now he was a drunk, just like Uncle Peter. Eleanor had pointed out that the weakness came from the Ingram side of the family and not from her side.

But David had worse things to concern him than his thankless son and wayward daughter. The final reckoning had come in on the financial state of Strathalmond Oils Ltd. and his own personal guarantees, and there was no longer any question about staying on in Strathalmond. It would have to go on the market. He had known this for some weeks now and he had agonised upon how to tell Eleanor.

Eleanor, for her part, could see the strain of worry on her husband. But all she could do about it was to work harder at her wifely duties, cleaning and polishing, cooking and tidying, as if she could clean away whatever it was that concerned him.

Since that terrible night before the wedding, she had not allowed herself to think about losing Strathalmond. It was a mistake. There was no question of them losing their house. It was unthinkable. Anyway, David had never raised the matter again and she was sure now that she had misunderstood him. It must be his work at the office, Cunningham, McCulloch & Ingram, that was worrying him. That was it, surely. After all, he wasn't getting any younger. He should cut back on his office hours, Eleanor thought. Yes, that was what he needed to do. She would talk to him about that.

Often, when David was away at the office and she stopped for her morning or afternoon coffee, Eleanor thought about the children. It used to be fun, showing them things, teaching Ann to sew and helping Jonathon put together a model ship that she had bought for him. And when they went on holiday to Morecambe or Scarborough, she would give them their pocket money and they would go whooping off along the front with her and David walking behind. Then they would go back to the guesthouse for tea, the place she had spent hours in selecting from the classifieds in the winter — the place that had no home-baking. Eleanor wanted no home-baked cakes, only bought ones.

These were good times. She had her children at home and they did what she told them. Why did the world steal them away from her? What had she or David done to deserve their betrayal?

Then she would finish her coffee and get back to her work, to make the house beautiful for her husband coming home.

Chapter
Twenty-one

❧ ❧ ❧

On the 17th day of August, 1965, Jonathon Ingram, in blue striped pyjamas, got out of bed and looked out the window of his flat at the sun edging up over Arthur's Seat.

He went to the table and made a pencil note, in his unique capital lettering, about cancelling milk and papers and returning a library book.

Then he sat back in his only easy chair, took a mouthful of pills, cut his wrists with a Gillette razor-blade, and pulled a plastic bag over his head, fastening it under his chin.

Jonathon, whatever else he may have been, was a belt and braces man. He had studied probability theory all of his young life, and he never left anything to chance.

A face looked down at him from his elastic band portrait on the wall. It was an evil face — the face of a monster from the id.

Forty-one hours later, at two o'clock in the morning, Big Pundy Ritchie, accompanied by his sergeant, banged on the front door of Strathalmond.

❧ ❧ ❧

The suicide of Jonathon Ingram, in his twenty-sixth year, plunged like a heavy fieldstone into the calm pool of Myrestane, sending its concentric ripples to the very edge of its society. Few were unaffected, and none were affected in the same way. For those at the edge of that pool, it challenged their attitudes to living. For those at the centre, it threatened life itself.

David Ingram never recovered from the death of his son. He went through the motions of living, but he was never alive. He came and went from his office and he sat in his greenhouse, but his mind never freed itself from guilt and remorse and a bottomless cavity of pain. Only a father who had lost a son could even begin to understand what David felt. Only a father who had abandoned that son could come close.

Eleanor cried every night into her pillow, and sat every day in front of the wide windows of Strathalmond, looking across the lawns. Sometimes she could see him, his freckles and short trousers, walking around the sundial, making adjustments to its mounting, and screwing his little face up at the sun. Then she would turn away. She never saw the dust collecting on the skirting boards any more.

She knew that it was her fault that her boy had done what he did. She wondered if it was because she didn't breast feed him when he was a baby. She should have done that, then he wouldn't have gone wrong. It was all her fault. She cried again.

Ann prayed for a stranger to talk to. Someone who was not family, not connected. Someone she could just . . . talk to about it. Her parents didn't want to talk. The Ingrams and the Rosses who came to the funeral nodded their sad heads and asked what had happened. They wanted the gory details of her brother's passing. She turned away from them, hating them, hating this whole world of ghouls.

And when she and Ian did talk, Ian was of no help to her, and her depression grew deeper by the day.

Their talk was of "what ifs". What if they had visited Jonathon more often? What if they had invited him to stay with them, and picked him up at the weekends? What if they had taken professional advice when they saw his deterioration? What if.......?

While Ann talked to nobody, Ian talked to his mother. Peg

Douglas said that there was no blame that could fall on anyone and that he should comfort that lassie he had married, and what a great tragedy had befallen her and her poor parents. But of his meeting with Jonathon in the pub, and what Jonathon had said, and what Ian had done to him, he never told a soul.

And he wondered about that, and how it had destroyed their friendship. What if . . . ?

Peg saw the tall, familiar figure pass her window before the knock came to her door. It was Walter Donaldson, and he came shyly into the lobby, pulling off his cap. "Ah jist came doon tae say that Ah'm sorry fur the trouble in yer family, Peg."

She made to invite him in, but he waived the offer.

"Naw, Ah'll no stay, hen. Thanks very much. But Ah jist wanted tae say that Ah ken it's an awfae thing, and maybe ye'll pass oan ma condolences tae the faither and mither, and the wee sister o' that puir laddie."

Then he retired slowly out the door, his cap still in his hand, and Peg watched him trudge slowly up through the housing scheme.

A long time later, when they had all got a lot older and some were no longer around, Hugh Donaldson would talk to Ann like that, and she would feel better, for it is only those, who have been at the centre of that pool, that can ever understand.

∿ ∿ ∿

A few months after Jonathon's funeral, David Ingram telephoned Ian at his office asking if Ian would meet him in the Castle Lounge after work as he had certain matters to discuss. Ian was surprised by the request, particularly as David Ingram had never really talked to him at any length before. He was even more surprised that his father-in-law should select a drinking establishment as a venue, considering that David Ingram had likely never been in one in his life — at least, according to Ann.

The two sat in the late afternoon silence of the quiet lounge bar, next to the bow window that looked over Princes Street towards the castle. David ordered a beer for Ian and a soft drink for himself, and Ian could see in his pale, haggard features the decline of a once strong man. What David saw was an alert young man, cheerful and interested, and entirely devoid of the shy poker face that he always wore in Strathalmond. "How is your apprenticeship going with Mason & Jardine?" David began.

"Fine, sir," Ian replied quickly. The "sir" was out before he realised it — part of his own unconscious recognition of the elevated status of a senior law partner — but he resolved to address David as "Mr. Ingram" thereafter. He was now part of the family and his notion of family didn't include calling his father-in-law "sir".

"Good, good," David replied. "And have you fixed up anything for when your apprenticeship term ends?"

"Not yet, Mr. Ingram." Ian said.

"Please . . . call me David," David said with a little smile, as he recognised Ian's quandary with the form of address. "I wondered if you might be interested in a position as Assistant Solicitor in my firm. I talked to your senior partner, John Mason the other day. He tells me that you have demonstrated quite an ability in the trust field, and you know Cunningham & McCulloch have one of the largest trust departments in town."

Ian was elated. Finding an assistantship in a good firm wasn't easy, and in Cunningham & McCulloch, impossible — without help, that is. So that's what marrying the boss's daughter can do for you, he reflected.

"That would be marvellous," Ian exclaimed, his face beaming. "Thank you very much. . . . David."

The older man nodded an acknowledgement and took a sip of his orange juice. He could feel the tightness in his chest again that had become more frequent in recent weeks. He knew what it was. His doctor had advised him to take things easy as stress was bad for his heart. "There is something else that I want to discuss with you, Ian," he continued. "It concerns Eleanor and Strathalmond."

Ian was taken aback, his face now serious and concerned.

"I'm not a well man, Ian, and I'm most concerned about Eleanor, should anything happen to me." As David spoke, he regarded Ian carefully. "What I am telling you must not get back to my wife." Ian listened with puzzled interest. Even if David feared for his health, Ian couldn't see a problem for Eleanor. After all, she had Strathalmond, and Ian had never thought of them as other than very comfortably off. As if reading Ian's thoughts, David went on.

"There is a large mortgage against Strathalmond and it takes every penny I earn to service it. As it is, we can no longer afford to live there, but I can't find the words to tell Eleanor that. If anything should happen to me . . . . well, that is why I wanted to talk to you."

Totally shocked by this revelation, Ian watched David's face. It was pale and lined like the face of a man who was already a ghost. He could see the great strain that was wrought on David Ingram by having to discuss such matters with a son-in-law, things he had never discussed in all his life with anyone, not even his own son.

"What I want, Ian, is for you and Ann to move into Strathalmond, and the house will be left to Ann provided that Eleanor will always have a home there. Ann will be the mistress of the house of course." While Ian was still trying to take in what had been said, David went on.

"As to whether you can keep the house, I don't know. Whatever money and investments and insurance proceeds there are, I will leave to Ann and you, and that will help to defray some of the mortgage debt. With a position as an Assistant Solicitor in Cunningham & McCulloch, and with Ann teaching, you might be able to pay the mortgage. I would be willing to attend with you at the bank to see if an arrangement could be made."

Ian's mind was racing to grasp all this. David was talking as though he were already dying, and Ian could see that the plan had been well formed in David's head. Ian would become an Assistant Solicitor with Cunningham & McCulloch — for some reason unknown to Ian, they had dropped the Ingram — and he and Ann would move into Strathalmond should anything happen to David. Eleanor could have her own suite, perhaps, which would allow everyone some privacy and independence. Ian liked the plan and found himself suggesting this private suite idea to David as he thought that it was such a bright observation.

"No! no!" David cut in. "Eleanor would have to live with the family, not be isolated in a suite." The thought of that clearly agitated David. Then, as if to reassure Ian, he added, " but Ann would be the mistress of the house."

Ian nodded in satisfaction. The two men had arrived at a deal. All that remained was for Ann to be advised of the arrangement. Before leaving the lounge it occurred to Ian to ask whether his post in Cunningham & McCulloch was conditional upon him following through with the rest of the plan, and he asked David this.

"Not at all, " David said. "The post is yours whenever you are ready to take it."

Ian was ashamed that he had, even for a minute, doubted the integrity of his father-in-law.

Ian talked to Ann that night. They had moved from Mrs. Hunky-Dory's flat in Holmes Road to a modern council flat in Myrestane. On hearing of her father's illness, she was most concerned and said that they must try to visit Strathalmond more often. When Ian laid related David's proposal, there was an entirely different reaction.

"What!" Ann erupted, while Ian was still in the course of explaining the arrangement. "Live with my mother in her house, and I would be the mistress! And she doesn't want a suite in the house! She wants to be in with the family! What can you and my father be thinking about?"

Ian couldn't understand what was wrong, but he felt that it was a good time to stay silent. His rather sheepish expression made his wife worse.

"Mistress, indeed!" she shouted.

When she had calmed down a bit, Ian slipped into the kitchen to make her a cup of tea. That was a thing that mostly worked with Ann Ingram, making her a cup of tea. Afterwards, when they sat at the table, she explained to her husband the great flaw in this marvellous plan of her father's.

"We have already told David that my mother is welcome to come and live with us if anything should happen to him. Haven't we? We have the room here, haven't we?" Ian nodded. "And what's wrong with that? Why can she not do that? Why do we need to move into Strathalmond?" Ann's anger was growing once more.

Ian could think of a dozen reasons for moving to Strathalmond. But it was more than reasons. For a boy from the Raws it would have been a triumph; a gigantic and unbelievable step up into a mansion. "Well . . ." he began.

"You can see what they are saying, can't you?" Ann went on. "Mother can't move in with us because they don't trust us to look after her. We might, after all, throw her out on the street. That's what they think of me. But if she owns the house, she maintains the control. As for that business of me being the mistress. . . . Ha! How could I ever be the mistress in mother's house? Why do you think I couldn't get away from her control quickly enough? And now you're asking me to go back? Back to Strathalmond! Back to mother? No! Ian. No! I won't even think about it. And I will tell father that myself. And if the job he is offering you depends on me moving to Strathalmond, you'd better turn it down now."

Sitting there listening to Ann, Ian was trying to understand. It was too bad, in a way, but he would consider her feelings first. He told her it was her decision and that she would get what she wanted, and to take it easy now or she might upset that little unborn baby Douglas that she was carrying.

David Ingram, as they say in Myrestane, "went doon the hill fast".

The death of his son killed him as sure as if it had been a gun to his head, as sure as it had killed his father, Old Sam Ingram, so many years before.

The next year he took a stroke and he couldn't speak. He lay in Myrestane Hospital for a month, paralysed down one side. Ian and Ann took Eleanor to see him every other day, and Ian cut his nails with clippers and looked into his wide, pleading, silent eyes.

Ian knew what they said. What would become of Eleanor? Who would look after her?

When he was released home, into the care of his wife, he lay for another three months in the little south-facing bedroom and Eleanor served him hand and foot. The fatiguing schedule that she created for herself brought with it her first relief from her suffering over Jonathon.

Then, in the Autumn, he took a heart attack, and died right there in his bed while Eleanor was in the kitchen preparing a special recipe that she was sure he would enjoy.

∞ ∞ ∞

About one month after David Ingram was laid to rest beside his son, Jonathon, in the Ingram plot in St. Nicholas Church cemetery, Jack Armstrong discharged himself from the little cottage hospital that nestled among the trees on the east side of Drumshorling Moor.

By "discharged himself" Jack meant that he escaped through a kitchen window, handing his suitcase down in front of him to the tall, thin man who was helping him. Drumshorling Hospital was a place for old people to die in peace, and there was only one way that they were meant to escape. Jack wasn't going to be one of them.

He walked to Myrestane Station, the tall man supporting him and carrying the case, then he leaned on Peg's front gate, his lungs screaming for air. Peg saw him from the window and rushed to the front door.

"I'm back, Peg, and I'm worse," was all Jack could say.

The tall man set down the case inside the gate, and, with a nod to Jack, he strode off up the road, his long grey hair blowing in the breeze. Peg went to the gate and took Jack's arm. "You're home, Jack. And you're staying home," she said.

Later, as Jack sat in his chair, his face grey and the lustre of his light blue eyes long faded, Peg asked him who the tall man was.

"I met him in the garden of the hospital at Drumshorling when I first went in. The gardener there said that tall fellow would help me if I ever wanted to go home. He lived somewhere on the moor. He just kind of turned up when I needed him this morning."

Jack had not too many days left to sit in his chair and look out at the bings. Barney O'Shea came to see him every night, with a bottle of beer or sometimes a dram of whisky.

On the small table by his chair, he kept his favourite book that he had bought in a second-hand bookshop in Edinburgh in 1942 for two shillings, *Burns' Complete Works — Kilmarnock Edition — Life and Notes by Wm. Scott Douglas.* For the time that was left to him, he read from its tattered pages.

> *O Why the deuce should I repine,*
> *And be an ill foreboder?*
> *I'm twenty-three, and five-feet-nine,—*
> *I'll go and be a sodger!*

In that way Jack Armstrong, the old soldier, just faded away at the finish.

Chapter
Twenty-two

ⁿⁿⁿ

Everyone goes home in the end, one way or another. Some go in the flesh, some in the soul. It's like the Scottish song,

> *O ye'll tak' the high road*
> *And I'll tak' the low road…*

Barney and Jeanie O'Shea went back to Inishennan a few months after Jack Armstrong was buried. They drove to Stranraer and took the car ferry to Larne.

Barney stood on the top deck, peering across to the "Ould Sod", the few remaining strands of his red hair plastered across his bald pate, and his belly stretching his white shirt tight as an Irish drum. Jeanie, small now and wizened, leaned against him, her arm reaching around his waist. Their children were all grown and away with children of their own, and scattered from Myrestane to London.

Barney and Jeanie meandered through the splendid greenery of Antrim and Derry and on into Donegal, savouring every minute of it. It was a strange feeling, the returning to Inishennan after half a lifetime.

There were people they looked at and didn't know, only to

find out that they were friends they had romped with across the mosses years ago. Others hadn't changed. They had the same faces on them that they had in the village school, with just a line or two here and there that the years had brought. Then there were the young ones, with the faces of their fathers and mothers, instantly recognisable.

Barney and Jeanie shared that feeling that had never left them about the place, that warm familiarity with a road, or a track, or the gap in a hedge, or the sweeping fall of the land where it drops into the Atlantic.

It was that feeling that everybody has for their own place — be it the graffiti-covered hoarding in New York, or the wreck of a Cuban village, or the yellow expanse of a prairie. It was the feeling that is called home.

"May you die in Ireland" was what Barney always said.

∾ ∾ ∾

In Myrestane, there were two widow women now who were left all on their own; Peg Douglas in her council house that sat on the brae looking north across the Beugh Burn towards a great rock on the horizon called Binny Craig, and Eleanor Ingram in the silence of her ancient mansion.

Strathalmond had been left in David's will to his daughter Ann, subject to the right of Eleanor to reside there for her lifetime. Ann visited her mother every day in the big empty mansion, pushing the first little Douglas, William Tosh Douglas, in his pram up the long driveway. She had told her father before he died that she had her own house and she wouldn't be moving in with her mother, and the subject had not been raised again. When the baby arrived, she had given up teaching, where she had tried valiantly every day to convert the language of her pupils. It is not "Haw Miss! See's a len' o' a ruler". It is "Please let me have the loan of a ruler, Mrs. Douglas". She sometimes wondered if it would ever change. Maybe it never should. But she never missed teaching, not for a second, and now she was at home with her little boy.

Ian had secured the promised position with Cunningham & McCulloch. He worked in the trust department, pouring over accounts of some of the same trusts that had formerly been in the care of David Ingram and Violet Walker. Nothing much had changed in Cunningham & McCulloch, and Ian constantly found himself thinking that there must be a better way to prepare these accounts, a faster more accurate way. If Jonathon had still been around, he could have devised a way, Ian thought.

Eleanor became more and more difficult. Her formerly beautiful face was now marred by a lack of sustenance brought on by her failure to eat regularly. Her decisions were erratic and she changed her mind every few hours. She made constant trips to see her solicitor in the city and she wouldn't talk to Ann about her business affairs. Ann tried to raise the question of Eleanor's ability to stay in Strathalmond, knowing the financial plight as described to Ian by David, but Eleanor would have none of it. At the same time Eleanor was obsessed with having enough to live on.

She took to living in the kitchen, moving a bed in from one of the many bedrooms, and she abandoned the rest of the house to the advancing ravages of the dust that she had once so abhorred. She picked out some of her finest antique furniture and sent for a man to come and value it. When he came, his valuation fell short of what she had expected, so she made a pile of the items in the front lawn and set fire to it, burning every last stick.

Ann was distraught with anxiety, and seeing its effect on her Ian sat her down to discuss a solution.

"Your mother can't stay on in that house," Ian said. "We don't know her financial position, but from what we do know it is unlikely that she can pay the mortgage your father told me about. She will have to be persuaded to sell up and come to live with us."

"She won't hear of moving in with us. I've already suggested it", Ann sobbed.

"Oh, Ian. What are we going to do?" Ian put his arm round her shoulders.

"It'll be all right," he said. Then, thinking aloud, he added, "maybe we could get her a little flat close to us. Then she would have her own place and you could keep a better eye on her. If that could be arranged, we would decide what to do about Strathalmond later, once she is out of it."

It came as a total surprise to Ann Ingram, that when she suggested the idea of a flat in Myrestane Eleanor showed an immediate interest.

"Of course it would have to have two bedrooms," Eleanor said, as she and Ann sat in the garden at Strathalmond discussing the move. "I don't want one of these poky little places with no room to entertain guests."

"Yes, Mother," Ann replied, wondering what guests her mother was referring to. No guest had been over the doorstep of Strathalmond since Jonathon died.

"And close to you and Ian," Eleanor went on, "but not next door, you know. I want to have my privacy." Ann repressed the irritation that her mother had always provoked in her.

"Of course, Mother. We wouldn't want that. I'm sure that we can find an entirely suitable place for you. I'll ask Ian to go to the Council office this week to see what's available." Eleanor smiled sweetly and Ann was relieved. At last, something would be done for Eleanor. The question of Strathalmond had not been raised, nor would it be. One thing at a time, Ann thought.

In the late sixties, council flats in Myrestane were not difficult to come by, and some preference was given to a widowed parent who had a child housed in the town. Ian spent an afternoon at the Council office and returned with full particulars of a two-bedroom on the ground floor, centrally-heated and with a small garden plot by the front door. Ann was delighted. She couldn't wait to visit her mother with the papers describing the flat, and the rental agreement. She walked up to Strathalmond, pushing the pram. It was her first happy day for a long time. She found Eleanor in the kitchen, still in her dressing gown, staring across a sea of papers and documents that covered the table.

"Council flat in Myrestane! You're not serious!" Eleanor

delivered the words with a sneering smile that stretched the thin white parchment of skin across her cheeks making her look ugly for the first time in her life. Her green eyes flashed at Ann, and Ann's heart sank. "How could you even suggest such a thing to your mother?" Eleanor went on, turning her attention back to the mess of papers on the table.

Ann walked down the drive between the tall trees, her white knuckles gripping the handle of the pram and tears blinding her eyes. Eleanor sat alone at the table. She thought she could see Jonathon working in the study and David coming in from the garden.

There was no cure for Eleanor Ingram. Her mind had wandered too far from reality, and no doctor or medicine can cure a broken heart.

Ann Ingram was sick at heart to witness the state of her mother.

~ ~ ~

In Myrestane Station, Peg Douglas sat at the window every day, looking up the housing scheme. Maybe Ian would come today. Maybe he would bring Ann and the wee boy. They're very busy, of course, these young ones of today. But maybe they'll come.

And sometimes they did come, and Ann told Peg about her mother. And Peg would look kindly at her and then into the fire.

"Aye . . . it's an awfae joab," was all she said.

Eddie McLean and Sandra visited Peg faithfully every week, and they would squirm in their seats when Peg sang the praises of her son and of the little Tosh Douglas.

Sandra never did believe that the child was their first. The way that that wedding had been rushed was clear evidence of that. Ann Ingram was pregnant when she got married. When no child appeared, Sandra was heard to say that they must have got rid of it. But she never said that to Peg.

In any case it can be a tiresome thing to have to listen to

the constant praises lavished on a sibling, and no one could really blame the McLeans for the growing bitterness that they nursed.

Peg had many other visitors, of course. She had friends in every nook and cranny of Myrestane. She was rich in that way, unlike poor Eleanor Ingram, a demented queen locked up in her castle.

∾ ∾ ∾

In the end, Eleanor had no desire to live any more. Like her son before her, she took her own life.

There used to be a man in Myrestane called Charlie Connolly. He was a money lender and ran a small pawn shop in the days when there was a great call for such services. When new customers came through his door, furtively sidling in from the street, their chins pressed down into their collars with shame, Charlie had a little story for them. He delivered it like an actor, in his Irish brogue.

"Do ye see this hat o' mine?" he would say taking the little pork pie of a hat off the top of his crown. "Well, I could take this hat now, and I could walk into the Myrstane Inn up the road there. Now this is the God's truth now, what I'm goin' to tell ye. I could take this hat, and I could throw it in the door of the bar." He demonstrated the throw with a flourish. "And it would hit four people that were customers of mine before it hit the floor. Now that's the God's truth, may He strike me down here where I'm standin'." He would make a quick, deferential gesture to the ceiling.

The object of Charlie's story was to make the borrower feel that he was not alone. There were plenty like him, though never a one would mention it.

Suicide, Ann Ingram discovered, was like that. It was a hidden, shameful thing that squirmed like a black serpent in the souls of the survivors. But it was common enough, and hardly a family in Myrestane had been left unacquainted with it, whether it had happened to their family or their friends.

In a way this one was different from before, for Eleanor had lived for her husband and her home, and what was one without the other? And what was she without them both?

When she took the overdose of sleeping pills in the kitchen of Strathalmond, her trials were over, and she smiled for the first time in a long, long while.

∾ ∾ ∾

When Ian and Ann moved to Strathalmond after Eleanor died, they did it for Ian's sake. It was Ann's house now and she knew that Ian Douglas wanted to live in it. For him, it was the realisation of a dream; to come from the Raws and Mrs. Hunky Dory's flat in Holmes Road to the great Ingram mansion with its long drive and its yew hedges and its history. It was a Douglas house, built on Douglas land, albeit centuries earlier, and that had to count for something. Ian didn't have to explain his feelings to Ann.

But Ann Ingram was moving in for her husband, not for herself. Strathalmond held nothing for her but the bitter memories of a family taken before its time. She hated it. She hated its kitchen and its drawing room, its study and all its fine bedrooms. Everywhere she saw the ghosts of her departed brother and parents.

Ann was more practical than her husband. While there was no immediate financial strain, David Ingram having ensured that they could continue to afford it, houses like this one could not be maintained for long by people who had to work for a living. They were a relic of the past, from the days when the Ingrams had money.

"The first Ingrams that lived here had ships. That's what grandfather told me," Ann said to Ian, as they walked around the huge garden. "Then later, they had land, part of the land that used to belong to the earl of Douglas who lived up there on the hill and owned half of the Lothians. Your ancestors maybe." They both laughed. "Finally it was shale that paid for Strathalmond. Now there are no ships, no land and no shale, so how long can we keep it on a lawyer's pay? In those days they had servants and gardeners. All we have, dear, is that old Hughie from Myrestane that you hired — hardly an estate manager — and your big ideas."

Ian knew she was right, of course. Too clever by half, this wife of his. In time they would sell out to the hotel group that had shown an interest. But not yet. Not for a while. For now it would be a Douglas house, and surely Ann would come to enjoy it.

ॐ ॐ ॐ

Peg Douglas moved into Strathalmond to live with her son and her daughter-in-law just when Spring came around again. Ann had insisted on it. Peg was getting old and frail and she needed to be looked after. But there was another reason for Ann's insistence. She would take in this widow no matter how much work it might involve. She would do for her mother-in-law what she had neglected to do for her mother.

Peg had her own room that Ann had fixed up for her. It was a bed sitting-room, with her own bed at one end, and her easy chair and china cabinet near the fireplace at the other end. There was a table where she could write her letters and a selection of chairs and coffee tables for the entertaining of her friends. It was the room that she had admired as a maid in Strathalmond — Rachael Ingram's room. Now it was her room.

From her window she could look out over the ancient yew hedge, planted centuries earlier, to the old castle ruins, and, looking left, she could just see the edge of the bing.

In the two years that she was there, her friends from the Raws and from the church plodded up and down the great driveway, and Peg entertained them graciously, sitting there like Mary, Queen of Scots newly arrived from France, meeting the locals. When the McLeans came, Ian and Ann stayed out of the way and let Granny Douglas do her boasting in private.

Peg started to write her life story in a notebook, and whenever she was interrupted by first one, then two, then three little Douglases, she laid down her pen and clutched these prattling grandchildren to her bosom.

One afternoon Ann was showing Peg the photographs in the Ingram family album when Peg caught her hand as she turned a page. There, at the door of Strathalmond, stood Colonel William Ingram with his wife and little boy. A serving girl in a black costume held the boy's hand.

"That's my father when he was a boy," Ann said. Peg put her finger on the serving girl.

"And guess who that is?" she said, smiling. Ann looked at Peg in wonder and Peg slowly nodded her head.

"Granny, it's you, isn't it?" Ann looked back at the photograph.

In her last few months, Peg started to hear things in her bed at night — sounds of men and animals, and shouting. Sometimes she would go to the window imagining that she saw soldiers, cavalrymen like Jack Armstrong. She thought she heard their cries sounding in the night. "A Douglas! A Douglas!"

Ann got pills from the doctor but Peg never took them, preferring to live with her dreams.

∾ ∾ ∾

When Peg died in 1972, all the old-timers of Myrestane turned out for her funeral.

The hearse purred silently down the driveway, bearing her away from the towering mansion of Strathalmond for the last time. Then it passed through the gates at the Miller's Wall and turned south towards Myrestane Station, passing over the Beugh and by the crumbling ruins of the Randy Raws. Turning once more, it skirted along the base of the bing and on through the village to St. Nicholas churchyard.

Ian stood at the graveside, hand in hand with Ann — for the old conventions of no women at the grave had passed, like everything else, into antiquity.

Sandra and Eddie were there, and their two girls with their husbands, and Ian could see Hugh Donaldson and Walter,

Mathie and Wee Tam McEwan, and many others, now retired, who were still plodding along.

He was glad of it, for he had laid out the spread in the Myrestane Inn, complete with the beer and the drams that Peg would have ordered.

When the service ended and the mourners were dispersing, a tall man pushed back his long white hair and walked out through the cemetery gates, striding off along the road towards Strathalmond, his hand holding a little book high up behind his back.

Permissions/Acknowledgements

Grateful acknowledgement is made to the following for permission to reprint previously published material:

George Garson: Excerpts from "No Idle Bread" by George Garson

Templecrone Cooperative Society Ltd.: Excerpts from "My Story" by Paddy the Coop. Reprinted in 1979 in the Republic of Ireland for the Templecrone Cooperative Society Ltd., Dungloe, by The Kerryman Ltd., Tralee.

The following work is gratefully acknowledged:

Mediaeval people: by Eileen Power Penguin Books 1937
[Out of copyright]

For generous help in the writing of this book I thank the following friends, relations and colleagues:

Marjorie Aitken
Susan Hannah
Peter Caldwell
Susan Aitken
Sandy Aitken
Sarah Yates
Peter Wardrop
David Kerr

Alex Aitken
1999

Glossary of Terms

aboot	about	fae	from
aff	off	faither	father
afore	before	feared	afraid
Ah	I	ferm	farm
Ah'll	I'll	first years	grade 7 students
Ah'm	I'm	fitba	football
ain	own	florin	two shillings
airm	arm	frae	from
auld	old	fu'	full
Aw	Oh	fur	for
awfae	awful	garron	small, thickset
awright	all right		horse
ay	always	gie	give
aye	yes	gloaming	twilight
bi	by	gonnae	going to
blaws	blows	grandfaither	grandfather
bookie	bookmaker	greet	cry
breeks	trousers	grund	ground
burn	stream	guid	good
cannae	can't	hadnae	hadn't
Cannie	Easy; Take it easy.	halfcrown	two shillings and
cauld	cold		sixpence
claes	clothes	hame	home
close	an access between	heid	head
	buildings	hen	an affectionate term
couldnae	couldn't		for a girl or woman
crabbit	cross,	hermless	harmless
	bad tempered	hiv	have
craic	fun (Irish)	hivnae	haven't
dae	do	hoo	how
daein'	doing	hoor	whore
dearie	dear	hoose	house
deid	dead	hud	hold
dinnae ken	don't know	hundredweight	112 lbs
dinnae	don't	jist	just
dirk	dagger	joab	job
dis	does	kail	broth of vegetables
disnae	doesn't		and meat
doo	dove, pigeon	ken	know
doon	down	kens	knows
drave	drove	kent	known
dug	dog	laddie	boy
efter	after	lang	long

lassie	girl
livin'	living
ma	my
mair	more
masel'	myself
mibbae	maybe
moarnin'	morning
nae mair	no more
nae	no
naw	no
neeps	turnips
no'	not
noo	now
o'	of
oan	on
ony	any
onywey	anyway
oot	out
ootside	outside
ower	over
packin' in	giving up, dying
piece	sandwich
pinkie	little finger
plaster	band-aid
poteen	home-made Irish liquor
puir	poor
R.S.P. C.A.	Royal Society for the Prevention of Cruelty to Animals
raw	row
roond	round
rushin'	rushing
sae	so
sang	song
shanks	legs
shaw neeps	cut the stem and leaves off turnips
shillin's	shillings
sodger	soldier
spurkle	a stick for stirring a pot
stey	stay
steyed	stayed
stone	fourteen pounds
stank	pool
tae	too, to
ta'en	taken
tear	bit of fun, prank
tenement	apartment building
tell't	told
thegither	together
twinty	twenty
wan	one
weans	children
wee	small, little
weemin	women
wey	way
whae	who
whit	what
wi'	with
wid	would
widden	wooden
widnae /widna	wouldn't
wis	was
wrought	worked
wumman	woman
yah	you
ye	you
yer	your
yersel'	yourself
yez	you [plural]
yin	one